THE
DEATH'S HEAD
CHESS CLUB

John Donoghue

Atlantic Books
LONDON

First published in Great Britain in 2015 by Atlantic Books,
an imprint of Atlantic Books Ltd.

This paperback edition published in Great Britain in 2015
by Atlantic Books.

10 9 8 7 6 5 4 3 2

A CIP catalogue record for this book is available
from the British Library.

Paperback ISBN: 978 1 78239 313 9
E-book ISBN: 978 1 78239 312 2

Printed in Great Britain by Clays Ltd, St Ives plc

Atlantic Books
An Imprint of Atlantic Books Ltd
Ormond House
26–27 Boswell Street
London
WC1N 3JZ

www.atlantic-books.co.uk

Contents

THE DEATH'S HEAD CHESS CLUB

1.

The Latvian Gambit

1944

Konzentrationslager Auschwitz-III, Monowitz

It is late afternoon and the camp is quiet. The biting February wind blows from the east and prowls along the alleys between the wooden barracks, waiting for the return of the inmates, an enemy in a long list of enemies. Everyone knows that the wind in Auschwitz speaks its own strange language. It does not speak of the outside world, of the sun on distant mountains, or snow falling lightly on city streets. It speaks only of what it witnesses within the electrified wire that surrounds the camp, of hunger and privation, of solitude among the multitudes that live there, and of death. Arc lights cut through the gloom to flood the parade ground with an unnatural brightness, creating sharp shadows between the fence posts that surround the camp. The camp is hungry. Hunger is another enemy, ever-present, heavy and gnawing, a ravening emptiness in the pit of every stomach that neither the bread ration in the morning nor the thin soup at noon can remedy.

Weariness is another enemy, but the camp cannot rest. Constant vigilance is needed to guard against possible infractions of the rules – rules that are unwritten, unknowable, unfathomable; rules which can be made up on the spot; rules where the only purpose is to increase the opportunities for misery. Each and every rule, whether written or unwritten, known or unknown, is another enemy: the camp is at war, and for each inmate the only measure of victory is that somehow they have managed to survive another day.

In his warm office in the *Kommandantur* building overlooking the camp, SS-Obersturmführer* Paul Meissner gazes out of the window, a cup of coffee in hand. The coffee is good quality, not the ersatz that the soldiers at the front get, for duty in the camps is arduous and essential to the wellbeing of the Reich. Meissner raises the cup to his lips and savours the richness of its aroma. It is a moment of quiet. His gaze lifts to the sky: iron-grey clouds fill his horizon. His leg aches: a sure sign – it will undoubtedly snow before morning.

Meissner is tall, even for a German. His hair is dark, but his eyes are a shimmering blue, disconcertingly so. He is a rarity in the camp – Waffen-SS; his collar bears the double lightning rune in silver on black, not the death's head emblem of the camp SS, the Totenkopfverbände.† He walks with a pronounced limp – a parting gift from a Russian tank. It is a badge of honour: few others in the camp have seen service at the front. Now he spends his days in Abteilung I, responsible to the camp Kommandant. His duties are concerned with overseeing the many satellite labour camps that fall under the umbrella of Auschwitz, mainly the old *Zwangsarbeitslager für Juden*, Fürstengrube and Blechhammer and others even further afield. He is responsible for the SS personnel, and two Scharführers and their teams work daily miracles for him with rosters of men and transport.

---

* See appendix for a table of SS ranks.

† The SS was divided into three main branches: the general or Allgemeine-SS; the military or Waffen-SS; and the concentration camp guards, the Totenkopfverbände, or Death's Head Units. Uniquely, the Totenkopfverbände wore a death's head emblem on their right collar tab.

Meissner's biggest headache is the IG Farben *Werke*, the labyrinthine Buna industrial complex that the Monowitz camp was built to serve. Its capacity to produce synthetic oil and rubber from the surrounding coal fields is crucial to the war effort, yet construction is months behind schedule; so far not a single drop of oil or gramme of rubber has been produced.

Without warning, the quiet is broken. The camp orchestra* has struck up a tune, a jaunty marching song. He searches his memory for its name but it eludes him. He glances at his watch. Where has the day gone?

Minutes later, their day at the factory over, the inmates start to enter the camp. The scene is almost comic in its absurdity: ghastly wrecks of men in filthy, blue-striped uniforms marching in time to the cheery melody of the orchestra. Some of the *Kapos*† have even got their men singing. They are led straight to the parade ground where they line up in columns, five abreast. The early arrivals will have to endure the cold while they wait. There are over 10,000 inmates and it will be a while before they are all assembled and the roll call can begin.

---

* An orchestra made up of inmates was established in the main Auschwitz camp as early as 1941. Others were subsequently formed in Birkenau and Monowitz. The orchestra played when the inmates left, and returned to, the camp each day. According to one account, the orchestra was required to play 'at all official occasions – for the camp commander's speeches, for transports and for hangings. It also served as the entertainment for the SS and the inmates in the medical barracks.' The women's orchestra in Birkenau was the most famous. Its leader was Alma Rose, a well-known musician, who died in Auschwitz in 1944.

† The SS used selected prisoners, the *Prominenten*, to run the camps for them. They were usually Germans sent to a concentration camp for a criminal or political offence. *Ältesten*, or elders, managed the living quarters; *Kapos* supervised the labour squads, or *Kommandos*. They were given privileges, providing they kept control of their fellow prisoners. In order to maintain their privileged status the *Prominenten* often acted with frightening brutality: there are numerous accounts of prisoners being beaten to death for some minor or imagined infraction.

Among the inmates is a recent arrival, from France. He has not yet acquired the haunted, hollow-eyed look of the camp, and, although he has lost weight and his uniform hangs loosely on his frame, his health is still good. He used to have a name, but that was in another life, a life that made sense beyond the daily struggle merely to survive. His name was Emil Clément, and he was a watchmaker. Now he is simply *Häftling** number 163291.

In the eyes of the Reich, Emil is guilty of a crime for which there can be no pardon: he is a Jew.

A hush descends on the parade ground. Roll call begins. The inmates must stand to attention and ignore the bitter fingers of cold that pinch at their emaciated limbs. The camp waits, gripped by numb anxiety. If the numbers do not tally, roll call will have to begin all over again. But not tonight. The Rapportführer† is satisfied and they are dismissed. One might expect to hear a collective sigh of relief, but no – the inmates simply move from one ordeal to the next. They do not have the energy to waste on sighing.

Emil collapses onto his bunk. Normally he spends his day in a machine shop, crafting tiny mechanisms for the repair of the many technical instruments that measure and regulate the processes that are the lifeblood of the Buna factory, much as he would once have created them for the workings of a fine watch. But today there was no electricity and he was reassigned to a labour *Kommando* unloading sacks of cement from railway wagons and stacking them in a warehouse. In his life he has never been so tired; every muscle and sinew hurts and his feet are raw from the

---

* Prisoner or detainee.
† An SS NCO responsible for conducting the roll call.

ill-fitting wooden clogs that the inmates wear so that even the constant clamour of his hunger is subdued.

He shares the bunk with another Frenchman, Yves. They arrived in Auschwitz on the same transport from the internment camp at Drancy, though they did not know one another before being assigned the same bunk. At first, Emil felt disgust at the thought of sharing his bed with another man, a stranger. Now he knows he is fortunate: it is the only time he is warm. They have become firm friends and look out for each other. If one of them is lucky and is able to organize some food – the most precious commodity in the camp – they share it, not like the other inmates in their block. Emil has noticed that most of them keep to themselves; their existence is so marginal, they cannot bear the thought of sharing anything. This solitariness is the source both of their weakness and of the strength of those in charge. Auschwitz is a camp divided against itself.

Yves climbs up to the bunk. They are on the top tier. 'Move over,' he says. Emil groans as he makes his tired limbs obey. Yves grins. 'I had a good day today.' He pushes something towards Emil. It is a hunk of coarse black bread. 'One of the Poles left a woollen jacket lying around. When no one was looking I organized it.' *Organize* is the camp slang for stealing. The inmates are forced to organize if they are to survive. And, in accordance with the absurd rules of Auschwitz, organizing is encouraged, but punished severely if the thief is caught. 'I smuggled it back under my jacket.'

The garment is a great prize, but risky. It would be difficult to keep concealed for any length of time: better to trade it. In the washroom in the corner of the camp that is furthest from the barracks of the SS men there is a thriving market. Every day, as soon as the roll call is dismissed, hundreds of inmates rush there, some to sell, some to buy. It is a buyer's market, for every stomach is empty, and the currency of the camp is bread. Those whose eyes are brittle with hunger can be persuaded to sell for the lowest prices amid the chaotic uproar of barter. Spoons and knives: each prisoner needs one, but the camp authorities do not provide them. They must be purchased. It is here that other items, that various prisoners have managed to organize, are also exchanged.

'What did you do with it?' Emil asks.

'I sold it to the block elder in Block 16. I got two bread rations for it.'

It is a fair price. They eat the bread in silence, savouring every morsel, even though they are painfully aware that every other inmate in their block is hungry. They will not be disturbed. It is a code among the inmates. They would all do the same if they had the chance.

Soon it is lights out and the camp settles into an uneasy slumber; in only a few hours its toil begins again.

Yves is thankful he has been paired with Emil. He is a gentle, cultured man. They talk endlessly about France before the war. Yves is also curious about Emil's passion for the game of chess.

'Explain to me again,' he says quietly in the darkness, 'about the Latvian Gambit.'

2.

THE DUTCH DEFENCE

1962

Grand Hotel Krasnapolsky, Amsterdam

The interview was approaching its conclusion. Still the interviewer, an old hand who knew how to wring the best and the worst from his guests, had not asked the question. At last, with the deftness of a conjurer, he slipped it in: 'What many of our listeners would like to hear about is your time in Auschwitz.'

The man sitting opposite him adjusted his lanky frame in the armchair and sighed. He glanced at the tape recorder as if he hoped that the spools might stop turning. Again, someone had asked the question; again, the hard stamping on the brakes, bringing the course of his life to an abrupt standstill. Auschwitz: after nearly twenty years, still it followed him everywhere. Bearing witness to the horror was a duty, but a heavy one. He had not expected to be confronted with it here. He raised his head to look at his tormentor. His eyes were a thin murky grey, like a sky threatening rain. They were eyes that seemed to look past the object of their attention, to depths and secrets that were best kept hidden.

The interviewer suppressed a shiver. Realizing that a silence had fallen between them, he felt compelled to break it. 'Your reluctance to speak about this is, of course, completely understandable...'

'Reluctance?' The word came out sharply, as if the man had been

7

caught in an untruth. 'No, not really. It is not so much reluctance, rather, it is not knowing what I ought to say. So much has been said already that there is perhaps little left to tell. It is complicated. If I start, where will it lead? And, of course, at the back of my mind I wonder what it is you really want.' Unconsciously, the man's long, slender fingers gripped the arms of his chair. 'Do you want to know what it was really like in an extermination camp, or do you want to hear lurid tales of what one had to do in order to survive?'

The interviewer knew his listeners would not want him to appear insensitive; he changed tack. 'In your book you wrote that you did not believe that any German who lived through the war could be untainted by what happened in the death camps. Guilt by association, you might say. Do you really believe that – that all Germans are guilty? Were there no good Germans?'

The question did not elicit the hoped-for response. The man bowed his head and ran a hand through his thinning hair.

The interviewer felt the need to prompt him. 'Mijnheer Clément?'

'It seems that everyone wants me to spend the rest of my life looking for a good German. Why? So he can apologize? There is no apology. You want a good German? Let me tell you, I saw none. Not one.' Clément enunciated the last words slowly and clearly.

Sensing there was something more, the interviewer persisted. 'You didn't mention it in your book, but isn't it true that it was a German who saved your wife's life?'

Clément looked sharply at his interrogator. 'Yes, it's true, after a fashion. I didn't include it in my book because I was writing about my experiences, not hers. But I will tell you what happened to her, if only to dispel the myth of the good German.' His voice had become harsh and tight, as if he were struggling to keep it under control. He took a sip of water before continuing.

'We both survived the camp, though neither of us knew that the other was still alive. It was months before I found her. Her registration card in Auschwitz said she was dead – "Shot while trying to escape" – usually a euphemism for dying under torture. But she wasn't dead; she was in Austria, in Mauthausen. She was in hospital. She had scarlet fever. If she hadn't been so weak…' His voice caught, and he coughed to clear it. 'All she wanted was to ask for my forgiveness. "What forgiveness?" I said. "You have nothing to be forgiven for. You are blameless." But she was insistent and, bit by bit, she told me what she had had to do to in order to live.

'Her life was saved by a note. Yes, a simple note. A note of the kind that could be written by anyone, for any number of reasons – a shopping list, a reminder, an apology, a demand for payment, an assignation – a tight little ball of paper that struck her lightly on the back of her head and fell to the floor. She knew it must have come from one of the guards. She covered it with her foot and glanced round to see who might have thrown it. There were two SS men nearby – it could have been either of them. She stooped to retrieve it and asked to be excused to go to the latrine. It contained three words: *Are you hungry?*

'It was a German, one of the guards. Yes, he saved her life, but at the cost of her dignity and self-respect. He saved her life, but it would have been better if he had not done so, for she felt she had betrayed not only me, but the memory of our children. How could she deserve life when they had perished? No more than me or any other survivor could she resist the instinct that called on her to choose life, but she could not forgive herself for surrendering to it.' Clément shifted in his chair, leaning forward and raising a forefinger to the other man as if to admonish him. His voice took on a hard, bitter tone. 'You ask if he was a good German—? Well, if it is good to take advantage of the helpless, those who have nothing, those who have been cast adrift without hope, then he was good. But as far as I am concerned, what he did was an abomination.'

Emil Clément wandered back from the Grand Krasnapolsky and the bustle of Dam Square to his own hotel, a humbler affair overlooking the Singel Canal. It wasn't far. His room overlooked a small bridge, over which cyclists seemed to glide in the dreamy way that the dwellers of Amsterdam had made their own.

Emil wondered at the persistence shown by the interviewer. He had not expected it. It wasn't as if he was a politician or a famous entertainer; he was a chess player, nothing more. He felt unsettled. Perhaps he should not have come straight back to his hotel. He stood at the reception desk, lost in thought.

'Is there anything I can do for you, Mijnheer Clément? Would you like your key?'

Emil glanced at the man behind the desk, a portly man in his sixties. 'Yes, maybe there is. Is there anywhere in the city where people play chess? You know, a city square, or a park, perhaps?'

The man smiled. 'Of course. You should go to Leidseplein. I'm sure you'll find a game there. It's quite a way, but you can take a tram from Dam Square; it's easy to find. '

Clément shook his head. 'Thanks. I'll walk. I could do with some fresh air.'

Lijsbeth Pietersen walked as quickly as dignity and high heels would permit along the gilded corridors of the Krasnapolsky. She held in her hand a piece of paper that was important, very important: it had the potential to wreck the World Chess Federation Interzonal tournament – due to start in two days' time – before even the first pawn was played. Lijsbeth took her responsibilities seriously. The Interzonal was important: its leaders would progress to the candidates' tournament and from there to the world championship.

At the door of the room that had been allocated to the tournament's chief arbiter she paused to compose herself before knocking. Inside, a man in a dark suit was standing by a window, idly watching the comings and goings of the people on the square below. He turned as she entered.

'Miss Pietersen,' he said, with a thin smile. 'To what do I owe the pleasure this time?'

With studied care she placed the piece of paper on the desk that stood between them, smoothing it onto the polished surface. 'I know you've seen this, Mijnheer Berghuis,' she said, her voice tight with suppressed anger. 'I would like to know why you didn't feel the need to inform me, and what you intend to do about it.'

Harry Berghuis slid his spectacles from the breast pocket of his jacket. In the past week Lijsbeth Pietersen had become something of an irritation. It was he who was the chief arbiter of the tournament; she was merely the administrator, a fact she seemed to find difficult to grasp. He seated himself at the desk and picked up the paper.

It was a copy of the draw for the first round of the tournament. He glanced at it, then let it fall back to the desk.

'I don't understand what you're so upset about,' he said. 'As to what I "intend to do about it" – I intend to do nothing. The games will proceed according to the draw, as they always do.'

11

She gave him a look that spoke much of her opinion of his intelligence. Taking a pen, she circled two names. 'Look.'

He looked again and shook his head in bewilderment. 'What?'

'Emil Clément and Wilhelm Schweninger will play each other in the first round.'

'You know, Miss Pietersen, you really are going to have to learn to express yourself better. You're not making any sense.'

'Emil Clément is the contestant from Israel. He's a survivor of Auschwitz. He wrote a best-selling account of his experiences in which he said there was no such thing as a good German.'

'And Schweninger is a German.' He gave her a dismissive look. 'So what?'

'Schweninger isn't just any German. During the war he worked in their Ministry of Propaganda.'

Berghuis sighed. 'And?'

Lijsbeth pursed her lips. Was Berghuis really so dense? 'To work in the Propaganda Ministry, he had to have been a member of the Nazi Party.' She took a step towards the desk and placed her fingertips on its surface, leaning over him. 'Am I starting to make sense now?'

Berghuis did not like her tone. He felt his face getting hot and reached for his collar, trying to loosen it, hoping that a reason to ignore what she was telling him would present itself. 'Lots of Germans were members of the Party,' he countered. 'Was he convicted of war crimes?'

'It doesn't matter whether he was or whether he wasn't. If the press get hold of this, they're going to have a field day.'

Berghuis picked up the piece of paper again, as if by looking at it the means to resolve the problem would leap out at him. 'Damn,' he said quietly. 'What do you suggest?'

'The only thing to do is to re-run the draw, making sure that the two of them do not meet unless it happens in the final.'

'No.' Berghuis shook his head. 'We can't do that. Notification has already gone out to all the contestants.'

'We can tell them there's been a mistake, that it needs to be re-done.'

'What kind of mistake? The draw was done in front of at least twenty people.'

Lijsbeth could not resist saying, 'Perhaps now you understand why you should have entrusted the job of doing background research on the contestants to me. There's more to it than creating happy family biographies for the press.'

Berghuis lowered his head. 'Yes, all right,' he acknowledged. 'But that's not what's important now. We have to work out what we're going to do. If we do a re-run, someone is bound to smell a rat, and then the press will definitely stick their noses in. No, we'll have to go with what we've got and pray for a minor miracle.'

'You mean do nothing and hope that nobody puts two and two together?' Lijsbeth rewarded her boss with a condescending smile. It was a small victory, but satisfying. 'Well, I'm sure you know best. You're the boss.'

At fifty, Emil Clément was tall and spare, with dark, receding hair and a closely cropped beard that hid the lower part of his face. Going down the hotel steps, he turned up the collar of his coat. Though it was April, a chill wind was blowing off the North Sea, bringing with it flurries of rain, somewhat different from the weather he was used to now.

He followed the canal southwards, almost to its terminus. He was looking for a street called Leidsestraat, and on reaching it he turned right

– after crossing three canals, he would reach his destination. He flinched as raindrops spattered on his face. Dark clouds were looming: he would be lucky to find anyone foolhardy enough to be playing chess in the square.

By the time he reached the eastern edge of Leidseplein it was raining heavily. The square was indeed empty, apart from a few hardy people hurrying across, some struggling with umbrellas or sheltering in shop doorways. He ducked into the nearest café.

The barman was wiping the counter top with a cloth that had seen better days. '*Nog regent het?*'

'I'm sorry,' Emil said in English. 'I don't speak Dutch. Do you speak French, or German?'

The barman smiled. '*Ja, Ich kann gut Deutsch sprechen.*'

Emil ordered a coffee and said, 'I was told I might be able to find a game of chess around here.'

The barman jerked his thumb in the direction of the parlour at the rear. 'You'll probably find a couple of games going on back there. They're regulars, mind, so you may have a bit of a wait before you get a turn.'

The coffee was placed on the bar and Emil handed over several coins. 'No matter,' he said. 'I'll be happy simply to watch.'

3.

The Polish Opening

November 1943
Oświęcim, German-occupied Silesia

Amid clouds of steam the train from Kraków groaned to a halt in the station in the small town of Oświęcim. SS-Obersturmführer Paul Meissner pushed open the door of his carriage and peered along the platform. There should be somebody there to meet him.

The stationmaster was about to put his whistle to his lips to send the train on its way when he saw an SS officer limping towards him. 'A moment, if you please,' the officer shouted. The whistle was lowered. 'I should be very grateful if someone could get my baggage off the train.'

SS officers were a common sight, constantly going to and from the camp, usually insufferable and demanding. But as the officer stood leaning heavily on his walking stick, the stationmaster detected a little humility in his bearing, and his eyes took in the Iron Cross on the officer's breast pocket.

'Of course,' he said. 'I'll see to it at once. Won't you have a seat in my office?'

Nearly an hour later, a shame-faced Rottenführer entered the stationmaster's office and stamped to attention. Meissner was not impressed by what he saw: the remains of a meal halfway down his tunic, collars that were curling upwards.

'Compliments of Hauptsturmführer Hahn, sir. I'm to take you to the officers' quarters.'

For long moments, Meissner did not speak.

'Your name, Rottenführer?'

'Eidenmüller, sir.'

'Well, Eidenmüller, let me tell you – you wouldn't last ten minutes in the Waffen-SS. A man who takes no pride in his appearance is unreliable. Next time I see you, I want you in a tunic that is clean and pressed, understood?'

The man stood ramrod straight. 'Yes, sir.'

'Good. Now pick up my bags and get me out of here.'

Ernst Eidenmüller had been in the SS for nearly two years. At first, his progress through the lower ranks had gone remarkably well. He was like a cat that always landed on its feet – 'Midas', his comrades called him: everything he touched seemed to turn to gold. He'd taken pride in his appearance then.

In June 1940, when the newsreels across Germany showed Hitler sightseeing in newly occupied Paris, Eidenmüller was not on the streets joining in the rapturous celebrations with his fellow countrymen: he was in a Leipzig police cell for possession of a stolen bicycle. His protestations of innocence availed him nothing: his accuser was a minor Party official. A year later he was charged with black-marketeering. Nothing was proven, but, with a previous conviction hanging around his neck, all it took was a word in the judge's ear from the local Gestapo chief and he was sentenced to eighteen months in a labour battalion. He braced himself for a tough time: everyone knew how hard life could be in the road gangs; instead, he found himself in an agricultural brigade.

His father was a Lutheran pastor, a severe man whose orbit he had been glad to escape, but he had given his son one sound piece of advice: 'There are three things you must never allow to control you – women, money, or the Nazis; above all, the Nazis.' Women had never been a problem: the kind of women he liked never seemed to be the kind that wanted to stay. As for money – Eidenmüller never had enough to be controlled by it. He had a taste for gambling. He was hooked on the thrill of it and never worried about whether he won or lost. That left only the Nazis.

The army wasn't keen to take convicted criminals into its ranks, no matter how minor the offence, but the SS was a different proposition, as long as recruits could demonstrate impeccable Aryan ancestry. Early in 1942, all the men in his barracks were ordered to assemble for a lecture in the dining hall. Waiting to address them was an SS recruiting officer. 'Healthy young men of German blood, your Führer calls you to do your duty…' He had harangued them in this vein for nearly an hour. They listened unmoved to the officer's words until he added that nobody would be allowed to leave the hall until they had pledged to join the SS – the first ten would be given the best postings. It was obvious there was no escape, so, with a shrug, Eidenmüller stepped forward. Along with nine others, he was assigned to the Totenkopfverbände and sent to Dachau for training; the remaining fifty were inducted to the Waffen-SS.

Eidenmüller soon realized he'd been lucky; life in the SS training barracks wasn't exactly a plate of *Zwetschgenkuchen** but neither was it backbreaking. The men were bored, they had money in their pockets,

* Plum cake.

and Eidenmüller had a way about him. He became the one who always knew how to obtain the myriad small items that would make life in the barracks easier. It wasn't that he delved or poked around or made lists; he simply had the knack.

He was appointed squad leader. He never had to bawl at the men. Because he always seemed able to find the things they wanted, they tried to please him – most of the time. At the end of training his promotion was made official, and Rottenführer Eidenmüller was posted east.

In Auschwitz, he was assigned to the pharmacy as a driver. He would collect medical supplies intended for the SS in the camp from the rail depot in Kraków, and, when required, make deliveries to the satellite camps. Medicines for the civilian population were in short supply and he set about getting friendly with one of the camp pharmacists and then acted as a go-between with a pharmacy in Kraków. His duties were light and soon he was running all sorts of errands for officers and senior NCOs. Collecting, carrying, delivering; his easy-going manner and his unerring nose won him friends in high places. Even Kommandant Höss had him collect packages from a warehouse in Birkenau to be delivered to an address near the railway terminal in Podgórze. Within months he had been promoted to Scharführer and more and more doors were opened to him.

When, late in the summer of 1943, Obersturmführer Morgen arrived, Eidenmüller knew the sleigh-ride was over. This was no ordinary SS officer, but an official of the criminal police, sent to investigate corruption in the camp. He ordered a raid on the NCOs' barracks. Eidenmüller's locker was crammed with soap and tubes of toothpaste. His explanation of how they had come into his possession was dismissed out of hand.

An SS court was quickly convened with the officer in charge of the

Auschwitz-I camp, Sturmbannführer Liebehenschel, as its president and Morgen as the prosecuting counsel.

Liebehenschel had already heard two cases that morning. One of the NCOs brought before him had had over a dozen expensive fountain pens in his locker. Collecting them was his hobby, he had insisted. It was obvious they had been pilfered from the possessions confiscated on arrival from the Jews sent to Auschwitz, but – Liebehenschel asked the prosecutor – was it important enough to require a court hearing? He ordered that the man should be disciplined by his commanding officer, with no further action. The next case involved the discovery of foreign currency. This was far more serious. The NCO was demoted to the ranks and transferred to the Eastern Front.

Then it was Eidenmüller's turn. Liebehenschel struggled not to laugh at the 'suspicious items' found in the NCO's possession.

'Soap, Herr Obersturmführer?' he asked Morgen. 'Suspicious? Really?'

The prosecutor drew himself up to his full height. 'Indeed, Herr Sturmbannführer,' he replied, his tone edged with astonishment that he should be asked such a question. 'Such a quantity could not possibly be for his own personal use. It is clear evidence of black-marketeering; a low crime, I'm sure you'll agree. Besides, the soap was of the type used by women and' – he looked pointedly at Eidenmüller – 'homosexuals.'

Eidenmüller winced. He was doomed.

Liebehenschel addressed him directly. 'The evidence against you seems pretty damning, Scharführer. What have you got to say for yourself?'

'Beg pardon, sir. The soap wasn't for me. It was for my girlfriend.'

'Your girlfriend? Just the one?' The officer was tempted to wink at the accused. Liebehenschel could not find it in him to send a man to the Eastern Front for possession of perfumed soap, but he ordered

Eidenmüller to be demoted and reassigned to a job where he would no longer be in temptation's way.

Later, as Eidenmüller packed his kit to go back to the troopers' barracks, somebody said to him: 'Look on the bright side – at least you didn't get sent to fight the Bolshevik swine.' That much was true, but for days afterwards Eidenmüller could not stop hearing his father lecturing him in the gloating voice he had hoped never to have to listen to again: '... above all, the Nazis.' He had been so right – the smug bastard.

'Fuckin' bastards,' the driver mumbled under his breath.

'What was that?' the officer beside him asked, sharply.

'Nothing, sir. I was thinking aloud, that's all. Beg pardon, sir.' Eidenmüller kept his eyes firmly on the road ahead, but his muttered imprecation seemed to have woken the officer up.

'Where exactly are you taking me?'

'To the *Stammlager*, sir. That's where officers are quartered. They're expecting you,' he added.

'They were expecting me an hour ago.'

'Yes, sir. Sorry, sir.'

'Out of interest, Rottenführer, why were you so late picking me up? Did you have an assignation over lunch?'

The driver reddened. 'No, sir. It was the motor pool, sir. Always having problems with it, we are, sir. If there's a big *Aktion* in Birkenau, they get priority.'

'And was there a big *Aktion* in Birkenau this morning?'

'Not that I know of, sir. Lack of spare parts is what I got told today. Still, you'll see how hand to mouth we have to live once you get there, sir. The military gets priority for most things, and we have to make do and mend as best we can.' When the officer did not reply, the driver continued: 'If I'd left it to them, sir, you'd still be waiting. As it happened, the Scharführer in charge of the motor pool owed me a bit of a favour, if you know what I mean. A quiet word in his ear and this car suddenly became available. Cost me a couple of packs of cigarettes, though.'

Meissner did not seem convinced by the driver's explanation, but said nothing more. It did not take long to reach the main camp, and the officer was pleasantly surprised at his accommodation: it was far more spacious and well appointed than he was used to. A servant had been assigned to him too, a short man with a shaven head. He wore a baggy, blue-striped uniform with a violet triangle sewn on its front.*

The small man lifted the baggage from the car and led the way to a small day room.

'With your permission, sir, I will unpack and put your things away.'

'What is your name?'

'Oberhauser, sir, though it's usual in the camp to use my number. I answer to 672.'

'You're German.'

'Yes, sir. From Elsdorf.'

'Really? I'm from Köln myself. It's a small world, isn't it?'

'Yes, sir.'

'Why were you sent here, Oberhauser? Political crimes?'

'No, sir.'

---

* The status of prisoners in the camp was denoted by coloured triangular badges worn on the breast of the tunic: green was for criminals; red for political prisoners, usually Communists; pink for homosexuals; violet for Jehovah's Witnesses; and, until the second half of 1944, a red triangle superimposed on a yellow triangle to create a makeshift Star of David was for Jews.

'You're not a Jew?'

'No, sir. I'm a Jehovah's Witness.'

'A Jehovah's Witness? I had no idea they were so dangerous.'

'Me neither, sir. May I carry on now?'

'Please do.'

An hour later Eidenmüller reappeared, this time in a clean uniform. 'Compliments of Sturmbannführer Liebehenschel, sir. The Kommandant asks would it be convenient for you to come to his office?'

The Kommandant's office was large but devoid of any personal effects, as if its occupant had only recently taken possession of it. Meissner brought himself to attention, raising his right arm stiffly in salute. '*Heil Hitler.*'

The salute was returned with rather less enthusiasm; Sturmbannführer Liebehenschel held out his right hand. 'Welcome to Auschwitz, Meissner. Please take a seat. Let me tell you I'm glad to have you here. I can use as many good officers as I can get.'

'Pardon me for mentioning this, sir, but my orders are that I should report to Obersturmbannführer Höss.'

'The Obersturmbannführer has been recalled to Berlin. He's been appointed deputy to Gruppenführer Glücks in the Concentration Camps Inspectorate. I have taken his place, with immediate effect.' The Sturmbannführer pushed his chair back and stood. 'But I am forgetting my manners. Allow me to offer you some coffee.'

The coffee was poured from an ornate silver pot, by another prisoner wearing a violet triangle. The Kommandant did not acknowledge the prisoner's presence, but spoke as he withdrew. 'Jehovah's Witnesses. The enlisted men call them "Bible-worms". We use them as servants. What else can you do with them? They could all walk out of here tomorrow if only they would sign the *Gottläubig*. We don't even expect them to believe it – just sign the bloody form that says they have no religious belief.'

'Are there many of them here?'

'No. A couple of hundred perhaps. The vast majority of the prisoners are Jews.'

'Is there any special reason why you use them as servants?'

'Well, for a start, they're good Aryans, but, to be honest, it's because they're the only ones in the camp who can be trusted not to rob us blind.' He laughed. 'I'm serious, Meissner. Probably the best advice anyone could give you is not to leave anything where it could be found by a prisoner. Turn your back on it for a second and it will disappear, I promise you.'

The Kommandant picked up a file from his desk and opened it. He struck Meissner as an affable sort. 'You're younger than I thought you would be, Meissner – I was expecting a hardened veteran after reading your service record. Most impressive. It says you single-handedly destroyed three Russian tanks with a disabled Wespe field howitzer.'

It was Meissner's turn to smile. 'That's not quite how it happened. It wasn't single-handed, the Wespe wasn't damaged, and the third T-34 was actually killed by one of our Tigers that joined the action in the nick of time. If not for them, I wouldn't have lived to tell the tale.'

'Still, you got an Iron Cross for it.'

'And this—' Meissner raised his walking stick.

The Kommandant closed the folder. 'Modesty. I like that in a man. I think you'll fit in well here, Meissner. In fact, I think I have the perfect challenge for a man of your obvious tenaciousness.'

'Which is?'

'I need someone to oversee the satellite camps. Not the day-to-day running of them – they're spread too far afield for that – but we have constant problems with personnel and transport; in fact, it's a bloody nightmare, a nightmare that we've been doing our best to ignore. Up to a few months ago our main concern was to increase capacity in Birkenau, but that's no longer a problem – we've got it running as smoothly as the Swiss railways. But now my orders are to increase armament production, and that means getting more out of the labour camps.' Liebehenschel stood and beckoned for Meissner to follow him to a map pinned to the wall. He tapped his forefinger on a particular point. 'Our biggest problem is here – the IG Farben *Werke*. It's one of Himmler's pet projects and it's months behind. I need people in place who will teach the Jewish scum what hard work really means. And that's where you come in. I need someone who's prepared to be single-minded, who will ignore the egos and tantrums of his colleagues – someone who will get the job done. This has top priority and you'll have my full backing. What do you say?'

Meissner's reply was immediate. 'I say yes, naturally.'

'Excellent. If you do only half as well as I think you can, you'll be a Hauptsturmführer by next summer – you have my word on it.'

4.

THE BENONI DEFENCE

Amsterdam

The note was waiting in Emil's hotel pigeonhole when he returned. He understood immediately what had lain behind the interviewer's question.

He had been paired with Schweninger.

Emil waited until the next morning before seeking out Miss Pietersen at the Krasnapolsky. She sympathized, she told him, but the rules were the rules. If he wanted to play in the championship, he must face Schweninger. He insisted on speaking to Berghuis. With a small, self-satisfied smile on her face, she accompanied him to the chief arbiter's office.

'Mijnheer Clément,' Berghuis said smoothly, 'I agree it is a most unfortunate situation, but we cannot change the rules because one contestant has personal difficulties with another. Think of the precedent it would create. No, I'm afraid that you must go ahead with the match or forfeit it.'

Before Emil could reply, a fourth person burst into the tournament office. Red-haired and overweight, he stood for a moment in the doorway to catch his breath, eyeing Berghuis accusingly. That he was furious was obvious.

'Did you hear the radio this morning?'

'No.' Berghuis cast an alarmed glance at his assistant but her eyes were fixed on Emil. Berghuis swallowed anxiously. 'Why?'

'Clément was interviewed by Piet de Woert on his culture show. He was asked if he maintained his view that there were no good Germans. He said that not only did he maintain it, but he gave his reasons why. It is an outrage!'

Lijsbeth Pietersen could see a disaster unfolding before her very eyes. Standing stock-still, her lips compressed into a rigid smile, she felt compelled to interrupt. 'Herr Schweninger, may I present Monsieur Clément?'

Her words had an effect similar to a car being driven off a cliff at high speed: they seemed to hang silently in mid-air while the people in the room struggled to understand what had happened.

Emil was the first to recover. He addressed the German in his own language. 'An outrage, you say, Herr Schweninger? If you consider freedom of speech an outrage, then I suppose you are right – what I said is an outrage, though I should have expected no less from one such as you.' He shook his head. 'But let me tell you what an outrage *really* is. It is when millions of people are murdered for no other crime than being born a Jew, including my mother and my children. That is what *I* consider to be an outrage, Herr Schweninger.'

'Perhaps it—' But Lijsbeth Pietersen did not get to finish.

'How dare you?' Schweninger bellowed, then turned on his heel and stormed out, slamming the door behind him.

The arbiter, the administrator and Emil Clément looked at one another.

'Well, I suppose it might have been worse,' Berghuis remarked.

'How?' Lijsbeth asked, shaking her head. 'How could it possibly have been worse?'

'Twenty years ago he could have had us sent to a concentration camp,' Emil said, acidly.

Berghuis could not hide his exasperation. 'Will you please stop saying things like that?'

Emil turned to face him. 'Why? Because they are true?'

'No. Because it is 1962. Hasn't anyone told you – the war is over. It is time to move on.'

Only Lijsbeth Pietersen remained calm. 'What is important is what we do about the situation. Mijnheer Clément, is it your intention to withdraw from the competition?'

Something had changed in Emil: minutes before he had been on the verge of quitting, but not now. 'Certainly not. I will play him and I will humiliate him and it will serve him right.'

Emil hurried back to Leidseplein, not seeing anything or anyone as he pushed his way past shoppers and office workers, not slowing his pace until he arrived, breathless, at the café.

The barman recognized him and smiled. 'Good morning, mijnheer. Coffee?'

'No. Something stronger. Cognac.' The barman glanced at the clock but said nothing. 'Is there anyone in who will give me a game this morning?' Emil asked when he had recovered his breath.

'I think so. By the way – did you know there is a big chess tournament in town? It was all over the radio this morning.'

Emil took the brandy and swallowed it in one. 'Yes, I knew.'

In the parlour a board was already set up, with an elderly man seated behind it, waiting.

'May I?' Emil asked. The old man nodded and, taking a white and a black pawn in his hands, held them out for Emil to choose. 'If you don't mind,' Emil said, 'I would like to play black.'

'Not at all.' The old man turned the board so the white pieces were on his side. He advanced his queen's pawn two squares.

Emil did not make a move but closed his eyes, allowing his hands to fall to his lap as if in prayer. He was still for a moment. 'Forgive me,' he said, when he opened his eyes. 'It's a little ritual I must go through before every game.' He moved his king's knight so that it stood in front of its bishop.

The old man immediately moved his queen's bishop's pawn forward two squares. Emil responded with the same move. The old man ignored the gambit and moved his first pawn forward one square. Emil moved his queen's knight's pawn forward two spaces. The old man took it.

'If you don't mind my saying so,' he said, 'that is a most unusual defence. I don't think I've seen it before.'

'No,' Emil replied. 'It is called the Benoni Defence. It means "Son of Sorrow".'

5

A Queen's Pawn Game

January 1944
Solahütte, SS country club, German-occupied Silesia

Despite the chill, Meissner did not feel quite ready to quit the veranda and go in for dinner: he had wanted a few moments of solitude to add a brief observation to his journal. His fellow officers enthused constantly about the SS country club and what a fine place it was for winding down after the rigours and stresses of camp duty, but this was the first time he had visited it. They had not exaggerated. Set on a hillside with spectacular views of the surrounding hills and forests, it was a haven of tranquillity; at least until the evenings, when, inevitably, after a few drinks, somebody would start on the piano, or an accordion, and the songs would begin. It put him in mind of happier days, before the war. There were even women here, SS-Aufseherinnen, supervisors in the women's and family camps. Meissner smiled to himself. They had taken quite a shine to him: his Iron Cross was like a magnet. He wondered if they would be quite so enamoured of his wooden leg. Taking a last drag on his cigarette, he flicked it over the balcony and went inside.

Dinner at Solahütte was informal, and he took a place at a table with Vinzenz Schottl, the Monowitz Lagerführer, and Erich Weber, one of the SS doctors. To their surprise, they were joined by the Kommandant, recently promoted to Obersturmbannführer. They stood as he pulled out a chair, but Liebehenschel insisted they should not stand on formality.

'Gentlemen, please. Here we are all comrades in the SS, no?'

Dinner was served by ranks of Polish waiters in immaculate white jackets. The dinner service was Königliche porcelain and the glasses Bohemian crystal. Afterwards, cigars and cognac were served.

A relaxed Paul Meissner exhaled a stream of grey smoke, appreciating the exquisite flavour. 'Where on earth do these come from?' he asked.

'Havana, I believe,' Weber said, whose father was in the diplomatic service. 'Via Portugal and Spain.'

'One of the privileges of serving in the Totenkopfverbände,' Schottl broke in. 'After all, there have to be some compensations for what we are forced to put up with.'

Meissner had heard such observations before. This time he demurred. 'I must say I find life here rather easy compared with fighting the Russians.'

'For you, maybe,' Weber said, tapping his cigar and letting the ash fall to the floor. He fixed Paul with a supercilious smile. 'My duties are perhaps a little more... taxing than yours.'

The hours Paul had spent in the field hospital were burned deep into his memory: the dirt, the blood, the cries of pain, and the ever-present sound of gunfire. 'Really? You are a surgeon, are you not?' The doctor nodded in assent. 'I wonder,' Meissner continued, 'when you last performed surgery under fire?'

Weber reddened and shot the Waffen-SS man an angry glare.

The Kommandant intervened. 'Gentlemen, please. Let us have no harsh words here. We are all doing our duty in the different ways that are demanded of us. Let us leave it at that, eh? Obersturmführer Meissner has not been here very long. It takes a while to get used to our ways, especially after the privations of the front.' He stood and raised his glass. 'I'm afraid

I can't stay, as much as I would like to, but before I go, a toast.' He pinged his glass with a silver teaspoon. Officers at every table rose to their feet and raised their glasses. 'The Führer.' He drained his glass.

Walking past Meissner, he placed a hand on the junior officer's shoulder. 'A quiet word before I leave, if I may?'

The Kommandant waited in the empty bar next door for his subordinate to catch up.

'I apologize, sir, if I…' Meissner jerked his head in the direction of the dining room.

The apology was waved aside. 'That? Don't worry about it. Weber is a patronizing ass. No, Meissner, all I wanted was to say is that even though it's been only a few months since you took over their administration, I'm aware of the improvement that has come about in the performance of the labour camps. Well done.'

A smile of relief crossed the junior officer's face. 'Thank you, sir. I'm glad to hear it.'

The Kommandant fished in his tunic pocket and pulled out a piece of paper. 'There was something else.' He handed the paper to his subordinate. 'As director of Abteilung I, your duties include responsibility for morale. I received this on Friday.' He indicated the slip of paper in Meissner's hands. 'It is a directive from the Reichsführer-SS himself, stressing the importance of morale and instructing that it should be improved. He is of the opinion that SS officers should take an active interest in higher culture.' He paused as an orderly approached with his greatcoat and cap. 'Now, I'm not suggesting that we go so far as to try and create an interest in opera or anything like that,' he continued, draping the coat over his shoulders, 'but we must do something to demonstrate that we have taken these orders seriously. I'll leave it in your capable hands.'

Meissner limped back to the dining room reading the orders. He resumed his seat. 'Look,' he said, looking at the men around him. 'I'm sorry if I, well ... if I said anything out of turn before.'

Schottl clapped him firmly on the back. 'Forget about it. You'll soon learn. What's that you've got?' he asked, pointing at the paper in Meissner's hand.

'Bloody WVHA.'*

'What do they want?'

'Seems the Reichsführer-SS is worried about morale in the camp system. We've been ordered to improve it ... *I've* been ordered to improve it – in Auschwitz, at least.'

'How?'

'Culture, so it would seem. We've all got to become more cultured. And I'm the one that has to make it happen.'

Schottl started to laugh. 'And you thought life here was rosy, didn't you? That'll teach you.'

Meissner could not help a sheepish grin. '*Touché*. But if either of you has any ideas, I'm open to suggestions.'

'I have one,' Weber offered. 'How about a chess club? The idea struck me some time ago. I play myself, but I never got round to asking if anyone else did.'

Meissner was doubtful: he had been thinking more along the lines of a choir. After all, singing seemed to be very popular at the country club. He turned to Schottl. 'What do you think?'

'Well, it's certainly cultural, no doubt about that.'

---

* *Wirtschafts und Verwaltungshauptamt*, the SS Economic-Administrative Main Office, which included the Concentration Camps Inspectorate.

'Do you play?' Weber asked.

Schottl shrugged but said, 'Of course. Who doesn't?'

Meissner pressed him: 'But do you think it would catch on?'

Weber was already warming to his suggestion. 'Yes, yes. The more I think about it, the better it gets. Officers who already play' – he indicated himself and Schottl – 'could take those who don't under their wings and show them the ropes. It could even be opened to the lower ranks. That would definitely be good for morale, wouldn't it – officers getting to know their men better?' He leaned back and took a mouthful of cognac. 'What could be better than chess? Wasn't it invented by a German?'

On Monday morning, Meissner was in his office at seven. Eidenmüller was there before him, a pot of coffee bubbling on the stove. Meissner had sensed that the Rottenführer would be useful to have around, and he had been right: he was a born fixer, a wizard at acquiring all sorts of items that were otherwise difficult – if not impossible – to obtain.

Meissner greeted his orderly by saying, 'What do you think about us starting a chess club, Eidenmüller?'

The Rottenführer kept his face deadpan. 'What, here, sir? In the office?'

'No, you idiot. I mean a camp chess club, for all the SS.'

'Officers *and* men, sir?'

'Yes. All ranks.'

Eidenmüller thought for a moment before replying, 'Well, I suppose it depends, sir.'

'Depends? Depends on what?'

'On whether we would be able to lay a few bets on it, sir.'

'A few bets?'

'Yes, sir. If the men were able to lay a bet or two on the games, I'm sure they'd be all for it. If they weren't, I wouldn't think there'd be much interest, to be honest.'

Meissner suppressed a smile. 'This is supposed to be adding to the cultural life of the camp, not creating opportunities for more of your shady dealings.'

Eidenmüller's features remained impassive. 'No, sir.'

'So, let me get this straight – if I allow betting on the games, you think a chess club would be popular?'

'Very popular, sir.'

'And who exactly would run this gambling enterprise?'

'I might know one or two people here and there, sir. I could ask around – with your permission, of course.'

Meissner merely grunted and sat down.

The orderly picked up the coffee pot and, filling a cup to the brim, placed it on the officer's desk. He turned to go.

At the door, Meissner called him back.

'Eidenmüller, while you're asking around, find out how many chess sets you can lay your hands on, will you?'

Eidenmüller smiled. 'It will be my pleasure, sir.'

6.

ZUGZWANG

Tuesday, 11 January 1944
Auschwitz-II, Birkenau

It is night and the train has stopped in the middle of a forest. Packed into fifteen cattle trucks, over a thousand people wait anxiously. There is no sound, apart from the wind howling through the trees and the freezing rain that gusts along the sides of the train. In every truck people are huddled together for warmth, for the wooden-slatted sides offer little protection from the biting cold.

It is still dark when the train resumes its journey. The regular *clack-clack* of the wheels, which has been a constant companion for close on a week, lulls nearly everybody back to a fitful sleep.

Less than half an hour later, the train stops for the final time.

Bright lights come on, assaulting the numbed senses of the passengers even through the wooden sides of the trucks. With a crash that has the quality of an explosion to those inside, the doors are thrown open and from the unnatural brightness outside comes the harsh, angry barking of orders shouted at people who do not understand them.

Beyond the opened doors is a long concrete platform. The passengers are forced out and herded away from the train. Possessions must be left where they fall. Now the passengers can see their tormentors: dark figures in the grey military uniform of the SS.

In one truck there is hesitation. A hand reaches up to the nearest person – an elderly man – and pulls at him roughly. He falls heavily onto the concrete below and rises uncertainly. He looks like he has broken an arm. One of the uniformed men calmly unholsters a pistol and holds it to the old man's head. A shot rings out. A woman screams. Her cry sounds disembodied, as if some banshee is shrieking in the dark beyond the floodlights. The body is kicked off the platform to fall beneath the wheels of the train.

It is as if a spell has been broken. To cries of '*Raus! Raus!*' the remaining passengers surge out of the trucks knowing that their lives depend on it.

On the platform an SS officer asks, '*Wer kann Deutsch sprechen?* Does anyone speak German?' Emil raises a reluctant hand. 'Come with me.' He is led to where several other officers are standing with an air of impatience, as if waiting in the cold for a bus that is late. A few more prisoners arrive. Each of them is told to go with an officer and translate orders.

Men are told to stand to one side and women to the other. The SS men separate out the elderly and children. Emil is anxious about his two boys, but the officer tells him not to worry: adults of working age will go to a work camp and the children will be sent to the family camp, where they will be cared for by those who are too old for manual labour. He says it with the weary calmness of a man who has given this reassurance a hundred times before.

It has the ring of normality, of truth. But it is the first of many lies in the land of liars. 'Family' is a word the Nazis have violated so that it has lost its natural meaning. In Auschwitz, 'family' means death.

With Emil interpreting, the officer sorts through the men who are fit for work. How old? Any special skills? It seems they have a quota to fill for able-bodied workers. Those with skills are an added bonus. Emil is lucky. He can speak German and is a master watchmaker. Emil sees that his wife, Rosa, has been told to stand in the column of women who have been selected for work. Their children, Louis and Marcel, are on the left with their grandmother.

All is now silent. One shooting is enough to subdue any resistance until one woman sees her children and breaks from the ranks to go to them.

A single blow from a rifle butt puts her on the ground.

'Stupid bitch,' one of the officers says as she rises unsteadily to her feet, wiping at the blood that runs down her face, then: 'Fine – let her go with them.'

The left column is marched away and disappears into the maw of the misty darkness that surrounds the area lit by the arc lamps.

Emil mouths a quiet, '*Au revoir*,' to his children. 'Be good for Granny.'

He does not know he will never see them again.

Emil is shaken awake by Yves. He was shouting in his sleep. Now he is crying, inconsolably. 'My children, my children,' he wails.

Yves tries to comfort him. If Emil does not quieten, the night guard will report him to the *Blockältester* and he will be punished for disturbing everybody's sleep.

'My beautiful boys…' Emil weeps. 'I don't even have a photograph of them. I can't remember what they look like.'

7.

ELOHIM AND THE
POWER OF JUDGEMENT

1962

Grand Hotel Krasnapolsky, Amsterdam

Friday morning saw the official opening of the World Chess Federation Interzonal tournament, to be followed by a formal lunch.

Rumours were rife that the German Grand Master would not show up for his opening match against the Israeli. At a hastily convened press conference, Harry Berghuis had answered all questions concerning the matter with: 'We shall have to wait and see.'

The vast hotel ballroom, with its spectacular high glass ceiling, had been cleared, and rows of tables set up, each with two chairs, a chessboard and a game-clock. There was an atmosphere of high expectation as a gaggle of arbiters stood opposite the entrance, waiting for the contestants to take their places.

All eyes were on table 7, where the game between Clément and Schweninger was to take place. Outside the entrance, the corridor was jammed with reporters and photographers. Rarely did the press show so much interest in a game of chess.

Wilhelm Schweninger pushed through the crowd, using his bulk to force people out of the way. To a shouted question: 'So, you won't be withdrawing from the competition, then?' he had roared, 'Of course not! What do you take me for – a coward? I'm not frightened of him or of any of the rubbish he spouts.'

There had been several notes in Emil's pigeon-hole at the hotel from journalists requesting interviews, and a telegram from his publisher. He had ignored them all; he had a game to prepare for. He had chosen to make a more discreet entrance than Schweninger, cutting through the hotel kitchens, arriving at the service entrance to the ballroom just before time.

At the appointed hour, the doors to the ballroom were firmly shut: no more contestants would be admitted. This created a buzz of expectation among the press outside, who assumed that the Israeli was a no-show. Inside, the tension was even greater as, without a word of greeting to one another, the two at the centre of all the attention took their places. An arbiter held out her hands concealing a black pawn in one, and white in the other. With a contemptuous shake of his head, Clément indicated that the German should choose.

Schweninger touched the arbiter's left hand. It opened to reveal white. Without ceremony he advanced his king's pawn two spaces and started the clock.

As he had in the coffee house, Clément composed himself in an attitude of prayer. He ignored the ticking of the clock, which seemed unusually loud. When he opened his eyes, he peered searchingly at his opponent for several moments, then moved his king's knight to sit two spaces in front of the bishop. Schweninger smiled. As he had expected, Clément's opening move was defensive, conceding the initiative to his opponent. He advanced his pawn one more space to attack the solitary knight. The knight moved to sit beside the pawn. The white queen's pawn moved forward two spaces. The black queen's pawn advanced one, offering itself to the white king's pawn. The German refused the gambit and attacked the knight again, this time with his queen's bishop's pawn. Clément allowed his knight to retreat to sit two spaces in front of its brother.

Harry Berghuis sidled up to the arbiter and whispered, 'How is it going?'

'Unbelievable. The German is using a three-pawn attack, and Clément is employing the Alekhine Defence.'

Berghuis raised an eyebrow. 'We might have expected Schweninger to be aggressive. But the Alekhine? That's reckless, surely. I don't think it's been seen in a major tournament for nearly twenty years. What is the Frenchman playing at?'

'Perhaps he knows something we don't.'

The night before the tournament, Emil Clément had retrieved a small velvet bag from his suitcase. It contained ten ivory tiles onto which were etched the first letters of the Hebrew alphabet. He emptied them onto a table, face down, and arranged them in the shape of the Sephiroth, creating the structure of the ten attributes through which the Divine Essence of Infinity is revealed. He turned the seventh tile, Netzah. He had chosen it because its significance was ambiguous: it could denote either 'victory' or 'eternity', and it lay beneath Hesed, the promise of mercy and healing. He turned the tile to reveal the letter ה – He – representing the sword of the Almighty and the strength that flows from the limitless power of God.

So be it: victory, not compassion.

His path now clear, Emil slept. When he discovered the next day that his game was to be played on table number 7, his faith in the power of the tiles was confirmed.

*

Emil's refusal to be drawn perplexed his opponent. Schweninger's attacking opening meant his pawns were now sitting in the centre of the board, to little purpose.

Having succeeded in unbalancing his rival, Clément set about his destruction with seemingly effortless calm.

His victory caused uproar. Schweninger's defeat had been accomplished in less than an hour.

8.

THE RÉTI OPENING

March 1944
Konzentrationslager Auschwitz-III, Monowitz

It is a Sunday, one of two rest days that are permitted each month. Warmer air is coming from the south and the chill of winter is fading. Though the warmth of the morning sun is slight, it is still pleasant, for the mosquitoes that plague the camp in summer have yet to emerge.

Emil is squatting on the bare earth beside the dormitory block, leaning back against the wall, enjoying the all-too-brief respite from work. He has been up for a while; on rest days, the inmates are permitted to use the washrooms, if there is any water available. He was one of the first into the showers and to go for lice control and have his head shaved. Now he is eating his morning bread ration slowly, trying to remember what it was like not to be hungry.

Time has no meaning here: it is too painful to contemplate the past and impossible to conceive of any future. There is only now, which is seared, like a brand, upon the consciousness; the struggle for this day, this hour, this minute, is all there is.

Yves settles beside him. He has lost much more weight than Emil, which is to be expected, for he works outside in a construction *Kommando*, while Emil has an indoor job that does not involve heavy physical labour. He eyes Emil's bread covetously, feigning indifference but failing.

42

Emil offers him some, but he shakes his head. 'One of us,' he says, 'has to live to get out of here, if only to tell the rest of the world what is happening.'

Emil holds the bread out again, but Yves pushes his hand back firmly. 'You're a good man, Emil, but if you have too many scruples you won't make it.'

'And if you end up a *Muselmann*,* it will help neither of us,' Emil objects, pushing the bread into Yves's hand.

Yves smiles. '*D'accord* – but only this once. And if anything comes my way...' He pulls a knife from under his jacket and cuts a chunk off before giving the rest back.

Yves's knife was a gift from Emil. Making knives has become Emil's métier in the camp. In the workshop to which he has been assigned, he has access to sheets of steel from which he fabricates and repairs various instruments for the Buna factory. The factory is a vast maze, as large as a town. Unknowable thousands toil here, coming and going constantly. In Buna, Emil sees the fable of the Tower of Babel, for many different languages are spoken, from across Europe and the East. In this shapeless tangle of concrete, iron and smoke it is in the nature of things to be insignificant and unnoticed, like an ant, and so it is easy for Emil to organize a small piece of steel, shape it and add a crude handle to make a knife. He manages one or two a week and sells them in the market. The going rate

* Slang used in Auschwitz to refer to prisoners who were so debilitated by starvation and abuse that they had lost the will to live: little more than skin-covered skeletons, wrapped in tattered blankets, they would sit or stand and stare vacantly, unaware, lost in the emptiness of their wretched existence, drifting aimlessly in the place between life and death, impervious to shouts or truncheon blows from *Kapos* to make them move. The word is thought to have come from a supposed resemblance to the kneeling posture adopted by Muslims in prayer.

is half a bread ration. It is something, but it is not enough, not for Yves. He is slowly starving to death.

Yves coughs, a long, laboured rasp, before saying, 'I have some news for you.'

'What sort of news?' Emil prays daily for news of his wife. He has heard nothing since they were parted during the selection on that first night. He harbours little hope for his mother and his children. He is certain they went up the chimney the day they arrived.

Yves hears the faint stirring of hope in Emil's voice. 'Nothing very important,' he says quickly, 'but something I think you'll be interested in. The *Blockältester* in Block 46 has a chess set. I'm told he plays every night.'

Emil leans forward eagerly. 'Whom does he play?'

'I don't know. But there's only one way to find out.' Yves finishes his bread and stands. 'I'll come with you.'

'No. I can manage by myself. You should rest.'

The blocks in Monowitz are all built to the same pattern: at the front, the door opens to reveal a small day room, furnished with a brick-built stove that offers some meagre warmth in the winter if wood can be found to fuel it. The day room leads to a much larger dormitory with rows of three-tiered wooden bunks in which the inmates huddle together to sleep. At Block 46 Emil stands respectfully at the entrance to the day room, cap in hand, and asks if he may speak to the *Ältester*. A short, stocky man comes to the door. He looks well fed, which is not surprising, for the block elder is a German and wears the green triangle of a convicted criminal on his uniform.

'What do you want?' The man draws on a cigarette. Even though it has probably been made with *Mahorca*, the dreadful adulterated tobacco that circulates in the camp, Emil eyes it enviously. He has not had a cigarette in months.

Emil clears his throat. 'I have heard that chess is played in your hut.'

'What if it is?'

'I like to play chess. Before I came here, I was quite a good player.'

'And you think you're good enough to join our little circle, eh?' The block elder belches, takes another puff of the cigarette and flicks the still-glowing butt at Emil's feet. 'What's in it for me?'

'I make knives.'

The elder glances at the red and yellow Star of David on Emil's chest. In an instant he weighs the value of what Emil might bring to his little fiefdom. 'No Jews,' he says, with a tight little shake of his head, and walks back inside.

Emil concludes that if he wants a chance to play chess he must do something extraordinary. Walking back to his block, he decides what he will do. It is risky, but it is worth it.

Yves cannot understand why Emil would take such a risk. 'If you are caught bringing it into the camp,' he says, 'you could get a dozen lashes, or more. I don't understand why you would do such a thing just for the sake of a game.'

Emil cannot make Yves understand the divine nature of chess. It is much more than a game. It is a connection with the intangible Wisdom of Creation; sublime; the possibilities limitless. It is the game created by the Ophanim to please God.

Emil would rather die than never play again.

The following Monday, he puts his plan into operation. At his workplace, he makes an offer to the civilian supervisor. Wartime shortages mean that items like watches are difficult for civilians to obtain, apart from cheap, unreliable ones. Emil asks if the supervisor has any watches or clocks that need mending. In return for one broken watch, Emil will mend two others, using scraps and tools from the instrument workshop. He does the work during the break that the prisoners are allowed for lunch. The supervisor is delighted with the result. Word gets around quickly, and it is not long before Emil is asked to repair watches for others.

Two weeks later, he returns to Block 46. Again he asks to speak to the *Blockältester*. When he comes to the doorway Emil shows him the watch he has repaired. 'I forgot to say that as well as making knives, I'm also a watchmaker.'

The *Ältester* is bemused. 'You'll give me this if I let you play?' He can hardly believe it – the watch is worth a lot of bread. 'Fucking Jews,' he says. 'I'll never understand them as long as I live.' But he stands aside and lets Emil in.

SS-Obersturmbannführer Liebehenschel leaned back in his chair and put his feet up on the desk, the chair teetering on two legs. Eidenmüller, newly promoted to Unterscharführer, having deposited two cups of coffee on the desk, came to attention, about-turned smartly, and marched briskly out of Meissner's office.

Meissner opened a filing cabinet and took out a bottle of Armagnac. He poured a generous measure into each cup.

Liebehenschel smiled as he watched the NCO's retreating back. 'I must say, Meissner,' he said, as a cup was passed to him, 'you've wrought quite a transformation in this place. As for that fellow, I thought he was incorrigible, but he's a new man. I've never seen him looking so smart. I don't suppose you've managed to put a stop to his thieving, too?'

'One thing at a time, sir, one thing at a time.'

The Kommandant laughed. 'Fair enough. Rome wasn't built in a day.' He took a sip of his coffee. 'Now, about this chess club. When you suggested it I thought you were mad, but I'm amazed at the way it's taken off. Everywhere I go there are people playing – according to my orderly, even the enlisted men and NCOs. It's extraordinary. How did you know it would be so popular?'

Meissner thought back to the confrontation he'd had with the Kommandant over the idea for the chess club. His suggestion had been met with a frosty response: '*When I asked you to take this on, Meissner, it was because I had gained some respect for your abilities and devotion to duty. And you come to me with this? A half-baked notion about some chess club? This is the SS, not the Boy Scouts. I passed you a serious order, endorsed by Himmler himself, and this is how you respond? Did you know that at Majdanek they have started a choir? Next time the Reichsführer visits, they'll be able to regale him with a bit more than the fucking Horst Wessel song. Here, he'll be able to watch a game or two of chess – if doesn't fall asleep.*'

But as the Kommandant had already observed, one of the young Obersturmführer's qualities was tenacity. He had stood his ground: '*With respect, sir, the order was to improve morale, not to provide entertainment for the Reichsführer.*' He had been dismissed with a dire warning that it had better work.

And it had – not least because of the widespread and sometimes heavy betting that went on.

'It was Obersturmführer Weber who convinced me, sir,' Meissner replied. 'After all, what could be more German than chess?' Now Meissner wanted to speak to the Kommandant about how the idea could be augmented by instituting an annual camp championship. Eidenmüller had come up with the suggestion, inspired – Meissner was sure – by the fact that it would greatly increase the turnover of his gambling monopoly.

But although pleased at the initial success of the chess club, the Kommandant needed convincing that a competition was a good idea. 'How exactly would it work? I'm not keen on the idea of the enlisted ranks getting cosy with their superiors over a chessboard.'

'No, sir. I thought we could run two parallel championships – one for the enlisted men and NCOs, and one for the officers. We could have a supreme camp champion, with the winners of the two competitions playing in a grand final.'

'What about prizes?'

'I think there should be prizes, yes, sir.' Meissner had already worked out what the prizes should be: for the runner-up, a five-day pass to Berlin, and, for the champion, two weeks' home leave.

Now he added the final twist, which he was sure the Kommandant's vanity would find irresistible. 'Once we have our two Grand Masters, we can issue a challenge to the other camps. The SS-Totenkopfverbände Chess Championship could become an annual event, hosted by K-Z Auschwitz. Would that not more than fulfil the directive to boost morale?'

9.

BISHOP'S OPENING

1962

Amsterdam

Apart from the first-round games that had yet to be concluded, Sunday was a day of rest for the contestants. Emil had a late breakfast and went out for a walk.

He had never been to a place like Amsterdam before. Its canals gave it a tranquillity that he had not expected – a quiet presence that had crept up on him, especially when the wind was still. The last flourish of winter was past and the trees that lined the canals were coming into bud. The sun peeked through the branches, throwing dappled shadows along the banks. People were up and working on house barges, giving them an airing and a fresh coat of paint, and the stalls at the flower market were full of daffodils and tulips.

Emil's walk led him further than he had been before, to Vondelpark. There, he rested for a while on a bench, watching the city go by. The young people on their bikes seemed particularly attractive, so carefree and full of life. It was well past noon when he decided to resume his journey, heading back towards Leidseplein.

The café, where he had become a regular visitor, was full of people out for a drink before Sunday dinner. On a row of tables outside, games of chess were in full swing. The old man he had played a few days before was standing by one of them, in animated conversation with a priest, a tall man with silver-grey hair.

When the old man saw Emil he waved. 'Good afternoon, my friend,' he said affably. 'We were just talking about you – about the strange defence you played, you remember? The Son of Sorrow.'

The priest turned. His face was drawn, its complexion sallow. Emil's first impression was that he looked tired, that he was somebody who had become old before his time. But a smile transformed his features, making it warm and welcoming.

The priest pulled off a black woollen glove and extended a bony hand. 'Hello,' he said, in a voice that was unexpectedly soft. No, Emil realized almost immediately, not soft – sickly. 'I was hoping I might meet you. Old Marius here has been telling me all about you, and the game you played. You made something of an impression on him. And your picture was in the paper – did you see it? Your victory over the German Grand Master made quite a splash. I'm a fan of chess, though I'm not much of a player. I think it requires a mind with more subtlety than mine.'

Emil took the proffered hand, but his greeting died on his lips. He had met the priest before, he was certain of it. His eyes were shockingly familiar: a blue as deep as the summer sky over Tel Aviv; clear as crystal.

'Hello,' he stammered finally, speaking in German without thinking. 'Emil Clément.'

A waiter was taking orders and the priest beckoned him over. 'Have you tried the advocaat?' he asked. When Emil shook his head he said, 'You should. They make their own here – a family recipe. If it were not sacrilegious, I should be tempted to say it was divine.'

He ordered three glasses.

'Forgive me,' Emil said, 'but I am sure we have met before.'

'Yes,' the priest replied, in a tone that suggested this was something he did not wish to discuss, 'we have. But, if you'll permit me to say, I think that this is not the time nor place to talk about it. For now, let us enjoy our drinks and perhaps watch a game or two of chess.'

'My parish is where the bishop lives,' old Marius announced proudly. 'He was sent here to convalesce – from the missions,' he added.

'Bishop?' Emil raised an eyebrow. There was no hint of exalted rank in the priest's apparel, which was plain black with the usual clerical collar.

'Here it's purely an honorary title,' the priest explained. 'My see is a long way from here – a province in the Belgian Congo.'

There was something in the priest's manner that Emil did not like, while his admission that they had met before was like an itch that he could not resist scratching. 'You said we had met before—? I know for sure I've never been to the Belgian Congo. Have you ever been to Israel?'

'No – but I think you might like the Congo if you were to visit. Leopoldville can be quite lively, and the interior has a reputation it tries hard to live up to.'

'Reputation?'

'Africa – dark and mysterious.' The waiter arrived with the advocaat. The priest raised his glass in a toast. 'To Africa.' He sipped appreciatively. When Emil left his untasted, the priest continued, 'I'm sorry – is it not to your liking?'

Emil set his glass down on a nearby table. 'No. What is not to my liking is a pointed refusal to answer a perfectly straightforward question.'

'I'm sorry,' the priest replied. 'I didn't intend to give offence. I thought it was for the best. It was a long time ago.'

'But where?'

'Auschwitz.' The word was like an electric shock. Their eyes locked and suddenly Emil knew. He barely heard the rest of what the priest said: 'My name is Meissner. Paul Meissner.'

Memory can play strange and sometimes unfortunate tricks. For Emil, the name was like a key that unlocks a door that leads to another, which in turn leads to another, then another, and so on, back, year after year, to the point in time before which his memory could not bear to travel: the spring of 1944. He saw the bishop as he had seen him then; and again, before he had disappeared. He remembered the crystalline blueness of his eyes, the certainty of his superiority, his imperturbable confidence. And now he had reappeared, as if the illusionist who had made him disappear nearly two decades ago had, at this very instant, decided to bring him back. Time stopped, anticipating the applause that would surely follow such mastery of the art of conjuring. And he was wearing the garb of a man of God – surely another trick? If Meissner had turned up wearing his SS uniform, it could hardly have been more shocking. Meissner had been a prince in the kingdom of liars, so this new identity also had to be a lie. No other explanation was conceivable.

Emil froze. He looked uncertainly from the bishop to the old man, to the other people milling around the front of the café. His brain sought frantically to find the words he had wanted to say to this man for nearly twenty years, but they would not come. Instead, he felt light-headed. The pavement seemed to take on the properties of a fairground mirror pulling his vision in and out of focus. He put out a hand to steady himself on a table edge but it slipped and with an almost inaudible gasp he fell, knocking drinks and plates from nearby tables onto the paving stones. At the edge of his consciousness he was aware of shouts of alarm, but they were distant, not part of his universe, from creatures that inhabited a dream world whose cries were foreign and unintelligible.

He heard again the lamentation that was the cry of Auschwitz.

10.

THE DESTINY OF A POISONED PAWN

April 1944

Kommandantur building, Konzentrationslager Auschwitz-I

Eidenmüller drove the *Kübelwagen* through the entrance to the *Stammlager*, passing beneath the blackened iron arch wrought with the words '*Arbeit Macht Frei*', before turning left to follow the road to the *Appelplatz*. He stopped to allow Obersturmführer Meissner to step down outside a two-storey building above which flew the emblem of everything the camp stood for: a black swastika in a white roundel on a scarlet banner.

The officer leaned heavily on his walking stick to push himself out of the car. 'Wait for me,' he said. He had an appointment with the Kommandant. He did not expect it to take long.

Inside, Meissner got quickly to the point: 'I have a suggestion to make, sir, that some may find shocking. Some might consider it disloyal but, please believe me, my motives are purely to do with the efficiency of the camp.'

Liebehenschel was intrigued. 'Shocking *and* disloyal? And all in one day. I can't believe that of you, Meissner.' He smiled and opened an intricate silver box that stood on his desk. 'Cigarette?'

Meissner took one and lit up. He exhaled a cloud of smoke upwards. 'The thing is, sir, that in order to sustain an acceptable work output, a certain amount of food is necessary. This holds true whether the worker is a German, a Russian, a Pole or a Jew. I'm afraid that the physical condition of many of the prisoners is poor at best, and this affects their ability to do strenuous work.'

Meissner's words prompted a searching look from his superior. 'You are quite right, Meissner,' the Kommandant replied. 'That is why our doctors work tirelessly to identify those who are no longer capable of doing what is required of them and have them eliminated.'

Meissner drew deeply on the cigarette. 'You'll forgive me for saying so, sir, but that approach is inefficient. It means that at intervals – which occur far too frequently – new workers must be inducted who have to learn skills that their predecessors had already acquired.'

'I take it you have a suggestion?'

'Yes, sir. I propose that the food ration be increased. That way we could get more work out of them for longer. It would be much more productive than the present system.'

The Kommandant flicked at the sleeve of his tunic, removing specks of ash that had fallen from his cigarette. 'You were right to bring this to me, Meissner,' he observed. 'With food at home strictly rationed, some of your colleagues would undoubtedly consider the idea of giving more food to Jews to be disloyal, and would be shocked that it had been suggested by a fellow SS officer. But I fully appreciate your motives.'

Meissner nodded, but did not tell his commanding officer what had brought about this sudden interest in prisoner rations. He had been taking some air a few days before, at the same time that the prisoners were being marched back from the Buna factory. A man had stumbled and fallen. The *Kapo* in charge had halted the squad and kicked and beaten the fallen man unmercifully.

Meissner had intervened. 'You won't get any work out of him if you kill him,' he'd said.

The *Kapo* had removed his beret and stood to attention. 'With respect, Herr Obersturmführer,' he had retorted, the sneer in his voice imitating that of many of the SS NCOs, 'that's all they're fit for. He's nothing but a dirty, lazy, idle Jew. Plenty more where he came from.'

Meissner had stared at the *Kapo*, his eyes drawn to the green triangle on his jacket: a criminal. So serious were his crimes that he had been sent to Auschwitz, where, in accordance with the perverse rules of the camp, criminals were put in charge of honest men and women.

Meissner had addressed the prisoner. 'What have you had to eat today?'

The prisoner had hung his head and not replied.

'He doesn't speak much German, sir,' the *Kapo* said. 'Italian.'

'Then translate, goddammit.'

The prisoner's voice could barely be heard. He'd had a ration of bread and a bowl of soup. No doubt the soup had been taken off the top of the cauldron and was thin, not like the thick soup at the bottom, where the chunks of potato and turnip settled. The *Kapo* and his cronies kept that for themselves.

Meissner had been furious. He had been charged with increasing the output of the labour camps but the poor food and capricious brutality were working against him all the time.

Now, Liebehenschel steepled his fingers thoughtfully. Meissner had a point, but the system for feeding the prisoners was long established – calculated to induce slow starvation among the Jewish slave labourers. There was nothing he could do to change it, no matter how much it might improve productivity. But he had to give the appearance of taking Meissner's concern seriously.

'Very well, Meissner, I'll speak to Dr Wirths about it. More than that, I cannot do.'

'He's the *Standortarzt*?'*

'Indeed.' Liebehenschel gave his subordinate a look that said he was dismissed, but Meissner did not move. 'There's more, Obersturmführer?'

'I've been checking the documentation relating to the acquisition of food. The records indicate that, in fact, enough food is purchased every day to provide an adequate number of calories for each prisoner. If the food isn't going to the prisoners, where is it going?'

The Kommandant sighed. Meissner was certainly tenacious, like a dog with a bone. Rather than answer immediately, he stood up and walked to the door, gesturing for Meissner to follow. In the doorway he paused and, turning to face the junior officer, said: 'You've never been to Kanada, have you, Meissner?'

April 1944
Konzentrationslager Auschwitz-III, Monowitz

Alarm is spreading through the camp. Typhus. It skulks in the shadows at every door looking for a way in. It is a pestilence feared by all. In the washrooms, there are signs in many different languages: *One louse is enough to kill you* – for that is how typhus ensnares its victims and spreads its foulness through the camp. The signs are among the many absurdities of Auschwitz, because the procedures for the prevention of lice are laughable. For the inmates, hot showers and soap are as rare as a visit from the Pope, yet lice are a deadly enemy, so when the inmates have time, they scour each other's bodies for the tiny creatures, squeezing the

* Chief garrison physician, with authority over the twenty or so other SS doctors in the Auschwitz complex.

life out of them between two fingernails. But now, it seems, there is an outbreak in Block 51.

Of course the camp is better informed than the SS doctors: all the inmates know the outbreak started two days ago. A man from 51 went to the infirmary after evening roll call. At first the symptoms are inconclusive. A day later, there were two more men from 51 with the same symptoms.

The SS doctors take no chances. On their command, the fate of the men is sealed: all three are sent to the gas chamber. This is to be expected. The sick men are resigned to their fate, and nobody lifts a finger to help them.

And now heavily armed SS men are marching through the camp, many of them with dogs. The camp bell is ringing, a sound that drowns out the camp's own frantic warnings. When the bell rings before sunrise it means: '*Out of bed. Rouse yourselves. Up, up, up!*'; when it rings at any other time of day, it is a command to return to your block and stay there.

In every block the inmates cower.

Emil is playing chess in Block 46 when the bell rings. He is winning but that is hardly surprising: since the *Blockältester* deigned to allow him to play, he has won every game. Nobody says a word when he leaves and walks like an automaton to his own block. Widmann, the *Blockschreiber*, is conducting a roll call. His pencil marks a tick against Emil's number. Inmates crowding around the door keep watch. It is the same in every block. The watchers shout into the block, reporting what is happening. The SS men march past without a glance in their direction. 'They are going past, they are going past.' The shouts are almost jubilant with relief. Bit by bit, more information trickles in from the door.

'They have stopped at Block 51.'

'They have sent the dogs in.'

'Now everybody is coming out.'

'They are marching them away.'

The SS doctors outside Block 51 come not as healers, but as executioners. Without regard for whether they are infected or healthy, all the inmates in the block are sent to Birkenau. Only the *Blockältester* and the other criminals who run the block for the SS are allowed the luxury of going to the infirmary. They will have to take their chances, but at least they are not going up the chimney.

The other inmates start to breathe again. They do not care whom fate has selected for death on this day, as long as it is not them. It is not because they are naturally cold-hearted. It is simply the way of things in Auschwitz. They deceive themselves, telling one another: 'It was their time; it is going to happen to us all eventually. Who has the strength to think about when it will be our time, as long as it is not now?'

A deep sense of shame runs through the camp. It has witnessed another barbarity. Its very conscience is defiled by what it has seen. It can no longer tell good from evil: there is no good, there is no evil – only life or death. Over 200 men are put into trucks and taken away. They will be forced into one of the gas chambers or shot. A day later their cold ashes will be scattered over the surrounding fields.

Emil finds Yves. Never before have they seen an entire block taken away to be murdered.

'It is an act of depravity,' Emil says, in the privacy afforded by their bunk space. 'Those were good men, healthy. These SS – some of them are doctors. Do they feel no shame?'

'Of course not,' Yves replies. 'If they did, they could not do what they do; it would be intolerable to them.' He is silent for a short while, then adds, 'Somebody must remember this day, to be a witness to it.'

Emil puts his head in his hands. He starts to weep, silent sobs shaking his body.

'What is it, Emil?'

The watchmaker searches his friend's eyes, as if hoping for forgiveness. 'I am scared that I have been infected by their corruption... if I were to look back on this day, it would be to say it was a day I played chess. This – *horror* – is too much to ask me to remember.'

Yves takes his friend's hands in his own. 'You mustn't think like that. This is not *your* shame to bear, but theirs. They do it because we are nothing to them. We are worthless. We are no longer even human beings. We are less to the SS than sacks of beans or potatoes. That is the truth of this place.'

But Emil is not satisfied. 'How did we become so worthless?'

'Have you not understood, Emil? Are you so caught up in your mystical other-world of pawns and kings that you have not seen that we are on a journey to nothingness?'

April 1944
Kanada, Konzentrationslager Auschwitz-II, Birkenau

Meissner surveyed the scene before him with seemingly calm detachment. He was in a large warehouse. Inmates scurried in with heavily loaded hand-carts, emptied their contents onto a large pile in the centre of the floor, then out again to return with a fresh load. An army of people, mostly women, some in camp uniforms, others in ordinary civilian clothes, delved into the pile, sorting it into a variety of categories: shirts, trousers, coats, dresses, jackets, hats, shoes, underwear, spectacles, suitcases, handbags – the last gleanings of the loot stolen from Jews from across Europe. Around the edges of the warehouse were mountains of these goods, waiting to be redistributed.

It was difficult not to show amazement at the scale of the plunder that was taking place before his eyes.

'Trains arrive daily,' the Kommandant said, in a low, matter-of-fact tone, 'sometimes two a day. Typically we can expect a thousand to fifteen hundred head on each train. They are compelled to leave their belongings on the unloading ramp. When they are inducted into the camp, they are relieved of their clothes and small possessions, like wristwatches or jewellery. Everything becomes the property of the Reich. It is all brought here to Kanada. All sorts of things find their way here. There is one Scharführer who spends every day doing nothing but sorting foreign currency. Every month it is sent to the Reichsbank where it is exchanged for Reichsmarks and the proceeds come back to the SS. Another is an expert jeweller who picks out choice items and grades precious stones. Gold and silver items are melted down.'

'Why is this place called Kanada?' Meissner asked.

Liebehenschel responded with a world-weary sigh. 'Because Kanada is a place of untold riches.'

'Why are you showing me this, sir? Does it have something to do with the discrepancy between the food that is purchased and the food that is distributed?'

The Kommandant stood aside to let a hand-cart pass. 'I'm afraid to say, Meissner, that not all members of the SS are as incorruptible as you. Some months before your arrival, the Concentration Camps Inspectorate initiated a commission of inquiry into corruption. Theft on a grand scale by SS officers was suspected. Some had their hands so deep in the honey pot that they were unable to get themselves clean again in time.'

He looked at Meissner. 'What I'm trying to say is that I'm sure there is still plenty of thieving going on, but it's more discreet, and on a considerably smaller scale. We try to control it by not allowing junior ranks to spend long periods of time here, but even officers are not always as trustworthy as they should be. Some of them collude with the prisoners – as you might have guessed. Valuable items that the prisoners find among the clothes and baggage are traded for food or privileges. What is happening with the rations in Monowitz is insignificant in comparison.'

April 1944

Technical workshop, IG Farbenindustrie Buna Werke, Monowitz

It is the day after the cleansing of Block 51. One of the Polish civilian workers brings a watch for Emil to repair. In return, he offers Emil a portion of his *Zivilsuppe* – the food prepared for the civilian workers – for the next two weeks. The watch is small and elegant, with a delicate movement. 'It belonged to my wife's mother,' the man tells him. 'She passed away a few weeks ago. It would mean a lot to my wife if I could get it fixed.'

Two words plunge deep into Emil's consciousness: 'wife' and 'mother'. He wants to shout, 'What about my mother? What about my wife?' He must keep such thoughts to himself. All morning, Emil keeps his thoughts locked in the vault of his mind, until the events of the previous day force their way in.

Everyone knows there is a camp for women. He hopes Rosa is there, but typhus is everywhere and the SS would have no more scruples over eliminating a block in the women's camp than they had had in Monowitz.

In an unguarded moment, these thoughts rush to the surface and Emil reveals his bitterness to the men at the nearby work benches. 'Did you see what happened to the men of Block 51 yesterday? It's only a matter of time before they do it to the rest of us. The SS are depraved,' he says. 'All of them.'

It takes only one to denounce him. Perhaps he is envious of Emil's newfound status with the civilian workers; perhaps not. Most likely he is simply starving. His reward is two rations of bread, riches beyond temptation to one suffering the hunger of Auschwitz.

As the men queue for the midday soup ration, the *Kapo* orders Emil to report to the Buna Rapportführer, SS-Scharführer Gessner.

Emil stands rigidly to attention, his cap held firmly in his hand, not looking at the SS man, eyes fixed on the wall ahead. The Scharführer is seated at a table eating his lunch: white bread and sausage. The rich smell of the sausage is torture.

The SS man seems to be in good humour. 'So, you are 163291.' For a moment he says nothing more, picking with his fingernail at a bit of sausage between his teeth. Then he reveals the depth of Emil's betrayal: 'The watchmaker.'

He pauses to let his words take effect. 'You thought I did not know about that, didn't you? Well, let me tell you, nothing happens in this camp that I do not know about.' He waits for Emil's reaction. When there is none, he continues: 'I have been informed that you said the SS is depraved.'

Emil feels his bowels constrict. His mouth goes dry and, instinctively, he swallows.

There is no point dissembling. Besides, he has made a promise to himself: he will not add to the lies on which the camp is built. 'Yes, Herr Scharführer.' His reply is not defiant, merely truthful.

The Scharführer leans back in his chair and slaps his thigh as if Emil has told him a great joke. A broad grin appears on his face and he laughs uproariously. There is a riding crop on the table. With great deliberateness, the Scharführer picks it up and, still laughing, comes from behind the table and strikes Emil viciously with it.

Emil falls to the floor, but he has seen what happens to prisoners who do not immediately get up: invariably, their punishment intensifies. Some are beaten to death. He picks himself up and stands to attention again. The skin on his face is split and blood runs from it, dripping over his chin onto his uniform. The pain is excruciating. Tears form in his eyes.

The Scharführer seems to approve. He walks in a circle around Emil, stopping once or twice to peer closely at the rough material of his tattered striped uniform.

Emil says a silent prayer that he has the correct number of buttons on his jacket and that there is not too much mud on his trouser bottoms. Although there are no facilities for the washing of clothes, punishments are frequently inflicted for having a muddy uniform. Emil tenses, expecting a second blow, but not knowing where or when it will fall.

The Scharführer speaks again. 'Your supervisor tells me you are a good worker. Can you believe he called you his "good Jew" and asked me not to beat you too severely?' Emil does not reply. The German continues: 'It astonishes me that you Jews do not understand the danger you pose to the Fatherland, especially after the Führer made it so clear. How can you be so ignorant?' He indulges himself with a second blow with the riding crop. He raises his hand to inflict a third but relents. What is the point? It is foolish to expect a Jew to understand – in fact, in a way, for a Jew to say the SS is depraved is a compliment. Everyone knows that in the twisted way that Jews think, everything is back to front: good is bad, rich is poor and depraved means heroic.

The Scharführer looks closely at Emil's face before dismissing him. 'If there could be such a thing as a good Jew, *Watchmaker*, I am sure you would be the one.' He laughs again. It dawns on him that what he has said without thinking is very funny. *A good Jew?* It is hilarious. But his humour quickly cools. 'Now, you stinking Jewish turd,' he says, his voice menacing and angry, 'get out of my sight before I change my mind and give you the beating you deserve.'

11.

QUEEN'S GAMBIT ACCEPTED

1962

Kerk de Krijtberg, Amsterdam

Emil awoke in a darkened room. Heavy curtains were drawn across tall windows. He was on a leather couch, with a blanket draped over him. Beside it was a small table on which stood a glass of water. As his eyes became accustomed to the gloom he was able to make out the features of the room. Opposite the couch was a heavy stone fireplace, above which was a large painting of the Madonna and the infant Christ. The picture was old, blackened from its proximity to the fire. The wallpaper was similarly smutted, adding to the impression of age. On either side of the fire sat tall, leather armchairs, their armrests rubbed to a shine, and horsehair stuffing peeking out in places where fingers had drummed times beyond counting. The hearth was home to a set of antique fire-irons. Against the wall opposite the window was a bookcase stuffed with ancient volumes and, above the door, a simple wooden crucifix. On the mantelpiece stood a clock in a brass case; as Emil tried to focus on it to see the time, it chimed four. Moments later, the door opened. Emil sat upright.

'Watchmaker,' the bishop said, his voice hushed. 'Welcome back. How are you feeling?'

Shocked, Emil struggled to make sense of what he had heard. 'Watchmaker? Nobody has called me that since…'

'No. But you didn't answer my question – how are you feeling?'

'I don't know. Awful.'

'You fainted. I suppose we could have called an ambulance, but on a Sunday it would have taken ages. The presbytery was not far, so I got a couple of volunteers to help bring you here. You've been out for quite a while. I was worried about you. I was about to call a doctor.'

Emil inhaled deeply, catching unfamiliar smells of incense and wax polish. 'Worried? Why would you be worried? You're not my keeper.' He got unsteadily to his feet. 'I should be going.'

The bishop barred his way. 'I don't think so. You should be resting. Let me help you – you've had quite a shock.'

Emil shook his head. 'Is that what you want – to help me? Why? So you can congratulate yourself that you came to my rescue again? No. I don't need your help, and I'm not staying.'

'I hoped we might take some time to talk.'

Emil was incredulous. '*Talk*? What could you possibly have to say to me that I would want to hear?'

Meissner retreated a little and bowed his head in an attitude of contrition. 'I thought perhaps I could start by saying I was sorry.'

'Sorry?' Emil found himself shouting. 'You are . . .' He stopped, unable to find words to express what he felt. 'We meet again after a gap of nearly twenty years and you think you can wipe away all that passed between us simply by saying *sorry*?'

'No, no, of course not. But it would have been a start.' The bishop moved aside, gesturing towards the door. 'Leave, if you wish,' he said, gently.

Emil's bitterness had been quick to erupt but Meissner's response had taken him by surprise. He had expected his anger to be met with more anger but, instead, the opposite had happened. His rage melted away; in its place he found the smouldering coals of what his life had become.

His anger could not always be trusted, but the coals could.

'Look,' he said, his voice becoming calmer, 'there is nothing we can say to each other that can possibly be worth saying, and as there is no changing what passed between us, I really do think it best if we go our separate ways.'

Meissner looked at him. 'It's for you to decide, naturally, but if you'll permit me to say, I do not agree with you that it would be best to go our separate ways. I think we have many things to say to one another, things that may be hard to say, but which nonetheless need to be said.'

Emil stood unmoving, casting his gaze around the room, taking in the odd variety of the knick-knacks that filled it, his mind seeking reasons to leave other than the bitterness with which he was filled.

'I would consider it an honour if you would stay to share my supper this evening,' Meissner said, breaking the silence.

'Why?'

From habit, the bishop's fingers strayed to the cross on his breast. 'Do you remember what you once said to me in Auschwitz? "There is no why. The outside world does not intrude here. We have been inoculated against it." For now, all I can tell you is that "Why?" is too complicated a question for me to understand.' He shrugged. 'For years now I have answered to an inner compulsion. I have tried to resist it, but without succeeding. I have told it I am not worthy, can never be worthy, but it does not listen to me. In the seminary they told me it was "my vocation", but I can't see it that way.' His voice took on a tone of almost desperate yearning. 'It is *more* than that. It is God's love working its way into the world, taking as its instrument something – someone – that once served evil, but moulding it to its own divine purpose. So to answer your question "Why?" in perhaps a simplistic way – because I am a sword that has been beaten into a ploughshare.'

1947

Kraków

In his prison cell, Paul Meissner was waiting for his lawyer. Meissner did not like the man. He was possessed of a colossal sense of his own importance.

For his part, Meissner's lawyer regarded his client with cynical disdain. That the German was a war criminal was obvious. The state was wasting its money appointing a lawyer to conduct his defence.

As usual, the lawyer had been late. 'If it were possible to find even one Auschwitz prisoner to testify on your behalf, that would make all the difference,' he now said, not bothering to suppress a yawn.

An exasperated Meissner retorted: 'Have you listened to anything I've told you? I had nothing to do with the prisoners. Why would I? I was an administrator with responsibility for the SS personnel in the satellite camps.' Angrily, he banged his fist on the table. 'I told you there was only one prisoner I had dealings with. *He's* the one you have to find.'

The lawyer made a show of consulting his notes. 'Ah, yes, "the Watchmaker". But you say you can't remember his name, only his number.'

'It's not a question of remembering or not remembering. Everybody called him the Watchmaker. But you must be able to trace him from the number.'

The lawyer was sceptical. '*If* the records were preserved, and *if* he survived.'

'Yes,' Meissner agreed, dejectedly. 'If he survived.'

But no trace had been found of *Häftling* number 163291. He had not been included in any records of inmates who had eventually turned up at other camps, like Mauthausen or Bergen-Belsen.

The lawyer yawned again. The case was hopeless.

The president of the court addressed Meissner's lawyer. 'Before the verdicts are read out and sentence is passed, does the defendant have anything to say?'

The lawyer stood. Drawing himself up to his full height, he adjusted his robes, grasping them in his right hand in a pose he imagined to be reminiscent of Cicero addressing the courts of ancient Rome.

'With the court's permission, my client would like to read a statement.'

In the dock, wearing trousers without a belt and a collarless shirt, ex-SS-Hauptsturmführer Paul Meissner rose to his feet. Only weeks before, his ex-commanding officer, Arthur Liebehenschel, had been condemned to death by hanging in this same court-room. But when Meissner spoke, his voice was clear and unwavering.

'I have not attempted to hide from the court the nature and extent of my activities in Auschwitz. Terrible crimes were committed there – unforgivable crimes. I do not seek to diminish the part I played, nor do I seek to evade my responsibility. I acknowledge that I am guilty of grave crimes, but I would like to put on record that I believe I did what I could to maintain my honour. Before I went to Auschwitz, I had no idea of what was going on in Birkenau. I learned about those events only gradually. I had nothing to do with anything that occurred there. I never set foot on the unloading ramp, and took no part in any of the *Selektionen*. Not one prisoner in Auschwitz died because of me. Once I realized I had no ability to change what was going on, I took what I considered to be the only honourable course of action – I requested a transfer back to active service, even though my old regiment was at that time fighting on the Eastern Front. All of this was recorded in my personal journal, which the court has graciously acknowledged. Many thought I was going to certain death, but that was preferable to being an accomplice in mass murder. When I surrendered, I did so as an SS officer and, unlike others, made no attempt to hide it. That, too, was a matter of honour for me. I did my duty. I do not ask the court for clemency and I am ready to accept whatever sentence is deemed fitting.'

It took only minutes for the president of the court to deliver the verdict and sentence: 'On the charge of genocide – not guilty; on the charge of complicity in genocide – not guilty. However, on your own admission, you are guilty of the hideous crime of slavery. You administered a system in which tens of thousands, mainly Jews, were used as slave workers, and although they did not die at your hand or at your command, still many of them perished. This is a crime that demands exemplary punishment.'

Meissner braced himself. The court did not have a history of leniency.

'You are sentenced to six years' penal servitude with hard labour. The sentence is to commence immediately.'

1962
Kerk de Krijtberg, Amsterdam

'Six years with hard labour. Little enough reparation for the part you played,' Clément said, breaking chunks of white bread into a thick vegetable broth.

'Little enough,' Meissner conceded. 'But not easy, especially with an artificial leg.'

'Not easy? Is that what you tell people? You should listen to yourself.

Not easy?' Emil stared at him in disbelief. 'Easier than we had it every day in Auschwitz, that's what I would say. Did they feed you sawdust bread and pig-swill? You should be grateful you had a wooden leg.'

'The leg lasted less than two months. The best craftsmanship German engineering could produce, and it fell to bits.'

Clément held his spoon before him, like a weapon, punctuating his sentences with it. 'You know what this sounds like to me? It sounds like you're feeling sorry for yourself. Did you know that when the Russians liberated Auschwitz, they found thousands of artificial limbs from Jews who were killed in the gas chambers? *Thousands*. Maybe you should have asked for one of those.'

'How could I? I had no idea they were there. Besides, the Poles had no intention of finding me a replacement. And it's pretty nigh impossible to do hard labour on crutches. They did try, of course, but no matter how often they beat me, I kept falling over. After a while the beatings stopped. In the end they put me in the kitchens. I was given a stool and a knife and I spent my days peeling and chopping vegetables. I got pretty good at it.'

'How the mighty are fallen.'

Paul did not respond to Emil's irony and they finished the soup in silence. Afterwards, the bishop busied himself clearing the dishes from the table.

'Six years,' Clément mused. 'It's no time at all. Who decided on six years? Not a Jew, I think.'

Meissner resumed his seat at the table. 'Actually, in the end I served only four years in prison. I think they were tired of me. I was unceremoniously deported to the British occupation zone, where I had to undergo de-Nazification.'

'What did that involve? Making you wear *tefillin* to see if you were struck with apoplexy, or eat matzos to see if you choked?'

Meissner sighed. 'No. They made me complete the *Fragebogen* – a questionnaire – and a series of interrogations. The British were suspicious of me. By then, relations between the West and Russia were at a low and they suspected I was a Communist plant; it was months before I got my *Persilschein* – my official exoneration. Only then could I look for work. I was offered a job in a ticket office on the railways, but I had already decided what it was I wanted to do. I asked to train as a priest in the Catholic Church.'

'So you swapped one organization that would look after you and tell you what to do, for another. Not exactly a hard life, it seems to me – being a priest.' Emil turned in his chair. 'Take this place, for example. You're not exactly living in ruinous poverty, are you? Quite the opposite, in fact.'

Meissner demurred. 'You can choose to see it that way if you want to, but that's not the reason I wanted to become a priest and I think you know it. If I'd wanted an easy option, I could have spent my days punching tickets at the Köln Bahnhof.'

'No.' Emil's fist came down hard on the table. 'For your information, I *don't know*. I don't know anything about you. For nearly two hours you've been parading your self-justification but without answering the most important question – *why*?'

The bishop shook his head. 'The same question as before. And I only have the same answer – the inner voice that will not be denied.'

'And such a voice – that only you can hear. Does the Church have no qualms about accepting convicted war criminals into its fold?'

'Of course it does. But the very foundation of the Church is in forgiveness.'

'Father forgive them...' Clément intoned.

'Yes. The Church rejoices in every sinner who repents.'

'Is that why you wanted me to come here, so you could ask my forgiveness? Let me tell you right here and now – you won't get it.'

The bishop reached across the table to grasp Emil's hands. The Frenchman pulled away as if fearing to be contaminated. 'Your forgiveness cannot help me, Watchmaker,' Meissner said. 'For me it is too late. The only forgiveness that counts is my own, and after nearly twenty years I am still unable to forgive myself. I tell myself better that I had been put in front of a firing squad than I should have stood by and done nothing. I know that I have God's forgiveness, but that is not enough for me. You must think me arrogant, but I promise you I am not. I am guilty. I am ashamed. And I will carry the guilt and the shame to my grave.' He looked keenly at Emil. 'What I hope is that I can help you to understand that the power of forgiveness will bring healing for *you* – not me, not anyone else.'

Clément's face soured. 'You sound suspiciously like all the people who have wanted me to find a good German, who insist that the war is over, that it is time to forgive and forget.'

'I am not here to tell you to forget. Nor do I want you to find a good German. But I beg you to listen to me when I tell you it *is* time to forgive – if you can find it in you.'

Emil found Meissner's reasoning impenetrable. 'You say I must forgive, but if it's not you I have to forgive, then who?'

'You must learn to forgive yourself.'

Again a silence fell between them. The bishop rose. 'Please wait here. I will bring coffee. That is one thing the Dutch are very good at.'

Emil surveyed his surroundings. The kitchen was large, with a big refectory table that would easily sit ten. It was true it was not exactly luxurious, but it had everything that might be needed to serve a large household, and it was spotlessly clean. On one wall was a photograph of a pope, though he had no idea which one; on two others, portraits of saints: he could tell by the golden halos that adorned their heads. He could find no connection between these representations of sanctity and Meissner's stubborn insistence on forgiveness. The priest clearly had little understanding of what Emil had gone through, still less of why he might think the very idea repellent. And yet . . . He was both intrigued and irritated: irritated that he had been put in a position where he felt he was not in control; intrigued despite himself to know more of what Meissner had done since being freed from prison. He wondered what he could have been doing in the Belgian Congo.

Meissner returned bearing an earthenware coffee pot decorated in garishly coloured tribal motifs, and matching mugs. 'I brought these back with me from Africa. If I have any prized possessions, it's these.' He set everything down and poured two cups of thick, dark liquid.

'Many Nazis escaped after the war to out-of-the-way places, mostly South America,' Emil observed. 'You fetched up in Africa. Some might see that as more evidence that you were trying to evade responsibility for what you had done.'

Meissner sipped his coffee, closing his eyes briefly, thinking. 'Some might, I suppose, if they were in an ungenerous frame of mind. But it wasn't my idea to go there, not at first. I was sent to a leper colony.' He paused, then continued softly: 'I was happier there than I have ever been. In Africa, where the people have so little, where one's grip on life is so tenuous, where ignorance kills more than any disease and famine can pounce without warning, there is a joy that has to be seen to be believed – the simple joy of living, of loving, and accepting the Lord's gifts without

75

question. I didn't want to come back. I wanted to live out my days with those people.'

Emil had listened without interruption. Now he said, 'Why *did* you come back?'

'Malaria. I tried to accept it as a trial sent to me by the Lord, but it was so severe I was incapable of doing anything. I was sent back to Europe to recuperate. But once I was here, it became clear that I have something more serious than malaria.' The bishop leaned forward, his face earnest. 'Watchmaker, I am dying. I have been sent home to die, and this is not even my home. I have leukaemia. I don't understand it fully, but it is a cancer that affects the blood. I have a matter of months, perhaps less, to live. But I still believe that God has a definite purpose for my life. Watchmaker, that purpose is you.'

12

ALEKHINE'S GUN

April 1944

Konzentrationslager Auschwitz-III, Monowitz

The evenings are lighter now and Yves has taken to sitting on the ground outside the entrance to the block, not coming in until it is almost time for lights out. The poor food and strenuous labour have reduced him almost to a walking skeleton. He is staring at the sky, fearing he may not awaken to see it again.

Inside, the *Stubendienst** finds Emil rocking slowly back and forth, praying, as he often does when he is alone.

'Watchmaker,' he says. 'Bodo sent me to find you. He wants to speak to you.'

Watchmaker – the name has stuck. Emil does not like it: it singles him out when his best protection from unwanted attention is anonymity.

Bodo Brack is the *Blockältester*, a thick-set man who is serving a life sentence for murder. He has never shown any interest in Emil before.

'What does he want with me?'

His errand done, the *Stubendienst* shrugs. 'What am I – his secretary?'

Emil walks slowly to the day room. He can't think what Bodo could possibly want with him, but it can't be anything good.

---

* Block orderly: a prisoner responsible for keeping the block clean and tidy. He was not expected to work outside like his fellow prisoners.

Emil removes his cap and stands to attention before the block elder. Brack has been in the camp for over two years, longer than anyone else. Everyone knows he is the kingpin among the *Prominenten* – the favoured prisoners who run the camp for the SS. He can arrange better food and even the vouchers that can be used to visit the brothel that the SS runs for the *Blockältesten*, *Kapos* and even the *Scheissministers*.* But not Jews. Brack does not like Jews. Ten minutes pass before he deigns to notice Emil.

'Watchmaker,' he says, pausing to lick his fingers after chewing on a lump of cheese. 'Is this block not to your liking? Do I not see to it that your every need is provided for?'

'Yes,' Emil replies anxiously, wondering where this is leading. 'This is a good block and you are a most considerate block elder.'

Without warning, Brack springs to his feet and with a back-handed blow to the face knocks Emil to the floor. 'You lying Jewish pile of shit,' he yells.

Emil struggles to his feet. 'Please,' he says, 'what have I done?' A second blow falls. Now Brack signals to his cronies who are standing nearby and they lay into Emil, kicking him repeatedly. All he can do is curl into a ball and try to protect his head with his arms. After a while the kicking stops and he is dragged to his feet. He stands unsteadily. Blood is flowing from his nose, and from the wounds inflicted by the Scharführer only days before.

'That,' Brack says menacingly, 'is only the beginning – unless you start to cooperate.'

'Yes. Of course I will cooperate, only please – tell me what I have to do.'

'Where were you the other day when Block 51 was cleansed?'

* Latrine superintendents.

'I was in Block 46.'

Bodo exchanges a knowing look with one of his cronies. 'And what were you doing in Block 46?'

'I was playing chess.' Emil looks beseechingly at his tormentor. *What harm can there be in chess?*

But Bodo is oblivious.

'Who did you play?'

Emil shakes his head. 'I don't know. The game was arranged by the *Ältester* in Block 46.'

'I happen to know the elder in Block 46. He's not as tolerant of Jews as I am. Yet he lets you play chess. What did you give him so that he would let you play?'

There is no point trying to lie. Brack already knows the answer to the question or he would not have asked it. 'I gave him a watch.'

'And where did you get the watch?'

'I did a favour for one of the German technicians in Buna. He gave me an old watch that was broken. I fixed it and gave it to the *Blockältester*.'

The German brings his face to within inches of the Frenchman's. 'But you forgot something, didn't you, you stinking Kike?'

Emil shakes his head. 'I don't know.'

The *Blockältester* hits him again, though this time with less force. 'Don't fucking lie to me, you Jewish pig-fucker.'

'Please. Tell me. What did I forget?'

'You forgot that before you make a gift to a *Blockältester* in another block, you must first make a gift to your own.'

One of Emil's teeth has been loosened – when he touches it with his tongue, he can feel it move. 'I'm sorry,' he says. A distant, fleeting thought occurs to him of how perverse it is that he should apologize to the person who has just inflicted a beating on him. 'How can I make amends?'

If he hopes that this will serve to mollify Brack, he is disappointed. 'I think you already know what you need to do,' Brack says, his words laden with contempt.

'Yes,' Emil acknowledges. 'May I go now?'

'You'll go when I say and not before. I haven't finished with you yet.'

Nervously, Emil swallows the blood that has pooled in his mouth and waits for the next blow to fall.

'From now on, you will not play chess unless you have my permission.'

Emil is not expecting this. It is as if a death sentence has been passed. But to protest would be to invite another beating.

Brack senses the effect of his words. 'I did not say you could no longer play chess. I said you could play only when I give my permission. From now on, you are playing chess for me.'

April 1944
Ministry of Public Enlightenment and Propaganda, Berlin
With a flick of his fingers, Wilhelm Schweninger launched the still-glowing butt of his cigarette into the street and pulled open the door to the Propaganda Ministry. His level of seniority did not entitle him to enter the building through the imposing portico of the Leopold Palace on Wilhelmplatz; instead, he passed beneath one of the tall, stone doorways that opened directly from Wilhelmstrasse.

With a nod in the direction of the uniformed doorman, he headed for the stairs that would take him to his office on the second floor.

For nine years, Schweninger has worked in Section III under State Secretary Hermann Esser, his every working day taken up with the propaganda opportunities offered by tourism. Unlike most of his contemporaries, a career in the armed forces or the SS had never been open to Schweninger. His father, Otto, was a farmer. At fourteen years of age, helping with the harvest, Wilhelm had trapped his hand in a baling machine. It had been so badly injured that amputation had been the only option. With a future working on the land impossible, the young Wilhelm had been encouraged to study, and he had gone to university in Heidelberg, where he had studied English. It was there that he had discovered his true calling: chess, giving himself over to the game so completely that he failed to complete his studies.

In order for any chess player to compete at a higher level, it was necessary to become a member of the Nationalsozialistische Deutsche Arbeiterpartei. Wilhelm's Nazi Party membership had proved doubly useful when, in 1935, in the run-up to the Berlin Olympics, the Propaganda Ministry had been looking for young Aryan men with a flair for languages to brief the foreign press. It had seemed the perfect solution for the twenty-two-year-old, who was already gaining a reputation as a fearsome chess player. The Propaganda Ministry was the biggest of the Reich ministries, so he had seemed set for an interesting career.

Even the war had not dampened his ambitions to become an international chess champion – not at first. Working in Section III afforded ample opportunities for travel, and having a position in the ministry meant that his talents in chess were encouraged, if only for their value as propaganda. Before he was thirty, he was the undisputed champion of Germany and had beaten several national champions from countries occupied by, or allied to, the Reich. But then had come the Allied landings in North Africa and the reverse of Germany's fortunes at Stalingrad. The work of Section III had become much more limited in its scope, as had international travel.

Of all the institutions in the Reich, the Propaganda Ministry was the most intolerant of defeatist talk and attitudes. But even so, now, at the beginning of 1944, the writing was on the wall for any but the most stubbornly myopic to see.

Wilhelm had never given voice to any of this, but, just lately, had decided that his career needed a new direction – one that would stand him in good stead after the war. He had learned that Herr Schweitzer, the graphic artist so favoured by Reichsminister Goebbels, was looking for an assistant. Under the pseudonym 'Mjölnir', Schweitzer's work could be seen all over Germany – striking posters that urged ordinary Germans to heroic feats, whether at the front or at home. The artist was held in the highest regard by all in the ministry. If Wilhelm got the job, it would transport him to the giddy heights of Section II, with its myriad opportunities in radio, film and the arts. His interview had been three days ago; he expected to hear the outcome today.

There was a definite spring in his step as he entered the office he shared with Georg Wetzel. Georg was in his fifties, a dour widower whose wife had been killed in a bombing raid. He now lived in constant dread of a letter from the army to tell him his son had been killed in action; so much so, his hair had gone completely white. Still, he saw himself as a father-figure to Wilhelm, and tried, in his clumsy way, to nurture his protégé's career.

With the insouciance of a circus performer, the younger man threw his hat on the stand and took his seat.

Georg spoke. 'Late again, Willi. It won't do. If Falthauser gets wind of it…' He jerked his head in the direction of the supervisor's office at the end of the corridor.

Wilhelm had heard it all before and shrugged it off. 'Couldn't be helped, old man. It was the bombing again. Tramlines are gone all along

Hohenzollerndamm. Anyway, I won't be having to worry about him for much longer.'

'If things carry on like this, there'll be nothing left to bomb, soon.' Georg looked longingly at the photograph on his desk of a woman and a teenage boy. 'If only the damned Luftwaffe did what they're supposed to do. It's every night now – every fucking night stuck in a cellar waiting for the one that's got your name on it and next day we're still expected to be at work on time. It's ridiculous.'

Wilhelm shot a warning look at Georg. 'Be quiet, you old fart, or you'll get us both in trouble. You know what the official line is.'

'I know what fat fucking Hermann's official line is...and he can stick it up his fat fucking arse.'

Schweninger made a show of opening his diary and going through it.

'And I don't know why you're bothering with that, either,' Georg continued. 'Word is, the Allies will be landing in France before the summer's out. How long do you think we'll be able to hold out after that happens?'

'Stop it, will you?' Wilhelm looked up in exasperation. 'You'll end up in a bloody concentration camp the way you're going. I heard the speech Doktor G gave from the Sportspalast. You should have too. "Total war is the demand of the hour," that's what he said.'

Georg snorted at the mention of Goebbels. 'Yes, and he also said that workers in government offices will work longer hours so that more of us can be sent to the fucking front.'

'Well, there's no chance of you being sent to the front – or me, for that matter. Anyway, as the Doktor said, it stands to reason that once the British and Americans are in France, they'll join with us and turn on the Russians – or face the prospect of Europe being overrun by the Bolshevik swine.'

The older man shook his head. The entire staff of the ministry had congregated to listen to Goebbels' New Year's speech on the radio, supposedly an act of solidarity. It had been a Friday and, instead of closing early, as it usually did, the ministry building had remained open; food and drink had been laid on, and wireless sets placed throughout the building so that everybody could listen. Timed to perfection, the dramatic final words of the speech had come only a minute before church bells across Germany started to ring in the New Year. The enthusiastic applause of the thousands of staff had changed to embraces, kisses and handshakes and cries of 'Happy New Year!' Georg had had to admit that the Reichsminister was very, very good: he had almost been convinced himself. The applause seemed genuine and spontaneous, though it was not always easy to tell.

Now, with bitter irony, Georg quietly echoed the Doktor's final words: 'Now, people, rise up and let the storm break loose!'

April 1944
Konzentrationslager Auschwitz-III, Monowitz

The camp is in darkness. All the doors are locked and the SS patrol the perimeter with their dogs and machine guns. In the bunk they share, Emil asks Yves what he thinks the *Blockältester* is up to.

Yves is more worldly-wise and astute than Emil, but he is completely exhausted and falls asleep mid-sentence. Emil prays he will make it to summer. Now that the biting cold of the Polish winter is past, he might have a chance.

Emil has an idea. It is common knowledge that Bodo has contacts with the SS. Emil will offer to repair their watches in return for extra food, which he will give to Yves. It seems a good plan, but Bodo is sure to want something in return.

Sleep comes slowly to Emil. He is aware of the night sounds of the block, the stirrings of his fellow inmates, the heavy, breathy sighs of hungry men sleeping, snoring; the occasional cry and the continuous to-ing and fro-ing of men to the toilet bucket. Emil needs to go to the bucket too, but waits. By now it must be nearly full, and he does not want to be the one who fills it and is then sent by the night guard to empty it into the latrine. At last he hears the sound of the door opening and the clang of the bucket against the doorframe as it is lifted out. In ten minutes he will be able to use it safely.

When the camp bell rings in the morning, it is still dark. The night guard switches on the light.

Although he has not slept well, Emil feels better. He has a plan, and he is sure it will work. He knows this because of the rules of Auschwitz: those who run the camp for the SS are all corrupt. They will agree to almost anything as long as there is something in it for them.

13

A CLOSED GAME

April 1944
Solahütte, SS country club, German-occupied Silesia

Obersturmführer Paul Meissner stood on the veranda looking out over the valley and inhaled deeply. He loved this time of year, and, standing there in the midst of the pine forest, it was difficult to imagine there was a war on.

Officers and NCOs were already arriving for the grand final of the camp chess tournament. Competition in the heats and the two semi-finals had been intense. Even Eidenmüller had tried his hand: 'I know what the moves are,' he had said. 'How difficult can it be?' Fortunately, he'd had the good sense not to bet on himself. Meissner had made an amusing entry about it in his journal. As far as he could tell, his Unterscharführer had made a killing, but this final game was more difficult to predict.

To everyone's surprise, among the officers, Otto Brossman, the taciturn Hauptsturmführer in charge of the first and second guard companies, had excelled. The SS had a reputation for being anti-intellectual, so Meissner had been surprised when Brossman had confessed that he had read widely about chess theory, and at Heidelberg in the 1930s had even taken lessons from the university champion.

'It's all about tactics,' he told Meissner. 'Attack, defend, entrench, retreat. Have you read von Clausewitz's *On War*?' Meissner admitted that he had. 'It's as he says – "War is very simple, but in war even the simplest things are very difficult." Chess is the same. The individual moves are very simple, but combining them to create a winning strategy is a different matter. And,' he continued, 'no two games are alike. Each one has its own personality, as individual as the players pitted against one other. It's so intriguing.'

Meissner was impressed. He liked Brossman. 'You'll make a worthy champion of the SS,' he said.

The other contestant, from among the non-commissioned ranks, was an even greater enigma. Oberscharführer Hustek was in the Gestapo, in the camp's political section. About forty years of age, with dark, greased-back hair and a heavily lined face, he had swept all competition aside. Little was known about him other than his reputation for brutality with the prisoners and his hatred of Jews.

'He's an evil bastard, that one,' Eidenmüller told Meissner.

The officer raised an eyebrow. 'Is that so? That's probably an advantage if you're in the Gestapo,' Meissner replied.

'And another thing – he's a sly one. You'll never know what he's thinking. I wouldn't trust him as far as I could throw him.'

Eidenmüller's judgement proved to be a sound one: Hustek had chain-smoked his way through every game, unnerving his opponents by staring at them unblinkingly until they made their move.

'I reckon that's something he's learned from interrogating prisoners,' Eidenmüller opined. 'More effective than any torture, I'd say.'

'Well, I think he'll find Hauptsturmführer Brossman a somewhat different prospect,' Meissner replied. 'He puts chess on a par with von Clausewitz.'

'Sorry, sir – von who?'

Eidenmüller was offering odds of two to one against Brossman. For the first time, Meissner bet on the outcome – a week's pay. *That will teach Eidenmüller a lesson when he's forced to pay up*, he thought with a grin.

The game was due to start at 19:30 hours. Twenty minutes before the appointed time, Brossman eased his way through the ranks of SS who had made the trip out to the country club. 'Hustek not here yet, then?' he asked Meissner.

Meissner shook his head, but before he could reply, the Kommandant entered the room, followed by a visiting senior SS officer.

Liebehenschel called out, '*Achtung!*' The hum of conversation ceased as the men in the room snapped to attention.

'Gentlemen,' the visitor said, 'please be at your ease. No need for any formality on my account.' The hum of conversation quickly resumed.

He surveyed the occupants of the room. 'You are to be congratulated, Liebehenschel,' he said in a confidential tone. 'I had my doubts that your chess club was really as popular as you had said, but now I'm here, I'm most impressed. The effect it's had on the morale of your men is obvious. I will tell the Reichsführer myself what a success it is.'

'Thank you, sir.' The Kommandant inclined his head. 'But credit must go to Obersturmführer Meissner. It was his idea and he is the one who organized everything. An excellent officer, if I may say so; it's a pity we do not have more like him.'

'I'd like to meet him.'

'Of course.'

Moments later the Kommandant was making the introductions: 'Herr Gruppenführer, may I present Obersturmführer Paul Meissner, head of operations for the satellite camps and the organizer of this competition.'

The Gruppenführer appraised Meissner. 'You are Waffen-SS? How is it that you ended up here?'

Meissner raised his walking stick. 'I was wounded in action, sir. Sadly, I'm no longer considered fit for active service.'

'And your Iron Cross. Where did you get that?'

'Kursk, sir. The Voronezh front.'

'Meissner rarely talks about it, sir,' the Kommandant interjected. 'He's far too modest. He took on four Russian tanks with only a Wespe field howitzer, and killed two of them before our Tigers came to the rescue. His action saved the other two Wespes that were under his command, one of which had already been hit.'

The Gruppenführer extended a hand. 'Well done, Meissner. It is a privilege to shake hands with you. You are a credit to the SS.'

'Thank you, sir. I did my duty, no more.'

'Gruppenführer Glücks is head of the Concentration Camps Inspectorate,' the Kommandant explained. 'He has travelled all the way from Oranienburg to watch the final, and I have asked him to present the prizes to our champions.'

Meissner smiled and glanced at his watch. 'With your permission, Herr Gruppenführer, the final match is due to start shortly. May I invite you and the Kommandant to take your seats?'

As Meissner spoke, Hustek arrived. Without acknowledging anybody, he took a seat at the game table that had been set up in the centre of the room.

Meissner was indignant – Hustek's insolence was insufferable. 'Oberscharführer Hustek,' Meissner barked, in his best parade-ground voice. 'Attention!'

Slowly Hustek raised his head and looked coolly at the officer. 'I don't have to take orders from you, Herr Obersturmführer,' he said. 'I'm Gestapo.'*

The room fell silent. Meissner's knuckles turned white as his hand tightened on his walking stick.

A voice came from the side. 'Really? Then perhaps, Oberscharführer, you'll take orders from me.' All eyes were on the Gruppenführer.

Hustek sprang to attention and saluted. '*Heil Hitler.*'

'Don't "*Heil Hitler*" me. You dare to insult a hero of the German people? Where's *your* Iron Cross, eh? I've half a mind to have you sent to the Russian front. Then we'll see what you're made of.'

Hustek swallowed. 'No, Herr Gruppenführer. I beg your pardon, sir. My behaviour was unacceptable. It won't happen again.'

The Kommandant glowered at the Oberscharführer. Everything had been going so well. 'Herr Gruppenführer,' he said, in a voice that was menacingly quiet, 'I would consider it a personal favour if you would permit me to deal with the Oberscharführer myself – after the conclusion of the competition.'

With a final glare at Hustek, the Gruppenführer took his seat. The game could begin.

* The Gestapo had a presence at Auschwitz because there were many political prisoners there, mainly Communists. In practice, the Gestapo operated above and outside the German legal code and were accountable only to themselves.

14.

TWO KNIGHTS

April 1944
Konzentrationslager Auschwitz-III, Monowitz
After roll call, Emil needs the latrine. Yves goes with him. The arrangements are primitive – a plank rigged above a pit, on which the *Häftlinge* must sit, shoulder to shoulder – and the stench is foul.

Yves settles beside Emil. He is worried about his friend after the beatings he has taken. 'Your face is a bit of a mess.'

Emil explores the scab on his cheek with his fingertips. 'I've been in better shape,' he admits.

Yves laughs hollowly. 'Haven't we all.' He holds out a bony hand for inspection. 'Look at me – I'm fading away to nothing. Jacqueline wouldn't recognize me if she saw me now.'

'Jacqueline?'

Yves looks away. The hurt inside had settled to a constant ache but now, in an unguarded moment, it has risen to the surface. 'My daughter.'

Emil finishes emptying his bowels. He pushes himself away from the plank and pulls his trousers up. He steps over to the tap to wash his hands. There is only a trickle of water but it will have to do. He is wiping his hands dry on his shirt when Yves joins him.

Gently, Emil puts a hand on Yves's shoulder. 'Jacqueline – it's a lovely name,' he says quietly. 'I wish you would tell me about her.' He squeezes the shoulder, every bone shockingly sharp under his hand. 'You know, here we are – we even share a bed...you would think we would know everything about one other – but we don't, do we? Not really.'

'She was...' Yves stops, an agonized travesty of a grin on his face. 'I can't.'

'It's hard to talk about them, isn't it?' Emil makes a point of looking his friend in the eye. 'But we must, otherwise they will be forgotten.'

Together they walk back towards the block. Their progress is painfully slow. Haltingly, Yves tells Emil something of his life before Auschwitz. 'My wife's name was Annette. We would have been married ten years in September. Jacqueline was our only child. She was eight when we got picked up in one of the mass arrests. There was only the three of us – no other family, you understand – Annette and I were both orphans. Funny that, isn't it? Both of us, orphans, I mean.' He pauses for breath; the simple effort of speaking is telling on him. 'Jacqueline was a beautiful child. Clever, in a quiet sort of way, and caring – always helping her mother. And then we got taken to Drancy. Annette was pregnant. The Germans didn't give a damn. We were put in a room with I don't know how many other people. And then Annette went into labour, about two months too soon. She haemorrhaged.' Yves runs a hand over his face. 'A doctor came. He said perhaps if she had been in hospital, she might have been saved. He was terribly sorry, he said. The baby didn't make it either. It was a boy – not that it makes any difference. So that left me and Jacqueline. She became very quiet after her mother died. It was like she had died too, inside, but was somehow managing to carry on, on the outside. I think she did it for my sake. After that, we were inseparable.

'Then there was the transport to Auschwitz. She was asleep when we arrived. When the SS bastards started hammering on the doors and yelling at us like mad people she got very frightened. Then we were separated. Jacqueline was screaming to stay with me until one of the guards went over with a dog that started snarling and barking at her, which only made it worse...' Yves stops. He cannot find the right words. He collects himself and continues, his voice hoarse: '... until an old woman came and said, "Don't worry, monsieur, I will take care of her until you can come for her." *Don't worry.* The most stupid thing I have ever heard in my life. How could I have let them take her away?'

Emil stops walking. His friend's anguish is raw, as if everything had happened only yesterday. 'Yves.' Once again he takes his friend by the shoulder. 'You can't allow yourself to think like that. There was nothing you could have done: they would have killed you right there.'

'Maybe.' Yves's face is a picture of inconsolable pain. 'But the thought of my little girl going to her death with nobody to comfort her is unbearable.'

'I know, but it's not your fault. You can't blame yourself for what happened.' Emil almost goes on to say: 'It was God's will,' but he stops himself.

'I hate them,' Yves continues, his voice hardening. 'When most people say they hate someone, they don't really mean it, but I do. We have had the most perfect instruction in the art of hatred, Emil, and we have a duty to put it to good use. One day, if God gives me the strength, I will pay them back for what they have done.'

The story is not so different from Emil's own, and he wonders how many of the men in Monowitz have a similar story to tell, of families torn apart, of women left to die, of children murdered in their thousands.

Bitterly, Yves goes on: 'You know how some of the prisoners suck up to the *Kapos* and the block elders, trying to curry favour? Mostly they do it for nothing more than a crust of bread or an extra ration of soup. But

I've promised myself – no matter what, that's something I will never do. It would be a betrayal. I would rather make a pact with the Devil. If there was a way to get back at the SS and the scum who run this place for them I would take it, and to hell with the consequences.'

Emil is silent.

'What about you?' Yves asks.

'Me?' replies Emil. How can he tell anyone about what he has lost, when the full depths of his grief are still unknown to him? *But Yves is my friend. My only friend*, he reminds himself.

'My wife was called Rosa – *is* called Rosa. When we arrived at the unloading ramp I saw she was selected for work, like me. She may still be alive. I pray she is. We had two boys, Louis and Marcel. The Germans took them away too, but at least they were with their grandmother. As for what became of them…'

September 1939
Paris

The word on everyone's lips was 'war'. Only last year, Britain and France had both fallen for Hitler's bluff over Czechoslovakia, and now the German Chancellor was making threatening noises over Poland. Emil was sure there would be no second climbdown, but surely Hitler was astute enough to see that? However, such thoughts were far from his mind as he walked briskly along the Rue Cambronne on his way home. Sometimes Rosa would put Louis in the pram and walk to meet him. He loved it when she did that.

Looking up, he saw her walking towards him in the shade of the trees that lined the street; she seemed lost in thought. He ducked into a doorway until she drew level with him, then jumped out to surprise her.

Smiling, she punched him lightly on the chest. '*Fripon*,' she said. Rosa linked her arm in his as they strolled homewards.

'Where's Louis?' he asked.

'At home with your mother.' She looked at him coyly. 'I've got something to tell you.'

'Really? What?'

'Oh, no, not so fast. You've got to guess.'

'Guess? You know I'm no good at guessing.'

Rosa laughed.

'All right ... I know. Le Quintette du Hot are playing at Le Chat Noir.'

'No, silly, you know they only ever play at Le Grosse Pomme, and anyway, they're in England at the moment.'

He grinned. 'I knew that. I was testing you.' He turned serious. 'War hasn't been declared?'

'Not yet.'

'I give in then. Come on, tell me.'

She smiled. 'We're going to have another baby.'

'Another baby?' Emil's face lit up with joy. 'When?'

'In May, the doctor says.'

Laughing, he took her hands and swung her round as if in a dance, all the way back to the apartment.

'*Maman*,' he yelled, running up the stairs to their door. 'Has Rosa told you the news? We're going to have another baby! In May! Isn't that wonderful?'

His mother greeted them not with joy but with foreboding. 'I take it you haven't heard the other news, then – France has just declared war on Germany.'

*

1962

Amsterdam

With a start, Emil woke. It was dark, and for a moment he could not remember where he was. His breathing was rapid and his heart was pounding. He must have been having a nightmare but he could not remember it. He lay back on his pillow and tried to settle again to sleep. But he could not get comfortable. The hotel pillow, which had been so soft earlier, was now solid and unyielding, despite the pummelling he gave it, and his limbs felt awkward no matter how he positioned them.

There was a reason why sleep had become so elusive: the conversation with Meissner and his ridiculous notion that the only way Emil could find peace was through forgiveness. And, more ridiculous still, that the person in need of forgiveness was himself. Emil rejected the suggestion. It was not he who had perpetrated such unspeakable evil. He was its victim. He turned again in the bed, his frustration and indignation mounting, but his attempt to relax was futile. Angrily he cast off the covers. Damn Meissner. To hell with him and his unassailable faith.

But there is no escaping the rules of Auschwitz. Everything is back to front. In Auschwitz the good are punished, the evil flourish, and the victims, not the perpetrators, are the ones who feel guilty. It is incomprehensible but true.

Emil had long ago lost hope that he would find anything to cleanse the past. And now Meissner had turned up, with his promise that hope could be rekindled...But hope was mocking Emil because it knew, as the priest did not, that the price of forgiveness was too high.

Forgive? He could not do it.

*

At breakfast, Emil found his appetite had deserted him. Coffee and two cigarettes left a bitter taste in his mouth as he headed to the Krasnapolsky and his next game in the tournament. He did not notice anything of his walk. He was preoccupied with the thoughts that had refused to let go of him during the night.

Could it be that he was denying himself the redeeming power that the universe had to offer because he could not forgive? Or, as Meissner would have it, that he was refusing to forgive? If there was the smallest grain of truth in what Meissner had said, he would be a fool not to pursue it. But *was* Meissner right? Where did his authority come from? It was true the Catholic Church preached a doctrine of forgiveness, but its actions gave the lie to this: to be a Jew was to be acutely aware of the harsh treatment they had received at the hands of the Church over the centuries, right to the present day, and all in the name of their loving, *forgiving* Saviour. 'Forgive' – it was an easy word to say. Too easy. The promise of hope that Meissner was holding out to him was an illusion.

Unable to sleep, and in an effort to see a way forward, Emil had cast the ten tiles on the points of the Sephiroth again, but the results had been unclear. A shadow seemed to have fallen over his powers of discernment and there was nothing he could do to see through it. The tile that was revealed when he turned it face upward was א – Aleph – which denoted the inaccessibility of the Divine Light. It told him there were some things that were beyond his understanding, and that for these he must have faith: but in what? He was a Jew, and despite all his searching of the Kabbalah, the religion of his fathers had done little to answer the questions that had raged in his soul for nearly twenty years. Surely it could not be telling him to have faith in the easy and convenient dogmas of the Catholics? Over the years, Emil had built for himself a subtle series of fortifications to protect the few certainties he had left. It was the only way he thought he could survive. Now Meissner had succeeded in planting a seed of doubt inside this fortress. Emil steeled himself to make sure it would not take root.

In the second round, Emil had been matched against Lopez, an Argentinean. Emil had researched a number of his past games, won and lost, looking for his strengths and weaknesses. The South American played in a traditional style, attacking through the centre of the board, like Schweninger. If playing white, he favoured the English Opening; if black, the Queen's Indian Defence.

Emil felt equal to either challenge, and he won comfortably. As Lopez congratulated him, he remarked: 'You surprised me, Monsieur Clément. You didn't use any of the defences you have employed at the top level in the last three years.'

Emil smiled a victor's smile, gracious but not condescending. 'That's the point, Señor Lopez – to be unpredictable.' The result of the match registered by the arbiter, and their moves recorded for posterity, Emil made for the exit.

Meissner was waiting for him at the door.

'Good morning,' he said, warmly. 'You won, of course?'

Emil nodded. He was not sure he wanted to talk to Meissner again. He tried to walk past, but the cleric fell into step beside him.

Emil stopped. 'Look,' he said, 'I don't want to appear rude, but I think we probably said enough yesterday.'

'You think we said enough?' Meissner looked appraisingly at Emil. 'Perhaps you're right. Who knows? I have spent quite some time since thinking about what we said. I wondered if you had.'

Emil hesitated before replying, but then said, 'I've been thinking about it for twenty years.' He strode off, leaving the other man behind.

'There is someone I should like you to meet, and, in the circumstances, the sooner the better,' the bishop called after him.

Emil stopped and half turned his head. 'Who?'

Smiling, the bishop limped forward to place a hand on Emil's arm. 'It's a surprise, but I think it will do you good.'

'I'm at that time in my life where surprises are rarely enjoyable.'

The bishop dropped his smile. 'I did not say it would be enjoyable. I said I thought it would do you good. Will you come?'

'I'd rather not. I need to spend some time reviewing the games of my next opponent.'

'Indulge a dying man,' the bishop replied softly.

Emil sighed. 'Very well. But I don't want it to take too long.'

'Not take too long?' Meissner shook his head. 'Watchmaker, this is likely to take the rest of your life.'

15.
WINDMILL

April 1944

Solahütte, SS country club, German-occupied Silesia

The game started. Hustek drew black. Every officer sneered at the Gestapo man for his boorish behaviour, willing Brossman to win, while every NCO winced with embarrassment but could not set aside their conviction that Hustek would triumph.

Meissner felt torn. As the game's arbiter, it was his duty to be even-handed but, by God, he hoped that the Oberscharführer would get his comeuppance.

For ten or fifteen minutes, the game progressed with little advantage to either player. Then Meissner spoke quietly. 'I should be obliged if you would stop doing that, Oberscharführer.'

'Doing what?'

'Staring so menacingly at Hauptsturmführer Brossman while he decides what move to make.'

'Don't worry about me, Herr Obersturmführer,' Brossman growled. 'I don't scare so easily.'

So intent were the spectators on the game – including the Gruppenführer – that the exchange was heard by everyone.

'I thought this was supposed to be a fair game, sir,' Hustek remarked, in an aggrieved tone. 'Is this how it's going to be – officers cosying up with each other to keep the lower ranks from winning?' He spoke quietly, but he knew his words would carry. He raised his face to stare defiantly at Meissner.

Hustek had castled to protect his king, and now Brossman brought up his queen to threaten the rook. If he moved forward one square he would take a pawn and have a direct diagonal route to his target. It took all Hustek's willpower to suppress a smile. The officer had walked into his trap. He moved his own bishop one space diagonally, threatening check, a move Brossman had to defend. However, Hustek's move also exposed his own queen. Brossman smiled, thinking Hustek had made a fatal error. He changed his tactic of attacking the rook to take the queen instead. It was Hustek's turn to smile. In three successive moves, he forced Brossman's king to move to avoid check, taking a pawn, a rook, and finally Brossman's queen.

The exchange greatly impaired the officer's ability to dominate the centre of the board. Minutes later, Hustek followed with a second windmill combination, this time taking a pawn, Brossman's remaining rook and a bishop.

Meissner was aghast. Would peasant cunning win out against an intellectual appreciation of the game? It seemed so. Brossman held on for another fifteen minutes, but his fate had been sealed the moment he had taken Hustek's queen.

April 1944
Ministry of Public Enlightenment and Propaganda, Berlin
As usual, Schweninger was late back from lunch. In the canteen he had met an attractive young secretary who had been impressed by his stories of foreign travel and international chess championships. She had been

wearing a V-necked woollen dress that exposed her cleavage enticingly whenever she leaned across the table. Standing over her, Wilhelm had not even tried to conceal what he was doing, taking full advantage of his height to peer down at her. That was what tourism was all about, wasn't it – taking in the sights? She had agreed to meet him for drinks and dinner on Friday.

In the office he found Georg in a sour mood. 'Late again, Willi. It really won't do, you know.' Schweninger rolled his eyes but said nothing. 'Falthauser's looking for you,' Georg went on. 'He didn't look happy.'

'Does that mean it's good news or bad news?'

The older man shrugged. 'Who can tell? He's such a miserable bastard.'

That was certainly true, Wilhelm thought to himself as he made his way from their cubbyhole to the large office at the end of the corridor.

'Come in,' was the crisp response to his knock on the door.

Wilhelm entered. It did not occur to him to be nervous. It had to be about his interview, and he was confident he had done well. 'You wanted to see me, Herr Falthauser?'

The supervisor looked up from a stack of papers piled on his desk. He seemed his usual, joyless self. 'Yes. It's about your application for the post of Herr Schweitzer's assistant.'

Wilhelm was aware of a change in Falthauser's demeanour. He seemed pleased. That could mean only one thing.

'I regret to inform you that your application was not successful.'

'Not successful? But…' Wilhelm was shocked. 'Are you sure there's been no mistake?'

Now the supervisor smiled. 'No mistake, Willi. You're here for the duration – better get used to the idea.' He turned back to his work.

Still stunned, Wilhelm turned to leave. Before he reached the doorway, his supervisor called after him: 'Who do you think you are – the second Max Amann?'

Wilhelm stopped. 'What? What do you mean?'

Falthauser looked up. 'Don't worry, you'll work it out – eventually.'

Wilhelm took his time walking back to the cubbyhole. He had been so *certain*.

'You look like you've just been given the sack, Willi,' Georg said.

The younger man slumped onto his chair. 'I might as well have been.'

'What did Falthauser have to say?'

'He asked me if I thought I was the second Max Amann.'

For moment Georg did not understand, then, with a sigh and a shake of his head, he gave a wry chuckle.

'It's not funny.'

Georg suppressed the laughter that was building inside him. 'Fucking Falthauser. What a fucking comedian. He couldn't be funny if his life depended on it, but this time...'

'Well, I'm glad you think it's so fucking hilarious.'

'Don't you see?' Georg said, grinning. 'It's his cock-eyed way of telling you why you didn't get the job.'

'No, I don't see. Tell me.'

'Because you're a one-armed cripple. Goebbels doesn't like cripples. It reminds him that he's one himself. It's not so bad if you're stuck down here out of sight in this hole, but anything else – forget it. Max Amann is the only exception.'

'What's so special about him?'

'Him and the chief go back a long way – and he publishes *Das Reich*.'

Understanding dawned on Schweninger. *Das Reich* was the weekly paper for which Goebbels wrote the editorial. 'And he's only got one arm?'

'He's only got one arm. Lost it in a hunting accident in the thirties. Some say Franz Ritter von Epp shot him deliberately.'

Wilhelm shook his head in disbelief. 'How the hell do you know all this stuff?'

The older man smiled. 'Well, when you've been around as long as I have…'

Scowling, Willi glanced around the cubbyhole. 'Christ, I'd rather be fucking dead.'

April 1944
Solahütte, SS country club, German-occupied Silesia
Summoning his reserves of dignity, Gruppenführer Glücks presented the awards – first to Hustek and then Brossman. He decided it was an opportune time to say a few words. He disliked speaking in public, fearing to say the wrong thing or to have his words misrepresented by a rival, but here he was on safe ground. Something big was about to happen to Auschwitz, and it was important to bolster morale in advance. Luckily, Himmler had recently made a speech on the same subject. Glücks had no qualms about plagiarism: the Reichsführer would take it as a compliment.

'Gentlemen,' he said. 'It is most gratifying to see such good spirits among our fighting men for – make no mistake – every man here is fighting a war every bit as much as any soldier of the Wehrmacht on the Eastern or the Italian fronts. Only our war is against a foe more wily, more insidious, more vicious than any Russian or American or Englander. Our foe is the Jew who, given the slightest opportunity, would betray our people and take from us our birthright. We must be stern – not only with our enemies, but with ourselves. We cannot permit ourselves to relax our vigilance for an instant, for to do so would invite disaster.

'It is a crime against the blood of the German people to be concerned for Jews in labour camps, or to make concessions that would make things still more difficult for our children and grandchildren. If someone says to you, "It is inhumane to use women or children to dig ditches or work in factories; I can't make them do it because the exertion will kill them," then you must reply, "If that ditch is not built, or if those armaments are not made, then German soldiers will die, and they are sons of German mothers. You are a traitor to your own blood."

'As for the difficult work you do here in Auschwitz, this is a page of glory in our history that can never be written, and the heroic part you have played will never be acknowledged. But *we* know how difficult it would be for Germany today – under bombing raids and the hardships and privations of war – were we still to have the Jews in every city as secret saboteurs and agitators.

'We have the moral right' – he paused – 'no, more than that, we have a *duty* to our people, to our blood, to destroy this race that wants to destroy us. It is no different to a doctor who exterminates a germ because if he does not eliminate the infection it will kill his patient. The Reichsführer-SS has said that any infection must be eradicated *without mercy* before it is able to gain a hold.

'This work is not easy, but it is our duty. We did not ask to be given this duty, nonetheless we take up the burden willingly. Despite all the difficulties we face and the enemies that would destroy us, we can be proud that we have carried out this most arduous of tasks in the spirit of love of our people, and that the work we do will cause no harm to our soul, our virtue or our honour.'

He raised his right hand. '*Sieg Heil!*'

The roar that followed was deafening. The men gathered round him must have shouted '*Heil!*' three, five, ten times.

With the clamour resounding in his ears, the Gruppenführer left the room, followed by the Kommandant.

Meissner waited until the noise abated before offering a hand to Brossman, saying, 'My commiserations.' He turned to Hustek. 'Oberscharführer,' he said, his voice curt, 'come to my office on Monday and I will make the arrangements for your leave.'

'Thank you, Herr Obersturmführer,' Hustek replied in a sneering tone. 'I can't tell you how much I'm looking forward to it.'

Meissner exchanged a glance with Brossman. 'Indeed, Oberscharführer,' he said, not bothering to disguise the irony in his voice, 'it must be almost as much as we are.'

Hustek froze. With studied insolence he placed his cap on his head and, without saluting, walked away.

The two officers watched as he made his way through the crowded room. Among all the NCOs present, only one congratulated the Oberscharführer, and left with him.

'The insolence of that man,' Meissner seethed.

'Gestapo,' Brossman replied, as if no other explanation were necessary. 'Don't let the bastard get to you. And if you want my advice, I would start watching my back if I were you. I think you've just made yourself an enemy.'

Meissner reached into his pocket for his cigarette case. He offered one to Brossman. 'I can take care of myself,' he said. 'Besides, after the Kommandant has finished with him, I think Hustek will want to keep a low profile for quite some time.'

*

The Kommandant enjoyed the use of a large house close to the main entrance of the *Stammlager*. That night, he hosted a dinner party for his senior officers, with Gruppenführer Glücks as guest of honour. Liebehenschel apologized for the poor quality of the food but, in reality, the fare was sumptuous compared with what most Germans enjoyed.

Glücks, who prided himself on being an instant judge of character, found the Kommandant a difficult man to assess: Liebehenschel was too familiar with his senior officers and Glücks sensed he was not a man to inspire much in the way of loyalty among his subordinates. But he could not fault his hospitality: wine flowed freely, followed by cognac and cigars, leaving the company in a relaxed mood.

When it was time for the officers to take their leave, the Gruppenführer asked the Kommandant's deputy, Sturmbannführer Richard Bär, to stay behind. While two orderlies cleared the dinner table, the three SS men retired to the sitting room.

Bär was the first to speak. 'I trust you feel your visit has been worthwhile, sir?'

The Gruppenführer rested his cigar in an ashtray and held out his snifter for a refill. 'It's always worthwhile to meet front-line officers and get from them the true picture of what we're up against. But I must confess that I had another motive in coming here. Your chess tournament merely gave me a convenient reason.'

'Oh?' The Kommandant poured a generous measure of spirits into his own glass.

'Yes. I've been putting it off, but I can delay no longer. Something quite extraordinary is about to happen, and I must make sure that all the pieces are in place to ensure its success.'

The two Auschwitz officers exchanged a glance. 'I'm sorry, sir,'

Liebehenschel said, 'I'm afraid I don't understand.'

'I want your honest opinion, Liebehenschel. Tell me – what's your position on the Jewish question?'

The Kommandant frowned. 'The Jews? I'm surprised you should ask me that, sir. Like any good German I think they're a menace and a blight on humanity.'

'Yes – but what do you think we should do with them?'

'I think we should make the swine work for the good of the Reich, like we are already doing here and in other camps.'

'But you don't think they should be exterminated?'

'I didn't say that, sir. Once they've outlived their usefulness, what else can one do with them? But I think it's inefficient simply to kill them out of hand. Surely it's better to get as much as we can out of them first?'

The Gruppenführer cleared his throat. 'It's being said in Berlin that you're not the right person to be the Kommandant of Auschwitz, that you're too soft on the Jews.'

The Kommandant sat bolt upright. 'And who is saying that?'

Glücks registered Liebehenschel's alarm. 'It doesn't matter. What matters is that it has reached the ears of the Reichsführer-SS.' He sighed heavily. 'Look, Auschwitz is the most important of the camps in the east. It embodies everything we're trying to do about the whole Jewish problem. The Kommandant of Auschwitz has to be like Caesar's wife – above even the slightest hint of suspicion. We simply can't have someone in charge who's soft on the Jews, or who is perceived as being soft on them.'

The Kommandant was affronted. 'Sir, if I have been soft on the Jews in Auschwitz, it is only because I had orders to increase the productivity of the factories. And it was only a few hours ago that you were telling me what a good job I had done.'

'Yes, but at the same time, the numbers being sent for *Sonderbehandlung** in Birkenau have fallen noticeably.'

Liebehenschel leaned forward, eager to explain. 'But if we want to keep the work camps operating at full capacity, we have to send fewer people to the gas chambers. It's simple arithmetic. Since the beginning of the year, all arrivals who are physically fit have been selected for work, and the results speak for themselves. It is on my orders that we have begun construction of an extension to the Birkenau complex to house them.'

The Gruppenführer's voice took on a conspiratorial tone. 'I am here to inform you that the situation has changed. There are plans to send many more Jews here – far more than will be needed for work in the labour camps. Capacity for special treatment at Birkenau must be increased dramatically.'

'Many more Jews?' Bär asked. 'But I thought we had practically emptied Europe of them.'

The Gruppenführer shook his head. 'Not quite. The French are dragging their feet, and it seems that in Denmark the Jews disappeared overnight. But these new arrivals are from elsewhere.'

'Are we permitted to know where?'

'Hungary. According to Eichmann, there are at least a million Jews there, and it has been decided to get them out before Horthy and the rest of his pack of cowards go over to the Russians.'†

---

* The SS rarely referred openly to the extermination of the Jews. Instead, the euphemism *Sonderbehandlung* – 'special treatment' – was used.

† Admiral Miklós Horthy was the regent of Hungary, effectively its ruler since 1920. Although an ally of Germany, up to this point in the war Hungary had permitted only limited persecution of Jews. In the spring of 1944, fearing that Hungary might surrender to the Russians, the German army was sent into Hungary, swiftly followed by SS units led by Adolf Eichmann, determined to round up the

Liebehenschel could hardly believe what he was hearing. 'And they are all coming *here*? It will take a year to process that many, at least.'

'We don't have a year. Eichmann says he can send us twelve thousand a day.'

Liebehenschel frowned. He thought he was used to the unreasonable demands of his superiors, but this—? 'No,' he said. 'It's not possible. Even with all the crematoria going at full tilt, we simply don't have the capacity to process so many.'

The Gruppenführer drained his glass. 'I thought that's what you might say. I'm sorry to have to tell you, but as of this moment you are relieved of your command.'

'What? Relieved of my command? But ... *why*? You said I was doing a good job. Surely ...' Liebehenschel realized he was gabbling and stopped speaking. A moment later, he resumed, his voice calmer. 'Naturally, I will follow whatever orders I am given, but ... who is to take my place?'

The Gruppenführer indicated Bär. 'You will be succeeded by your deputy. He will take over responsibility for the day-to-day running of the camp, but it was felt in Berlin that a more experienced hand should take charge of processing the Hungarian Jews. Obersturmbannführer Höss will return temporarily, specifically for this purpose. The operation is code-named *Aktion Höss* in his honour.'

Bär raised his glass in salute. 'Thank you, sir. I will do my best to live up to my new responsibilities.'

'And what is to become of me?' Liebehenschel asked, quietly.

The Gruppenführer reached across to squeeze the ex-Kommandant's

....

Hungarian Jews and transport them to Auschwitz. There were far too many for them to be assimilated into the labour camps: the vast majority were sent to the gas chambers immediately on arrival.

arm. 'No need to look so downcast. You are to be the new Kommandant of Majdanek. You'll have a fortnight's home leave, then take up your new position on your return.'

'And when does all this start?'

His task done, the Gruppenführer permitted himself a small smile. 'Tomorrow.'

16.

FIANCHETTO

1962

Amsterdam

In his hotel near the Oude Kerk, Wilhelm Schweninger was packing to go home. He had hoped his return would be triumphant, but it was not to be. He was not sorry to be leaving: the hotel's attempt at modern décor merely made it look drab, and he was still smarting from his defeat by Emil Clément. In his wallet he had a ticket for the 16:17 train from Amsterdam Centraal to Berlin, where he intended to get numbingly drunk.

There was a knock on the door. He looked at his watch and sighed. The porter was too early: check-out wasn't until 11:30. 'I'm not ready yet,' he called in German, knowing the porter spoke it fluently. 'Come back in a quarter of an hour.'

'I'm sorry, Herr Schweninger,' a voice replied, also in German. The long narrow corridor beyond the door gave it an odd echo. 'But could you spare a few minutes of your time? It's rather important.'

Schweninger dropped a shirt on the bed and opened the door. 'Oh,' he said, surprised. 'I wasn't expecting a priest.'

'I must ask you to forgive the intrusion, Herr Schweninger. Allow me to introduce myself. My name is Paul Meissner.'

Schweninger did not stand aside to let the priest in. 'What can I do for you, Father?'

'It's more what I can do for you,' the priest replied.

'And what is that, exactly?'

'I offer forgiveness for your sins.'

Schweninger shook his head. 'I'm sorry, Father, I'm no longer a believer, and you've caught me at a bad time. I am about to leave Amsterdam.'

'I know. That's why it's important that I speak to you now.'

'You're talking in riddles, and I've got a train to catch. If you don't mind—?' Schweninger tried to close the door.

Meissner put his shoulder against the door and spoke quickly: 'My SS number was 1214958 and my Party membership number was 6374971. You joined the Party in 1934 and your membership number was 1265409. Although you held a position at the Propaganda Ministry, you were never inducted into the SS because of the injury to your hand.'

Schweninger paled but then grew angry. 'What is this? Are you trying to blackmail me? Well, you can forget it – I have owned up to my past and put it all behind me.' He pushed at the door again.

Meissner put his foot against it. 'It would be a strange sort of blackmail, attempted by a priest, would it not? I revealed my own history to you to show that I too am tainted by a previous life that will not let me be.'

'Look, I don't know how you know all these things about me, but I don't respond to threats. Now if you don't go, I'll call reception and have you removed.'

'I'm not here to threaten you, Herr Schweninger, far from it – I'm here to help you. If you'll allow me to buy you lunch, I will tell you everything. Afterwards, you will be quite free to catch your train, I promise.'

There was something in the tone of Meissner's voice that made Schweninger hesitate. He stepped back from the door, allowing it to swing open.

'Let me be sure that I understand what you are saying, Father Meissner,' he said. 'If I listen to your story, you will buy me lunch and, afterwards, you will not try to stop me from getting my train.' Meissner nodded. 'In that case, why not? But I warn you – I have a healthy appetite.'

Schweninger picked up a jacket and stepped out into the corridor. Followed by the priest, he walked along it to the door to the stairs.

'What exactly is all this about?' he asked, as they walked.

'There is someone I would like you to meet. He's waiting for us in a restaurant on Oudekerksplein.'

May 1944
Konzentrationslager Auschwitz-III, Monowitz
Meissner had a letter, from France. The envelope was creased and thumb-print-stained. It had clearly taken some time to reach him. It took him some moments to recognize the writing.

I Abteilung
SS Panzer Artillerie Regiment 2
2nd SS-Panzergrenadier-Division Das Reich
Montauban, 12 March 1944

My dear Paul,

I'll bet you're surprised to hear from me. You must have thought I was dead! To be fair, that wouldn't be so far from the truth, but you know I'm not given much to writing. I tried to see you when you were still in the field hospital but they told me I was too late and that you had already been sent back to Germany. Nobody seemed to know where you had ended up and there were still many Russians to fight. After you went on your little holiday they counter-attacked in force. You probably saw something of it in the newsreels but you can't get the sense of what it's really like from them, can you? You know what I'm talking about. You don't get the smells – the earth burning around you, the tightness in your belly when you see a squadron of T-34s heading towards you, and the elation when you're surrounded by a dozen burning tanks and you've come through unscathed. You'll be pleased to know that old Schratt is still making life hell for the junior officers. In case you didn't know, he was the one that pulled you out of the Wespe after you were hit…

Meissner looked up and stared out of the window. *Old* Schratt? Not so old. He couldn't have been more than three or four years older than he was himself. He could picture him clearly: his helmet pushed back on his head and a chin like a rifle butt. It was good to know he was still well. He was one of those soldiers that every regiment needed – he had probably been born wearing jackboots. He had terrified Meissner when, as a young officer, he had arrived to take command of the unit. The Scharführer had taken him to a quiet corner and made it clear that it was he who was in charge – not some wet-behind-the-ears Untersturmführer foisted on them by a tin soldier in headquarters who had nothing better to do. What Schratt taught Meissner was far more important than anything he had learned in officer training. He had taught him how to keep himself and his men alive. 'How much you care for your men every day is exactly how much they'll care for you when it really counts.' And the Scharführer had been right, as he had been about everything else. And now it seemed that old Schratt had saved his life.

… Well, the good news is that now we're on holiday too. The division was pulled out of the line and as a punishment for not fighting hard enough we have been sent to France. We are stationed in Montauban, about 50 km north of Toulouse. I must say the French make a bit of a change from the monumental stupidity of the Ukrainian peasants. Most of them don't like us, of course, but it doesn't stop them trying to sell us their cheese and wine. And the women, Paul – you should see the women. Real beauties.

You probably won't have heard that Knocken and Ernst Bock are both dead. Knocken was killed in a bombing run by some half-blind Stuka pilot who couldn't tell the difference between the Ivans and his own men. Of course that lunatic Hempel ordered us not to shoot at the stupid fucker, but what the hell, we did anyway. And Ernst got caught in the open when we came under mortar fire. I yelled at him to get down but he kept on running. Stupid bastard.

But that's enough bad news for one letter. The good news is that I have been promoted to Sturmbannführer. Can you believe that? If war is crazy this is surely all the proof you need. So here I am. The Das Reich is to be refitted as a full Panzer division and I am on holiday enjoying the French sun and wine and women. Whoever said war is hell got it completely wrong – if this is hell, all I can say is I'm glad I spent my life as a sinner. You'll also be glad to hear that Schratt has managed to keep most of your old unit together. On the odd occasions I bump into him – incidentally, he's a Sturmscharführer now – he always asks whether I have any news of you.

You're still missed here, Paul. I ought to say it's despite the way you used to go on at us about duty and honour, but I think it's probably because of it. If you ever manage to get some leave, try to get down here and visit your old comrades.

Sincerely,

Your brother in arms

Peter Sommer

1962

Amsterdam

Emil had taken a table at the rear of the restaurant, telling the waiter that he was meeting a colleague – possibly two – for lunch. He could not stop himself from looking at his watch. Twenty minutes, Meissner had said, and it had been nearer thirty. He still wondered why he had allowed the priest to convince him to come but, he had to admit, Meissner could be very persuasive.

While he was waiting, he tried to recall the first time he had met Meissner. To his surprise he found his recollection imperfect. He had thought it etched deeply into his memory, and it was a shock to find how elusive it had become.

The door to the restaurant opened and two men entered. With the light behind them it was difficult to tell whether it was Meissner or not, but then Emil saw the walking stick. With a start, he realized who was with him.

Angrily, he stood up. 'You have misled me,' he said. 'I knew I shouldn't have trusted you. What you thought you could achieve by bringing *him* ...' He raised a finger to point at Schweninger.

'Do not worry,' Schweninger replied in frosty recognition. 'I have no more wish to be here than you.' He directed a curt nod at Meissner. 'I think it best if I forgo your offer of lunch, Father. I will bid you good day.'

'Please,' Meissner said. 'Enough of this ridiculous posturing, both of you. If you won't even talk to one another, how can you expect anything to change?'

'I never said I expected anything to change,' Emil said.

'And as far as I am concerned,' Schweninger said, 'Herr Clément and I have nothing to say to each other.'

'Nothing to say? Are you so determined to be enemies? It is my belief that you both have much more in common than either of you realize or would care to admit. Is the idea of talking to each other really so terrible?'

Behind Schweninger, a waiter was hovering hesitantly. 'I have a suggestion,' Meissner said. 'Let us at least have lunch and I will tell the beginning of a story that I pray will bring us to at least a little common understanding.'

Emil and Schweninger exchanged a mutually suspicious look. Schweninger shrugged. 'What the hell,' he said. 'I've come this far and, anyway, I'm starving.' He looked directly at Emil. 'How about you, Herr Clément? Is the promise of a free lunch enough for you as well?'

Emil frowned. There was something that did not feel right about sitting down calmly to lunch with two former Nazis, and the memory of his angry exchange with Schweninger was still fresh. How could Meissner think there could be any rapprochement between them? It would be easy to walk away. And yet, last night, when he had cast the tiles, they had told him to have faith; in what, he still did not know. For a moment he hesitated but then, quietly, he sat down again.

Relieved, the waiter stepped forward. 'Would any of you gentlemen like something to drink?'

They ordered beer. Meissner and Schweninger seated themselves.

Meissner spoke first. 'This is a long and complicated story,' he said, 'and Herr Schweninger has a train to catch later this afternoon, so we must try to keep to the point. I don't think any of us knows the full extent of it, so we will all have something to tell. Let me start by saying that Herr Clément and I knew each other during the war. We were both in

Auschwitz – I was an SS officer and he was a prisoner. In normal circumstances, it would have been extremely unlikely that our paths would ever
have crossed, but in Auschwitz nothing was normal.'

The drinks arrived.

'So what was it that brought you together?' Schweninger asked.

Meissner made no attempt to respond. He looked to Emil.

Emil sighed. 'Chess,' he replied. He lifted his glass to his lips and drank
deeply.

Schweninger seemed unconvinced. 'Chess? In Auschwitz?'

'Yes. It was played among the prisoners. Apparently I was one of the
better players.'

A smile played fleetingly on Meissner's lips. 'One of the better players?
Come now, I never took you to be one for false modesty.' He turned to
Schweninger. 'The perception of the other prisoners was that he was so
good it seemed he had almost magical powers. He was their talisman,
their unbeatable champion. I can't begin to tell you about the problems
he caused me.'

'This is fascinating,' Schweninger said, dropping his pretence of disbelief. He took a sip of his beer. 'Did you know that late in 1944 I was
approached by the SS and asked if I would play a chess match in Auschwitz?'

Meissner smiled. 'Yes, I did know. The request came from me. But
then I was transferred back to my old unit. I never found out whether
the game took place.'

Schweninger's eyebrows lifted. 'From you? Then you would know who
my opponent was to have been.'

Meissner looked from Schweninger to Clément. Understanding
dawned on both men.

'Are you gentlemen ready to order?' the waiter asked.

17.

Ruy López

SS Officers' quarters, Konzentrationslager Auschwitz-I

On Sunday evening, Meissner was in his quarters in the *Stammlager* half listening to a programme of light music on the wireless. The music was doing nothing to improve his mood. *I ought to be celebrating*, he thought. Before leaving, Gruppenführer Glücks had commended him both for his efforts to improve morale and for the results of his work with the satellite camps. Added to this, Liebehenschel had been as good as his word and had recommended him for promotion to Hauptsturmführer, which Glücks had been happy to confirm. He had also been given a week's leave.

If it had been longer, he might have attempted to get to Toulouse to see his old comrade, Peter Sommer. The truth was, he was ambivalent about going home. He felt changed by the war, tempered and reshaped in its furnace, and the old certainties that he had once happily shared with his parents and his fiancée now seemed distant and unimportant. All the same, he felt he should spend a few days with them. It worried him that he hadn't heard from them for a couple of weeks, though with the bombing, disruption of the postal service was becoming more frequent.

On top of that, he was sure somebody had been looking through his journal. It could only be Oberhauser. His servant denied it, of course, but Meissner could not shake off his suspicion, despite the reputation for honesty that the Bible-worms enjoyed. In future, he would make sure to keep it locked away.

Now, Oberhauser was folding his clothes prior to packing them. Knowing that it was practically impossible for his servant to write home, Meissner had offered to take a letter back to his family for him. His servant was such an odd character; Meissner could not understand his stubborn devotion to his incomprehensible religion. 'Why,' he had asked, 'do you not simply say that you no longer hold your beliefs? That is all that is required for you to be able to go home. Nobody will care if you continue with your beliefs, as long as you do it in private.'

But Oberhauser had been adamant. 'Jehovah's Witnesses are commanded to live in the truth,' he had replied. 'If I did as you suggest, it would be a lie. Better that I should lose my life in the service of Jehovah than to even pretend to turn my back on Him.'

Oberhauser was sewing the insignia of Meissner's new rank onto his uniforms when Eidenmüller arrived to inform his superior that Oberscharführer Hustek had departed for Berlin earlier that day. Meissner took it as a subtle reminder that it was time for him to make good on the wager he had made on Brossman to win.

'It all went so well,' Meissner observed, 'until the end.'

'You mean the wrong man won, sir?'

Meissner smiled wryly. He wondered where Eidenmüller's unconscious knack of lightening an atmosphere came from. He went into the bedroom to retrieve his wallet, passing Oberhauser on the way. 'Did you hear about our little tournament, Oberhauser?' The servant nodded. 'No doubt you disapprove that Unterscharführer Eidenmüller made so much money out of it?'

'It's not my place to approve or disapprove, sir.'

Meissner returned to the sitting area and counted a number of notes into Eidenmüller's hand.

'Did you know, sir, that chess is also played in the camp by the prisoners?'

Meissner regarded his servant with surprise. It was rare for Oberhauser to volunteer anything without being spoken to directly.

'By the prisoners? No, I didn't. Where on earth would they get a chess set from?'

The servant held his sewing up to the light to check the stitching. 'I couldn't say, sir.'

'I assume it is the *Blockältesten* and *Kapos* who play?'

'No, sir. It's mainly the politicals and some of the Jews.'

'The Jews? Really? I wouldn't have thought they'd have the strength.'

'No, sir, I suppose not. But they say that one of the Jews is so good his talent is unnatural. I heard one of the *Blockältesten* say he was unbeatable.'

'Unbeatable, eh?' Meissner found the idea highly amusing. 'What do you think of that, Eidenmüller? It wouldn't be too healthy for your gambling enterprise if there really *was* a player who was unbeatable, would it?'

Eidenmüller smiled broadly. The chess tournament had indeed made him a lot of money. 'Oh, I wouldn't say that, sir. Nobody's unbeatable, especially not a Jew. After all, it's us who're the master race, not them.'

'Sounds to me like you think we ought to issue a challenge.'

'Definitely, sir. Can't have a Jew going round thinking he's unbeatable, can we?'

'No,' Meissner agreed, 'I don't suppose we can.'

*

1962

Amsterdam

The conversation over lunch was polite, if reserved. Schweninger said little as the other men talked about their time in Auschwitz, but ate heartily.

'I always wondered,' Meissner said, as the waiter cleared their plates, 'why people called you "Watchmaker".'

Emil looked at him, surprised. 'Because I made and repaired watches. Before I was sent to Auschwitz, I had a shop in Paris. Then, at the camp, because I had those skills and could speak German, I was put to work in a technical workshop. Word got about, and before long I was repairing watches for the SS guards and the civilian supervisors.'

Schweninger's disbelief resurfaced. 'You spoke German?'

'I grew up in Metz.' Emil took a swallow of beer. 'It was only later that I moved to Paris. Although my family was French, until I was six, Metz was part of Germany. In the 1930s, there were many in Metz who wished they were still under German rule and who wanted to follow the example of the National Socialists regarding how they treated the Jews. He paused. 'One day my mother was knocked to the ground by a group of men wearing swastika armbands. They screamed at her that she was a filthy Jew and that the time when the Jews got what was coming to them was fast approaching. Even though the men were arrested, my mother was very frightened. We decided it was time for us to leave.'

His words were followed by an awkward silence. Neither German could meet Emil's gaze.

Schweninger mumbled, 'Yes, I suppose it could not have been very easy for you, but things were worse in Germany.'

'Worse?' Emil snapped. 'Worse for whom?'

Schweninger bowed his head, embarrassed. 'For the Jews. Things were bad for everyone, but for the Jews...'

Gently, Meissner tried to steer the conversation. 'I can imagine things must have been awful. But still, it must have been a difficult decision to pack up your entire family and leave.'

'It was not such a difficult decision. My father had died in the war, fighting for the Kaiser. He even won an Iron Cross. My sisters both died from influenza after the war. There was only myself and my mother. We sold the family pawnbroking business and I set myself up as a watchmaker in Paris, near the Gare Montparnasse. It was there that I met my wife.'

1935
Paris

Emil adored Paris. After the dour, narrow streets of Metz it was open, bright and exciting. He and his mother had taken an apartment off the Boulevard Garibaldi, with its overhead Metro line, not far from the shop he was renting in Montparnasse.

After two years, the business was starting to take off, and an expanding coterie of discerning clients was sending family and friends to buy watches made by the young master craftsman from Metz. Emil was also gaining recognition in Parisian chess circles. That had not been so easy – there were some who did not welcome Jews, but his uncanny brilliance won many people over.

But, for once, chess was not the centre of his life. The twenty-three-year-old Emil had become a regular at Le Chat Noir, a jazz club off the Place d'Anvers. Jazz was not the only attraction. There was a girl, Rosa. She was like no woman he had ever met before. She was intelligent, witty and overflowing with a simple, infectious joy. Emil was in love.

Le Chat Noir was not like its bigger rival, Moulin Rouge, with its extravagant burlesques and tableaux. Patrons of Le Chat went there for two things – the heady beat of jazz, and to dance as if their very lives depended on it.

One night in September, dripping with the joyous perspiration of dancing, Emil ordered champagne for his circle of friends.

'Champagne?' Rosa said, her eyes sparkling. 'That's extravagant.'

'Tonight I feel like being extravagant,' Emil said, smiling first at Rosa, then at everybody else. 'Tonight is the most important night of my life.'

'I agree that the news that Duke Ellington is coming back to Paris is a reason for champagne,' somebody said, 'but surely that doesn't make it the most important night of your life.'

'It's my birthday, too,' Emil said.

'Your birthday?'

A waiter arrived with two bottles of champagne, another with a tray of glasses. With a flourish of gushing froth the waiter poured until all had a glass. Somebody began to sing 'Happy Birthday'. In an instant the entire audience had taken it up, then a clarinet and a muted trumpet, and within moments the whole band was playing it. Everybody was laughing and cheering and toasting in pure, hedonistic rapture.

Rosa pulled Emil to her and kissed him. 'You never told me it was your birthday,' she said quietly, her lips against his ear. 'I didn't get you a present.'

Eyes bright with happiness, Emil said, 'The best present you could give me would be to make me the happiest man alive.'

Rosa's eyes widened as Emil went down on one knee. The band was still following its own unfettered variations of 'Happy Birthday' and he had to shout over them: 'Rosa, will you marry me?'

She took his face in her hands. Tears started, tears of joy. She couldn't hold them back. 'Marry you?' She pretended to hesitate, until she saw uncertainty playing on his face. Her beautiful, full lips parted in the widest of smiles. 'You idiot. Yes, of course I'll marry you.' She laughed.

Emil got to his feet. He waved at a waiter. 'More champagne,' he shouted. 'Listen, everyone! We're getting married! Rosa has no idea what she's letting herself in for, but we're getting married.'

The next day he had told his mother. He had expected her to share his enthusiasm.

'Married?' she said, as if she couldn't believe it. 'You're getting married?'

Emil was so excited he couldn't keep still. He smiled and nodded and played with his place setting, unfolding and folding his napkin. 'Yes, Maman. Married.'

But his mother did not share his excitement; she did not leave her place to kiss and congratulate her son. Instead, she said, 'And who is this girl you're getting married to? What do you know about her?'

'Only that she's the most beautiful woman I have ever seen. I love her, and she loves me. That's all that matters.'

His mother tut-tutted and shook her head. 'But what do you know about her family? Is she Jewish?'

With that question the joy inside Emil seemed to shrivel away. 'No, Maman, she's not Jewish. She's a Catholic.'

'A Catholic, you say? And what do her parents say about her marrying a Jew? What if they disapprove? How will you marry her then?'

Emil tried to smile but he had not expected his mother to take this attitude. 'She doesn't need her parents' permission to marry – she's over twenty-one. Besides, she doesn't live with them. She's from the south.'

'So you are going to marry this girl, a Catholic from the south who's

126

gone past the right age for marrying and who doesn't live with her parents. Please don't tell me you've picked up some dancer in a cabaret and made her pregnant.'

The disapproval in his mother's voice was hard to bear. 'Maman, please don't be like this. She's not a dancer, and she's not pregnant. I hoped you would be happy for me. We're in love.'

'Hmph,' his mother snorted. 'So much in love that you couldn't bring her home to meet your mother.'

'I'm bringing her home to meet you today, Maman. I beg you, please don't be difficult, for my sake. Once you get to know her you'll love her as much as I do, I promise.'

His mother reached a hand across the table to touch his. 'You are my son, all I have left in the world. Naturally, what I want is for you to be happy. But there are so many things that need to be sorted out. For starters, where will you get married – will it be in a synagogue or in a church?'

'You are right, of course.' Emil took his mother's hand and squeezed it reassuringly. 'There are many things that need to be sorted out. But for now let us put them all to one side while you and Rosa get to know one another.'

In the end, their union was blessed in neither church nor synagogue: they settled for a civil ceremony followed by a small reception in a restaurant owned by one of Emil's friends. His mother's reluctance thawed over the months and her fondness for her daughter-in-law seemed genuine.

For their honeymoon, Emil took Rosa to Switzerland, to Basle, where he introduced her to Walter Nohel, now in his late sixties, to whom Emil, at the age of fourteen, had been apprenticed.

'Meister Nohel taught me to play chess,' Emil told her. 'Most people think that chess is merely a game, but it is more than that. It was created by the angels to please God.'

Nohel had also introduced Emil to a deeper understanding of his own religion, to the Kabbalah; something Emil had never spoken about, even to his mother. It was in his contemplation of the Kabbalah that he had found the most profound revelations about the game of chess – how it connected him with the divine thoughts of angels and how he could draw on their strengths when he played.

That there was a close bond of affection between apprentice and master was plain to see. One evening, at dinner, Nohel said, 'I have been thinking about retiring. I have had a reasonable offer for my business from Adolf Boeckh. You remember, he has that place on the corner of Koenigstrasse.'

Emil remembered it only too well. Its windows were always brightly lit and the merchandise festooned with trinkets and gewgaws, 'lacking in taste and decorum' his master had always said, calling it 'Boeckh's Bazaar'. And now it seemed that Nohel's elegant establishment would suffer the same dreadful fate.

It seemed obvious that his master was tempted by the offer, but was most reluctant to see his life's work come to nothing. 'How are you finding Paris?' Nohel asked. 'Is your business prospering?'

'Better than I could have hoped for. I have an excellent location in Montparnasse, and a clientele that is growing steadily.'

'And a reputation,' Rosa added.

'Of course,' Nohel agreed sagely. 'But would you not consider coming back to Basle? I would much rather hand the business over to you than to that nincompoop, Boeckh.' He regarded his former apprentice hopefully. 'It is well established and profitable, and I wouldn't expect you to pay me out all in one go – you could buy the business in stages, over a few years.'

He was smiling now, warming to the idea. 'Don't give me an answer now; take time to think about it. Come back and see me again before you return to Paris, eh?'

Later, Emil and Rose talked about it. It was tempting, but Basle was no match for Paris.

'Is there even a Le Chat Noir in Basle?' Rosa asked.

'If there is a Le Chat Noir in Basle, it must be well hidden,' replied Emil. 'So well hidden that I was here for seven years and still I could not find it. Basle is probably the dullest city in the world. After Metz,' he added.

1962
Amsterdam

'It seems quite extraordinary that in the midst of so much privation you managed to play chess.'

Schweninger's words brought a sharp look from Meissner. 'I assure you it's quite true.'

'Please don't misunderstand me. I'm not questioning the veracity of Herr Clément's story. All I'm saying is that it's extraordinary, that it seems almost an extravagance, in a place where there was no room for such things.'

'I don't think it's possible to understand unless you were there,' Clément said. 'Everything was extraordinary. The mere fact of survival was extraordinary. The depths of deprivation we suffered were unbeliev-able. Many times I have asked myself the question, "How can men be so lacking in pity that they can subject their fellows to such brutality?" Yet it happened every day.' He shivered. 'Different people did different things to survive. I played chess.' He looked at the German. 'I wonder what you would have done if it had been you instead of me.'

'Since I was not there, it is hardly a fair question. I'm sure I would have been able to find something.'

'Find something? Like what?' As Schweninger shrugged, floundering, still Emil pressed him: 'No, I really want to know.' His voice took on a commanding tone. 'Tell me – how exactly do you think you would have survived?'

Schweninger coloured. 'You're not the only one who managed to survive,' he retorted. 'You ask me what I would have done – I would have conformed. Followed the rules. Kept my nose clean.'

Clément smiled. 'Followed the rules?' He shook his head. 'Like I said, it's not possible to understand if you were not there.'

Schweninger appealed to Meissner. 'Well, I was not there and that can't be changed. Herr Clément says it's not possible for me to understand.'

Meissner signalled to the waiter to bring coffee. 'I'm not sure it's possible for anyone really to understand the paradox of Auschwitz. Even those who were there.'

'The paradox? What paradox?'

'The conditions in Auschwitz were appallingly degrading, yet prisoners and guards alike came to accept them as normal. It was as though we had entered another world, where the normal rules of civilization were suspended. The prisoners were utterly at the mercy of those in any sort of authority. You might expect there would have been some sort of solidarity among them as a result, but that was not the case. The need to survive was so acute that some prisoners would prey on their fellows without giving it a second thought. And yet...' The priest paused while the waiter placed cups before them.

'And yet?' Schweninger urged.

'And yet there were places where the human spirit continued to burn

130

brightly. That was why the Gestapo were there in force – to extinguish all hope before it could take hold. But they could never put it out completely.' He lifted a cup to his lips but put it back down without drinking. 'And that is why I think Herr Clément played chess in Auschwitz, because, for him, it was an affirmation of his humanity.'

Schweninger turned to Emil. 'Is that true?'

Emil sighed. It seemed plausible, but was it true? With a shake of his head he replied, 'I really don't know.'

Schweninger frowned, and ran a hand through his hair. 'Tell me,' he said, 'how it was that the two of you came to meet.'

'You need to be a little more patient,' Meissner replied, 'or you won't understand the extraordinary circumstances that brought us together.'

18.

AHLHAUSEN'S OPENING

May 1944

Konzentrationslager Auschwitz-III, Monowitz

Bodo Brack had not merely survived in Auschwitz for two years; he had thrived.

During the Weimar years,* Brack had made a good living organizing muscle for the Social Democrats for their brawls with both the Communists and the Nazis. He did not care for politicians and their posturing; all that concerned him was what he could make from them. In 1929, sensing a bigger game was to be had in Berlin, he had left Hamburg for the capital. Joseph Goebbels had been appointed Gauleiter† for the city – an entirely unofficial position until the Nazis came to power – and had immediately started a vendetta against the chief of police, Isidor Weiss. Misjudging the mood in the city, Brack had decided the greatest profit was to be made from the Communists, who were being bankrolled by Stalin.

---

* The period of democratic government in Germany from the end of the First World War to the enabling Act in March 1933 by which the Reichstag granted dictatorial powers to Hitler and, as a democratic body, voted itself out of existence.

† During this period, when the Nazis were aiming for electoral success, a Gauleiter was no more than a regional Nazi party leader. The Gauleiter of Berlin was a key position if the Nazis were to make inroads in the capital. Nazi tactics included attempts to discredit every element of the Weimar government, including the police, who would often try to prevent Nazi actions against their political rivals.

In the summer of 1931, the Communist *politburo* in Berlin decided that a deliberate provocation would tip the balance in their favour. The police were thought by many to be the puppets of the Social Democrats and were unpopular in Communist areas. An example was to be made. In August, a car stopped outside the Babylon Cinema near the Bülowplatz. Two men got out and gunned down three policemen.

The Communists waited for the popular uprising to happen, but they underestimated Goebbels' ability to use the crisis to his advantage. He put on the mantle of righteous outrage: it was intolerable, he said, that law and order had so declined that policemen doing their simple duty of protecting the citizens of Berlin could be gunned down with impunity. He promised swift justice.

The full weight of the Nazi network of informers was put behind discovering the identities of the killers. Within days, the newsstands proclaimed that three men were wanted for murder: Bodo Brack, Erich Mielke, and a third, as yet unnamed, man. The reward for information leading to their capture was huge.

Mielke, a high-ranking member of the Communist Party, was spirited out of Berlin to Moscow. Brack had no such luck.

It was not the police who found him, but Nazi Brownshirts. While relations between Goebbels and the police chief might have thawed over this matter, the Gauleiter was not prepared to share the credit for apprehending one of the killers. Brack was in an apartment in the Fischerkiez district. In twos and threes, the Brownshirts made their way there, their uniforms concealed under overcoats. Despite the hot weather, nobody noticed how strange this was. When the building was stormed, Brack received a brutal beating, but was nonetheless delivered to police headquarters alive.

In court, the prosecutor demanded the death penalty, but the judge was a Communist sympathizer. Brack received a life sentence with hard labour.

When the Nazis came to power, they proved to have long memories. In 1936 they established a concentration camp north of Berlin where their political opponents could be incarcerated away from public view. One day, Brack was brought from his cell and handed into the custody of two men in black SS uniforms. He was taken to Sachsenhausen. There his head was shaved and he was given new prison clothes: a coarse, blue-striped uniform with a green triangular patch on the breast and a prison number beneath: 11442. He still wore that number.

The SS understood that the most efficient way to operate a concentration camp was to get selected prisoners to run the camp for them. They created a system of *Ältesten*, or elders, who would manage the living quarters, and *Kapos*, who would supervise the labour squads. These *Prominenten* would be given privileges but would keep them only by maintaining an iron control over their fellow prisoners. They would do anything to avoid losing their positions. If ever they were returned to the status of an ordinary prisoner, their lives would be short indeed as their fellow inmates exacted revenge. The system resulted in extremes of violence as the *Ältesten* and *Kapos* competed to curry favour with their SS masters, who imposed few limits on their brutality.

If the Nazis thought that incarceration in Sachsenhausen would be the end of Brack, they were mistaken. He discovered that among the prisoners, those with a green triangle could prosper. Greens were convicted criminals. They fared much better than prisoners with red triangles, the Communists, or homosexuals or Jews. In the camp, Brack discovered his natural milieu. It was as if somebody had been able to enter his mind and, on finding his greatest aptitude, had created for him the perfect playground. Instinctively, he knew how to make the system work for him.

Where the Communists refused to cooperate with the camp authorities on principle, and the SS loathed the homosexuals and Jews, criminals like Brack became natural collaborators, and he rose rapidly in the camp's perverse hierarchy. In 1942, in return for a promise to commute his sentence from life to fifteen years, he agreed to be moved from Sachsenhausen to Auschwitz.

Brack started as a *Kapo* in the original Auschwitz camp, the *Stammlager*, but things did not turn out as he had expected. Brack's record – suggesting Communist sympathies – had come with him. In the Nazi pantheon of hatred, this was almost as bad as being a Jew. He was taken to an interrogation room in the punishment block.

Like most of the buildings in the *Stammlager*, the punishment block was brick built, and two storeys high. Brack was taken up unlit stairs to the upper floor. Dark stains on the bare walls and concrete floor bore witness to what he could expect. Two SS men strapped him into a heavy chair.

He had been there for about twenty minutes with a single guard for company when the door opened and a man entered: a dark, thick-set man with a heavily lined face, and thick, greasy hair. Klaus Hustek was Gestapo, and a Communist-hater of the highest order.

As soon as Brack saw him, he recognized someone with as little regard for his fellow man as he had himself.

'How is it,' Hustek asked, in a hushed voice, 'that you have managed to insinuate yourself into this camp as a Green, when you are a known Communist terrorist?'

'Herr Scharführer,' Brack replied, trying to keep his voice calm, 'I was convicted of murder. I did not kill because of any political convictions, but because I was paid to do it. I have no interest in politics,' he added.

His response earned him a hard slap across the face. 'No lies, Brack. Understand? I can tell when you're lying. Now tell me, who did you bribe to get the green triangle?'

The Scharführer seated himself and lit a cigarette, all the while staring at the prisoner with unblinking, heavy-lidded eyes.

'Nobody, Herr Scharführer,' Brack protested. 'How could I bribe anybody? What would I have that anybody would want?'

Hustek made the slightest of gestures and the guard hit Brack from behind with a cane, raising an angry weal on his right cheek. A nod, and the blow was repeated; then again, and again.

Brack tried to pull away from the blows, but it was futile. In under a minute, his face had become a bleeding, purple mess.

'That's enough.'

A bucket of water was thrown over the prisoner.

Hustek took short, thoughtful puffs on his cigarette as he gazed at his prisoner. Brack's attention flitted between the guard, who now stood beside the Scharführer, and the window that looked across to a similar barrack block perhaps twenty metres away.

The Gestapo man's voice brought him back. 'You know, it does not do to make an enemy of me.' His voice was quiet. In different circumstances it could almost have been mistaken for being friendly.

Brack tried to speak but his throat was thick with fear and his mouth full of blood. Fearing to spit it onto the floor, he had swallowed. Forcing a cough, he replied, 'Please believe me, Herr Scharführer, I have been in Sachsenhausen since 1936, and nearly four years in Spandau before that. I am not a Communist, and I have not bribed anybody.'

Hustek ground out his cigarette butt beneath his jackboot. 'Today is your lucky day. Today I believe you.' He raised his face to look directly at the man strapped to the chair. 'But I want you to be very clear about something – from now on, you belong to me. Every breath you draw in this camp will be at my pleasure. I will permit you to live, but in return you will do something for me. You will be my eyes and ears wherever you go in this camp, and you will report to me everything you see and hear. Is this understood?'

'Yes, Herr Scharführer.'

Hustek held a hand out to the guard and was handed the cane. With a back-handed swipe he brought it across Brack's already battered face. 'I did not hear you properly, Brack. What did you say?'

Brack spat a gobbet of blood onto the floor and shouted, 'I said yes! I will do anything you ask.'

'Good.' Hustek stood and walked to the door. Opening it, he said to the guard, 'Have him assigned to Block 14. It is a rat's nest of Polish Communists.' He turned to Brack. 'I want results, and I want them fast.'

Delivering the results Hustek had wanted was easy. Brack's reputation as a Communist who had killed three police stooges and the obvious evidence that he had been badly beaten meant it was not difficult to get the Poles to trust him. Within a fortnight, six of them were lined up against the wall outside the punishment block and shot.

Brack did not lose any sleep over it. For the next year it became his task to work his way into the confidence of new Polish prisoners as they entered the camp. He was not looking only for Communists: Hustek wanted information about the Polish underground, the black market, smuggling rings – anything, and Brack delivered. Yet there was no respect between him and the Gestapo man. Brack had a nose for how people felt about him and he knew that Hustek considered him scum. His opinion of Hustek was the same. He hated Hustek for the hold he had on him, and in the long darkness of winter nights he schemed endlessly about the day he would get his revenge. When Hustek was promoted to Oberscharführer, he gave Brack one of the vouchers that the *Prominenten* could use in the camp brothel. Brack got an hour with a Polish whore and cursed Hustek savagely for it.

In August 1943, while the Battle of Kharkov was at its height, Brack was transferred to the Monowitz camp. He was surprised at how far it was from the *Stammlager* and he calculated that Hustek would never bother to make a special trip all the way to the other side of Oświęcim to find him.

Despite being in thrall to the Gestapo man, Brack had not done badly, and he was determined to do even better for himself in Monowitz. Better than any of his fellow Greens he knew how to organize a gang of thugs and, before long, his status as unofficial Führer of the camp underworld was secure.

Nearly a year later, one of Brack's fellow *Prominenten* told him about a Jew who had given him a watch so he could play chess. At first, Brack was merely curious, but when he learned the Jew was from his own block, he became angry. He could not allow such a slight to go unpunished: the Jew had to be taken down a peg or two. He deserved the beating he got. But now the Jew puzzled him. Brack could understand that people would want something to distract them from the constant misery that existence as a *Häftling* entailed, but chess? The Poles played it, he knew, and some of the politicals, but a Jew? He should have been too exhausted at the end of every day. In truth, Brack's refusal to allow Clément to play had been more about asserting his control over the Frenchman, but he had soon started to wonder how he might make a profit from this foolish game.

Like himself, many of the *Prominenten* spent much of their time in idleness, desperately bored, amusing themselves by baiting prisoners and occasionally getting a ticket for the brothel. Now, he wondered if it was possible to get them interested in chess.

If he had been in the *Stammlager* he could have organized items from Kanada to give as prizes, but the camp economy in Monowitz was confined within such tight boundaries that, apart from brothel tickets, it was hard to think of anything that his fellow Greens would value enough. The *Häftlinge* were another matter: almost anything was of value to them as long as they could exchange it for food, but that wasn't going to be much use to him. No, try as he might, he could think of no way to turn the game to his advantage.

He sent for the Watchmaker. 'Give me the watch you promised and you can play your stupid game.'

The Frenchman held out something wrapped in a piece of cloth. 'I was already on my way,' he said.

Brack opened it slowly. It was a pocket watch. 'You gave Muckermann a wristwatch,' he snapped.

Emil knew he had to choose his words carefully; he had been dreading this moment. 'I beg your pardon, Herr Brack. I assumed a man of your eminence would prefer something more fitting to his stature.' His heart had sunk when the Polish foreman had given him the ancient timepiece. But it had polished up quite well, and although the case was brass, not gold, it had a handsome crest engraved upon it, and a pleasant chime that Emil had managed to restore. Emil reached across to demonstrate. 'It chimes every hour,' he said, turning the hands to make it sound.

Brack actually smiled. This set him apart. It also told the other *Prominenten* that the Watchmaker belonged to him. And it was then that it suddenly occurred to him how he *could* benefit from chess: the *Häftlinge* were all slave labourers – slaves without owners, but that would change. There must be many good chess players in the camp. He would make it his business to find them, and then he would set them against one another, like fighting cocks – no, not fighting cocks, something more refined than that . . . like *racehorses*. And the games would become entertainments that he, Bodo Brack, would put on, an affirmation of his dominance.

1962

Amsterdam

Schweninger leaned forward, puzzled. 'Let me be sure I understand,' he said. 'The prisoners who played chess were slaves, playing at the orders of this brute, for the entertainment of his fellow criminals . . . like the gladiators of ancient Rome?'

'Precisely,' Emil admitted.

'I would have refused to play,' the German stated flatly.

Meissner rolled his eyes. Emil said, 'I have not the slightest doubt that that is exactly what *you* would have done, but it would have changed nothing, and I would most likely have been killed.'

'Then I would not have played as well as I could have. I would have ruined their sport.'

Emil looked hard at the German. 'I was not playing for their pleasure. I was playing for *me*. I was playing because chess was something the SS could not take from me. With or without chess, we were slaves. This way, at least, I got to play the sublime game.'

Schweninger sniffed and shook his head dismissively. 'This Brack.

Do you know what happened to him after the war?'

'Yes. But that would be getting ahead of myself. You said you wanted to know how the bishop and I met for the first time.'

Meissner raised his hand a little as he shook his head. 'Please. I would be most grateful if you would stop calling me "bishop". My name is Paul.'

'And my name is Emil, though you persist in calling me "Watchmaker".'

Meissner winced. 'Yes. You are right. I am sorry.'

Emil nodded curtly. 'So, I first met *Paul* in late May or early June—'

'I can tell you the date exactly. It was a Sunday. The twenty-first of May 1944.'

'How strange that you can remember so precisely.'

'Not really. It was my mother's birthday.'

'My mother was killed in Auschwitz. Did you know *that*, Paul?' Emil's voice cut through the café; several diners turned to stare. 'She celebrated her last birthday in 1943,' he continued, more softly.

A silence fell between them.

The exchange had made Schweninger feel uncomfortable. At a loss for something to say, he glanced at his watch. 'My God,' he said. 'Have you seen the time? I've missed my train.'

Instinctively, Emil and Paul checked their watches. 'Dear Lord,' the priest murmured, distractedly.

Schweninger scratched his cheek thoughtfully. 'Herr Clément...' His voice thickened and he coughed to clear it. 'Would you be offended if I offered my condolences?'

Emil's eyes were now closed, but he gave a slight jerk of his head.

Schweninger's chair scraped on the floor as he pushed it back from the table. 'I'm sorry, but I must leave. If I don't get back to my hotel, they will let my room go.'

Meissner reached across the table to touch Schweninger's sleeve. 'Don't worry about that. It's my fault. I insist you stay with me at the Krijtberg.'

'Is that a hotel?'

The question provoked a surge of anxiety in the priest: he wanted Schweninger to remain in Amsterdam, for now, at least. 'No,' he replied. 'It's a place run by my order. It is a church with a house attached, which is usually occupied by priests like me, home on leave from the missions. There are only two of us there at the moment – the parish priest and myself. Most of the bedrooms are empty. It would be no trouble to put you up.' He breathed a quick prayer that his powers of persuasion would prove to be as strong as ever. 'The rooms are perhaps a little spartan compared with your hotel, but they're clean, and the housekeeper gives us a hearty breakfast each morning. What do you say? Will you give it a try?'

19

THE NAJDORF VARIATION

Emil made his way back to his hotel. Meissner had asked him to meet them later, but he was not sure he wanted to.

The late afternoon sun was bright, but gave little warmth as Emil stood on a bridge over the Singel Canal, wondering what he was doing. Schweninger and Meissner had both been Nazis, committed to the dream of a German Empire lording it over the rest of Europe. Slavery had been the least of many crimes, and yet Schweninger had immediately protested that he would never have submitted to it, as so many had.

Did he have a point? For the life of him, Emil did not know. The realisation shocked him: *he did not know*. Until today there had been a sharp clarity in his consciousness, especially in his hatred of the Germans, that he had nurtured, as a parent would a child, until it was almost the only thing that gave him any meaning. Hatred and chess: was that the sum total of his existence? *Meissner is right*, he thought grudgingly. *What kind of a life is that?*

He stared at the water below him, and saw a stranger staring back at him from its murky stillness. He heard the voice of Yves, as clearly as if he were standing beside him: 'One of us has to live to get out of here, if only to tell the rest of the world what is happening.'

Well, he had done that. He had fulfilled his duty to the thousands who had perished in Auschwitz. Nobody knew for sure how many they were:

at his trial, Kommandant Höss had claimed the death toll ran into millions; so many that the numbers were distant, abstract – they were not real people, they were figures to be entered into a calculating machine, like an exercise in accounting. And Emil had done his duty. He had testified. He had written his book. He had borne witness to the horror…Still it was not enough. Nothing he did could free him from the aching loss and guilt. Meissner was right about that too, he realized now. It was not enough to bear witness. He had to make people understand the truth of existence in a death camp; how it penetrated every consciousness, poisoning every experience, twisting every thought.

Painful as it was, Emil decided he would tell his story to Schweninger. Then perhaps the German would understand. And perhaps he, Emil, would find some peace.

Perhaps.

Tuesday, 6 June 1944
Konzentrationslager Auschwitz-II, Birkenau
Something terrible is happening. The camp senses it but cannot see it. It is hidden, concealed in unknown depths. The camp has felt this pulse of pain and terror before, but never with such intensity, repeating over and over. The camp is searching for the source, determined to find it, frantically extending tendrils of consciousness along the pathways and between the many huts of Birkenau. It is transmitted through the concrete posts that have their roots deep in the earth, and along miles of electrified wire; there is a whisper of it in the railway siding where, every day now, the cattle cars unload their human cargo.

We follow the rails inwards from the arch, beneath which the trains enter the camp. Ahead, there is a grove of birch trees. Their silvery trunks reflect the sun to make patterns on the grass below. We listen. All we can hear is the rustling of the leaves and the sigh of an early summer breeze. Then we see them: a column of people standing quietly in the birch grove, queuing outside a low, red-brick building dominated by a large chimney. Thick smoke pours into the sky, a black stain on its pristine summer blue. There is an unfamiliar smell, cloying and unpleasant. Around the building, sheltered by the trees from prying eyes, are grassy lawns, and the people are there: men, women, and children, patiently waiting their turn to descend into a stairwell that takes them below ground.

They proceed in a calm, orderly fashion, with no pushing or jostling. They have been told they have been brought to this place to take a shower.

'A shower?' a voice asks incredulously. It is a woman. Her nervousness makes her voice a little too loud. She did not intend for the SS men who stand around with dogs and machine guns to hear her. She is suspicious of the Germans. They are not known for their good treatment of Jews, and the set-up seems rather elaborate for something as simple as taking a shower.

Smiling indulgently, an officer calls to her. 'Where have you come from?'

'Debrecen.' The officer's eyebrows lift as if to repeat the question. 'In Hungary,' the woman explains.

'And how much time did you spend on the train?'

'Six days.'

He nods sagely. 'Six days cooped up with I don't know how many other people and you don't need a shower?'

Despite all that their experience has taught them about the SS, people nearby cannot help but smile.

'We are not barbarians, you know,' the officer continues. He looks more closely at the woman, who wishes now she had never opened her mouth.

She is young, in her twenties, and beneath the dirt and matted hair, she is quite attractive. 'What did you do before you came here?' he asks.

'I was a seamstress.'

'A good one?'

She blushes. 'Of course.'

'Men's or women's clothes?'

'Women's. Mostly undergarments.'

Again she is on the receiving end of his indulgent grin. 'Well, here you'll learn to make men's clothes. We are short of *good* seamstresses.' When he says 'good', he catches her eye and winks. 'We need as many as we can get to make uniforms for our troops.'

She does not seem convinced so he addresses the people nearby: 'Are there any more of you who are skilled at making clothes?' A couple of hands are raised.

The officer points at a man who is cradling a young child in his arms. 'How about you,' he says. 'What did you do?'

'I was a shoemaker.'

'Can you make military boots?'

'Of course.'

'Then you'll do well here.' The officer spreads his arms wide as if to embrace the people around him. 'We are not fools,' he says. 'We know good work when we see it, and we reward it. So let's be practical. Put away your doubts. You are in a work camp. After your shower, you will be given your assignments. I give you my word as a German officer.'

His speech is reassuring, but the people do not know that they have entered the kingdom of lies, and it is thus that the camp finds them, shuffling down concrete steps into a long underground chamber, where they are told to undress: men, women and children all together.

There are pegs with numbers where they hang their clothes. They are told to remember the number so they will be able to find their belongings afterwards. Many try to cover their nakedness with their hands as they shamble along the corridor to the shower room. There are very many of them and they are crammed in tight – too tight. Suddenly, the doors are slammed shut and there is the distinct sound of heavy bolts being shot home.

The lights go out.

Voices are heard in the darkness: 'What is happening?' Some call to their loved ones. Some start to weep. Children cry and cling to their mothers and fathers. Then there is a harsh, scraping noise from above, and a shaft of light penetrates. It reveals fearful faces staring upwards at the noise.

Above, SS men wearing gas masks have removed grilles from ducts that lead down to the shower room. In their hands they hold tins marked with a skull and crossbones. From the tins they pour granules of a powdery substance into the ducts. It falls lightly on those standing below – a fine, soft grit. It gives off a sweet, sickly smell.

The grilles are put back. Below it is dark again. Then somebody gasps: 'I can't breathe!'

Then another: 'Gas. Poison gas!'

People start to yell. Those nearest the doors hammer on them frantically, begging to be let out. There is a surge of panic towards the doors. Children and old people are crushed. Now many are screaming, especially the women and children. For a few short minutes the noise is deafening. When it abates someone can be heard saying Kaddish, the Jewish prayer for the dead. Some succumb to the poison less quickly than others, but in a matter of minutes, they are all silent, all dead.

Afterwards, the mouths of many of the victims remain open, as if their screams continued after death.

By the end of this summer day, nearly 4,000 lives have been extinguished. The only concern among the SS who have orchestrated this murder is that the corpses must be removed and burned before the next consignment arrives the following day.

All that is left in the underground chamber are the last traces of gas and rows of empty clothes hanging mute, in accusing ranks. Those, and the silence of a thousand absent voices.

A wail of grief passes through the camp at the horror it has just witnessed; a long keening wail that nobody hears: not the SS men who run the camp; not the thousands of prisoners who yet endure; not the camp orchestra which plays its absurd, cheerful tunes at the start and end of each day; not the birds that have deserted the trees that surround the camp; not the earth itself on which the camp lies.

Only the wind hears it, but it is only one cry among many, and before it can be remembered, it is lost.

1962

Kerk de Krijtberg, Amsterdam

Dinner in the presbytery was a frugal affair: onion soup followed by boiled potatoes and fried herring.

'I do enjoy herring,' Meissner said good-naturedly, 'but why did the good Lord have to give them so many blasted bones?' He grinned at Emil, pleased that the chess player had decided to return.

Schweninger was silent, chewing stolidly; as always, his appetite came first, conversation, later.

Afterwards, they retired to the same gloomy lounge where Emil had woken from his fainting spell.

'I think perhaps it's my turn to take up the story,' the priest said, offering cigarettes to his guests. 'There are two sides to every tale, after all.'

He held a taper to the glowing coals in the fireplace to get a light, then settled into an easy chair, inhaling deeply on his cigarette before starting to speak. 'You might be surprised to hear that I was not brought up to hate Jews. My parents were staunch Catholics and it was only when I was inducted into the Hitler Youth that anti-Jewish sentiments were demanded of me. But my parents never took the rhetoric too seriously, so neither did I. When I got to Auschwitz, as far as I could see, the work that the Jews were doing was badly needed by the Reich, and it did not occur to me that the new Kommandant, Sturmbannführer Bär, would object to the idea of pitting this "unbeatable" Jew' – he gestured at Emil – 'against our SS chess champions. After all, as my orderly, Eidenmüller, would have said, we couldn't have a Jew thinking he was invincible, could we?'

When neither Emil nor Schweninger commented, he continued. 'I was due to go on leave back to my family in Cologne, but when I got to the station in Oświęcim I learned that Allied bombing had severely disrupted rail traffic from Silesia to Germany, so I had to put off my journey. The following Sunday was a rest day in Monowitz, so I summoned Eidenmüller and told him I wanted to take a look at this Jewish chess marvel for myself.'

May 1944
Konzentrationslager Auschwitz-III, Monowitz
It was the first time that Meissner had entered the section of the Monowitz camp in which the prisoners were confined. At the administrative office, he learned the number of the block where *Häftling* number 163291

had his bunk. Accompanied by the *Blockführer* – an SS NCO – and Eidenmüller, he walked briskly through the camp.

At the *Blockführer*'s shout of '*Achtung!*' the inmates in the block sprang to attention.

At the rear, a small man slipped unseen into the dormitory. His eyes lit on a boy, perhaps fifteen years old, said to be Brack's *Piepel*,* though nobody mentioned it openly. The man grabbed the boy by the scruff of the neck.

'Where's Bodo?' he rasped.

'Block 39.'

'Not so loud. What's he doing there?'

'The Watchmaker is playing the one they call the Flying Dutchman.'

'Right. I need you to get him. Tell him I sent you and that there's an SS-Hauptsturmführer in his block. What he wants I don't know, but Bodo better get back here fast. Got it?'

In the day room, Meissner looked around, amazed. He had not realized how primitive the interiors of the blocks were. He had imagined them to be somewhat like the barracks of the SS enlisted men: basic, functional, but not completely bereft of any comfort. What hit him instantly was the smell. He knew that in the Buna factory many of the civilian workers used the word '*Stinkjude*' when they spoke of the camp inmates; Meissner had thought it a term of derision. It was not. It was a reference to the sickly sweet stench of men who lived packed tightly together and who had not had a proper wash for months.

'Where is the *Blockältester*?' the SS NCO roared. Nobody seemed to know.

---

* Teenage boys were used as personal servants by some of the *Prominenten*. Some were exploited for sexual gratification.

'Send somebody to find him,' Meissner said, before jerking his head to Eidenmüller to follow him back outside. 'Jesus Christ Almighty,' he spluttered once they were out. 'How do they manage to live like that?' The officer fished in his tunic pocket for his cigarette case.

His orderly struck a match, cupping his fingers to protect it from the breeze. 'Thank God we get plenty of fags, eh, sir? They're the only thing that makes the smell bearable.'

Before they had finished their cigarettes, they were approached by a clean-shaven prisoner. He stood to attention, pulled his cap smartly off his head and announced himself: '*Häftling* 11442, *Blockältester* Brack, Herr Hauptsturmführer. At your service.'

Meissner was astonished. It was the first time he had ever seen a prisoner wearing an immaculately clean uniform. The green triangle looked as if it could have been sewn on that morning.

Before Meissner could say anything the SS NCO joined them. 'Where the hell have you been?' he yelled. Brack did not flinch. This was another first for the officer. He had only ever seen prisoners shrink with fear whenever they were addressed by an SS man.

'Beg pardon, Herr Unterscharführer. I was … watching a game of chess.'

'*Chess?* What the fucking hell are you talking about, chess?'

'It's all right, Unterscharführer,' the officer said. 'That's why we came. I wanted to see this particular game of chess myself.' Smiling, he let the still-glowing remains of his cigarette fall at his feet and gestured for Brack to lead the way.

They followed the immaculate, blue-striped uniform for about 200 metres. Meissner noticed that Brack had well-polished boots rather than the rough wooden clogs that the rest of the inmates had to wear.

The *Blockältester* stopped at a block with a small plate bearing the number 39 nailed to its front. He pulled open its rickety wooden door. Meissner peered inside. What he saw was identical to the block they had left moments before, with a brick stove offset from the centre, and a narrow window set in the roof to let in a little light. The only difference was to his right, where a chessboard had been placed atop a wooden crate, with two men seated on smaller crates, one to either side. Crowded around them were perhaps thirty or forty men: some on the floor, some on makeshift chairs, some standing.

With a groan of rusting hinges, the door opened, flooding the interior with light. Brack held the door open for the SS men, shouting '*Achtung!*' as he did so. All eyes turned to the door. At the sight of Meissner's uniform, the prisoners sprang to their feet.

The SS NCO pushed his way to the front. 'What's the meaning of this?' he screamed. 'I'll have you all flogged!'

Meissner stood watching the scene in an almost detached way. Most of the spectators bore green triangles on their jackets, with one or two red triangles among them. The two men at the chessboard each had a red triangle over a yellow one – Jews.

The players stood rigid, eyes straight ahead. Senior officers rarely entered the prisoners' barracks. When they did, it was usually SS doctors come to make a *Selektion* of the sick and exhausted to be sent to the gas chambers. No Jewish inmate ever thought such a visit might be for their benefit. The presence of an SS officer was always an occasion for fear.

'Unterscharführer,' Meissner said crisply, 'thank you for your assistance. You have been most helpful, but I'll take it from here.' He paused and turned to Brack. '*Blockältester*, I see there is a game of chess under way. I'm a great admirer of chess, and I would like to watch the rest of the game. Tell these men to carry on as they were and to pretend that we are not here.'

1962

Kerk de Krijtberg, Amsterdam

'Is that how it happened?' Emil said. 'I had forgotten.'

Schweninger could not help himself: 'Forgotten? How could you forget something like that?'

Shaking his head slowly, Emil turned to the German. 'Only someone who had not been in Auschwitz could say such a thing. When an SS officer came to the block, the important thing was whether they were there for a *Selektion*. Fear drove all other considerations from your mind.'

Schweninger frowned. 'I do not understand what you mean by "*Selektion*".'

Keeping his eyes on the hearth, Meissner spoke in a low monotone. '*Selektionen* were how the SS carried out their mandate to maintain production in the armaments factories, while at the same time keeping the gas chambers operating. At regular intervals, SS doctors, accompanied by squads of soldiers, would be sent into the camp to pick out those who had been debilitated by ill health or starvation and who could no longer carry out the work that was required of them. They were sent to the gas chambers in Birkenau. There were so many Jews coming in on transports from all over Europe that there was never any problem replacing them.'

'And you knew about this?' Schweninger asked.

Meissner nodded, his eyes fixed on the red-glowing coals. 'Not at first, but eventually I came to realize what was happening. How could I not?'

'And you went along with it?'

'What else could I do?' Meissner shrugged, then looked up. 'At one point I tried to persuade the Kommandant that the arrangement was inefficient, that if we improved conditions for the prisoners, the productivity of the arms factories would improve. But it was made clear to me that if I persisted, I would be labelled as a Jew sympathizer and things would go badly for me.'

'Badly for you?' Clément was appalled. 'We were starving. Freezing. Exhausted. We were outcasts. The suffering inflicted on us is beyond my ability to describe. Yet you thought things could go *badly* for you? What would they have done – take away your brothel privileges?'

'I never visited the brothel,' Meissner said, stiffly. 'I tried to do what I could. Not one prisoner was sent to the gas chamber because of me. Not one.'

'How noble of you,' Clément mocked, his lip curling. 'You were still part of a system that sent innocent people to their deaths. You have blood on your hands as surely as if you had herded them into the gas chambers yourself.'

'Do not presume to think, Herr Clément, that I have not reproached myself for my failings.' The priest's voice was brittle with shame. 'And I will continue to do so for the rest of my life.'

'But still,' Schweninger said, after a pause, 'was there nothing you could have done?'

'I managed to save one life, and for me, that had to be enough.'

'And whose life did you save?'

The question was answered by Emil.

'Mine.'

20.

THE ALBIN COUNTERGAMBIT

May 1944

Konzentrationslager Auschwitz-III, Monowitz

The result of the match was a foregone conclusion – the Watchmaker had defeated the Dutchman even before the arrival of the SS men, but was stringing it out for the benefit of Brack and the other *Prominenten* who had started to follow the games that were now being played.

Everyone knew that the Watchmaker belonged to Brack, but he had let it be known that he had no objection to other block elders or *Kapos* taking an inmate under their wing to pit them against his champion. But it was not Brack who had spread the word that the Frenchman was unbeatable: that was Pasinski, a Pole who claimed to have beaten the German champion in the 1936 Chess Olympiad in Munich.

Pasinski had been in the camp since the liquidation of the Warsaw ghetto in 1943. He had a gift for scrounging, and it was this that enabled him to survive when most of those who had entered the camp with him perished. Before the war, he had harnessed his natural shrewdness into a formidable talent for chess, and he had been looking forward to playing the upstart Frenchman he had heard about.

Pasinski had drawn white and made a conventional enough opening move: advancing his queen's pawn two spaces. The Watchmaker copied his move, blocking the pawn. The Pole had then advanced his queen's bishop's pawn two squares, offering a sacrifice to black. Clément had ignored the gambit and moved his king's pawn two places, to stand beside its brother. The Pole had taken this second pawn, allowing the first black pawn to then advance one place to stand before the white queen, creating a wedge in the white defence.

In only six moves, Pasinski had lost the initiative and, with it, the game. Later, he claimed to have known of the countergambit the Watchmaker had employed, but it was unheard of for it to be played at senior level – if any other player had made the same move, he would have lost, the Pole had insisted.

According to Pasinski, the Watchmaker had an insight into the thinking of his opponent that was uncanny. That was what made him unbeatable.

When the game with the Dutchman was over, Eidenmüller told Brack to have the Watchmaker brought to Meissner's office. 'But get him shaved and showered and in a clean uniform first. Is that clear?'

It was an hour before *Häftling* number 163291 found himself standing nervously to attention in the office of an SS-Hauptsturmführer.

The aroma of coffee in the room was tantalizing. The SS officer was stretched out in his chair, his feet up on the desk, watching the smoke from his cigarette as it rose slowly to the ceiling. An Unterscharführer poured coffee for the officer then took up position by the door.

After surviving nearly five months in the camp, Emil Clément knew better than to utter a word to an SS man until he had been directly addressed, and so he stood, rigid, his eyes fixed on the wall behind the officer, with a strong urge to scratch where the rough cloth of his new uniform was making his armpits itch.

1962

Kerk de Krijtberg, Amsterdam

'So you remember being summoned to his office?' Schweninger asked, indicating Meissner with a tilt of his head. 'But you had no idea why. Amazing.'

'Not so amazing,' Clément countered. 'It was merely another of the absurdities we faced every day. I guessed – after the elaborate cleansing I had been forced to endure – that it was not to inflict any punishment on me. I assumed it was probably to do with my skill at repairing watches.'

'Were you afraid?'

'Of course.' Emil shook his head in disbelief at the naivety of Schweninger's question. 'Always. Everyone who had not lost their senses was afraid. Every time you were spoken to by an SS man, it was like a game of cat and mouse. You weren't supposed to look at the SS man, but you had to, to try and guess what he wanted. You tried to work it out from how he was looking at you, or the way he was holding himself, or the way he spoke. If he was shouting you knew he was angry over something and that you were likely to get a beating. And while a beating on the spot could be painful, it was not as bad as a whipping.'

'Presumably for serious infringements of the rules?'

Clément spread his hands. 'Of course. Some men were so careless as to get mud on their trousers or lose a button from their jacket. I saw men flogged for that.'

Schweninger winced. 'But you didn't think that was what was waiting for you this time?'

The Frenchman nodded. 'No, but it was always a possibility. You feared even to speak. Anything you said could be twisted and used against you. You listened hard to try and work out whether there was some hidden

157

meaning that you needed to understand so that you could give the answer the SS man wanted to hear, but it was almost impossible – anything you were told could be a lie, and the SS man was like a rottweiler, eager to pounce on any unguarded word and punish you for it.'

'And that was how you felt the first time we spoke?' Meissner asked, his voice barely audible.

Emil nodded.

'I'm sorry,' the priest said hoarsely. 'I had no idea.'

May 1944

Konzentrationslager Auschwitz-III, Monowitz

The Hauptsturmführer took his feet from the desk, stubbed out his cigarette in an ashtray fashioned from a shell casing and addressed the prisoner: 'Your name?'

'Clément, Herr Hauptsturmführer. Emil Clément.'

'And where are you from?'

'France.'

'I'm told you are an excellent chess player. Is that true?'

For a moment Emil's guard faltered: instead of staring at the wall, he let his gaze fall to look at the officer.

'Chess player? I'm sorry, Herr Hauptsturmführer, I don't understand.'

'It's a simple enough question. Are you a good chess player – yes or no?'

'I think so. I mean – yes, Herr Hauptsturmführer.'

'You speak good German for a Frenchman.'

'Yes, Herr Hauptsturmführer. Originally I was from Metz.'

'Almost a German, then, eh?' Grinning, the officer reached across his desk for his cup and took a sip of coffee.

Emil fixed his eyes once more on the wall.

THE DEATH'S HEAD CHESS CLUB

The coffee seemed to help the officer get his thoughts in order. 'How long have you been playing chess?'

'Since I was about fourteen years old.'

'And have you ever played at national or international level?'

'No, Herr Hauptsturmführer, I have not.'

'Are you sure? That seems hard to believe, when I'm told that you have beaten at least one international-level player here in the camp.'

'Who told—?' Emil checked himself. 'It should not be so hard to believe, Herr Hauptsturmführer. Before the war it was not so easy for a Jew to get onto the French team – after the fall of France, impossible.'

'Did you know that we hold a chess tournament among the SS personnel here in Auschwitz?'

'No, Herr Hauptsturmführer. I did not know that.'

'How would you like to play against the SS?'

The question did not make sense; Emil struggled to understand it. There was always a trick question; everyone knew that. Perhaps this was it, the question that would lead to a flogging, or worse. What was the right answer? If he said yes, they would tell him he was an uppity Jewish turd and beat him for sure. The correct answer was surely no. It would show them that he knew his place; that he was not so stupid as to think of challenging the established order, even if invited to do so.

'Well?'

'It is not my place to think I could play against the SS, Herr Hauptsturmführer.'

Meissner leaned forward. 'Not play? Are you quite sure? I could make certain privileges available to you if you did.'

Emil licked his lips, his mouth suddenly dry. 'May I have permission to speak frankly, Herr Hauptsturmführer?'

The officer looked surprised that he should even ask the question. 'Please do.'

'Your privileges have no meaning for me, Herr Hauptsturmführer. How long do you think I would be able to hold on to them? And if I beat one of your SS men, I do not think I would survive for long – I would be pulled out of my work *Kommando* and beaten to death, or there would be a *Selektion* and I would be one of those sent up the chimney.'

Meissner frowned. He had not anticipated such a flat refusal of the chance of better treatment. 'So you refuse to play?'

'Respectfully, Herr Hauptsturmführer, I must.'

'What if I give an order that you must play?'

'Then I will play, Herr Hauptsturmführer, but not to win.'

Exasperated, Meissner stood. 'Are you really so deluded as to think you have a choice in this matter?'

But *Häftling* number 163291 stood his ground. 'One always has a choice, Herr Hauptsturmführer, if you are prepared to accept the consequences.'

1962
Kerk de Krijtberg, Amsterdam

'So you did refuse, after all. That took courage. Well done.'

Schweninger's words brought Emil up short. Was it approval he heard in the German's voice? 'It was not a matter of courage, Herr Schweninger,' he replied coolly, 'merely survival. I did not see how I could comply with this incredible suggestion and live.'

The German reached across and patted Emil's forearm. 'Please,' he said, his voice unexpectedly warm, 'enough of the "Herr Schweninger". Call me Willi – everybody else does.'

The clock on the mantelpiece chimed ten. Meissner looked at Emil.

'Do you have a match tomorrow?'

'No. Not until the day after.'

'Then may I offer you gentlemen a nightcap?'

His offer accepted, Meissner left the room and returned minutes later with three glasses and a bottle of Kümmel. 'It's Dutch, I'm afraid,' he said. 'Not as good as German, but not undrinkable.' He poured three generous measures. '*Prosit*,' he said.

Meissner and Schweninger clinked glasses. They held their drinks together, waiting for Emil to join the toast. Emil did not stir; instead, he stared at the colourless liquid in his glass. Meissner and Schweninger exchanged an uneasy glance.

Slowly, Emil raised his hand. '*Prosit*,' he murmured.

The men drank deeply, appreciating its satisfying warmth as it went down. 'So, where were we?' said Meissner.

Schweninger used his glass to point at Emil. 'Our friend had just refused your kind offer to play chess against the SS.' He took another sip of the liqueur. 'For which I congratulated him.' He winked at Emil then took a pack of Camels from his pocket, put one between his lips and offered the rest to his companions.

'Yes,' the priest said, taking one. 'But it was not long before he changed his mind, was it?'

21.

THE BALTIC DEFENCE

May 1944

Konzentrationslager Auschwitz-III, Monowitz

Unterscharführer Eidenmüller was furious; he could not remember the last time he had been so angry. The gall of that stinking Jewish piece of shit. Christ, no wonder everybody hated the ungrateful swine. He had stood listening to the exchange between the Hauptsturmführer and the filthy pig-fucker with growing disbelief, wanting to march across the office and give the little prick a good beating right there and then. But he knew the Hauptsturmführer wouldn't have stood for that, so he had been forced to let the bastard go. For now.

Eidenmüller made himself calm down. His boss wanted a game of chess. He would see that he got it.

He waited a week before returning to the block where the Jew had his billet. The day room was empty apart from the *Stubendienst*, who was slowly pushing a brush across the uneven floorboards. The brushstrokes quickened when the man saw who had entered.

'Where's Brack?'

The prisoner stopped what he was doing and came to attention, holding the brush pole like a rifle. The sight almost made Eidenmüller laugh. 'Block 19, Herr Unterscharführer.'

At Block 19, Eidenmüller pulled the door open and looked in. Brack was engaged in a desultory conversation with three other Greens. 'Brack,' Eidenmüller called. 'A quick word, if you don't mind.'

The obsequiousness Brack had shown in front of Meissner was gone. 'Yeah? What about?' he said, blinking as he came out into the bright sunlight.

'Let's go for a little walk.'

Curious, Brack fell in beside the SS man as they sauntered towards the parade ground.

'Tell me about this Jewish chess player of yours,' Eidenmüller said.

'The Watchmaker?'

'Is that what they call him? Why do they call him that?'

''Cause that's what he does. He fixes watches.'

'For the prisoners?'

Brack gave him a *Don't be so bloody stupid* look. 'What do you think?'

They continued a few paces without speaking until Eidenmüller said, 'You know, my boss wanted to set up a game between the Jew and some of our SS chess players.'

Brack stopped, astonished. 'Why would he want to do that?'

'Word's got out, Brack – know what I mean? I'm not saying it's your fault, but it's a funny thing, word getting out. Once it's out, it won't go back in again.'

'What the fuck are you talking about?'

'"Unbeatable", Brack. That's the word. Your Jew chess player. Fucking "unbeatable". Can't have that, can we? A fucking unbeatable Jew? So someone's got to beat him, only it can't be a put-up job. Everybody would know straight away if it was. So my boss wants to put him against some of our best SS chess players and, believe me, there's a couple of really good ones. Only there's a problem, isn't there?'

'A problem?'

'Yeah. The stinking little Kike doesn't want to play, does he?'

They walked on a little further.

'What is it, exactly, that you want me to do?' Brack asked.

'He's a decent sort, my boss, you know,' Eidenmüller said, ignoring the question. 'So he wouldn't take too kindly to it if he thought I had done anything to frighten his precious little Jew boy into playing. So I won't tell you what to do. You know your business. Just make sure the ungrateful little fuck agrees to play.'

'What's in it for me?'

Eidenmüller smiled broadly. 'Well, first, you get my undying gratitude. Second – when was the last time you had a decent drop of Schnapps?'

Emil and Yves are walking back to the block after evening roll call. Their progress is painfully slow. Yves has returned from the Buna factory completely spent. Every night, some prisoners are carried back by their fellows. Most of these will be earmarked for *Selektion*.

For days now, Emil has been expecting his friend to be one of them.

'Let's try to get you into the *Krankenbau*,'* Emil urges Yves. 'You can say you fell and twisted your ankle and that it can hardly support your weight. They won't be able to prove otherwise. The doctors are Jewish. They'll take pity on you. All you need is a few days of rest, and you'll be a new man.'

His words are hollow and he knows it, but, to his surprise, Yves agrees and joins the long queue outside the sick bay. For days, he has spoken of nothing but food; he dreams constantly of feasting. Yet when Emil offers him half his bread ration, Yves will not take it.

* Infirmary.

Emil helps his friend to sit on the ground and lean back against the wooden wall. 'Give me your bowl,' he says, 'and I'll fetch your soup ration. I'll be back before you know it.'

It is not far from the K-B to their block. As Emil gets to the front of the line, however, the prisoner doling out the soup calls out: 'Here he is. Tell Bodo.'

Emil is pulled out of the line and into the day room. At a word from Brack everyone clears out, leaving only Emil, Brack, his pimp, Widmann, and half a dozen heavies.

It is obvious that something is wrong.

'You've got a fucking nerve, you ungrateful piece of Kike shit,' says Brack.

Emil does not reply.

'Who the fuck do you think you are?'

Still Emil gives no answer.

Brack shouts, almost screaming. 'I said – who the fuck do you think you are, you stinking stupid Jew!'

And Emil knows he is going to die.

1962

Kerk de Krijtberg, Amsterdam

The housekeeper put her head round the lounge door. 'If you don't need me for anything else, Father, I'll be off.'

'Of course. Did you make up the bed for Mijnheer Schweninger?'

'Two beds, Father, I made up two beds – I thought you had two guests staying. And I've laid breakfast out ready in the morning for you.'

'Thank you.'

'Only I won't be in tomorrow, as it's my day off.'

'Thank you, Mrs Brinckvoort. I'm sure we'll manage splendidly.' As the housekeeper closed the door behind her, Meissner turned to Emil. 'You heard what she said – there's a room for you if you want it. Why don't you move out of your hotel and stay here for the rest of the tournament? You and Willi would probably enjoy picking over the games together.'

'Just a minute,' Schweninger interjected. 'I only agreed to stay here for one night, not for the duration.'

'As you wish. It was just a thought.' Meissner picked up the coffee pot. It was empty. 'More coffee, anyone? It won't take a minute.'

The two chess players contemplated the glowing coals in the hearth while they waited for the priest to return from the kitchen. He seemed to be taking a long time.

Eventually, Emil broke the silence. 'For years I've wondered,' he began, haltingly. 'I mean, I've read about it in books, but I've never asked someone who was there, somebody who was part of it . . .' His voice tailed away.

'What is it that have you wondered, Herr Clément?'

Emil took a deep breath. 'How could intelligent people like you and Paul have allowed yourselves to be so hoodwinked by Hitler that you ended up criminals?'

Only yesterday, this question would have caused great offence. Now Schweninger took it philosophically. 'What a question,' he replied. 'I've asked myself the same question many times, and the truth of it is very disheartening. People have talked about the failings of our politicians and the terrible effect on Germany of the Depression and the war reparations, but the fact is that too many of us *wanted* to say "Yes!" to Hitler. We knew he was dangerous, but he promised to lead us to our rightful destiny. Who could say no to that?' He sighed, heavily. 'At first there was no real shape or form to the danger, but then the Nazi Party wormed its way into every nook and cranny of our lives, watching us and controlling us: the Brownshirts, the youth movements, the artistic societies, the propaganda machine – even the postal service, and, later, the Gestapo. It was like you were facing a colossus that was willing you, inciting you, imploring you to say "Yes!" without knowing what "Yes!" meant. But despite the undercurrent of fear, it was exhilarating, liberating. The Führer knew what needed to be done and all we had to do was to leave everything in his capable hands. Then all would be well and we would be strong again – one people, one blood, united in a common purpose, marching together to a marvellous future where the old uncertainties would be banished. If you had been part of it you would understand. It was irresistible.'

Emil shook his head slowly. 'No, I could never have been part of it. I was a Jew.'

Meissner returned. 'Coffee?'

'No, thank you,' Schweninger said, pushing himself up from his chair. 'I think I'll go to bed.'

'So early?'

But the mood in the room had soured; the feeling of fellowship that had been growing was gone.

'What about you, Emil, will you stay the night?'

'No. I think I should go back to my hotel.' He stood and stepped past Paul to the front door, retrieving his coat on the way.

Meissner followed him. 'Will we see you tomorrow?'

Emil stopped in the open doorway. 'I don't know. Perhaps. I need time to think. It's been a long day. Things might seem different tomorrow.'

'I'll pray for you.'

'Thank you. But I'm not sure what value the prayers of a Christian have for a Jew.'

'Christians and Jews both pray to the same God.'

'So it is said.' Emil turned away. 'Goodnight,' he called back.

As always, Meissner awoke early. He washed, put on a cassock and hobbled down the short flight of steps from the presbytery to the deserted street. He eased himself onto a bench overlooking the canal. With only birdsong for company he lit a cigarette, but it tasted bitter in his mouth and he threw it into the water. He twisted around to face the church with its double doors and twin spires and its dedication to St Francis Xavier. The Jesuits had been there for over three centuries – clandestinely for two of them. He usually took inspiration from their tenacity in keeping faith with Dutch Catholics after Holland had become avowedly Protestant, but not today. He sighed, spent a moment longer in the company of the birds and then stood.

Taking a key from his pocket he unlocked the church door and went in. He wondered whether he had done the right thing in bringing Emil and Willi together. It had gone better than he had expected until he had left them alone. Then something had happened, but what? He limped to the altar rail. The smell of polish and candle-wax usually made him feel he was coming home. He knelt, joining his hands in prayer, but he found the words that were supposed to bring serenity had become mechanical and bereft of meaning. He looked at his watch. It was still not seven o'clock. He decided he would say Mass.

In the sacristy he put on an alb and draped a stole over his shoulders. From a cupboard he took a little wine and a single communion wafer. He went back into the church and stood at one of the side chapels, dedicated to the Virgin. 'Holy Mother of God,' he murmured, 'please help me to do the right thing.'

He put the cup of wine and the wafer down on the altar cloth, genuflected and crossed himself. '*In nomine Patris, et Filii, et Spiritus Sancti . . .*'

Meissner returned to the house feeling better, as he often did after saying a solitary Mass. *Ask, and it shall be given unto you.* Well, he had asked. Now it was in the good Lord's hands. Schweninger was still not up so he busied himself making coffee and frying bacon. The smell would surely wake his guest.

Within minutes Willi entered the kitchen, rubbing his eyes.

'I thought I heard the front door open before,' he said.

'It was me. I went into the church.' Quickly he changed the subject. 'Coffee?'

Over breakfast neither of them spoke about the previous evening. When they had washed the dishes and settled down for a smoke, Schweninger said, 'You never said what made Herr Clément change his mind.'

'No. And if it's all right with you, I think it would be better to wait for Emil to tell you himself.'

Schweninger leaned across the kitchen table to tap the ash from his cigarette into an ashtray. 'Fair enough,' he said.

They fell into a companionable silence until, after a while, the priest said, 'Why don't you tell me about what you did in the war. Ministry of Propaganda, wasn't it?'

Schweninger nodded. 'That's right. Section three – Tourism.'

'And you spent all your time in the ministry in the same section?'

'Yes. I liked being there at first, it was quite glamorous, especially during the Olympics, and there were opportunities for travel. But after a while I came to realize I was going nowhere. Even when I applied for a transfer, for which I was well qualified, I never got it. I was a bit slow working it out, but eventually it dawned on me that I had a stain on my record that I would never be able to erase.'

'You think somebody had it in for you?'

Schweninger stubbed his cigarette out, so hard that the butt disintegrated in his fingers. 'It's the only explanation.'

'Do you know who it was?'

'Oh, yes. I'm convinced it was the Malicious Dwarf himself, though naturally he considered himself above telling me to my face.'

'Malicious Dwarf – you mean Goebbels?'

Schweninger nodded. 'Yes, the old club-footed devil.'

'What happened?'

August 1936
Munich

It was a disaster: complete, unmitigated and humiliating.

Berlin, 1936. Germany was hosting the Olympic games. The year before, there had been a flare-up of anti-Jewish agitation which had led to the passing of the Citizenship Law and the Law for the Protection of German Blood and Honour, the so-called Nuremberg Laws, which robbed Jews of their citizenship and barred them from participating in civic life. When the German Chess Federation – the Grossdeutscher Schachbund – proposed a chess Olympiad to coincide with the Olympic games, the International Chess Federation, FIDE, announced that anti-Semitism in Germany meant they could not take part in a German Olympiad. In a cynical move, Germany agreed to suspend its ban on Jews being allowed to compete and the FIDE General Assembly voted to leave national federations free to decide for themselves whether to participate.

Although the *Schach-Olympia* 1936 was an entirely unofficial event, more teams competed than in any previous Olympiad, and the Nazi authorities considered it a great propaganda coup. Jewish masters from many countries took part, including Boris Kostić, Lodewijk Prins, and the young Polish genius, Mendel Najdorf.

Making his first appearance on the German team was a young player, Wilhelm Schweninger, whose daring – some said reckless – play had brought him rapidly to national attention. He seemed to embody the fever of optimism that had infected Hitler's Third Reich. Since the Nuremberg Laws had barred Jews from membership of the German Chess Federation, Germany had fallen in international rankings. Schweninger, convinced of his innate superiority, used his new connections within the Propaganda Ministry to tell the home audience that things were about to change: he was hailed as the face of the resurgent German chess movement which would soon take its rightful place at the forefront of the world game.

The young Schweninger's play was as swaggering and aggressive as everyone expected. In the first round he was paired with a similarly callow Jewish player from Latvia. Schweninger won convincingly and was lauded in the German press as living proof of the superiority of Aryans over the Jews. In Munich a dinner was quickly given in his honour, and he even received a congratulatory telegram from Goebbels. Schweninger allowed himself to imagine a meteoric rise within the ministry. He would be courted by the rich and famous, and beautiful women would hang on his every word.

He was able to enjoy his new-found celebrity for exactly one day.

In the second round he was matched against another Jew – the legendary Najdorf. The Pole had given his name to a variation on the Sicilian Defence. Naturally, Schweninger expected his opponent to make use of his famous move and was taken by surprise when, instead, Najdorf opened with a simple Queen's Gambit and proceeded from there to terrorize the young German, bringing the game to its inevitable conclusion with astonishing speed. At checkmate, Najdorf gave his opponent a cold look of contempt.

Utterly demoralized, Schweninger tried to maintain his dignity. 'Congratulations, Herr Najdorf,' he said, extending a hand to his opponent.

Najdorf ignored it. Without a word, he turned his back and walked away.

Simmering with resentment, Schweninger shouted after him: 'The time is coming, Herr Najdorf, when Jews will get the same treatment that they like to dish out themselves. Then we'll see whether you think you're too good to shake my hand.' But the victor merely continued his progress to the exit. Furious, Schweninger yelled after him: '*Heil Hitler!*'

But that was not the worst of it. Two countries, Poland and Hungary, fielded teams made up entirely of Jews. The German team was beaten comprehensively by both of them.

Goebbels was said to be incandescent with rage. It was a propaganda disaster and Wilhelm Schweninger was its centre.

1962
Kerk de Krijtberg, Amsterdam

'So Goebbels would not forgive you for being beaten by a Jew?'

'To be fair, I think it was probably more than that.'

'Fair? To the man who ruined your career?'

A ghost of a smile crossed Schweninger's lips. 'It was never much of a career, really. I did a good job shepherding the English journalists around the Berlin Olympics, but that was pretty much it. After that I was never much more than a glorified pen-pusher. I think that what so enraged

Goebbels was that I had used my contacts in the ministry not so much to create good propaganda for the German team, but to aggrandize myself. If I had been successful, all would have been well. As it was, I had the misfortune to come up against Najdorf.'

'He's here now, you know, in Amsterdam.'

'Najdorf? Yes, I know. I had thought I might introduce myself, and apologize for my boorish behaviour all those years ago, though I doubt he'd remember now.' Schweninger stood. 'Excuse me, I need the bathroom.'

When he returned, Meissner was at the sink, washing the dishes. 'What happened after Munich?'

Schweninger leaned on the counter, watching as the priest scoured a frying-pan. 'I was determined not to let a single setback define my career as a chess player. By 1940 I was the undisputed champion of Germany, but by then Goebbels had more important things to occupy his time than a chess player who had allowed himself to be beaten by a Jew. I further developed my attacking style, which I had based on the writings of Spielmann, even though he was also a Jew. If I could have played against him there would have been no argument about my being champion of both Germany and Austria, but he fled to Sweden.'

'It seems you were fated to have your career shaped by Jews, and now you get beaten by another one. Does it make you feel bitter?'

'No. If I'm honest, I had only myself to blame for what happened in Munich. I was arrogant and simply not good enough. But in my defence, I was only twenty-three. What I can't explain is how Clément managed to beat me so convincingly here in Amsterdam. I thought I was better than that. It's quite chastening to discover otherwise.'

'You should have seen him in Auschwitz.'

*

By midday, Emil still had not turned up, so Meissner suggested they walk to his hotel.

'I'm afraid Mijnheer Clément is out,' the receptionist informed them.

'I think I know where he'll be,' Meissner said.

22.

THE MUNICH GAMBIT

1962

Leidseplein, Amsterdam

It was a bright spring day. The two men retraced their steps along the Singel Canal. Dodging bicycles and trams, Meissner guided his companion over several bridges until they reached the open square that was the Leidseplein. Under trees that were coming into bud, a number of tables had been set out with chessboards. Meissner pointed to one that was opposite a café. 'There he is,' he said.

They walked across. 'I thought we might find you here,' Meissner said, smiling broadly.

Emil looked up from the chessboard, squinting into the sun.

'May we?' Schweninger asked, pointing to a chair.

Emil didn't answer; instead, he looked questioningly at his opponent. He was playing against a teenager who seemed a little anxious at the intrusion.

'Please don't mind us,' Meissner said. 'We are simply admirers of the game. If we're putting you off please say so, and we'll leave you alone.'

'No, Father, that's fine,' the youth replied.

The game proceeded slowly. With each move – both his own and his opponent's – Emil explained what was happening. The key to winning, he explained, was to anticipate what your opponent was going to do four moves ahead, but to make your own moves unpredictable.

After a while, the youth said, 'In four moves you are going to win.'

Emil smiled. 'Excellent, though that's not quite what I had in mind when I said you should think ahead. But may I say well done – you are thinking like a chess player already.'

The teenager started to rise, but Schweninger reached out to grasp his arm. 'Do you know who it is you're playing?' The youth shook his head. 'Herr Clément is the champion of Israel, though he's really French. In a week or so he is going to win the international championship.' He looked at Emil meaningfully. 'Some say he's unbeatable.'

The teenager was impressed. 'Really? If I'd known, I wouldn't have…'

Emil chuckled. 'Then I'm glad you didn't know. Thank you for the game; I enjoyed it.'

A waiter arrived. 'That walk has given me an appetite,' Meissner announced. 'Shall we have some lunch?'

Over a lunch of bread, cheese and beer, Schweninger said, 'This morning I asked Paul why you changed your mind about playing chess against the SS. He said I should ask you.'

Emil frowned. 'Did he?'

June 1944
Konzentrationslager Auschwitz-III, Monowitz

'You've changed your mind?' Meissner looks closely at the *Häftling* standing to attention before him. His face is discoloured and when he opens his mouth, a tooth is missing. He looks like he has taken quite a beating. Meissner sighs. This is decidedly not what he had wanted.

'Why?' he asks.

The reply astonishes him. 'Pardon me, Herr Hauptsturmführer,' Emil replies, 'but last time we spoke you mentioned certain privileges that you could arrange if I agreed to play. I do not ask for anything for myself, you understand. I ask on behalf of a friend.'

'A friend? And who would this friend be? Not *Blockältester* Brack, by any chance?'

Emil shakes his head. 'No, Herr Hauptsturmführer. It is the man I share my bunk with. His name is Yves Boudeaud. His number is 162870.'

'And what do you want for this friend of yours?'

'Something very simple. He is in the *Krankenbau* at the moment, recovering from an injury. The truth is he is starving and exhausted. He will die if nothing is done to help him. He is a good man. All I ask is that when he is discharged from the sick bay he is assigned to work in the kitchens. There the work will be lighter and he can get better rations.'

Meissner shakes his head, puzzled. He had been expecting a request far more extravagant – this is too small a thing to ask. There has to be something more.

'Is that it? Nothing else?'

Emil hesitates before answering. When he speaks, his voice betrays him by cracking. 'My wife and children, sir. I don't know what has happened to them but if they are still alive, I would like similar arrangements to be made for them.'

Meissner pauses, weighing his reply. 'I'm afraid I can't promise that. If they are alive they will be in Birkenau; I have no jurisdiction there. But I will grant your other request – your friend – on one condition.'

'Certainly, if it is within my means.'

'Oh, I have a feeling that it is well within your means. The condition is that you must win.'

Emil takes a moment to consider what the officer has said. 'I don't understand. Why is it so important to you that I win?'

'You mistake my purpose. It is not at all important to me that you win. However, it is essential that you *play* to win. Otherwise it would not be a true contest and the outcome would not be valid.'

Emil finds the officer's reasoning difficult to fathom. Surely the SS would want a Jew to be beaten? But does it matter? To him, it is simple: if – when – he wins, Yves will live; otherwise he will surely die. 'I see,' he says. He doesn't see: what the officer has said makes no sense. Frantically, Emil's brain rearranges the officer's words, as if they were pieces on a chessboard, looking for some hidden meaning, a move he must see through. 'But *if* I win,' he continues, choosing his words deliberately, 'Yves will be assigned to the kitchens – permanently? And you give me your word that he will not be selected to go up the chimney?'

'That's an additional condition,' Meissner points out. 'What you are saying now is that you will be playing for your friend's life. That is a heavy responsibility.'

'Maybe so,' Emil concedes, 'but still I must do it. He would do the same for me.'

'In that case, I will do as you ask. Your friend will be assigned to work in the kitchens and I will have it marked on his *Häftling-Karte** that he has been designated *Schutzhäftling*† and exempt from the *Selektionen*.'

'Then I will play.'

The prisoner bows and walks out of the room.

As soon as he is down the stairs, Meissner shouts for his orderly.

'Did you have anything to do with that?'

---

* Prisoner card.
† Prisoner in protective custody.

Eidenmüller's face, as he stands in doorway, becomes home to an expression of pained innocence. 'Me, sir? What, sir?'

'The prisoner, Eidenmüller. He's been beaten. I sincerely hope it had nothing to do with you.'

'The prisoner, sir? You mean the one who was in here just now? The Watchmaker?'

'"Watchmaker"?'

'That's what they call him, sir.'

'Well, then, yes, you idiot, the Watchmaker.'

The orderly gives a theatrical shake of his head. 'No, sir. Definitely not, sir. It must have been that *Blockältester*, sir. Brack, I think his name was, sir. Nasty piece of work. Didn't like the look of him, sir, not one bit.'

'Well, do something for me will you, Eidenmüller? I want you to go and see this Brack yourself. I want you to tell him from me that from now on, this Watchmaker is to be left alone. He's under my protection, and if anything happens to him I will make it my business to see that exactly the same thing happens to Brack. Got that?'

'Yes, sir. Got that, sir. Loud and clear, sir.'

1962

Grand Hotel Krasnapolsky, Amsterdam

Emil's next game in the tournament found him pitted against a Hungarian who was playing on the American team. Emil drew white and started the game by moving his queen's pawn forward two spaces on the board. The Hungarian responded by bringing out his king's knight so that it sat two squares in front of its bishop. Emil advanced his queen's bishop's pawn to stand beside its brother. The Hungarian moved the corresponding pawn to block it, offering it as a sacrifice to white. Emil ignored the gambit and advanced his first pawn one space, offering a countergambit to the black knight. The exchange of a knight for a pawn is not equitable, so the Hungarian advanced his queen's knight's pawn in a third gambit. Emil took the pawn. His opponent moved his rook's pawn one space and Emil took that too. The Hungarian fianchettoed* his queen's bishop to take Emil's pawn.

Watching from the sidelines, Schweninger whispered to Meissner. 'What is he doing? Doesn't he see he's been led into a trap?'

'A trap? How? He's a pawn ahead in the exchange. That's good, isn't it?'

'No. White always starts with the initiative but now he has lost it. Look how much more developed the Hungarian's position is, and the threat his bishop poses along the diagonal.'

Emil, however, was fully aware of what his opponent was doing. He was playing a variation of the Benoni Defence that Emil himself favoured when playing black. He had seen this variation before, in quite different circumstances, when there had been far more at stake.

June 1944
Konzentrationslager Auschwitz-III, Monowitz

Emil has to wait until he has finished work for the day before he can visit Yves in the K-B to give him the news. Yves is still weak, but he is more alert and his eyes have lost the dull sheen of desperation. Emil tells him he looks better already, before excitedly telling him of the deal he has made with the SS officer.

'So,' Emil says, feeling easier than he has for months, 'when it is time for you to be discharged you will be assigned work in the kitchens, and

---

* The fianchetto is a developmental move where the pawn in front of a knight is moved forward one or two spaces and the bishop occupies the space behind it, giving the bishop freedom to move on the long diagonal that the move has opened.

if there is a *Selektion*, you will not be among those sent up the chimney.'

But Yves's response is not what Emil expected.

'And what if you lose?'

'I will not lose.'

'But you might. What you are saying, Emil, is that if you lose, in all likelihood I will be in the next *Selektion*, and if you win, I will owe my life to you.'

'Yves, trust me – I will not lose.'

With a fervour that Emil has not seen for a long time Yves says, 'I do trust you, Emil, but that is not the point. Do you not understand? My life is not yours to bargain with. I am not a piece on a chessboard for you to play with.'

Emil is shocked at his friend's reaction. 'But you said one of us had to survive to tell people about this place.'

'I meant you, Emil, not me. I did not – do not – expect to survive. Look at me. I can't go on for much longer. A few days, a few weeks, maybe.'

'No. Yves, please. Listen to me. This will work. It will.'

'No, Emil. I will not let you do this thing. I do not wish my life to be saved because of the whim of some SS officer. What he gives today he can just as easily take back tomorrow.'

Emil is distressed by his friend's stubbornness, and his fingers pluck unconsciously at the fraying hem of his sleeve. 'I do not think he will take it back. He gave me his word.'

Yves is incredulous. 'He gave his word? To a Jew? And you believed him? Surely you know by now that none of the Germans can be trusted. They are liars, all of them. He is probably laughing at you as we speak.'

Emil pleads with his friend: 'Please, Yves. Let me try.'

'No. I forbid it.'

Emil is caught in a trap set by the kingdom of lies: to save his friend's life he must abandon the truth, something he promised himself he would not do. He tells Yves he will do as he asks, that he will play for his own life. By the time Yves is out of the K-B it will be too late for him to do anything about it.

Back at Emil's block, Bodo Brack has been summoned by the *Blockführer*. He is handed a piece of paper.

'What is this?'

'Notification of a change of status of one of the *Häftlinge*. Prisoner 162870 Boudeaud has been designated *Schutzhäftling* on the orders of Hauptsturmführer Meissner. Your *Blockschreiber* will amend his record accordingly.'

'Why has his status changed?'

'I have no idea. All I have are my orders.'

Back in the block, Brack hands the paper to Widmann. 'Who is this Boudeaud?' he asks.

'He's a Frenchie. Him and the Watchmaker share a bunk. Thick as thieves, the pair of them.'

'And what's so special about him?'

'Nothin' 's far 's I know. He's in a bad way, though, has been for weeks. Not long for this world, I wouldn't think. He's been in the K-B for the past few days.'

Later, when Emil returns to the block, Bodo grabs his collar and pulls him outside.

'What the fuck have you been playing at?'

'Playing at? I don't know what you mean.'

'Your bum-boy. Don't pretend you don't know who I'm talking about.

The one who shares your bunk. Are you so stupid you thought I wouldn't find out?'

'I still don't know what you're talking about.'

That earns him a slap across the face. 'Don't mess with me, you stupid cocksucker,' Brack screams. 'How the hell did you manage to get your arse-fucking friend designated *Schutzhäftling* on the orders of an *SS* fucking Hauptsturmführer?'

Emil explains, bracing himself for a beating, but when he finishes Brack simply dismisses him. Emil does not know what to make of this but takes his opportunity to get away. 'Scheming little bastard,' Bodo says under his breath, to Emil's retreating back.

The game takes place two days later. Yves is still in the infirmary. Emil is cleaned up and taken in a truck to the *Stammlager*. He sits in the back with an SS guard. The driver does not seem to care and drives recklessly, throwing his vehicle around with no consideration for their wellbeing. Emil is shaken and nauseous when he arrives. He is marched to the enlisted men's barracks, where a large room has been set up with a table and chessboard at its centre.

Emil is left waiting in a corridor where he is told to remove his cap and face the wall. As people pass, some make a point of shoving him into the wall or punching him. He is on edge, not knowing when the next blow will fall, and time passes painfully slowly. Eventually, he hears a voice he knows.

'Watchmaker.' It is Hauptsturmführer Meissner. 'Come with me.'

The room is full of SS men, mostly NCOs, but there are one or two officers. Emil does not recognize any of them. He is led to the chessboard. 'Your opponent will be here shortly,' Meissner tells him.

Emil has never been among so many SS men. He stands to attention and fixes his gaze on a wall.

Somebody brings a stool. 'Sit,' he is told, as if he were a dog. Holding his cap in both hands, Emil sits.

His opponent arrives, an SS NCO. On his collar he has the twin pips and bands that signify he is a Hauptscharführer. He is a heavy-set man with a wart on his chin and piggy eyes peering out from deep folds of fat.

'Must I go through with this, sir?' the NCO asks Meissner.

'Yes, Frommhagen. This must be a meaningful contest and you were a finalist in the enlisted men's championship. It is your duty to uphold the honour of the SS.'

The NCO rolls his eyes. Meissner is called away and Frommhagen appeals to Eidenmüller. 'Just 'cause someone said the Kike's unbeatable? Doesn't look that special to me. Why not just have him shot and have done with it? Happy to do it myself, if your boss is too squeamish to do it.'

Meissner rejoins them. 'Let's get on with it, shall we?'

Meissner holds out his hands in the usual manner of choosing which colour each player will get. Frommhagen chooses. He draws black. Emil starts the game by advancing his queen's pawn two spaces.

Emil's confidence has withered away. The knowledge that he must win or Yves will almost certainly die weighs heavily. The stool is uncomfortable and after he has shifted his weight nervously for the third time his opponent growls, 'Keep still, goddammit, you stupid Yid.'

Emil recalls perfectly his words to Yves: 'Yves, trust me – I will not lose.' Now he is frightened he will not be able to keep his promise.

After ten moves Emil is one pawn up but his opponent's position is better developed and his bishop threatening Emil along the diagonal greatly limits the unpredictability that is Emil's greatest strength.

1962

Grand Hotel Krasnapolsky, Amsterdam

Emil watched blankly as his opponent pushed down the tab on the game clock. The Hungarian's opening moves had been unconventional and disconcertingly effective. Emil peered at him, half expecting to see a resemblance with an SS-Hauptscharführer with a wart. He felt unsettled; no doubt because of all the time spent with Meissner raking over the past. Well, if he got through this stage, he would have to put a stop to that, at least until after the interzonal was over. Progress to the world championship was at stake. But first he had to beat the Hungarian.

The night before, when Emil had cast the tiles, he had uncovered ח – Heth – which signifies the Benelohim, the Sons of God. He had taken that as a sign of God looking benevolently on him, and he expected it to mean that he would win again. Now he was reeling at how easily he had fallen into to his opponent's trap. Luckily, progress from this stage in the tournament did not depend on the outcome of a single game, but on the best of three; still, he racked his brains for a way out of the position the Hungarian had created. The clock was ticking. If he advanced his king's pawn, black would bring his bishop across to take the white bishop. Emil would take it with his king but that would leave his king exposed, which would concede the initiative to his opponent still further. He could bring out his queen's knight, but that would still leave him without any immediate attacking options. Theory told him to play safe, but every fibre of his instinct told him that was what his opponent wanted. Without making a conscious decision, his hand settled on his queen's bishop and moved it kingside to threaten the black knight still nestled on the back row. It was not a conventional move, but it might make his opponent hesitate. If he could just gain a little space, he might at least salvage a draw...

Somewhere a floorboard creaked. In the hushed atmosphere it was surprisingly loud. The sound brought him back to another game.

It was the last thing he wanted to be thinking of, but the memory sprang into his mind unbidden. He could see again the bright red tributaries in the nose and cheeks of the SS man; he could smell the sauerkraut and beer on his breath and hear the shouts as his comrades urged him to see off this nuisance Jew.

The Hungarian saw the threat to his knight. He moved it, taking the lone white pawn in the middle of the board, but it was a fundamental error.

With a silent whoop of delight, Emil advanced his queen to capture the knight. The exchange left him dominating the centre of the board. It was not the way he liked to play, but his chances of winning had improved markedly.

Afterwards, Schweninger was voluble in his praise for Emil's victory: 'Such clever opening play by black,' he said. 'So unconventional. I can't ever remember seeing it before. Respond to it as you ought – as Emil did – and you're in trouble before you know it. Almost impossible to get out of it without a major concession. What Emil did was a master stroke: bold but eccentric; your opponent thinks they've missed something, and you're able to take the initiative back.'

'I've seen it before,' Emil said. 'It's called the Volga Gambit. I never expected to see it here. It caught me by surprise.'

'Where did you see it?' Meissner asked.

'In Auschwitz. In the first game I played, the Hauptscharführer used the same opening. I've no idea where he might have come across it. It took me by surprise then, too. It was the first time I had seen it and I remember thinking what a clever opening it was and wondering what I was going to do about it. There was an awful lot riding on that game.'

'Fascinating,' Schweninger said. 'You know, it's just occurred to me – I have an idea where he might have seen it.'

Emil responded with a sceptical look. 'Really? Where?'

'1936. In the Munich chess Olympiad. I'm sure it was Thorvaldsson who played it, though it was taken up afterwards by Eliskases. It was called the Munich Gambit then.'

23.

THE FRENCH DEFENCE

From the journal of Hauptsturmführer Paul Meissner

SUNDAY, 11TH JUNE 1944 It seems I have made something of a miscalculation. Sturmbannführer Bär is quite furious with me. He is adamant that I should have consulted him before pitting a Jew against a member of the SS. He wanted the Watchmaker shot out of hand for having the temerity to win. He was not mollified when I explained that I had put the Jew in a position where he could not afford to lose. Nor was he impressed when I tried to convince him that the game was essential because of an idea that has sprung up among the Jews in the camp that one of their number is unbeatable. An idea cannot be defeated by shooting bullets at it, I said. Hauptscharführer Frommhagen was the weakest of the finalists in the camp championship, and the Watchmaker had trouble beating him. It seems likely that if he is pitted against our stronger players he will meet his match, and the 'unbeatable' Jew will soon be forgotten. The thought of the Jew pitting his wits against the likes of Hustek almost makes me want to pity him. At least the Kommandant agreed that we now have to go ahead with the further games – though he is still not happy about it. I told him that if he finds what I have done is so objectionable, he could arrange to have me transferred. He said that with *Aktion Höss* running at full tilt there was no question of a transfer. It seems I am indispensable, at least for now. Even so, I will write to Peter Sommer to see if there is any chance of my old regiment taking me back. It seems likely they'll soon be in the thick of the fighting in France – if they're not already. Goebbels vowed the enemy would be pushed back into the sea within a week, but there's precious little sign of that happening. The Führer promised Germany would never have to fight on two fronts again, and now we are fighting on three. Is this defeatist talk? If I knew what was good for me I would destroy this journal, but there is something that stops me from doing that. I tell myself it is the voice of reason. Heaven knows, that is a rare commodity these days, especially here. There is no reason, only orders. As for this Jew, I am reluctant to admit it, but there is something about him that is unsettling. His chief concern was for his friend, not for himself. That is what I might have expected from comrades who have faced death together in the heat of battle, not from a Jew mired in the filth of avarice. I begin to wonder whether all that has been said of this race is true, or whether, like Lot in the city of Sodom, the Watchmaker is the one good man among an evil multitude.

1962
Amsterdam

Narrow though Emil's victory had been, Meissner insisted they celebrate. He told them of a small, family-run restaurant on the Oude Turfmarkt that served marvellous Italian food. It was not far, perhaps a ten-minute walk. He would buy them dinner.

Walking through the lobby of the Krasnapolsky they encountered Lijsbeth Pietersen.

189

'Good evening, Mijnheer Clément,' she said. She had a book in her hand. 'I bought a copy of your book. I wondered if you would mind signing it for me, if it's not too much trouble—?' Her eyes lit on his companions. 'Oh. Mijnheer Schweninger. I wasn't expecting to see you. I thought…' Lijsbeth trailed off.

'You thought what, Miss Pietersen?' Schweninger enquired.

'I just thought…the two of you…' Lijsbeth flushed.

'Perhaps you thought that Herr Schweninger and I did not have so much in common that we would seek out each other's company?' Emil suggested gently.

'No – that is, I mean…'

'Let's just say that we have reached an accommodation,' Willi said. 'We have found that it is better to talk to each other than shout at each other.'

'So you…'

'We are talking, Miss Pietersen, and that will have to do for now,' Emil said, extending a hand for the book. 'By the way, have you read it?'

'Yes. It's very moving. It's hard to believe that people could have done such terrible things.'

'Yes, it is, isn't it?' He wrote something on the first page and handed it back. '*Au revoir,* Miss Pietersen.'

The three men descended the steps of the hotel and crossed Dam Square, going through the archway that led on to Rokin. The streets thronged with people and the air was filled with the tinkling of bicycle bells as their riders threaded their way through the crowds. The evening sun reflected off the windows of the bars, which were full of people having a drink after work.

'It's quite amazing, this city,' Emil said, ignoring for a moment Willi's discourse on the merits of an attacking style. He stopped to gaze at a row of ancient gables opposite. No two were the same. The occasional modern building intruded among them, looking clumsy and conspicuous. 'Why would they do that?' he asked, pointing at one. 'You know – put such ugly concrete blocks like those where they don't belong.'

'It was the air raids,' Meissner said. 'If one of the old buildings was destroyed, the Dutch saw no point in trying to hide it by creating a replica. The new constructions are monuments to what they went through during the war.'

'Makes sense, I suppose,' Schweninger said, walking on. 'As I was saying,' he continued, 'in my opinion, Capablanca will probably prove to be the greatest player of this century. The simplicity of his attacking play and the speed with which he made his moves were really quite…' He realized he was talking to himself and stopped. Looking back, he saw Meissner doubled over, holding onto a lamppost for support, and Emil, concern etched on his face, standing beside him, a hand on Meissner's shoulder.

'What's the matter?' Willi said, walking back as quickly as his bulk would allow.

Meissner waved a hand. 'It's nothing,' he said. His face was contorted with pain and his voice little more than an agonized whisper. 'Only an affliction that comes on me from time to time. Don't worry about it – it will soon pass. Malaria,' he added.

But it did not pass.

They were not far from a bar with its ubiquitous green-and-white 'Heineken Bier' sign, so Willi went in to borrow a chair.

Meissner smiled weakly. 'So, "Watchmaker",' he said. 'Now I am the one in need of help. I wonder, do you think we could forgo dinner? I would be grateful if you could help me to get back to the Krijtberg.'

Despite the coolness of the evening, beads of sweat stood out on the priest's forehead.

Willi returned with a chair. 'I'll find us a taxi,' he said.

Back at the presbytery, it took both men to help Paul from the taxi to the door. Willi rang the doorbell repeatedly. They could hear footsteps in the hall and the housekeeper calling, 'All right, all right.'

'Dear God,' she said, when she saw them. Quickly she stood to one side so they could move past her. 'What's happened?' She crossed herself.

'He's really not well,' Emil said. 'I think you should call for a doctor.'

By the time they managed to get him to bed, his nose had begun to bleed. Having summoned the other priest in the Krijtberg, the housekeeper had taken up station at the side of the bed and was tearfully trying to stem the blood. Father Scholten, a dour Belgian, stood at the foot of the bed praying, his lips moving soundlessly as he passed a set of beads slowly between his fingers. When the doctor arrived they all moved downstairs to the kitchen.

It seemed as if he was with his patient for a long time.

'How is he, Doctor?' the housekeeper asked when he came down, her voice tremulous with worry.

'I've given him some laudanum and he's resting now. You should let him sleep. What he needs is a bit of peace and quiet.' He took one of the housekeeper's hands in his own. 'He's very ill, Mrs Brinckvoort, but you knew that,' the doctor said gently.

'But he'll make a full recovery, surely?' Willi asked.

The doctor shook his head slowly. 'That's highly unlikely. Of course, we all pray for a miracle, but I'm afraid there's little more that medical science can do.'

'For *malaria*?' Schweninger's voice had in it more than a little outrage.

How could doctors in Holland be so far behind their counterparts in Germany?'

A look of comprehension crossed the doctor's face. 'Is that what he told you? Yes, I can understand that. He would not want your sympathy.'

'If it's not malaria, what is it?'

'It's leukaemia,' Emil said. 'He's dying.'

June 1944
Konzentrationslager Auschwitz-III, Monowitz
It is two weeks since the Allies landed in France. After hard fighting, the British have advanced as far as Caen and the Americans have succeeded in reaching the western side of the Cotentin Peninsula, isolating Cherbourg. Hitler has forbidden the local commander, von Schlieben, to retreat to the fortifications of the Atlantic Wall, leaving him no option but to stand and fight until his men are exhausted or dead.

Although it is isolated in the coalfields of Silesia, the camp is aware of what is happening over a thousand miles away: news is brought by Polish workers in the Buna factory. The camp is jubilant. In the years since it was established, it has not known a moment like this. In their compound beyond the wire, the British prisoners of war can be heard jeering at the guards.

The inmates do not know how to celebrate but there is no stopping the slender seedlings of hope from germinating. The prisoners have an unaccustomed spring in their step as they are marched off in their work *Kommandos*, and the jaunty tunes played by the camp orchestra no longer seem so ludicrous. Emil is one who has already broken the rule that says hope is forbidden in Auschwitz, and for him the news adds substance to his optimism.

Still, for some days he has been unhappy. When Yves was discharged from the K-B and assigned to the kitchens, he knew immediately that Emil had not been true to his word. Angrily, he accused Emil of betraying his trust. It was a strange form of betrayal, Emil told him, that saved the life of a friend, but Yves would not listen.

There is a rift between them and Yves has moved his bunk. Emil now shares with an Italian, a tall, taciturn man who does not respect Emil's space.

The companionship that Emil shared with Yves is gone. Emil prays that his friend will soon forgive him. The news coming from France buoys him and he decides that when he gets back from the factory this evening, he will seek Yves out and ask again for his pardon.

On their return from the Buna complex the prisoners sense a change. The camp is fearful. Dread and foreboding stalk its pathways as the inmates are made to wait on the parade ground after evening roll call.

At the head of the *Appelplatz* is a gallows. Three empty nooses hang from its cross-beam. Several SS officers stand watching. The Watchmaker recognizes the tall form of Hauptsturmführer Meissner, leaning on his walking stick and looking distinctly like one who wishes he were somewhere else.

The roll call is completed unusually quickly. The Rapportführer tallies the count. It is three short. Instead of ordering a re-count, he reports to the Lagerführer who responds with a curt nod. With a flourish, the camp orchestra strikes up Mozart's 'Rondo alla Turca'. They play well, and some of the officers standing around the platform smile appreciatively.

There is a stirring among the men massed there, as three bruised and bloody inmates are led out, their hands tied behind them. They have ropes around their necks and they are pulled along by SS troops like dogs. The Lagerführer gives a sign that the orchestra should cease playing and mounts the steps to the scaffold. He shouts at the assembled thousands. Though only the front ranks can hear him, he knows that before the parade ground has emptied his words will have been repeated a thousand times.

'These men are thieves,' he yells. 'They have been caught stealing food. This is a crime against the generosity of the German Reich, which sees fit to provide you with your daily bread. It is also a crime against *you*. The food they took was your food. By filling their bellies there is less for *you*. Such a monstrous crime calls for exemplary punishment.'

Emil is frantic. Yves was not present at the roll call. The SS men force the prisoners to lift their heads. Emil thinks he is going to be sick. The prisoner on the right is Yves.

The Rapportführer reads aloud the names and numbers of the three men. The nooses are put in place and pulled tight. The orchestra resumes its obscene parody of jollity. Stools are kicked out from underneath the condemned men and the camp watches helplessly as they kick and writhe, choking in their death throes.

Tears stream down Emil's cheeks but he is no longer sure whether he is crying for himself or for his friend.

And all for a few rotten potatoes.

Meissner is angry. Walking away from the executions, he catches up with the Lagerführer and pulls him around. 'Was that absolutely necessary?'

Obersturmführer Vinzenz Schottl regards the superior officer with a disdainful smile. 'Of course it was. They were caught stealing food. They said they had some ridiculous notion of doling out an extra ration to prisoners who were starving. An example had to be made.' Schottl tilts his cap back and puts his hands on his hips in an attitude that, in an enlisted man, would be considered insolent. 'But why would you care about the fate of a few worthless Jews?'

'One of them had been designated *Schutzhäftling* – on my orders.'

The Lagerführer sees his superior in a new and unflattering light. 'Really? Why would you do that?'

'I had my reasons. Why did you not respect his status, or at least speak to me about it?'

'I had no idea. I assure you there was no note of it on his *Häftling-Karte*.'

Disgusted, Meissner turns and walks away. The junior officer calls after him. 'Herr Hauptsturmführer, you should take care that people do not start to call you a Jew-lover.'

24.

THE TORRE ATTACK

1962

Amsterdam

A man is standing on Gerard Doustraat, outside the synagogue. He has a *kippah* on his head but hesitates to go inside. The building's purpose is obvious from the Star of David set in the window at the top of the gable, yet still he hesitates. He feels he has no business there. But he has an overwhelming urge to pray, and has learned that it was in this very synagogue that Rosh Hashanah was celebrated in 1943, before the last Jews of Amsterdam were deported to Auschwitz.

He senses a connection with this place, but he wonders whether it is because of the time he spent in Auschwitz, or whether it is because he is simply a Jew who cannot escape his people's history.

A man comes out. He has an iron-grey beard and wears the wide-brimmed hat of an Orthodox Jew. 'Good morning,' he says, in Yiddish.

The man in the street has not spoken Yiddish for nearly twenty years. 'Good morning,' he replies in Hebrew.

'Welcome,' says the Jew, extending a hand. 'Shmuel Jacobsen. I'm the rabbi here. Are you new to the area, or visiting?'

'Visiting,' the man replies absently.

'Would you like to come inside?'

'I don't know.'

The rabbi has business elsewhere, but is reluctant to leave if this person who has found the synagogue needs his help in some way. Eventually the visitor breaks the silence.

'A friend of mine is dying. Cancer. I feel very bad about it. I don't know what to do.'

The rabbi gives a reassuring smile. 'Why do you feel bad about it? You are not the cause of his cancer. You should perhaps do your best to bring him comfort during his last days, and when he is gone you should rejoice in his memory, but you should not feel bad about it. It is the will of God.'

'I can't help it. The last time a friend of mine died I was not the cause of it then either, but I have carried the guilt of his death with me ever since. It has been a heavy burden. I do not wish to carry it twice over.'

'Would you like to come inside? Talking about it might help.'

The visitor shakes his head. 'No. Thank you. I've been talking about it for days already. So far it hasn't helped. I was drawn to this place, but now I'm here it doesn't feel right.'

The rabbi brings his hands together, his fingers steepled, like a Catholic saying a prayer. He taps his lips with the tips of his fingers, wondering. The man is obviously troubled. 'Doesn't feel right?' he asks. 'That's quite something for a Jew to say about the synagogue.'

For long moments the man looks away: at his feet, up the street, searching the trees for birds, anything but meet the rabbi's calm gaze. 'It's complicated,' he replies.

'Complicated?' The rabbi's eyebrows lift and he smiles. 'Everything about being a Jew is complicated.'

The man shakes his head. Slowly, he rolls up the left sleeve of his coat to reveal a tattoo on his arm. Six numbers: 163291.

The rabbi sighs. Understanding dawns. 'Which one?' he asks.

'Auschwitz.' In his mind's eye, the man sees the concrete posts and barbed wire of the camp standing between them, a barrier that is all the more impenetrable because its physical presence is long gone.

'We should talk,' the rabbi says. He puts a hand on the man's upper arm and guides him inside.

June 1944
Konzentrationslager Auschwitz-III, Monowitz

It is two days since Yves was executed. Now everybody knows what happened. With two others, he had stolen a basketful of bread from the kitchen and was taking it around the camp to the *Muselmänner*, those prisoners who had yielded to despair. It was a plan doomed because of its crazy folly. Nearly every *Muselmann* ignored the bread that was held out to them: they did not know what it was they were being offered. They were beyond any help that an extra ration of bread might bring.

It was inevitable that the three men would be caught and punished. Emil wonders if that was why Yves did it: determined to hold fast to the last threads of his dignity, refusing to allow another to decide whether he lived or died. Emil aches with guilt. If he had not made the bargain with the Hauptsturmführer in the first place...

A voice tells him that Yves would be dead anyway: one more day of hard labour would have finished him off. He would have been carried back to the camp by his workmates, already dead or destined for the next *Selektion*. But Emil cannot listen to this voice. The voice of reason has no place in Auschwitz. It is overwhelmed by the twisted logic that tells him that, in addition to his mother and his children, he is now responsible for the death of his friend and he must carry the burden of it to his grave.

Emil has been summoned to see the Hauptsturmführer again. He does not wish to go but cannot refuse. A *Kapo* he does not know marches him to the building and the two of them wait in a corridor, Emil with his face to the wall. After a while the orderly arrives. He gives the *Kapo* a cigarette and tells him to smoke it outside.

Once the *Kapo* has gone, the orderly speaks to Emil. 'I don't know that I should be speaking to you,' he says. His voice sounds harsh to Emil, rough and uneducated. 'Seeing you are nothing but a stinking Yid. But my boss is interested in you. Why, I don't know, but he is, and he's my boss, so I've got to go along with it. But he's a good sort, my boss, so I don't like to see anyone trying to put one over on him. He says you struggled to beat Hauptscharführer Frommhagen. Tell me, is he right? Did you struggle or did you make it look harder than it was?'

'I struggled,' Emil replies, speaking to the wall.

'So how d'you think you'll manage playing one of the officers? 'Cause that's what the boss has got in store for you next.'

'I–I don't know,' Emil stammers. 'It depends.'

'Depends, does it? What exactly does it depend on?'

'If I told you, you wouldn't believe me.'

'Try me.'

'It depends on whether the angels speak to me.'

The SS man bangs Emil's face against the wall, making his nose bleed. 'Fuckin' Kike,' he says angrily. 'I should have known I was wasting my time.'

1962
Gerard Doustraat, Amsterdam

The rabbi leaves Emil to wait in a small room furnished with a couch, chairs and a coffee table. It is a place where couples come to talk about their wedding arrangements and the bereaved make plans for funerals. He returns with two cups of tea and hands one to Emil. 'Tell me about your friend,' he says.

'Which one? The one who is dead or the one who is dying?'

'Does it matter? Either of them; both of them. Whatever you think is important.'

'My friend who died,' Emil says, 'was my bunk mate in Auschwitz. We arrived on the same transport. He was starving to death. I tried to save him. I made a pact with a German, one of the SS, but still they killed him. It was 1944, a summer's day. For him there was no *chevra kadisha* to care for his body, no *tahara*, no readings from the Torah, no *kevura*. His body was thrown into an incinerator. There were no seven days of mourning and no *matzevah* to mark his passing. As far as I know, he has no relatives to light the *yahrzeit* candle. I am the only one who remembers him.'

The rabbi lays a hand on Emil's arm. It is a gesture of consolation, of shared grief, of natural compassion. 'And your friend who is dying now,' he says, gently. 'Is he also someone from Auschwitz?'

Emil raises his eyes to the rabbi's. 'Yes,' he says, 'but not in the way you think.'

'How then?'

It is too easy for Emil to revisit this sorrow: if the sky has a certain colour to it, especially at dusk; or if he finds himself in a large crowd; an orchestra playing Mozart; or something as simple as stale bread: all these things can trigger the memories that surge forward, uninvited. He sees three suspended bodies silhouetted against the sky, the ropes seemingly as insubstantial as silken thread. He sees Meissner talking to a fellow SS officer; he sees the multitude of prisoners surrounding him, subdued by yet another savage demonstration of the power of the SS; he sees the barbed wire that surrounds the *Appelplatz* and the SS barracks beyond. His vision of all of these things has remained crystal-clear, as if he were still there, yet he cannot recall the faces of his own children. He sees them only as he saw them for the last time, as they walked into the shadows, hand in hand with their grandmother, not looking back, and he remembers his last words to them: '*Be good for Granny.*'

'It is the SS officer with whom I made the unholy pact.'

The rabbi's hand falls away from Emil's arm. 'And your survival – was that a result of this pact?'

'Yes.'

'But not your friend?'

'No.'

'And did this officer have anything to do with your friend's death?'

Emil shakes his head.

'But neither did he prevent it?'

'No.'

'I can see how you may owe a debt of gratitude to this man for your life. But friendship – that is a different matter.'

'As you say, a different matter.' Emil gets to his feet. The memories are threatening to overwhelm him. 'Thank you, rabbi,' he says.'

'I hope I have been of some help.'

'I hope so too.'

There is no quick route from Gerard Doustraat to the Singel Canal and the Kerk de Krijtberg, and the walk takes Emil some time. He is not alone on his journey. For companions he has both the living and the dead; voices he cannot quieten, words that howl in his consciousness.

Friendship – that is a different matter.

The rabbi is right. There can be no friendship with Meissner. How could there be?

There is no forgiveness. I cannot forgive.

No. There are some things that are beyond forgiveness; some things that are beyond redemption. Sometimes it takes courage not to forgive because it is easier to forgive, but it is not the right thing to do.

Your forgiveness cannot help me, Watchmaker.

Damn Meissner. What had possessed him to interfere? He had no right.

I would rather make a pact with the Devil.

These words ring in his mind like the bell of an ancient church tolling for the souls of the departed. Yves had seen everything with extraordinary clarity. He would never have countenanced an accommodation with the Nazis and their henchmen.

There is no why.

But there is. The why is Auschwitz and the tens upon tens of thousands who starved, suffered and were murdered. If the dead could speak, would they forgive? And he can almost hear them: all those who waited patiently to go down into the gas chambers, those who collapsed from starvation or who were beaten to death, those who succumbed to the depths of winter or the bullets of the SS on the death marches: their voices clamour to be heard.

I can help you to understand that the power of forgiveness will bring healing for you.

No. I do not need to be forgiven. I did nothing wrong.

My life is not yours to bargain with.

The memory of those words is like a betrayal. They cut through all the familiar certainties he has erected to protect himself.

Forgive me.

Two simple words that are etched into his memory, diamond bright, never dimming. Now they call to him: remote voices broadcast on a Tannoy, a choir singing a lamentation, a crowd at a football match, cheering; no one voice is discernible, until he finds himself again at his wife's bedside in the days before she died. The voice is hers. *You have nothing to be forgiven for*, he tells her, helplessly; *you are blameless*.

How did she understand what he did not?

He finds himself on the bridge that crosses Vondelpark and realizes he is not far from Leidseplein. He has no idea how much time has passed since leaving the synagogue. It feels like hours. He stops, his hands gripping the metal railings that line the bridge, holding tightly. He wants to shout, to the cars and vans going past, to the cyclists, to the people strolling in the park below. He wants to shout, 'Enough! Leave me be! Let me have some peace. Haven't I suffered enough?'

Suddenly, the wind that has been shrieking through his mind stops. The clamour of the voices ceases. The only sound is the breeze soughing through the trees nearby. He is left with a single thought: the *why* of Auschwitz. The dead are waiting. He has a duty to serve them, but their suffering is at an end. He cannot suffer for them. Nor would they want him to. They would want him to live.

He does not consciously come to any decision. It simply happens. What he said unwittingly to the rabbi is true: *A friend of mine is dying*. Since Auschwitz, he has been afraid to allow any bonds of friendship to grow, but now they have taken him by surprise. Emil is engulfed by a surge of emotion: he feels lighter, certain, free. He cannot say how it has happened, but he knows it to be true.

Paul Meissner is his friend.

1962

Kerk de Krijtberg, Amsterdam

The housekeeper showed Emil into the bishop's room. The curtains were pulled closed and the room was in semi-darkness.

'He's quite weak,' she said in a low voice. 'He wakes for a short while and then falls asleep again. I think it's the laudanum.' She turned to go. 'Try not to get him too excited. If you need anything, I'll be in the kitchen.'

Emil pulled a chair up to the bed and sat down. Meissner's eyes were closed. He seemed to be in a deep sleep. Emil bowed his head. Understanding dawned on him: *this* was the place for him to pray, not the synagogue.

He started to speak, quietly. 'I went to a synagogue today, the first time in years. I thought I had questions for which only God would have an answer. I was wrong. I had the answers myself, only I did not know it. I found the answer in a word I spoke without thinking – I told somebody that you were my friend. Such a small word for such a big thing. As soon as the word was uttered I knew the truth of it, like a shaft of light that pierces a dark sky.

'I had a friend who died in Auschwitz, the best friend I ever had. I tried to save his life but he would not let me, he would not abandon his dignity. He was hanged as punishment for stealing food. Do you remember? You were present at his execution; I saw you. Do you remember what we spoke of the next time you summoned me to your presence? It was not an easy exchange of words.

'I remember being marched into your office. I had blood dripping from my nose. You saw it and glared at your orderly. "He fell," the orderly said. I could see from the look on your face that you did not believe him. You dismissed the orderly and offered me your own handkerchief.' Emil fell silent for a moment. 'You would not have known how beautiful it was to feel again clean, white linen between my fingers. I was reluctant to soil its purity by using it to wipe away the blood. I wanted to keep it so I could take it out occasionally as a reminder of what it was like to be clean. And I remember what you said—'

'I am sorry about your friend.' The words came out in a hoarse whisper as Meissner reached a trembling hand across the bedspread to take Emil's. 'That's what I said, didn't I?'

Tears clouded Emil's eyes. 'Yes, Paul. That's what you said.'

June 1944
Konzentrationslager Auschwitz-III, Monowitz

'I am sorry about your friend,' the officer says, for a second time.

Emil says nothing. He holds the handkerchief to his nose.

'I did not break my word to you,' the officer continues. 'It seems there was an administrative error.'

'Pardon me – an administrative error?'

'Quite so. It is unfortunate, but these things happen in times of war. I'm sure you can understand.' The officer's speech is stiff and formal, as if he is aware how hollow his words must sound. 'But you must have something to show for your victory. I will see to it that the status of protective custody is entered in your record instead.'

'Unfortunate? Is that all you can say? My friend is *dead*.' Emil looks to see if the orderly is listening, but he is gone. 'You make it sound as if I had been playing for a toy at a fairground. I was playing to save my friend's life and now he is dead.'

The officer's voice remains tightly controlled. 'I kept my side of our bargain. Your friend knew what he was doing. I am not to blame if he was so careless with his life. I have treated you fairly.'

THE DEATH'S HEAD CHESS CLUB

Emil cannot believe what he is hearing. Does this officer not know that they are in Auschwitz and that there is no such thing as being treated fairly?

'May I have permission to speak honestly?'

The officer gives a slight nod.

'You say you have treated me fairly. If you were treating me fairly you would have greeted me with respect, offered me coffee, a cigarette. There is a gulf between us that is impossible to bridge. Why am I even here? I have been convicted of no crime, yet my children were taken from me and are most likely dead; my wife, too, may be dead. I am a slave forced to live and work in the most primitive conditions in return for starvation rations, and you say you have treated me *fairly*—? You are indifferent to me and to my fate and to the fate of all the thousands who suffer and die every day.'

Meissner can see the truth in Emil's rebuke, but to admit as much is impossible. 'I did everything I could, but the matter is now closed. No purpose can be served by discussing it further.'

'Then why did you summon me?'

'I want you to play another game of chess.'

'Why? So you can dupe me again?'

'Do not provoke me, Watchmaker. I did not dupe you the last time. The matter was out of my hands. I have almost been accused of being a Jew-lover.'

Emil does not reply. His nose has stopped bleeding. He folds the hand-kerchief and tries to hand it back. Meissner waves it away.

'About this other game of chess,' he says. 'This time you will play against one of the officers.'

Emil will not be taken in a second time. 'I will not do it.'

'I offer you the same terms as before. If you win, you will save a life.'

Emil's head snaps up. 'My wife,' he says. 'I will play for my wife.'

Meissner frowns. 'I've already told you – I have no authority in Birkenau, only here in Monowitz. You must choose someone else.'

'But there is no one else.'

'Nobody whose life is worth saving?'

'I did not say that. I don't know anyone else well enough to choose.'

'Then choose somebody at random. You could draw lots. I don't care how or who you choose, but I want it done quickly.'

Emil knows he has no choice in the matter. Win or lose, he will be forced to play, as he was before. 'How can I be sure that whoever I pick this time will be protected?'

'I will supervise the entry in their camp record myself.'

Emil is beaten. 'How will you know who I have chosen?'

'Tell your *Blockältester*. He will get word to me.'

'I'm thirsty,' the bishop said, hoarsely.

A glass of water stood on the cabinet next to the bed. Emil went to pass it across but Meissner shook his head. 'Help me to sit up.' He grimaced with pain as Emil gripped his arms and pulled him upright. 'I don't like this laudanum,' he said. 'It clouds my thinking.'

Emil offered the glass again. Meissner took it and drank thirstily. 'You tell it exactly as I remember. I have reflected many times on our conversations in Auschwitz.' He paused, collecting his thoughts. 'You remember I told you the other day I thought God had a final purpose for my life?'

'Yes. You said that purpose was me.'

'I did not say so then, but I'm also sure that although He had no part in sending you to Auschwitz, once you were there, God also had a purpose for you.' He looked searchingly at Emil. 'No matter how you might try, you cannot evade God's purpose.'

'What purpose can He possibly have had for me in that place?'

'It was me.' Meissner saw the look of incredulity on Emil's face. 'Please, do not think me so egotistical. Catholics believe that there is more rejoicing in Heaven over one sinner who repents, than over ninety-nine righteous persons who do not need to repent. I was that sinner, and it was you who set me on the path to repentance.'

Emil stared at him. 'Now I am confused. Before, we talked of forgiveness but now you add something else. Which is more important – forgiveness or repentance?'

Meissner took another sip of water. 'For a sinner such as me, without repentance there can be no forgiveness. After the war, when I was awaiting my trial for war crimes, I realized it would not have been possible to seek forgiveness of God in Auschwitz because He had been shut out as surely as all of us were shut in. Auschwitz was a fortress designed to keep God and mercy and compassion as far away as humanly possible.'

'So you repented, and God forgave you.' Emil closed his eyes for a moment, to reflect on what Paul had said. He was missing something. 'But you said that was not enough. What else did you need?'

'There was – and is – only myself.'

Emil rubbed a hand over his face. He felt drained. *My life is not yours to bargain with.* 'And have you been able to forgive yourself?' he asked.

'Not yet. Perhaps never. But I must hope. Otherwise, I am lost.'

'That is what I used to tell myself every day in Auschwitz.'

'And now?'

'Now I wonder whether the hope I held on to so fiercely was worth the price I have had to pay for it ever since.'

'I'm sorry to hear that.'

'There's that word again. And it's still too small, too feeble, for what you need it to do.'

Meissner fell back exhausted. Emil stayed with him for a few minutes and then went down to the kitchen.

The housekeeper was at the stove, stirring the contents of a large pan. 'I'm making some broth for the bishop,' she said. 'The doctor said it was important to try and keep his strength up. Would you like some?'

'Thank you, that's very kind of you.'

'Mijnheer Willi came back while you were talking to the bishop. He said he didn't want to disturb you. Would you mind finding him and telling him that lunch is ready?'

Emil climbed the stairs again in search of Willi's bedroom. He tried two empty rooms before he found the right one. Inside, Schweninger was seated at a small table, writing. He looked up when Emil entered the room.

'Good afternoon,' he said brightly. 'How is the patient?'

'As well as can be expected, I suppose. Lunch is ready if you would like some.'

By the time they got down to the kitchen, Father Scholten had returned from saying the midday Mass. Mrs Brinckvoort ladled generous portions of steaming broth into three bowls and they seated themselves around the table. The priest said grace, and a second prayer for the recovery of Paul Meissner.

'Father,' Emil said hesitantly, 'a day or so ago, the bishop asked if I would like to stay here. At the time I said no, but if it's all right with you, I have changed my mind. While he's so ill, I would like to be close by.'

'Of course,' the priest replied. He turned to the housekeeper, who was setting a bowl of broth on a tray. 'Mrs Brinckvoort, could you make up a room for Mijnheer Clément?' He turned back to Emil. 'If you don't mind my asking, how is that you and the bishop came to be such good friends?'

With a wan smile Emil replied, 'I'm not sure you could call us "good" friends. But friends, certainly. As to how, I have been asking myself the same question. I suppose it's because we went through quite a lot together during the war.'

Before the priest could reply there was a loud crash from upstairs. Mrs Brinckvoort was first out of the door.

They found the bishop on his knees on the landing, the housekeeper trying to help him up. 'He fell,' she announced, unnecessarily.

'Please,' Meissner said weakly, 'don't make a fuss. I needed the toilet, that's all, and I thought I could make it on my own.'

'Here, let me,' Emil offered, taking Meissner's arm and hoisting it around his shoulder. He spoke to the others. 'I'll shout if we need help.'

The two of them edged along the landing to the bathroom. Emil eased the sick man into the lavatory and helped him to unfasten his pyjamas. 'I'll wait outside the door,' he said. 'Shout when you're finished.'

It was a struggle getting Meissner back to bed, but he insisted Emil should not call the others for help.

When he was settled on his pillows again, gasping with pain, Meissner reached across to grasp Emil's arm. 'Thank you,' he murmured. 'I know things look bad, but I'm not finished yet. These episodes come and go. I will be up and about again before you know it. In the meantime, keep talking to Willi. He is not so bad as you think.'

Later, Willi offered to help Emil move his things across to the Krijtberg. In Emil's hotel room, he noticed the small ivory tiles inscribed with Hebrew letters. 'What are these?' he asked.

Emil put them into a soft leather pouch. 'I'll tell you later.'

Afterwards they went to a bar and ordered beer. They sat in an uncomfortable silence, sipping occasionally at their drinks. After a while Emil asked, 'Before we played, did you analyse any of my previous games?'

'Of course. I obtained the records of many of your games, looking for the moves you favour, trying to discern any pattern to your play.'

Emil took a sip of beer. 'And did you? Find any pattern, I mean.'

The German shook his head. 'It was strange. Your play seemed very methodical. I was convinced you must play to a system, but I couldn't work out what it was – every time I thought I could detect a pattern of play, it vanished. It seemed to be taunting me. "Here I am," it was saying. "Look closer." It was like a wisp of smoke from a cigarette – it hangs in the air and then a door opens and it is gone.'

Emil smiled. 'Of course I have a system – perhaps more of a philosophy than a system. But I learned in Auschwitz to keep things to myself. It's hard to break the habit.'

'A philosophy? That's even more intriguing, but you should not keep it to yourself.' Willi regarded him earnestly. 'The game of chess is bigger than either of us. You should tell people about your philosophy, and see what happens when they add their own ways of thinking to it.'

'That's the problem. I don't really understand how it works myself. When I draw on it, it doesn't tell me what moves to make – it's more what my mental approach should be.'

'Is it a form of meditation?'

Emil did not answer. Instead, he reached into his jacket pocket for some cigarettes and, taking one, lit it. Exhaling a cloud of smoke upwards, he offered the pack to Willi and said, 'I suppose you could say it was something like that, yes.'

Willi took a cigarette. 'Look,' he said, holding it loosely between his fingers, 'if you think it's none of my business, all you have to do is say so.' He put the cigarette to his lips.

'No, it's not that, not exactly.' Emil ran a hand through his hair. 'It's just that I've never told anyone before…'

With his good hand, Willi lit up and inhaled deeply. 'Fine. I'm not trying to pry. It was you that mentioned it.'

'My system is based on the Kabbalah.'

'The Kabbalah?'

'Yes. It's a Jewish mystical science based on the Hebrew alphabet. You remember the tiles you found earlier? On each of them is inscribed a letter that signifies one of the powers of the orders of angels. In some way I feel as if I am able to connect with the power and I don't have to think about what moves I should make. I simply know.'

Schweninger gave a wry smile. 'You're playing with the hand of God. That doesn't seem fair.'

Emil shook his head. 'Not the hand of God – the power of angels. It's a little different.'

'But still hardly fair.'

'No, I suppose not.'

'Some people might say you were deluded.'

'Yes. And they might be right.'

'How does it work then, this Kabbalah?'

Emil took a moment to gather his thoughts. 'The night before an important game, I cast the alphabet tiles with the letters facing down and arrange them in a pattern. I pick the one that feels right. The letter that is revealed represents the order of angels I should call on.'

Willi's eyes narrowed. 'What letter was I?'

'The fifth letter, He.'

'And what did that mean to you?'

'"He" signifies the sword of the Almighty and the strength which flows from the limitless power of God. To me it meant I could be confident of victory.'

'But how did it influence the way you played?'

'I sensed it meant I should appear to play cautiously. I already knew of your reputation for aggressive play and thought that if I held back, you would think me timid and press all the harder and not see the trap I set for you. And it worked, did it not?'

Willi grinned, shaking his head. 'That's too subtle for me.' He drained his glass. 'Another beer?'

25.

THE COLLE SYSTEM

June 1944
Konzentrationslager Auschwitz-III, Monowitz

Bodo Brack had a conundrum. Its name was Widmann.

Brack had little liking for the *Blockschreiber*, but he was useful. Widmann knew people, influential people on the outside. He had been convicted of attempted murder, but before that he had made his living as a pimp, and it had been a good living. He had not been one to hang around street corners stumping up business for cheap whores; his girls were high class and catered to a rather exclusive clientele: senior military officers and civil servants. All had gone well until a low-ranking Gestapo type had decided Widmann was doing a little too well, and that he should share his good fortune with others. Thinking he would be able to rely on his clients to protect him, Widmann had shot the Gestapo man and left him for dead. The problem had been that Widmann was not much of a killer and his intended victim survived to testify. Soon after Widmann's arrival in Auschwitz he had started plying his trade again, sucking up to the guards and quickly becoming the leading dealer in *Mahorca*, the adulterated tobacco that he traded for the coupons the SS gave out for the camp brothel.

Brack cared little for Widmann's enterprise, but he knew that the war could not last indefinitely and that to have such contacts outside the camp could prove invaluable. Widmann had been a *Kapo* in charge of a construction *Kommando*. It was brutal work, not at all to his liking, and so Brack had seduced him simply by asking him to be his *Blockschreiber*. The duties were light and did not involve marching to the Buna factory in the driving rain of a Polish winter: Widmann had accepted without hesitation.

However, Brack was now realizing, it was one thing to keep Widmann close in Auschwitz but another to rely on him when the war was over. He needed to find a way to tie Widmann to him, but so far the answer had eluded him.

His musings were interrupted by the arrival of Eidenmüller. He handed a bottle of Schnapps to Brack, and gestured for the *Blockältester* to follow him outside.

'Don't you like the sunshine?' Eidenmüller asked.

'Not really. Anyway, not much of a view, is there?' They laughed. 'What do you want this time?'

'It's the Watchmaker.'

'What's the little bastard done now?'

'Nothing. My boss wants him to play another game. Against an officer this time.'

'And the stupid fuck has refused to play again, is that it?'

'No, he's agreed to play.'

'Then what?'

Eidenmüller stopped in the shade of a birch tree. 'It's like this, Brack. I run a bit of a betting syndicate and I lost a packet on the last game.'

'Because the Yid won?

'Yeah. Made a bit of a miscalculation. I said to myself, nobody's unbeatable, especially not a runt of a Jew watchmaker. And Frommhagen, the one he beat, he's not half bad. So what I need to know is this – how good is this Watchmaker really?'

'It wasn't me who said the Watchmaker was unbeatable,' Brack said. 'It was a Pole who said he played in some big-shot chess tournament in Munich back in '36. According to him, the Watchmaker would have beaten anybody who played in the tournament. He said he reckoned the Watchmaker had supernatural powers he was so good.'

Eidenmüller hawked and spat. 'Bullshit.'

Brack shrugged. 'Maybe. Who knows?'

'He'll be playing an SS officer next time. Who would you put your money on?'

Brack sniggered. 'Who do you think?'

Eidenmüller glanced at the sun and grimaced. 'Thought as much.' He started to walk away.

'Hang on,' Brack called after him. 'What's he get if he wins this time?'

'Same as before – he gets to save somebody's life.'

'How?'

Eidenmüller stopped and gave Brack a puzzled look. 'I thought you knew – when there's a *Selektion*, they'll be protected.'

Understanding registered on Brack's face. 'Right. So – whose life?'

'Anyone he likes.'

Anyone he likes . . . Eidenmüller's words set the cogs whirring in Brack's brain. By the time he got back to the block he was beaming.

He had found the answer to his conundrum.

Word of Emil's victory over one of the all-powerful SS has circulated around his block, and some of his fellow prisoners have had the audacity to mention it to the *Kapos* in their work *Kommandos*. Most are rewarded with a kicking or a sharp blow from a knotted rope, but this has not prevented the whispers from spreading: the Nazis are not unbeatable.

When Emil returned to the block that evening, Brack was waiting for him.

Seeing him, Emil's stomach contracted to a tight knot of anxiety: the fearful beating he had received at the hands of the block elder remained an acutely painful memory. Why would Brack be waiting for him? The only thing he could think of was that Brack had been told to stop the whispers at their source.

To Emil's alarm, Brack put an arm around his shoulder as if they were the best of friends, and led him away from the block so they could not be overheard.

'You know, Watchmaker, I think you and me got off on the wrong foot. I said to myself, Bodo, you and the Watchmaker ought to be friends, good friends. You'd like that, wouldn't you? Fact is, I've got a bit of a proposition for you.' He patted Emil's shoulder clumsily. 'We both know this war ain't going to last for ever, don't we? Well, I reckon if you help me and I help you, the both of us will live to survive it.'

Emil eyed the *Blockältester* suspiciously. 'What do you want?'

'I want us to help each other, that's all. Look, I've been doing a bit of digging around. I know a lot about you. I know you got a wife in the camp, for example.'

The expression on Emil's face told Brack that he had hit his target.

'She's dead,' Emil muttered. 'I'm sure of it.'

'What if she's not? What if I was in a position to help her? What would you do for me in return?'

Emil searched Brack's face, trying to fathom whether the *Blockältester* was sincere. 'Anything,' he said, his mouth suddenly dry. 'I'd do anything.

Is she still alive?'

'She is. At least, her name hasn't appeared on any of the death reports.'

'Where is she?'

'In Birkenau.'

'Can you get a message to her?'

Slowly Brack shook his head. 'It's chaos there. There's a big *Aktion* going on. Thousands of Jews arriving from Hungary every day, and all of them going straight up the chimney.'

'If it's chaos, how can you help her?'

'I might be able to get her extra rations.'

'What do you want me to do?'

'Simple. Keep playing – and winning – at chess. I know about your deal with that SS officer – I get to choose whose life you are playing for, and I will do what I can for your wife.'

'You want to choose whose life I play for? What if I say no?'

Brack smiled, an unctuous leer. 'You wouldn't want to do that, Watchmaker. Think about your poor wife. Besides, that's not the only way I can help you.' He stepped away, expecting Emil to follow, but the Watchmaker did not move. Brack jerked his head in the direction of their block. 'Come on,' he said.

Brack led Emil to the line for the evening soup ration. He took Emil straight to the front and said to the inmate who was doling out the soup: 'In case you didn't know, this is the Watchmaker and he's a friend of mine. In future he's to get his soup ration from the bottom of the pot, not the top, got that?' He gestured for Emil to hold out his bowl. The ladle dipped to the bottom and came up heavy with chunks of potato and turnip. 'Give him two,' Brack ordered. He winked at Emil. 'So, Watchmaker. Do we have an understanding?'

Like a drowning man, Emil's hunger rose instantly to the surface, gasping for air.

He gave a little bob of his head.

Later, Widmann asked Brack what he was up to. 'Insurance,' came the reply. 'I've got a proposition for you. Some of the Yids in here are bound to have rich relatives in England or America, only they can't get word out to them. But *we* can.' He stepped closer to Widmann and lowered his voice, explaining the deal he had just struck. 'Every time the Watchmaker wins a game, I've fixed it so that I get to choose which life he saves. So, we're going to have an auction – the Yids can bid against each other for their lives. We get word to their relatives in return for a large deposit into a Swiss bank account.'

Widmann grinned. 'I like the sound of it. What exactly are you proposing?'

Brack passed a bottle of Schnapps over. 'A 70–30 split. I've got the Watchmaker, you've got the contacts. All you have to do is get word out to the relatives. What do you say – deal?'

Schnapps or no Schnapps, Widmann was not to be bought so cheaply. He took a large mouthful of liquor and gasped appreciatively as it went down. '70–30 doesn't sound like such a good deal to me. 60–40 sounds better.'

Brack laughed and spat on the palm of his hand, extending it to Widmann. 'It's a deal. If we play this right, there'll be plenty for both of us. By the time we get out of here, we'll have made ourselves some serious money. But' – he pulled Widmann close, his strong, heavy hand closing around the *Blockschreiber*'s, squeezing it until the other man winced. 'Don't ever think of double-crossing me,' he growled. 'If you do, you'll wake up one day trussed like a goose ready for the oven – 'cause that's where you'll be going.'

Widmann pulled his hand away, rubbing it gingerly, eyeing Brack with alarm. 'Don't worry, Bodo. You can trust me.'

'Trust you? I don't think so. But as long as you remember which side your bread's buttered, we'll get along fine.'

1962
Kerk de Krijtberg, Amsterdam

After supper, the bishop insisted on coming down to the sitting room. The housekeeper fussed and muttered but Meissner would not be denied.

'The doctor—' she objected.

'—has been wrong before, Mrs Brinckvoort, and will no doubt be wrong again. It makes me feel much better if I am able to sit and have a civilized conversation with my friends.' He pointed at the antique cabinet that stood against the wall. 'If you look in there, you will find what's left of the bottle of Kümmel. I should be very grateful if you would pour me a large one.'

'But the doctor—'

'To hell with the doctor. If you won't get it…' He looked pointedly at Willi.

Schweninger stood. 'It will be my pleasure.'

Not used to being on the receiving end of harsh words from the bishop, the housekeeper stalked out of the room.

'A toast,' Meissner said, raising his glass, an ironic smile playing on his lips: 'To life.'

*

The next morning, Emil and Willi set off for the Krasnapolsky and the next game of the tournament.

'Did you cast your tiles last night?' Willi asked. When Emil nodded he asked, 'What was the result?'

Emil shook his head. 'The tiles do not always give a clear answer. Last night was one of those occasions. I could not understand what they were trying to tell me. Today I will have nobody to rely on but myself.'

'How does that make you feel?'

'It usually makes me feel quite alone, but perhaps today not quite so much.'

'You will win,' Willi stated confidently. 'I have a feeling about it.'

This time Emil's opponent drew white. He started innocuously enough, advancing his king's pawn one square and his queen's pawn two squares before bringing out his king's knight.

Schweninger had found a chair from where he could see the game. Half an hour later, Lijsbeth Pietersen sat beside him. 'What's happening?' she whispered.

'It's very different from the last game,' he told her. 'The Hungarian is playing defensively, right from his first move. It's as if he knows he can't win but wants to avoid being humiliated. In my opinion, Herr Clément is certain to win.'

'Mijnheer Schweninger, do you mind if I ask you a personal question?'

'It depends on what the question is.'

'Last week, you and Mijnheer Clément were at each other's throats. Now you seem always to be together. What has brought about this transformation?'

Schweninger leaned back in his chair, smiling. 'Chess. That is what has brought us together.'

Miss Pietersen pursed her lips primly. 'Mijnheer Schweninger, if you didn't want to tell me, all you had to do was say so. Please don't mock me.'

'I'm not mocking you, I promise. I don't understand it myself but, for the first time in my life, I have been given a glimpse of the real power of this game.'

'By Mijnheer Clément?'

'Yes. By Mijnheer Clément.'

Although the game dragged on for over two hours, its end was never in doubt. Afterwards, Emil and Willi walked without speaking along the Singel Canal. When they reached the Krijtberg, Willi walked straight up the steps but Emil loitered on the street.

'If you don't mind,' Emil said, 'I need to spend a little time alone.'

'Of course. Are you going to the Leidseplein?'

'Yes, I think so.'

'I should have known.'

Back at the Krijtberg, Meissner was in the sitting room, a shawl wrapped around his shoulders. He seemed to have aged years in a matter of days, though his eyes were bright and alert. 'How did it go today?' he asked, as soon as Willi entered the room.

'Emil won.'

'Naturally.' Meissner twisted stiffly in his chair and peered down the corridor, like a naughty schoolboy keeping a look out for the teacher. 'Willi, could I trouble you for a cigarette? Mrs Brinckvoort has hidden mine.'

They sat in companionable silence, staring at the hearth and blowing smoke at the ceiling.

'You know, if Mrs Brinckvoort catches us, there'll be hell to pay.' Meissner laughed and started to cough.

'I suppose.' Willi flicked his cigarette butt into the fire. He looked troubled.

'Is everything all right, Willi?' Meissner asked.

'No. It's not – not really.' He paused, then announced: 'I'm thinking of giving up chess.'

'Giving up chess? In the name of God, why?'

'Until a few days ago I thought chess was simply a game, a game with rules that could be understood and which, with sufficient dedication, could be mastered. I thought I was a master; fellow players in my own country honoured me by calling me "Master". But it is an empty title.' He raised his head to give Paul a quizzical look. 'I wonder how well you really know Emil Clément. To him, chess is not a game or even an art – it is an act of worship. It is not something to be mastered, it is something to be *lived*. I do not think I can compete with that.'

26.

THE TROMPOWSKY ATTACK

June 1944

Konzentrationslager Auschwitz-I

Unterscharführer Eidenmüller was fuming. Brack had been told to make sure the Watchmaker had taken a shower and was in a clean uniform. He had done neither. The prisoner stank; he could not be taken to the officers' mess in that state – Meissner would have apoplexy. But Brack had insisted it was not his fault: there was no water in the prisoner showers and clean uniforms were unobtainable. Eidenmüller's solution had been to use the showers in the enlisted men's barracks, but there was nothing to be done about the uniform. He promised himself he would give Brack hell for dropping him in it like this.

The Watchmaker stood facing the wall outside the entrance to the officers' mess waiting for the Unterscharführer. He could scarcely believe his luck: a shower with hot water – and soap. It was as if he had been permitted to indulge himself in the most decadent of luxuries. For the first time in months he felt clean, and when he breathed in, it was the tang of soap he could smell, not the sourness of the *Häftlinge*. It was almost criminal that he had had to put his filthy rags back on.

Inside, the Unterscharführer found his officer. Meissner looked at his watch. He spoke sharply. 'Why are you so late? You should have been here a quarter of an hour ago.'

Eidenmüller looked straight ahead. He could take no liberties here, in front of so many officers. 'Beg pardon, sir. I had to take the prisoner to the enlisted men's barracks for a shower.'

An officer standing next to Meissner grimaced. 'A Jew having a shower in SS barracks? I'm surprised you didn't cause a riot.'

'Me too, sir. But the Hauptsturmführer's orders were that the Jew should be cleaned up before being brought here and the water in the prisoner washrooms has been cut off.'

'Where is he?' Meissner asked.

'Outside, sir. Waiting for permission to come in.'

'What are you waiting for? Bring him in.'

The murmur of conversation stopped abruptly when Emil entered. SS officers lined the walls; most had been drinking. Malevolent eyes followed the Watchmaker's progress to a table that had been set up in the middle of the room. Emil stopped close to Meissner and stood to attention. The silence was broken by a snigger. Meissner gave an angry look.

Somebody spoke. 'Well, for Christ's sake, what are we coming to? A fucking Yid – in here?'

Then there was a shouted '*Achtung!*' and all eyes turned to the door where the Kommandant, Sturmbannführer Bär, was now standing.

'Gentlemen,' he said, loudly, 'what we are about to witness is evidence of the truth of National Socialist principles in practice – a practical demonstration of the superiority of Aryans over the Jews. For that we must tolerate this unpleasant intrusion.' He wrinkled his nose as if offended by a smell. He looked directly at Meissner. 'Herr Hauptsturmführer, I'd like to get this over with as quickly as possible.'

The Watchmaker was given a small bench to sit on. He drew black.

His opponent wore on his left collar patch the three silver pips of an

THE DEATH'S HEAD CHESS CLUB

Untersturmführer. He waited with an air of nonchalance until Emil had settled himself, then ground out his half-smoked cigarette beneath the heel of his boot before advancing his queen's pawn. The Watchmaker responded by bringing his king's knight to sit in front of its bishop's pawn. The SS man brought out his queen's bishop to threaten the knight.

Meissner watched impassively. He could not see much of an advantage in what his fellow officer had done. If the Watchmaker did not move his knight, the white bishop would take it, but would then itself be taken. It seemed a careless move on the SS man's part.

Before the Watchmaker's arrival, Meissner had tried to counsel the junior officer against being overconfident – in vain. Only six months before, Untersturmführer Kurt Dorn had been in the SS officer-training school; after two months in the *Hundstaffel* at Mauthausen he was sent to Auschwitz. Dorn was typical of the new breed of concentration camp officers: what he lacked in intelligence he more than made up for with unconditional obedience. Meissner did not think he had emerged so brainwashed after his time in officer school. Perhaps it was different for the Waffen-SS: they had to be able to think – their enemies could fight back. Dorn's arrogance was monumental. He was delighted to play, he told Meissner; it gave him the opportunity to show a Jew pig where he belonged – in the dirt with all the other pigs.

It is one of the cardinal rules of chess theory that the same piece should not be moved twice in succession in the opening phase of a game. Emil violated that rule now, and with his second move placed his knight to threaten the bishop. In only two moves Dorn had contrived to lose the initiative and was on the defensive. The game was already as good as lost.

The last moves of the game were played in oppressive silence. Emil did not dare to take his eyes off the board so hostile had the air around him become.

With a surly flick of a finger Dorn tipped over his king to concede defeat. 'A fluke,' he said, sulkily. He stared menacingly at the Watchmaker. 'Either that, or you cheated.' Emil said nothing. He dared not meet the SS man's gaze. 'Set up the board and we'll play again,' the officer ordered.

Meissner strode over. 'Are you quite sure you want to do that, Herr Untersturmführer? I saw no evidence of cheating. Perhaps you...'

'There will be no second game.' It was the Kommandant. 'Get the Jew out of here.'

Eidenmüller hustled the Watchmaker away. The Kommandant glared at Meissner. 'Herr Hauptsturmführer, you will report to me first thing on Monday morning.'

1962
Kerk de Krijtberg, Amsterdam

'So,' Willi said, 'you won your second game with ease. No wonder the SS officers were angry. You gave their noses quite a tweaking. You could at least have made it look difficult.'

Emil pushed the remains of his breakfast away and reached for a cigarette. 'It was not so easy as that,' he replied. 'For a start I was very afraid. It's quite daunting to be in a room where every person really does want you dead. I could sense their eyes on me, imagining a pistol held to the back of my head. That's all it would take, they were telling themselves, and this inconvenient Jew could be forgotten.' He paused, unconsciously rolling the cigarette between his fingers. 'If I had been matched against an experienced player, there might have been some pattern to his play which I could have used to delay the inevitable conclusion, but this man had little real idea of chess and there was no thought behind his moves. For him to have reached the final of the camp contest must have been sheer luck, no more. He was the author of his own defeat.'

'He lost because of his own arrogant carelessness,' Meissner said. 'There were many like him in the Totenkopfverbände. What else would you expect, when all they had to do was watch over starving prisoners and herd women and children to their deaths?'

His words had a sobering effect and for a while they sat in silence, until Willi asked, 'What about the angels – did they come to your aid on that occasion?'

'Angels?' Meissner rasped.

Willi levelled a finger at Emil. 'Our Watchmaker believes he is able to call on angels for guidance. A most unfair advantage, I would say.' He smacked his leg and laughed.

Meissner gave Emil a curious look. 'I always sensed there was more to you than meets the eye. Tell me about your angels.'

With an unlit cigarette dangling from his lips Emil stood, picked up the kettle and carried it to the tap. He filled it and waved it at the others, spilling a few drops of water on the tiles. 'Anyone else want more tea?'

'Yes,' Meissner said, 'but stop avoiding the question.'

Emil struck a match to light the gas. Setting the kettle on the flame he stooped to get a light for his cigarette, blowing out a cloud of blue smoke after it caught. 'It's not such a mystery,' he said. 'I have created a system based on the Kabbalah. Each of the orders of angels has a specific attribute. I meditate on the attribute and it guides my style of play.'

Meissner nodded, as if he had stumbled on an insight that had long eluded him. 'Going back to Willi's question, what did the angels tell you on that occasion?'

'It was not so easy to summon them in Auschwitz; I had no tiles to cast.'

Willi leaned forward, eager to hear what Emil had to say. 'So, what did you do?'

'I had to find a number at random, to correspond with a letter from the Hebrew alphabet. I was with your orderly…'

'Eidenmüller?'

'Yes. I counted the number of times Eidenmüller called me a Yid. The number corresponded to Zebaoth, the God of hosts whose power is represented by the order of angels called Principalities. I knew immediately I should sweep my opponent aside without regard for any other consideration.'

The whistle on the kettle started to shriek. Emil turned off the gas and made the tea, stirring the leaves to make it strong. He looked over at Meissner as he did so. 'After seeing how angry the Kommandant was at the result, I could not understand why he let you continue with more games,' he said, adding milk to their cups and, for the bishop, sugar.

'Yes. That proved to be an interesting conversation.'

June 1944
Konzentrationslager Auschwitz-I

Meissner was outside the Kommandant's office at 7 a.m. He had spent most of Sunday working out what he was going to say, though what he couldn't admit to his superior, or perhaps even to himself, was that he had started to feel a grudging respect for the Watchmaker.

It was almost nine when Bär turned up, accompanied by a senior officer who followed Bär into his office. The Kommandant seemed preoccupied until he said, 'Ah, Meissner. There you are. Good of you to come.' He pointed at the other officer. 'I don't think you've met

Obersturmbannführer Höss, have you?' Meissner clicked his heels and brought his arm up in a salute. 'The Obersturmbannführer was the original Kommandant of Auschwitz. He's back temporarily to oversee the *Aktion* involving the Hungarian Jews. The results have been really quite impressive.'

'A privilege, sir,' Meissner said, with a deferential dip of his head towards Höss, wondering whether the Kommandant had completely forgotten the chess game.

'So impressive,' Bär continued, 'that the Obersturmbannführer has proposed the *Aktion* be intensified. Eichmann tells us he can send an additional transport every day, but we don't have sufficient men at this end to process them. Yours is the only section with any men to spare. You have such a genius for organization I'm confident you'll be able to manage if we take, say, fifty men and their NCOs off you. We wouldn't need their officers – would we?' he concluded, with a questioning look at the senior officer.

'Sir,' Meissner objected, 'may I respectfully remind you that the order to give priority to armaments production came from the Reichsführer-SS himself? I don't see how we can maintain capacity if you take so many men.'

'Nonsense. Where's that never-say-die spirit the SS is famed for?' The Kommandant gave his subordinate a condescending smile. 'Anyway, after the stunt you pulled on Saturday I'd have thought you'd want to do something to try and retrieve your reputation.'

'My reputation, sir?'

'Let's not mince words, Meissner. You're a bloody good officer – too good to be true, some are beginning to say. You don't want people to start thinking you're a Jew-lover.'

Meissner was indignant. 'Sir, I protest. It's not a question of loving or hating Jews. It's a question of duty. And my duty has been – and I assume still is – to produce as many bullets, shells and steel helmets as possible.'

Höss joined in. 'You are quite right, Meissner,' he said, mildly. 'It is indeed a question of duty. Your duty – *our* duty – is to follow orders without question. The orders to intensify the *Sonderbehandlung* of the Jews from Hungary come from the very highest level. I'm sure I don't need to elaborate. Time is short; the Hungarians are wavering. They may surrender to the Bolsheviks at any time. So this takes precedence over all other considerations, wouldn't you agree?'

There was only one acceptable answer. 'Naturally, sir.'

'Good. That's settled then.'

'Now, about the Jew chess player,' Bär added.

'Ah, yes, as I was saying on the way over, such an interesting idea,' Höss said. 'Though it doesn't seem to have worked terribly well so far.'

'Sir,' Meissner said, 'I think I can explain why things have not gone as expected.'

Bär took a seat and invited the senior officer to do likewise. 'Please do,' he said, acidly.

'In the first game, it was clear that Hauptscharführer Frommhagen was reluctant to take part. The Jew must have been able to discern this and take an advantage from it.'

'You can hardly blame the Hauptscharführer for being reluctant to play a Jew,' Höss remarked. 'One can understand it could have been quite distasteful to him.'

'Then how do you explain what happened with Dorn?' Bär demanded. 'He was more than eager to teach the Jew a lesson.'

'Quite so, but he underestimated his opponent. A fatal mistake when dealing with Jews in my experience, sir.'

'Nonetheless, I think you should bring this experiment to an end,' the Kommandant said. 'Immediately.'

'As you wish, sir, naturally.'

'I'm not sure I would agree,' Höss intervened. 'This Dorn, the one whose overconfidence led to his defeat – has it not occurred to you that in what he did there is a potent metaphor for the kind of difficulties that beset the Party?'* Meissner and Bär exchanged a puzzled glance. 'Consider,' Höss continued, 'although chess is a serious intellectual duel, Dorn was foolish enough to take his victory for granted. Don't you see? National Socialism suffers from the same problem. If it is not constantly confronted, it will grow complacent and die of hardening of the arteries. And the SS – as the Party's natural protector – should be in the vanguard of this challenge.'

Bär shifted in his chair, his discomfort at the senior officer's words only too evident.

'Don't pretend to be so shocked,' Höss continued. 'It's hardly heresy – one sees these kinds of ideas expressed almost every week in the *Schwarze Korps*.† In my opinion, what Hauptsturmführer Meissner is doing should be applauded as a bold experiment designed to challenge complacency within the SS and at the same time expose the very real danger posed by the Jews, who will take advantage of any weakness they perceive on our part. With the Jew taking full advantage of his natural slyness, it is working exactly as one would expect, and should continue to its natural conclusion.'

'Which will be?' the Kommandant asked.

---

* Nationalsozialistische Deutsche Arbeiterpartei – National Socialist German Workers Party – the full name of the Nazi Party.
† The official newspaper of the SS.

'The defeat of the Jew at the hands of the SS, of course. But only when we begin to take him seriously.'

There was no mistaking the look Bär gave Meissner: *This had better work*. 'Very well,' he said. 'But from now on, Meissner, it will be your responsibility to make sure our men do not underestimate the cunning of their opponent.'

'That should hardly be necessary,' Höss observed.

'No, sir,' Bär replied, 'but if it's all the same to you, I would prefer to leave nothing to chance.'

27.

THE ENGLISH OPENING

June 1944

Cologne

The rail lines running west from Kraków had been repaired, so Meissner was at last able to go home on leave. He had written to his parents to let them know he was coming, but they hadn't replied; indeed, it was over a month since he had last heard from them, but he wasn't unduly worried: Allied bombing was still severely disrupting all but the most urgent communication throughout Germany.

The devastation that met him in Cologne shocked him to his core: as a living organism, the city had all but ceased to exist. He was used to the carnage of battle, but this was different: it was his home, the place that had nurtured his hopes and dreams. For as far as he could see, apart from the cathedral, all that remained of the city was rubble and the skeletons of buildings gutted by fire that had fallen from the sky in an avenging hail. It was only eight years since he had left to go to university. Then it had been a bustling metropolis of over three-quarters of a million inhabitants; now it was a ghost-town, reeking of the stench of a dead city: escaping gas, smoke and exposed sewers.

His childhood home on Friedrichstrasse was a charred ruin. Of his parents and his fiancée there was no sign. He knew he should have been frantic for news of them, but the sheer scale of the desolation overwhelmed him, numbing his emotions. They could not have survived.

The Reich records bureau had no information, and all he could discover from the civilian defence centre was that the area had been hit by incendiary bombs about six weeks earlier. Now all that remained was the blackened form of the cathedral with its twin spires still reaching upwards to Heaven, miraculously preserved in the very midst of the inferno as if by the will of God Himself.

Meissner stood on the cathedral steps and watched a small number of people as they straggled in for Sunday Mass. The world had become incomprehensible to him. What kind of faith, he wondered, could draw people to this place on such a day: the desperate devotion of those who prayed for salvation before they too were consumed by fire, or the hubris of those who could not believe that they were deserving of God's wrath and who begged fervently for Him to send this rain of destruction elsewhere? And what had happened to his own faith? Was it lost, or simply hiding? The Lord knew he had seen enough for it to shrink to nothingness: the horrors of the Eastern Front and Auschwitz were more than any man should be asked to witness. But to see hell visited upon his own home, on his own family – that was too much to bear. He knew he should have been feeling grief, anger, sorrow, fury, but the truth was he felt nothing. He was empty.

The only certainty was that nothing remained for him there.

He took a last drag on his cigarette and flicked it to the ground before turning his back on the cathedral doors.

Meissner had been ordered to report to the WVHA, the SS economic and administrative HQ, on his way back from leave, to give a first-hand report to Glücks on the status of the armaments factories within the Auschwitz sphere of control. It was the last thing he felt like doing. After the devastation he had just witnessed, it seemed pointless.

There was a tension within the higher echelons of the SS, with the RSHA* and its fixer, Eichmann, set on the extermination of as many Jews as possible, and the WVHA wanting workers for its slave factories. The war situation was becoming increasingly desperate, but nobody seemed willing to make a decision as to which of these contradictory demands should take precedence. Of all the actors in the drama, Meissner understood least the role of Höss. In the WVHA he was second in authority only to Glücks, yet he was carrying out the mandate of the RSHA with quiet yet unstoppable efficiency.

There were no trains to be had to Berlin, but Meissner managed to hitch a ride to Potsdam with two SS officers. They were both SIPO† officials and besieged the Waffen-SS man with questions about his experiences on the Eastern front and in Auschwitz.

'I intended to go to the east myself, to serve in the Einsatzgrüppen,'‡ one of the SIPO men confided, 'but I was told the quota for this region was already full. Then we began to hear the stories of how the work was affecting the men who did go – how they had to be plied with drink in order to carry on and how many were driven to suicide. I was glad in a way that I was spared all that.'

'That's why the extermination camps were set up,' the other added. 'To find a cleaner way of eliminating the Jews.'

* Reichssicherheitshauptamt: SS Reich Main Security Office. The delivery of the 'Final Solution of the Jewish Question' was in their remit.
† Sicherheitspolizei: the State Security Police. Its officers were members of the SS.
‡ SS death squads that followed the army into Poland and Russia and conducted mass killings of Communists and Jews.

'And it seems to have worked,' the first one said. 'Look at you – being in Auschwitz doesn't seem to have done you much harm.'

'I'm not involved in the liquidations,' Meissner replied, trying to keep his tone neutral. The SIPO was notorious for finding dissent and sedition in the most unlikely places, even among war heroes. 'I'm based at the main work camp. My responsibility is to keep the armaments factories running, so you could say I am more interested in keeping Jews alive than in killing them.'

'Does that not bring you into conflict with your fellow officers?'

Meissner frowned. 'Yes, from time to time.'

'And how do you deal with it?'

'I tell them I'm following orders, same as they are.'

From Potsdam he got a train into the centre of Berlin, and from there begged a ride with the daily courier between SS headquarters and the WVHA offices in Oranienburg.

Gruppenführer Glücks seemed less interested in the state of the slave factories than he was in the performance of Obersturmbannführer Höss. Meissner sensed the Gruppenführer disliked his deputy and wanted information that would undermine him. It was not an intrigue in which Meissner wanted to become embroiled, and he kept his answers short and evasive. He knew it would not commend him to the head of the concentration camps but, as he saw it, unless a miracle happened to save Germany from total defeat, this was hardly something he needed to worry about.

The final leg of Meissner's journey back to Kraków found him alone in a train compartment. He had had plenty of time since leaving Cologne to reflect on where his fate had led him. The Nazis had lied. The whole edifice was built on lies. Mentally he ticked off the lies of which he had personal evidence: the Bolsheviks were sub-humans who would be defeated easily; no enemy bombs would fall on German cities; Germany would never be asked to fight on two fronts again. And then, there were the Jews. How many lies had been told about them? They were beyond counting. And he had swallowed those lies, all of them. What did that make him? A fool or an accomplice – or both?

In Berlin he had obtained writing materials and, using his valise as a table, he started to compose a letter that he hoped would help him make his escape.

Abteilung 1

Konzentrationslager Auschwitz

30 June 1944

Dear Peter,

It seems an age since we faced the Ivans together at Voronezh, but it's actually been less than a year. Hard to believe, I know. Do you remember how we said we would laugh in the teeth of death? That was a lifetime ago. Duty in the K-Z is much less dramatic than fighting in the front line, but it has to be done. The amount of material we are able to contribute to the war effort is quite staggering. The workshops for which I am responsible produce thousands of steel helmets, bullets and shells every week – imagine how you would fare without them – and I am told that the first production of synthetic oil in the Buna *Werke* here at Auschwitz is only weeks off. Your Panzers will need that oil, so don't be too quick to look down your nose at me, even if all I have become is a glorified factory manager.

I have to confess I have not found life easy in Auschwitz. Most of the officers in the Totenkopfverbände look down on the Waffen-SS as brainless apes who can hold a rifle, but not much else. The way they see things, theirs is the more difficult and more important task. They have been entrusted with the struggle against the eternal enemy of Germany, even though they can't fight back. I'm talking about the Jews, of course. When you're facing a squadron of enemy tanks, everything is simple. It's a case of kill or be killed. The Ivans know that as well as we do – no quarter expected, and none given. When we were indoctrinated in officer training, I accepted what we were told about the danger posed by the Jews, but I never dreamed it would come to what I have witnessed here. Do not doubt me when I tell you that thousands of Jews – men, women and even children – are killed every day. There is no let-up in the slaughter.

I tell myself that I am fortunate. I am not in the camp where the killing is done and I am not involved in this brutality. In fact, I am quite insulated from it. But that does not absolve me from the guilt in which I must share because I am here and do nothing to prevent it. I tell myself that it would be futile – what would I achieve other than getting myself shot by the Gestapo? But the little rats' teeth of remorse are gnawing at me without mercy. The absurdity of it came to me recently. I got a lift from a couple of SIPO men and I told them that because I was involved in armament production I wanted to see Jews spared for work in the factories, not killed as soon as they arrive. That's what my life has come to – an SS officer in a death camp who is trying to keep the prisoners alive when everybody else wants them dead. Behind my back it is being said that I am a Jew-lover.

I must get away before I become like the rest of them. My honour is all that is left to me now. I have just returned from Cologne. Mother and Father and Maria were killed in an air raid. Do you think there is any way in which I could return to the regiment? At least then I could hope to be killed in action.

The compartment door was pulled open. A railway conductor stood in the opening, a hand extended for Meissner's ticket. The SS man turned over the page so the conductor would not see what he had written before reaching into his breast pocket for his travel authorization. The conductor gave it no more than a cursory glance before clipping its edge and passing it back with an apology for disturbing the Hauptsturmführer.

When the man had gone, Meissner read the pages through. With a shake of his head he tore them up. Everything was wrong. All except one thing. He must find a way to escape.

1962

Kerk de Krijtberg, Amsterdam

Emil awoke not remembering where he was. It took a few moments to orientate himself. His room was unlike anywhere he had ever stayed before. It was furnished simply, with a narrow bed, a wardrobe, some drawers, a writing table and chair, and in a corner, a prie-dieu with a crucifix affixed to the wall above it. Emil knew of the Catholic devotion to the cross, but still, its presence in the room unsettled him: the suffering Saviour with His promise of redemption among whose last words were, '*Father forgive them, for they know not what they do.*' Every time the cross caught his eye, it brought those words back to him. After a moment or two, he could not stop himself from glancing in its direction every few minutes, as if daring it to utter the words aloud.

It is not the Jewish way to kneel to pray, but Emil did so now, lowering himself onto the prie-dieu. He was unsure of what shape his prayer should take. Before his encounter with Meissner in the Leidseplein his life had been simple but certain. He carried the burden of Auschwitz with him everywhere and had become used to its grim companionship. He had long known that the camp was a living, breathing organism, painfully conscious that an outpost of hell had been planted in the fragment of earth on which it stood. The camp was both a victim and a witness: watching, waiting, weeping: keeping a tally of the crimes that were visited within its boundaries, yet powerless to prevent or punish them. It was this certainty that had given direction to Emil's existence for nearly twenty years. It was his duty to bear witness, never to forget, never to forgive. But it had made his life a bitter one, something to be endured, not relished.

Something Meissner had said the other night came back to him now. *But I must hope. Otherwise, I am lost.*

It dawned on Emil that *he* was lost. The rules of Auschwitz had blinded him, especially the rule that forbade hope. Even at so great a distance in time, he was unable to tell where he was or see where he was going. His life was meaningless. His devotion to chess had kept him going, but it had become mechanical, something against which he could measure himself, a disguise for the true condition of his soul.

He raised his eyes to the figure on the cross. 'Is that it?' he mouthed silently. 'Is that how a Christian prays – by listening?'

The bronze eyes stared sightlessly back at him. Emil shook his head and pushed himself up from the prie-dieu.

He found Meissner in the kitchen. His cheeks were brighter and he seemed a little less frail than the day before.

As Emil took a seat at the table, opposite Meissner, he decided to tell him about his encounter with the crucified Christ. He was not sure how he expected the priest to respond – perhaps with a discourse on the nature of the redeemer and redemption. After all, Meissner had been a missionary: it was his job to win souls for Christ.

Instead, Paul asked, 'What was it you wanted when you knelt before the cross?'

Emil was taken aback by the question. 'What makes you think I wanted anything?'

Meissner smiled. 'In my experience, prayer is something that most people reserve for times of great need. They stand before God as a supplicant, begging for His intervention.' He sighed. 'That's not how it works, I'm afraid. Most of the time, the best you can hope for is an insight of some sort – a revelation, I suppose you could say. It seems to me that is what has happened to you. Something has been revealed to you, but it is up to you to decide what to do about it.'

Emil shook his head. 'I think I was hoping for more than that.'

'Like what?'

'I don't know. I thought that someone like you – a priest – would be on more intimate terms with God; that you would know what He wanted you to say.'

'But there's the very problem, don't you see? It is not God's way to be so direct. Both of us are searching for the same thing – forgiveness – but it seems determined to elude us. And when we turn to God for an answer, He is silent – but why? Since I met you again I have thought of little else.' He leaned over and took Emil's arm, looking at him intently. 'But there *is* something I have come to understand. Forgiveness is bound up with hope. If you cannot hope, you cannot forgive. In my faith, to abandon hope is a grievous sin. It is hope that we must both rediscover, before we run out of time. And my time is running out.'

28.

THE KING'S PAWN GAME

July 1944

Konzentrationslager Auschwitz-III, Monowitz

Nobody knows how news travels so quickly, but the atmosphere in the camp is transformed by the Watchmaker's defeat of a second SS officer – for a few days, at least. There is a whiff of pride among some of the inmates, especially those in Emil's block: one of their number has taken on the invincible SS and beaten them – again. And, as if good news is contagious, there is also a rumour that has spread around the camp – that there will be no more *Selektionen*. But it is no more than a cruel delusion.

Such false prophecies are common currency, but the Watchmaker is real and those Jewish prisoners who still harbour secret hope in their souls speak of him in a wistful manner, like some past glory that has all but been forgotten but which is suddenly remembered. It is no secret that when he wins a chess match against the SS, a prisoner – a Jewish prisoner – will cheat the gas chamber. Now, wherever he goes, he is hounded by a straggle of inmates who shamble in his footsteps, as if following their messiah, some of them bold enough to tug at his sleeve, hoping to attract his attention and become the next one to be nominated. He is their champion; his is the solitary act of defiance against the indignities that are heaped on them every day. He is even said by some to possess magical powers. Shouts of encouragement follow his every step. Even some of the

Kapos greet him respectfully when he passes by, an unheard-of privilege for a Jew.

Brack is delighted with his protégé. Emil is given a bunk to himself, with clean straw and an extra blanket. When he leaves the block in the mornings, the *Stubendienst* inspects Emil's tunic to ensure it has the prescribed number of buttons.

Emil is troubled by all the attention. Almost since he first entered the camp he has had a companion in whom he could confide, but now he is alone. He does not trust Brack. There is no honour among thieves, even less among murderers. He is only too familiar with Brack's reputation for casual brutality. He knows of the incident last year when one of the newly arrived politicals pushed back angrily when the Ältester shoved him out of the soup queue. A red triangle on a prison tunic denotes a far higher status than does the crude star worn by the Jews, but that did not stop Brack from ordering his minions to hold the Communist's head in the soup until he drowned. The soup men then continued to dole out the ration as if nothing had happened.

No, Brack's newfound concern for Emil's welfare is a patent pretence. His life has improved immeasurably, but for how long? Emil is still not sure exactly what Brack is getting out of this, but there must be some advantage to him or he would not be doing it. As soon as Emil's usefulness is over, he knows he will be abandoned.

Emil is also more than a little worried that, since the game against Untersturmführer Dorn, he has heard nothing from Meissner.

One evening, Emil is stopped on the way back to his block from roll call by a Dutch Jew. He tries to give Emil his bread ration. When Emil refuses it, he says, 'But there must be something I can do to thank you.'

'Thank me? For what?'

'For saving my life. I am the one whose life you won from the Germans in your last game of chess.'

Appalled, Emil steps back. 'Do not try to thank me. Do not think for one moment that this is something I am doing willingly. I have been forced into this as with everything else in this place. As far as I am concerned, it is just another of the cruel tricks that the Germans like to play on us.'

The man shakes his head. 'I cannot agree with you, my friend. Your courage strikes at the heart of this evil regime. According to the Torah, he who saves one life saves a thousand, and that is the truth of it.'

'Courage?' Emil says. 'Please, do not mistake coercion for courage. When I entered the place where I played against the SS officer I was so full of fear that I almost lost control of my bowels. I do not know how I managed to win. That somebody's life should depend on my performance in a game of chess is an outrage.' He stops and raises his hand to point at the *Kommandantur* building beyond the electrified fence. 'Only the SS could devise a scheme so monstrous that we, its victims, would consider ourselves its beneficiaries.'

But the Dutchman is adamant. 'You are wrong, my friend. The very existence of this place is a contradiction. Every aspect of life here is the opposite of what it is on the outside. We cannot judge what happens here according to the rules of a civilized society. Here there is no right or wrong, only survival. It is a duty to survive, and every life that is saved is a victory.'

Emil can see that the man is not open to argument and tries to move past him, but the Dutchman catches Emil by his sleeve and holds fast to it. 'I do not know your name, my friend – I only know they call you the Watchmaker. My name is Kastein, Avram Kastein, of Rotterdam. Before the war I was a wealthy man. When this is over, if you survive, come to Rotterdam and look for me. I will not be hard to find. You will find me more than generous.'

In his zeal to show his gratitude he tries to take Emil's hand, but Emil is horrified by the Dutchman's words. He cannot bring himself to collude in such a bargain. For him to accept payment would be an act of betrayal. How could he profit from the place where his family was exterminated? How has this man permitted himself to be so corrupted by the perversion that is Auschwitz to even think of making such an offer? Without a word he pulls out of the Dutchman's grip and turns to run away. But Kastein calls after him: 'Herr Brack said you might be difficult, but my word is my bond. If we survive this, remember, no matter what, no matter when; I pay my debts.'

But Emil is no longer listening. He understands now how Brack is choosing the people whose lives will be put at hazard during his games, and the knowledge chills him.

An orderly stepped into Sturmbannführer Bär's office and waited for the Kommandant to acknowledge his presence. After some minutes, he was eventually forced to say, 'I'm sorry to disturb you, sir. Hauptsturmführer Meissner is here. He's asking to speak to you.'

Bär closed the file he had been reading. 'Meissner? I thought he was still on leave.' When the orderly made no reply he said, 'Very well, show him in. And have that Bible-worm bring us some coffee.'

Bär observed Meissner closely as he limped into the office, leaning purposefully on his walking stick. He did not stand to greet his subordinate, but waved him towards a chair.

'I wasn't expecting you back so soon,' he said. 'Anything wrong?'

'Nothing more than thousands of other Germans have had to put up with, sir.' When Bär gave a quizzical look Meissner continued: 'I went home on leave. It's been bombed. There's nothing left.'

'Nothing?'

A muscle twitched in Meissner's jaw. He shook his head.

A prisoner wearing the violet triangle of a Jehovah's Witness entered bearing a tray with a jug and two cups. The Kommandant waited until he had put it down, then told him to get out.

'How are you doing?'

'I'll manage.'

The terse tone of Meissner's response prompted the Kommandant to scrutinize his officer more closely. He could not help but notice how tightly Meissner was gripping his walking stick and wondered whether it was to stop his hands from trembling. 'I can arrange for more leave if it would help.'

'No. Thank you, sir. But there is something else you can do for me.'

The Kommandant raised a cup to his lips and took a sip before replying. 'Yes? What?'

'You can approve my request for a transfer back to active service.'

Bär narrowed his eyes and leaned back in his chair. 'There are many, including the Reichsführer-SS, who would say that what you do here *is* active service, and essential to the war effort.' He shook his head. 'I'm sorry, Meissner, but it's out of the question. The Hungarian *Aktion* is in full swing. You simply can't be spared.' He took another sip of his coffee, as if to indicate that the subject was closed, but Meissner was not deterred.

'With respect, sir, I don't really care what Reichsheini* might have to

---

* Himmler's nickname among the SS. It was not used in an affectionate way, especially among the Waffen-SS, where respect for Himmler was often scant.

say on the matter. It is my prerogative to request a transfer, and you have no good grounds for refusing it.'

'No good grounds? You think so?' Bär frowned. Meissner's obstinacy was verging on impertinence. 'Face facts, Meissner. Even if you could find a unit to accept you – bearing in mind that you are not fully able-bodied – have you any idea how difficult it would be to get a replacement for you? On the rare occasions I can get an officer sent here, all I get are the dregs – office clerks, schoolmasters and postmen with a grudge, who only want to wear a uniform to impress the women back home. They're unreliable and ill disciplined. I'm sorry, but I cannot support your request. You're far too good an officer for me to let go.'

Meissner stiffened. He had set his mind on getting away from Auschwitz. 'I am an officer in the Waffen-SS,' he said through gritted teeth. 'I enlisted to fight the enemies of the Reich, not to play nursemaid to Jews.'

'If you're referring to the problem of the chess player you seem to have adopted, there's a simple answer: get rid of him. Make sure he is included in the next *Selektion*, then forget about him.'

'I can't do that, sir. It is a question of honour.'

There was a brief silence. 'In that case, I can do nothing to help you.'

1962

Leidseplein, Amsterdam

Meissner had rallied and insisted he needed to get some fresh air. He said he would like to go with Emil to what he smilingly referred to as 'the best chess club in Amsterdam'. He was not up to walking, so they took a taxi to the Leidseplein. Willi had some business to take care of and said he would meet them there.

When they arrived, Emil ordered coffee and rolls and then they went through to the lounge at the rear of the bar. Meissner eased himself into a chair at one of the tables with chessboards sitting on them and leaned his walking stick on the wall behind. Emil took a seat opposite and started to set out the pieces.

'Would you like to play?'

'Me?' Meissner said. 'Against you?' He laughed.

'Why not?'

'I won't give you much of a game, will I?'

'It doesn't matter. We're playing for the love of it.'

'In that case, yes. I would like to very much.'

Meissner drew white and moved his king's pawn forward two spaces. 'It's hard to believe that, after all these years, I'm actually playing the famous Watchmaker at chess,' he said.

'Yes, who would have thought that a humble Jewish *Häftling* would come so far?' Emil mirrored Meissner's move.

As he did so, Willi came in, carrying a tray with their order. 'The barman asked me to bring this through,' he said, glancing at the board as he deposited the tray on a nearby table. 'Aha. A double king's pawn opening. Interesting.' He pulled up a seat beside Meissner. 'Did you know, Paul, that there are only twenty opening moves that white can make? The king's pawn game is a powerful opening. You have a dominating position in the centre of the board and both the queen and the bishop are set free.'

'That's a nice thought,' Meissner said.

'What is?'

'That a bishop could be set free.'

Willi smiled self-consciously. 'I was thinking,' he said. 'We should get on with the story.'

'In case I don't make it to the end?' Emil and Willi exchanged a worried look. Paul started to laugh but it quickly turned into a cough.

'No, of course not,' Willi said. 'I want to know how our friend fares when he has the entire weight of the SS thrown at him.'

'Well,' Emil said with a grin, 'as you can see, I'm still here, and the SS isn't, so I suppose that must tell you something.'

'It's interesting,' Meissner said, 'the notion of freedom. It's something I've spent a lot of time thinking about since the war, and not because of the years I spent in prison.' His voice caught and he cleared his throat. 'It's not something I speak about much, but after Emil won his second game I went home on leave, to Cologne. It changed my life.'

Willi took a bite of a ham-filled roll. 'Really? In what way?'

'It set me free,' Meissner replied simply, reaching for his coffee. 'You must bear in mind,' he continued, moving his king-side knight, 'that I was no stranger to devastation. I fought at Kursk, perhaps the bloodiest of all the battles in the east. I saw plenty of action – real action – but nothing prepared me for what I found at home. I thought I had already seen hell on earth, but I was wrong. Cologne was the real hell, because it was my home. I have never seen anything like it. The destruction was terrible. Terrible.'

Paul's voice had fallen to a whisper, so Willi said quietly, 'And your home?'

'Gone.' Paul sighed heavily. He delved into a pocket, brought out a handkerchief and blew his nose loudly. When he continued, his voice was thick with emotion. 'Everything – everyone – had been taken from me. I had nothing. No, that's not quite true. I still had the SS. That was my home then. But not the SS of the camps – they were a disgrace, a squalid bunch of petty crooks out to make as much as they could out of the "Final

Solution".' He winced at his own words. 'I wanted no company with *them*, you understand. I wanted to make my escape, back to the Waffen-SS, back to my old regiment, back to where once again I could serve with honour.'

'Honour?' Emil broke in. 'It seems incomprehensible to me that someone should talk about serving with honour in an organization like the SS.'

Meissner reached across the board to squeeze Emil's hand. 'I can understand why you would think that, Emil; and my service in Auschwitz does me little credit, I know. I confess I was convinced that National Socialism, with its values of order and unity and obedience, was the salvation of the German people. I thought I could contribute to the struggle without becoming tainted by it.' He looked away. 'I was wrong. I thought the SS was an elect order carrying out the work of Providence. I was wrong about that too, but I hoped that if I could get back to my old unit, I would be able to regain my self-respect.'

'And is that how it worked out?' Emil asked, coolly.

Meissner bowed his head. 'No.'

29.

GIUOCO PIANO

Friday, 21 July 1944

Konzentrationslager Auschwitz-III, Monowitz

Rejoice, rejoice! Hitler is dead, assassinated in his field headquarters in East Prussia. For the first time anyone can remember, the inmates are not marched off in their work *Kommandos* after morning roll call, but are returned to barracks. The SS guards are out in force, patrolling the camp perimeter with dogs. Their weapons are not slung over their shoulders, but are held at the ready, fingers hovering over the triggers. They look jumpy and wary. The rumour mill is grinding away, its stories becoming more fantastic with every hour: Hitler was shot by his own guards, Göring has been killed by a bomb, Goebbels has been strung up in the street by an angry mob. Gradually the inmates come out into the sunlight and congregate along the wire, watching the guards, wondering.

Hours pass. The noon soup ration is delivered. This serves to pull the prisoners back into the body of the camp, for nobody can ignore the call of hunger, but they eat quickly, too curious about this unprecedented state of affairs to stay away from the wire for long.

They do not know that in Berlin a battle has been fought at army headquarters between soldiers loyal to the officers who plotted to kill Hitler, and Waffen-SS units whose allegiance to the Führer is beyond question. But now it seems that nobody is above suspicion: even senior members of the SS have been implicated.

The camp guards do not know any of this, either. They have been told they are on high alert for fear that Polish partisans may attempt to break into the camp and free the prisoners. Naturally, the guards regard the milling thousands along the perimeter fence with suspicion.

As the day lengthens, even though no prisoner has been permitted to exit the camp, the order is given for evening roll call. But the prisoners do not stray from the wire. A day spent in idleness scanning the horizon has given many an itch for freedom. By now they have heard the rumour that an attack by partisans is imminent and they do not want to let slip the chance to escape. They tell themselves the partisans must be concealed in the trees to the south, waiting until they are at full strength before they launch their attack, or perhaps they are waiting for nightfall, for it would be foolish to risk an assault in broad daylight.

The camp bell is rung, a signal for the inmates to return to their blocks. Some automatically start to walk back. Others turn their heads for a moment but are unwilling to relinquish the positions they have occupied. This day is like no other. They do not want it to end in another capitulation. Now a group of guards is walking towards the fence. They are waving their arms and shouting furiously for the prisoners to disperse, threatening them with dire consequences if they do not obey. Dogs are barking, straining at their leashes, fangs bared. Some prisoners, emboldened by the rumours, dare to shout back, hurling obscenities and curses. If words could kill, no guard would be left standing.

Without warning a machine pistol is fired, a long burst of automatic gunfire that does not finish until a metallic click indicates that the magazine is empty. The noise echoes through the camp, alerting prisoners, officers, and guards alike, but it is not the partisans attacking. Where the shots have been fired, men lie dead or wounded, some screaming, blood spreading across the patchy grass. A few prisoners run, but most look on stupidly, frozen into inaction. With an angry grimace, the guard who has fired his weapon releases the empty magazine and replaces it. In a deliberate gesture he tilts back his helmet and wipes his brow with his sleeve, as if he has completed a difficult task to his satisfaction. He turns to his companions and jerks his head in the direction of the remaining prisoners. With approving smiles the rest of them raise their weapons.

There is no need to give any order: when he fires again the others follow suit, a lethal hail that hits the defenceless mass and fells them instantly. Now all the prisoners are running for their lives without a backward glance to see how many have fallen.

In a matter of seconds, it is over.

The guards are laughing. 'Fucking Kikes,' one says, reloading his weapon as they walk away, leaving the carnage behind them. 'They never learn.'

In his office, alerted by the sound of gunfire, Hauptsturmführer Meissner is inspecting his pistol, making sure there is a bullet in the chamber, before putting it into its holster. Calmly, he puts on his service cap, collects his walking stick and limps quickly to the outer office. Bewildered NCOs and men are away from their desks, peering out of the windows. None is armed or ready for action.

'All of you,' Meissner barks, 'get away from the windows.' Sheepishly the men return to their desks. 'Who's the senior rank here?'

A Scharführer calls out. 'Me, sir.'

'Grawitz, isn't it? Send a runner to Hauptsturmführer Brossman. Tell him we're ready to assist and await his orders. Then get the men armed and assembled downstairs. Quickly. I'll be back in five minutes. Eiden-müller, you're with me.'

Without another word Meissner heads for the stairs, the call to action too strong to resist, his orderly following in his wake. They reach the guard room next to the main gate without incident. There they find Ober-sturmführer Schottl, the Lagerführer. He is shouting into the mouthpiece of a telephone.

'What's happening?' Meissner demands.

Schottl regards his superior with contempt. He has not forgotten their exchange at the hangings. 'Nothing that you need to worry about, *sir*.'

'Thank you, Obersturmführer,' Meissner replies coldly, 'but I think I'll be the judge of that. It sounded to me like automatic fire, several weapons. Do you know where it came from?'

When Schottl does not reply, Meissner turns to an NCO. 'You, Ober-scharführer – where did it come from?'

'The southern perimeter, sir, as far as we can tell.'

'Thank you.' Meissner turns to Schottl and gestures to the door. 'Shall we?'

With a glare at the Oberscharführer, Schottl says, 'Don't you think it would be better to stay here, to have a central post of command?'

'In my experience,' Meissner replies, 'nothing beats an on-the-spot assessment. But if *you* think…'

Schottl immediately grasps the veiled implication of the Hauptsturm-führer's words, as do the rest of the men in the guard room. 'No, sir. Of course not. After you.'

It does not take long to reach the site. It is a massacre. A squad of four guards and an Unterscharführer are already there.

'Do you know what happened?' Meissner calls.

'No, sir. We only just got here ourselves.'

Meissner rolls a corpse over with the toe of his boot. There are three bloody entry wounds across its chest. 'Better see if any of them is still alive.'

But Schottl objects. 'Sir, don't you think we should be preparing for an attack? We were put on alert to expect a partisan raid. This could be part of it.'

'I doubt it,' Meissner observes. 'If it were partisans, it would be dead Germans lying here, not prisoners. I think somebody has been a little trigger-happy.'

'Sir,' one of the guards shouts, 'here's one still alive. What shall I do with him?'

'If he's able to talk, ask him what happened, then get him to the infirmary.'

But Schottl will hear none of it. 'There's no point asking a prisoner what happened – all they know how to do is lie. And we'll not waste our time taking them to the sick bay.' He pulls out his pistol and strides over to where the wounded man is lying. Without a word he puts it to the man's head and pulls the trigger.

Meissner is disgusted, but there is nothing he can do. He is only an administrator and Schottl is the Lagerführer. He turns away. He is not squeamish; he has seen many men killed, but never before in such a casual manner. 'Let's go,' he says to Eidenmüller, 'before I do something I'm bound to regret later.'

On their way back, Eidenmüller asks, 'Is it true, sir? Has somebody tried to kill the Führer?'

'I'm afraid it is. And from what I've been told, it seems there were many involved in the conspiracy. No doubt the details will come out over the next few days, but I am assured that although he has been injured, the Führer lives.'

They run into the guards commander, Brossman, leading a platoon of men. 'I don't suppose you have any idea what's happened?' Meissner asks.

Brossman stops, letting an NCO lead the men on. 'It seems there's been an unfortunate accident,' he says, flinching as a shot rings out. 'A loose finger on an over-sensitive trigger, shall we say?'

'More than one loose finger, I would have said,' Meissner replies, as another shot pierces the evening air.

'What's happening now?' Brossman asks, referring to the gunshots.

'More "unfortunate accidents". Obersturmführer Schottl is proving to be particularly accident-prone.'

'Little shit,' Brossman says.

'Yes.' Meissner turns to Eidenmüller. 'We've left the men waiting. You'd better go and tell them the panic is over. I'll be back soon.'

As Eidenmüller hurries off, Brossman jerks his head in the direction of the sporadic gunshots. 'Do I need to see it for myself?'

Meissner shakes his head. 'No, not unless you want to see the scale of the carnage.'

'How many?'

'At least a hundred, and Schottl is doing his level best to add to the count.' Meissner reaches into his tunic pocket and extracts his cigarette case. Opening it, he takes one and offers the case to Brossman, who pulls out a lighter. Both men inhale deeply, enjoying the bite of the smoke as it hits their lungs. They turn their backs on the slaughter and head back towards the SS buildings.

'How did you manage to end up here, Otto?'

Brossman puckers his lips and puts a finger to them to remove a strand of tobacco. 'Fucked if I know,' he says. 'I was a Scharführer in Mauthausen. They sent me there because I was qualified as a mining engineer. But once I got there that didn't seem to matter. I was put in the guard detail and the next thing I know, I've been sent to the *Junkerschule* in Bad Tölz.'*

'Really? I was there myself. When were you there?'

'1940. And you?'

'Not until the autumn of '41.' Meissner takes up the thread again. 'And after officer training, you came here?'

'No. I was sent to Poland. Until September '41 I was on Globocnik's staff in Lublin. God, he was a vicious bastard, I can tell you. With the invasion of Russia I expected to be sent east with the Einsatzgrüppen, but luckily for me, I suppose, I found myself posted here. At that time there was only the *Stammlager*, and a few thousand Russian POWs that we put to work constructing the camp at Birkenau. I was put in charge of the guard company, and I've been here ever since. How about you?'

Meissner grins self-consciously. 'I only ever wanted to be in the Waffen-SS. Death or glory, that's me. I contemplated a career in the Luftwaffe, but in my last year at university a Waffen-SS officer came to speak to us. They were the Führer's shock troops, he said, the imperial guard of National Socialism. That was good enough for me.' He was silent for a moment. 'Everything was so much clearer then than it is now.' He let his cigarette butt fall from his fingers. 'Otto,' he continued, 'I've been meaning to speak to you about this damned Jewish chess player. Will you take him on? I should warn you – he's good. He struggled against Frommhagen, but I think it was only because of nerves. He beat Dorn easily.'

---

* Bad Tölz was one of three SS *Junkerschules* – officer training schools.

It is a warm evening. Brossman takes off his cap and wipes the sweat-band with a handkerchief. 'Dorn? He's worse than Schottl. I don't know what the SS is coming to when they let pricks like those two in.'

'So, how about it? Will you play against the Jew? Only make sure you beat him, or Bär will have me shot.'

Brossman glances at the sky and sniffs. 'Can you smell that? It's the crematoria at Birkenau. Never quite get used to the smell, do you? Between you and me, Paul, I'm sick of it. Sick of the war, sick of all the killing. I think we may have made a mistake about the Jews. We're never going to get rid of them all, so why are we even bothering?' He shakes his head. 'Yes, I'll play your Jew, and I'll even do my best to beat him, but I'm not making any promises.'

'For his sake I hope you do beat him.'

'Why?'

'Because after you he would face Hustek.'

'Christ. I wouldn't wish that on anybody. Not even a poxy Yid.'

'Quite. But on the other hand...'

'Yes?'

'I've seen the Jew play. I'm no expert, but I think he may be quite exceptional. What if he beats you and Hustek, too? Then what?'

The sound of another shot breaks the calm. Brossman scowls. 'Luckily for me,' he says, 'that's not something I'm going to have to worry about.'

1962

Leidseplein, Amsterdam

'I remember that night very clearly,' Willi said. 'Talk about panic. We didn't know what was going on. The ministry building was surrounded by soldiers and we were told we couldn't leave. Joey the Cripple was frantic, expecting to be hauled out and shot any minute. Then, at about seven o'clock, there was a telephone call from the Führer. The officer in charge of the men outside came into the building and spoke to him. Everything changed after that. We were ordered to tune in to the radio for an emergency broadcast. That's when we learned what had happened. There had been a bomb, but Hitler had survived. The traitors were holed up at the General Army HQ. The people of Berlin were ordered to stay off the streets. We weren't far from the army headquarters and, a little while afterwards, we could hear the gunfire, very clearly. Then, shortly after midnight, Skorzeny arrived with SS troops and it was all over.'

'I have often wondered what would have happened if Hitler had not survived,' Paul said.

Willi pondered for a moment. 'The obvious thing would have been for the army to take over and negotiate a peace,' he said wistfully. 'We probably wouldn't have been occupied by the Russians.'

'Perhaps, then,' Emil said, 'it was better that he did survive. If Germany had not experienced such a catastrophic defeat as she did, it would have been only a matter of time before another Hitler emerged and the whole disaster was enacted again.'

'I do not think we would have let such a thing happen.'

'I wish, Willi' – Emil's voice was suddenly harsh – 'that I could share your confidence, but having experienced what a person like Hitler and his henchmen could inflict first-hand, you'll forgive me if I say that no price would be too high to make sure it could never happen again.'

30.

THE CHIGORIN DEFENCE

August 1944
Konzentrationslager Auschwitz-III, Monowitz

It is not the place of a *Häftling* to seek an audience with an officer in the SS, but nearly two months have gone by since the game against Dorn, and still there is no word from Meissner. Even Brack is showing signs of unease. It is some relief then, when, finally, word reaches them that the Watchmaker must report to the Hauptsturmführer without delay.

A *Kapo* escorts Emil to Meissner's office. Meissner is alone – even Eidenmüller is absent. The SS man seems distracted. He sends the *Kapo* away, and Emil stands at attention, waiting. Meissner limps to the outer office and returns bearing a pot of coffee and two cups. 'Please take a seat,' he says, and, filling a cup, hands it to the dumbfounded prisoner.

'Thank you,' Emil manages to say, as he sits. He takes a sip from the cup. It is too hot, but the smell of it is intoxicating. It is *coffee*, real coffee.

'Cigarette?' A pack is handed over. 'Keep it.'

Emil's hands tremble as he tears the pack open and puts a cigarette between his lips. He has nothing to light it with and waits, until the officer points to a box of matches on the desk.

Emil inhales deeply, savouring the first rush of nicotine. It is some moments before he realizes he is being watched. 'Why are you doing this?' he asks.

'The last time we spoke you accused me of being uncivilized. That is far from the truth. Germans are a civilized people. But we have allowed ourselves to come under the control of a bunch of gangsters. That is our disgrace and your great misfortune. There is little I can do about that, but I have decided I can put up with it no longer. I am not permitted to leave my post, but I will no longer play the game according to their rules.'

'*Their* rules?'

'They used to be my rules too, but no longer.'

Emil looks away, stunned. He wonders if he is dreaming. For an SS officer to talk to him in this way is unthinkable.

'Are you playing some kind of game with me?'

There is an edge to Meissner's voice when he replies. 'No. No more games, Watchmaker.'

Emil searches for a reply but can find nothing. He feels as if he is alone in a deep cave, groping blindly, trying desperately to understand the words that flit around him, like bats, in the darkness. He wonders if he is being tested and responds by saying, bitterly: 'It does not matter whether you are playing a game with me or not – nothing can change my situation. Not until you Nazis and all you stand for have been utterly destroyed.'

The SS officer stiffens. For a moment his eyes rest on a photograph of Hitler that adorns the wall. 'I know,' he says. 'I'm sorry. Truly.'

Meissner's words are shocking, astounding. They hit the Watchmaker with the force of an earthquake: whole cities topple and fall into dust.

Emil is bewildered by the transformation that has come over the SS man. He hears his own voice as if it were coming from the next room: 'Sorry? Dear God. Do you expect me to believe that? You give the impression of being sincere, but for all I know this is simply some new and refined cruelty that you have dreamed up. How do I know there will not be some bolt from the blue – that all of a sudden, some punishment will descend on me without warning?'

Meissner does not reply. Instead, he pushes himself up and walks to the hat stand where his belt is hung. Taking his pistol from its holster he pulls back the action and puts a cartridge into the chamber. Then he hands it to Emil.

'It's loaded,' he says, 'so be careful with it.'

'What do you want me to do with this?'

'Whatever you like.'

'But why?'

'I want us to pretend, for a while, that this is not one of the circles of hell and that we are two civilized men having a civilized conversation.'

'And which circle of hell do you think we are in?'

'Isn't it obvious? The ninth one.'

'The ninth one? Heresy?'

Meissner shakes his head. 'No. Treachery.'

Treachery. The word rumbles like an aftershock. Emil becomes aware of the pistol in his hand. It feels strange. It is heavy, its black metal smooth to the touch, and cool. He sees it as though through a magnifying glass: there are traces of grease around the moving parts and blemishes on the handgrip where it has been damaged, perhaps in battle. Gingerly, he rests a finger on the trigger. It would be child's play to shoot the SS man; at this range he could not miss.

If Yves were alive, what would *he* do? The answer is certain: he would kill the German. But Emil is not Yves and the certainties that once guided his life have all been torn away: if he killed Meissner, would that mean he had descended to the same level? And – the most uncertain of all his uncertainties – what if Meissner is sincere?

There is a clock on the wall above the door. The Watchmaker glances at it. He has been here for thirty minutes and there has been no bolt from the blue.

Gently, he puts the pistol on the desk.

Meissner smiles, but it seems out of place.

'What do you want from me?'

'I want you to fulfil the Führer's direst warnings about the Jews.'

'I don't understand what you're talking about.'

'Watchmaker, you are one of the most dangerous prisoners in the camp. I'm surprised the Gestapo hasn't taken an interest in you.'

A look of alarm crosses Emil's face. 'Why would they? I'm not political.'

'Of course you are. Every Jew is political, because, according to the Führer, every Jew is part of the international conspiracy against Germany.'

'Ah, yes. The international conspiracy,' Emil says scathingly. 'I was an ordinary person doing what I could to make my way in the world, a watchmaker with a tiny shop in Paris. What danger did I pose to Germany? How could you even think that I could be part of a worldwide conspiracy? The idea doesn't stand up to any rational examination.'

'You would say that, wouldn't you?' Meissner opens a desk drawer and lifts out a bottle. 'Cognac?'

'No, thank you. In my state it would probably kill me.' Emil inhales deeply, catching the warm aroma of the spirit as the officer pours himself a generous measure. 'All right, then,' he continues, 'what about the poor, uneducated peasants in the Ukraine? Most of them have never set foot outside their villages. How could they be part of an international conspiracy?'

Meissner taps his nose with a finger. 'Ah. That's the clever part. *They* were an enormous Fifth Column. For years they have been lying dormant, waiting patiently, lulling us into a false sense of security. But when they got the word, they would rise up and overwhelm the German people.'

'How can you believe that?' Emil asks in wonderment. 'It's nothing more than a hate-filled fantasy.'

'I agree. But don't you think it's strange that among the nine circles of Dante's hell, not one of them represents Hatred?'

Emil's eyes stray to the half-empty bottle of cognac. Meissner catches the look and smiles wryly. 'I've not been drinking, Watchmaker. Not yet.'

'I would like more coffee, if there is any left.'

'Of course. Help yourself.'

While the Watchmaker refills his cup, Meissner picks up the pistol and resets the safety catch. 'I almost wish that you had shot me,' he says.

'Shoot you? Why would I do that?'

'Because I am your enemy.'

1962

Kerk de Krijtberg, Amsterdam

Emil brought the coffee pot from the stove and refilled their cups. 'Every time I have coffee it reminds me of that time in your office,' he said. 'I have never known coffee to taste so good, before or since. It was exquisite.'

'But what was it,' Willi asked Meissner, 'that you wanted Emil to do?'

'It was quite straightforward, though I hadn't thought it through fully at the time.' Meissner's face relaxed as he thought back, retrieving the memories. 'It took a while to sink in how rattled the Kommandant was by Emil's victories. As Höss said, this was a test of National Socialism, and a challenge to the complacency of the SS. Bär didn't see it that way – he considered it a dangerous experiment that should be brought to an end. Then I realized they were both right. I knew that Emil had an extraordinary gift and that, no matter what we did, he would win. This would expose one of the fault lines in Nazism – that the idea of the master race was a myth; a fantasy built on nothing more solid than the sinister delusions of a megalomaniac. I remembered the ideological lectures we had in the SS training school. We were told that the Russians were sub-human, but then we saw what they were like on the Eastern front: they were the same as us. We had been lied to. What if we had also been lied to about the Jews? I think it was in Cologne that I realized none of it made any sense. That was when I knew I wanted Emil to win.'

Meissner took a sip of coffee, putting his thoughts in order. 'The next game was to be played in the middle of August. I wanted it to be in the officers' mess again, but Bär vetoed that. He wanted it played in the prison block in the *Stammlager*, where nobody would see it. Hardly fair to Emil of course, but that was the intention – to intimidate him – all the prisoners knew what went on inside its walls. Naturally, none of this prevented Eidenmüller from taking bets' – Meissner smiled briefly at the recollection – 'which he told me were heavier than ever. But what came as a complete surprise was who turned up to watch.'

August 1944
Konzentrationslager Auschwitz-I

A room on the upper floor of the prison block in the *Stammlager* has been emptied.

Otto Brossman has heard tales of this place, though he has never been inside before: of cells below ground so narrow that it is possible only to stand in them; of prisoners locked in basement cells and left to starve to death in the darkness. It is said that some cells have been bricked up to entomb their occupants.

The room itself is intimidating. The plaster on the walls is painted a pale creamy colour, but it is discoloured in many places by dark stains. It is not difficult to imagine what goes on in there.

A single table and two wooden chairs have been set up in the middle of the room. A chessboard stands waiting for the players to arrive.

'I think the Jew is going to find this place more than a little daunting,' Brossman says in a low voice.

'That'll make two of us,' Meissner replies.

The Watchmaker is escorted in by Eidenmüller. Meissner nods to his orderly but pointedly ignores the prisoner.

'Is that it?' Brossman asks.

'Yes. The Kommandant did not want any spectators. He also insisted that you have an advantage. There will be no draw to see who gets which colour. You get to choose.'

'Then I choose white.'

The SS man advances his queen's pawn two spaces. Without hesitation the prisoner makes the same move. The SS man brings up his queenside bishop's pawn to stand beside its companion. The prisoner brings out his queenside knight. The SS man brings out his kingside knight. The prisoner moves his queen's bishop across the board. White pawn takes black pawn and the prisoner retaliates by taking the white knight with his bishop. Black bishop falls to a white pawn and with that the black queen is out to take the white pawn in the centre of the board. All this has taken place with almost unthinking rapidity.

White is ahead, just, and Meissner is holding his breath.

Play is interrupted by the sound of a heavy footfall on the stairs. A shadow looms on the landing and in walks Oberscharführer Hustek.

'Oh,' he says in mock surprise. 'I didn't think you would have started already. I'm sorry to be late, but then I didn't receive an official invitation.'

'What are you doing here, Hustek?' Meissner asks, already knowing the answer. 'The Kommandant wanted this game to be a quiet affair, not a crowd-puller.'

'But I'm not a crowd, am I?' Hustek replies. 'I'm only me. When I heard what trouble you had gone to over this little game, I thought to myself it's about time I took a closer look at this unbeatable Jew. So here I am.'

'Clear off, Hustek. That's an order.'

But Hustek is not to be deterred. With a smile sweetly laden with disdain he says, 'I thought we had already agreed, Herr Hauptsturm-führer, that since I'm Gestapo, I'm not answerable to you. Besides,' he says, almost as an afterthought, 'seeing as how I will be the next person to play the Jew, unless by some miracle he manages to lose tonight' – he sniggers – 'I have Sturmbannführer Bär's permission to be here. If that's all right with you, Herr Hauptsturmführer?'

Meissner fixes his eyes on the Gestapo man, taking in the cocky smile and pose of casual insubordination. He glances at Brossman to catch a look of resignation as it flits across the other officer's face.

The prisoner keeps his attention fixed on the chessboard.

'Don't worry about me,' Hustek adds. 'I'll be quiet as a mouse. Pretend I'm not here.'

'Fine,' Meissner says, making a tactical retreat. For now.

Hustek takes up position against a wall, lights a cigarette and says not another word; but he watches. Unblinkingly.

Before the game, Emil had sought out Brack. 'I want to know whose life I'm playing for this time.'

'None of your business,' Brack says.

'I think it is. I need to know the person who will go up the chimney if I'm unlucky enough to lose. I want him to look me in the eye and tell me he understands what a risk he's taking.'

'Oh, he understands all right,' Brack says. 'Same as every other Yid in this place. On the one hand, there is the certain knowledge that, sooner or later, one of the *Selektionen* will get them and they will never be seen again; or, on the other hand, they can gamble that you really are unbeatable – which is what they all think anyway – and that for reasons that frankly are beyond their comprehension, a life will be saved.'

'I still want to see him.'

'Afterwards,' Brack insists. 'You can see him afterwards.'

1962

Kerk de Krijtberg, Amsterdam

'Those early moves were played at a breathtaking pace,' Paul remembered.

'I can imagine,' Willi replied. 'Such an unconventional response. The SS officer must have come with a well-prepared game plan, yet you took him by surprise. When did you pause for breath?'

'Only after he took my bishop.'

'It must have been a terrifying ordeal. In my wildest dreams I would never have thought of a game of chess being played in a torture chamber, with a man's life at stake.'

'It was very tense,' Meissner said. 'The stakes were extremely high – more so than we realized at the time. I knew that if Emil won it would create more trouble for me, but at the same time in my mind I was urging him on. Brossman gained the early advantage and I was more nervous than I would have been facing a Russian tank. I can't speak for Emil, but the spectre of the Gestapo witnessing the whole affair made it difficult to draw breath. I could guess what Hustek usually got up to in that room. Eidenmüller had asked around about him, and what he discovered was not flattering, even by the standards of the Gestapo.'

Willi shuddered. 'I never met anyone from the Gestapo – not that I know of, at least,' he said.

'Lucky you. But Hustek…simply being in the same room with him made you feel uneasy. If you had met him on the street you would have known immediately that he was someone to avoid.'

'I agree,' Emil added. 'I never felt such malice in any of the other Gestapo I encountered.'

'Other Gestapo? You never mentioned that,' Meissner said, with some surprise.

'Why would I? You never asked me how I came to be in Auschwitz.'

'I assumed you were sent there because you were a Jew. I'm afraid I never thought beyond that.'

'No, I don't suppose you would. There must have been ten thousand Jews in Monowitz, with ten thousand tales of how they came to be there. You had no reason to ask me about my story.'

October 1943
Annecy
Emil returned from the town dripping wet from the downpour: another fruitless errand. Every time he went he ran the risk of being picked up. Annecy was not a large town and strangers were soon noticed.

In the confusion following the fall of France, Emil had taken his family south, to Rosa's parents in Périgueux. In late 1942, when the Germans moved to occupy the Vichy territories, Emil managed to get a letter to

Meister Nohel in Basle asking for sanctuary. His old master had replied quickly: 'Come at once,' he had written, 'before the round-up of Jews gathers pace.' But Emil's mother was ill. Her ankles were swollen and she had been feverish. The doctor said she could not possibly travel. So they had delayed until the following summer. Even then it had not been an easy journey, heading for the Swiss border shepherding two young children and an ageing mother, trying to avoid attention.

Near Annecy, they had come upon a farmer out early to bring in his cows. Emil told him they were heading for Geneva. The farmer said they did not have far to go, perhaps fifty kilometres, but the border was heavily guarded. He offered them shelter in his barn and told Emil of a café in town where he could make contact with the Resistance, who might be able to guide them. He told Emil to ask for Jacques. If, in reply, he was told that Jacques had gone away to care for his sick mother, he should then say that he had heard that Madame Blanchard was making a good recovery and that he hoped Jacques would be back soon.

Every day for four days Emil had returned to the café, asking its patrons if they knew Jacques. All he had got were blank looks. It did not bode well. They would have to move soon, before somebody told the Germans about the persistent stranger asking for a man he did not seem to know.

When he got back to the barn, it was empty.

Trying to bring his pounding heart under control, Emil inched around to the farmhouse. There were two vehicles in the yard: a small military car of the type used by the Germans and a black Renault. Emil smelt the acrid tang of cigarette smoke. A German soldier was lounging against one of the farm buildings, blowing smoke rings to ease his boredom.

From inside the house Emil could hear his children crying. He had two choices: to save himself, or to try and bluff his way out of the situation.

Ignoring the soldier, he strode into the house.

The ground floor consisted of a single room, with a large fireplace and cooking range along one wall and a table opposite; in the corner was an ancient dresser crammed with various items of crockery.

Although the room was large, it seemed crowded. In one corner was his mother, his wife and their two sons; in another, the farmer and his wife. Around the fire were four men: two in military uniform, one in civilian clothes and a French gendarme.

'What the hell is going on?' Emil demanded.

The answer came from the man in civilian clothes. His French was adequate, though his accent was execrable. 'Who are you, monsieur?'

'My name is Emil Clément.' He looked anxiously at his wife. The brave face that Rosa had been wearing for the sake of the two boys fidgeting nervously with her skirt, crumpled. Her eyes pleaded silently for him to find a way to rescue them. His mother was beside herself, her lips trembling and her hands twisting and re-twisting her handkerchief. The sound of Emil's voice startled his children and they started to cry again. 'And this is my family. I demand to know what is going on.'

The gendarme intervened. 'Monsieur,' he said, almost apologetically, 'this is Herr Hefelmann. I'm afraid you must go with him.'

'Why? I have done nothing wrong.'

The gendarme shrugged. 'Nonetheless, monsieur...'

'I *demand* to know what is happening!'

Emil's outburst brought a smile to the face of the man in civilian clothes: a mocking, insincere smile. 'I am Obersturmführer Hefelmann. Gestapo,' he added, with a touch of malice. 'You, monsieur, are under arrest.'

'On what charge?' Emil appealed to the gendarme. 'I have a right to know.'

'You have no rights,' the Gestapo man snapped. 'You are a Jew.'

1962

Kerk de Krijtberg, Amsterdam

'For nearly a week, off and on, we were interrogated by the Gestapo. Where had we come from? How had we travelled? Where had we stayed? Who had helped us? The same questions, over and over and over. First me, then my wife, then my mother. I think it hit my wife the hardest. She had never experienced anti-Semitism and simply could not comprehend what was happening. "Why?" she kept asking – over and over.' Emil looked up. 'To this day, if she were to walk in and ask me that question, still I would not be able to answer her.'

'We were conditioned,' Meissner said quietly. 'Brainwashed, lied to and conditioned to obedience.'

'But why were you conditioned? How did such a hatred of Jews arise?'

'It was not only Jews. The Nazis hated Communists, homosexuals, Gypsies.'

'You still have not answered my question.'

'That is because I do not know the answer.'

Willi interrupted. 'Were you tortured?'

Slowly Emil shook his head. 'There was no need. They had my children. I told them everything I could.'

'What were their names? Your sons, I mean.'

'Louis and Marcel. Louis had his fifth birthday while we were in the prison in Annecy. Marcel was three.'

Emil lowered his head into his hands, unable to continue.

31.

THE JANOWSKI VARIATION

1962

Amsterdam

In the morning the three of them took a taxi to the Krasnapolsky.

Reaching the top of the hotel steps, Meissner pulled on Willi's sleeve. 'Hang on,' he gasped. 'I need a moment to get my breath.'

Willi eyed him warily. 'Are you sure you're well enough to be out like this? The doctor said...'

Meissner's face creased – Willi could not tell if it was with pain or irritation. 'If the doctor had his way, he would have me in an invalid's chair in a sanatorium somewhere. I'm fine, really, so please stop fussing.'

In the next round of the tournament Emil was drawn against an Englishman, David Abramson.

'Is he a Jew?' Willi asked.

'I have no idea,' Emil replied. 'Does it matter?'

Willi shrugged. 'I was wondering whether your Kabbalah would be effective against another Jew.'

The game was tough. The Englishman drew white and, in keeping with his nationality, played the English Opening, advancing his queen-side bishop's pawn two spaces.

'Good. An orthodox first move,' Willi whispered in Meissner's ear.

Emil's response was not: he brought out his kingside knight's pawn.

Willi smiled. 'I should have expected this by now,' he said. 'Once again he knows his opponent will have a well-structured game plan, so he sets out to stymie it immediately with an unconventional move.'

Two hours later, the game was still in progress. The two spectators moved to the hotel lounge for coffee and sandwiches. 'Don't the players get a break?' Meissner asked.

'Of course, if they request it. But Emil would not dream of joining us – he will want to maintain his concentration.'

The game continued almost to the time limits imposed by the competition and ended in a draw. The players parted amicably and would play again the next morning.

'How many more rounds are there to play?' Paul asked Emil, as the three of them waited on the hotel steps for a taxi.

'If I beat Abramson? Only two.'

'So this is a quarter-final?'

'I suppose it is, yes.'

'I hadn't realized.'

'Me neither.'

Back at the Krijtberg, Mrs Brinckvoort had left a stew for them to warm through for supper. Hungry after missing lunch, Emil wolfed his meal. After doing the washing up, he excused himself.

'Where are you off to?' Meissner asked.

'It's obvious, isn't it?' Willi called from the pantry, where he was drying the dishes. 'He's going to cast his tiles.'

'Are you?' Meissner asked. He continued in a mildly amused tone: 'You know the Church has a strict injunction against fortune-telling and the like?'

'It's not really a question of simply casting the tiles,' Emil tried to explain. 'It's not like a witchdoctor throwing bones or a fortune-teller reading tea leaves. It involves meditating on the will of God. I have to be open to the Divine will. If I'm not, then no amount of casting of tiles will help.'

'I think I understand,' Meissner replied. 'And I would really like to see how it's done sometime.'

'More to the point,' Willi said, 'how did you do it before your match with Brossman? And how did the game end? I've been waiting all day to hear.'

'It's getting late, Willi,' Meissner said. 'It's a long story and Emil has an important game tomorrow. Perhaps that should wait until after Emil has won this round.' He glanced slyly at Emil. 'But I should still like to see how you do it.'

Emil brought the tiles down from his room and placed them face down on the kitchen table. He arranged them vertically in a column of three, then a column of four then another column of three. 'This is the shape of the Sephiroth,' he said. 'Put simply, each of the ten placements represents a different manifestation of the infinite will. But the different manifestations do not signify that God's will might change or has changed; rather, it is our ability to perceive the Divine will that changes. The highest point corresponds to the infinite creative will. The others are aligned with wisdom, understanding, knowledge, compassion, judgement, beauty, eternity, submission and accomplishment. After I have meditated, I decide which of the tiles I should turn.'

'Which one will you choose tonight?' Willi asked.

'None of them.' He turned to Paul. 'I would like you to choose.'

Paul had not expected this. 'Are you sure? What if…'

'I'm sure, Paul.'

Meissner stood over the table, pondering his decision. 'Which one signifies compassion?'

Emil pointed to the third tile in the central column. 'That is called Tif'eret,' he said. 'It balances the two positions above – Gevurah, signifying severity and Hesed, which is unconditional kindness.'

Meissner turned the tile. 'What letter is that?'

'Beth.'

'What does it mean?'

'It belongs to the order of angels called the Ophanim. In its most literal sense, it denotes the selflessness of wisdom. What it means tonight, I have no idea.'

August 1944
Konzentrationslager Auschwitz-I

Brossman was unable to maintain his early advantage. Once the opening flurry of moves was over, the Watchmaker found a way to strike deep into his opponent's territory. At checkmate, Brossman stared at the board for several minutes, trying to work out where he had gone wrong.

At a gesture from Meissner, he and Brossman left the room. Eidenmüller followed with the Watchmaker. Not a word was spoken.

Oberscharführer Klaus Hustek stayed behind, musing over what he had witnessed. He did not share Meissner's opinion of Brossman's ability as a chess player, but there was no doubt the Jew was good. Well, he would have to do something about that. Hustek prided himself on being methodical. He did not prejudge the wretches who were brought to him for interrogation – that was merely a charade to put them off balance. Even so, in his estimation Meissner had been taken in by the Jew and would do his utmost to protect him. He would have to find a way to neutralize the Hauptsturmführer.

The next morning Hustek asked to speak to the Kommandant. He sensed that Bär was extremely uneasy about the chess games with the Watchmaker and adjusted his own attitude accordingly, making it almost the complete reverse of what it had been at the final of the SS championship: he was respectful and deferential.

'Don't get me wrong, sir,' he said. 'It's not that I don't want to play the Jew – I do. I want to put him in his place, good and proper. It's just that I want to prepare thoroughly and, what with all the rumours flying around after the attempt on the Führer's life, I need to be able to devote myself to hunting out any conspirators who may be hiding here. So what I suggest is that the game against the Jew is delayed for a month, or perhaps longer.'

Bär agreed. 'Do you have a date in mind?'

'Yes, sir. October the thirteenth. And I would like the game to be played at the Solahütte, with your permission, of course.'

When the news was relayed to him, Meissner was baffled. 'Delayed until October?' He checked the calendar. 'Friday the thirteenth? What's he playing at?'

Eidenmüller had noticed the change that had come about in his commanding officer since his return from leave: he was pensive and kept to himself much more. Eidenmüller had tried in his clumsy way to discover what was troubling his boss, but had been rebuffed.

About a week after the game between the Watchmaker and Brossman, Eidenmüller was in the SS barracks in Monowitz looking for Unterscharführer Hoven, one of the few SS men who had bet on the

Watchmaker to win. Eidenmüller owed him money and he never welched on his bets.

Hoven was a hopeless gossip who was in charge of prisoner records for the Monowitz camp. As he watched his winnings being counted out, he could not suppress the urge to pass on his latest titbit: 'Bet you don't know who's been taking an interest in your Watchmaker,' he said, with a knowing smirk.

Eidenmüller looked up sharply. 'He's not my Watchmaker.'

'But you've made a packet out of him, haven't you?'

'Business, purely business. Anyway, who is it that's taking an interest in him?'

'That Gestapo creep, Hustek.'

'Hustek?' Eidenmüller said, raising an eyebrow. 'That's not so surprising. He's next in line to play the Watchmaker.'

'I'd say the bastard's been doing more than taking an interest, if you get my meaning.' Hoven tapped a bony finger against his nose.

'Bastard—?' Eidenmüller asked, curious.

'You've never been interrogated by the Gestapo, have you?' When Eidenmüller shook his head, Hoven continued: 'I have – by Hustek. Calling him a bastard is too good for him in my book. It was because of him I got demoted and sent here. I had a cushy little number, with benefits, you might say, before he shoved his nose in.' He curled his lip in disgust. 'Fucking Gestapo. They're all of them bastards, if you ask me.'

Minutes later, a frantic Eidenmüller was outside Meissner's office. But he couldn't go in – the Kommandant had arrived before him, and Eidenmüller could easily guess what he was saying. He could not have been more wrong.

'The planes,' Bär was saying, 'are American, apparently from bases in

Italy. Now that we're within their range, we can expect more than reconnaissance flights in future. What arrangements are in place for air-raid protection?'

Meissner stumped across to a filing cabinet and extracted a thick file. 'The shelters for all the camps are listed and designated on maps in here, sir,' he said, passing it across. 'We have given priority to the Buna *Werke*, with concrete blast walls and underground shelters sufficient for the civilian and SS personnel.'

'But not the prisoners?'

'No, sir. In accordance with policy, they are considered expendable. With more shipments arriving daily, it is a simple matter to replace any casualties.'

'Good. And what about your Watchmaker?'

'*My* Watchmaker, sir?' Meissner watched the Kommandant's face carefully for what it might reveal, but his expression was stony. 'Naturally, there is no special provision for him. In the event of an air raid he will have to take his chances, same as all the other prisoners.'

'Good.' The Kommandant stood and put on his cap. When he reached the door he said, 'It would be ironic, would it not, if the Watchmaker became a casualty of what he might consider "friendly" fire?'

As soon as the Kommandant had left, Eidenmüller entered. Meissner was peering at a large map of the Buna complex pinned to one of the walls. He barely looked up.

'Sir. Something important you should know.'

'It'll have to wait. I have to make an inspection of the air-raid-protection installations in Buna. If it's urgent, get Untersturmführer Schneider to deal with it.'

'I can't, sir. It's about the Watchmaker.'

*

Hustek had wasted no time getting on with his plan, and he was pleased with the progress he had made. What he had told the Kommandant about the need to hunt for anti-Hitler renegades within the camp was nonsense, of course – if they had been included in the conspirators' calculations at all, the camps were no more than an embarrassment to them. What Hustek wanted was time to find ways to put pressure on the Watchmaker. And he thought he had found the perfect way.

Employing the simplest of police investigative procedures, he went to the archive of prisoner records. All slave-labourers in the camp were registered; when they died, that was also recorded and cross-referenced to the original entry. It would be easy for Hustek to discover the Watch-maker's real name, the date he had entered the camp and where he had come from. Then all he had to do was to look for another prisoner with the same surname who had arrived on the same transport. They were almost certain to be related.

Unterscharführer Hoven had good reason to be wary of Hustek. A year earlier, he had been among those assigned to work in Kanada, where he had fallen under suspicion of misappropriating items of jewellery. He had been interrogated by Hustek. While it was out of the question that violence would be used against a fellow SS officer, still, the Gestapo man had frightened him. Hoven had indeed been purloining choice items for months, but he kept his mouth shut, and in the end nothing was proven. On Hustek's recommendation, however, he had been demoted and trans-ferred away from the source of temptation. Since then, he had nursed a grudge against the Gestapo in general and Hustek in particular, though he had been able to do nothing about it – yet.

When Hustek walked through his door, Hoven was so startled that it had registered immediately in Hustek's finely tuned index of suspicion. Did Hoven have something to hide – again? It was possible – probable, even. Hustek made a mental note to follow it up.

'I'm looking for information about the Watchmaker,' Hustek said.

'The Watchmaker?'

'Don't pretend you don't know who I'm talking about.'

'No. Of course not.' Hoven licked his lips. 'Everyone in Monowitz knows the Watchmaker. What did you want to know?'

'Just get me his record and then forget I was ever here.'

'What are you going on about?' Meissner demanded irritably.

'It's Hustek, sir. Unterscharführer Hoven in the records section told me. Hustek has been nosing around for information about the Watchmaker.'

'I don't see what's so shocking about that. Hustek's Gestapo. It's exactly what I'd expect him to do.'

'Yes, sir. I mean, it's more than that. Hustek wanted to know what his name was, where he came from, what transport he arrived on – everything. It's not the Watchmaker he's interested in, it's who came to the camp with him.'

Realization dawned. 'His wife.'

'Exactly, sir. And I wouldn't give much for her chances if Hustek finds her.'

'No,' Meissner reasoned, 'that's not what he's up to. If he finds her, he'll use her to make the Watchmaker throw the game.' Angrily, the officer slammed his hand against the wall. 'So obvious! Why didn't I think of that?' He gave his orderly an appraising look. 'And what about your friend, Hoven – did he give Hustek the information he wanted?'

Eidenmüller had never seen his boss so agitated. 'No, sir. Not yet. He said it would take a few hours to retrieve it from the archive. Hustek said he would go back tomorrow.'

'Do you know where she is?'

'That's where we might be able to pull a flanker, sir. Hustek didn't ask Hoven anything about the wife – must have his own way of finding out where she is. But Hoven has the records of all the prisoners assigned to the satellite camps – which come under your jurisdiction, sir.'

'And?'

'We found her. She's in the munitions factory at Rajsko. If we move quickly, we can get to her before Hustek.'

Rosa Clément is not in the munitions factory. She is in the *Krankenbau* in the women's camp in Birkenau. She has the *durchfall* – starvation-induced diarrhoea – and she is not fit for work. She will have rest and extra rations for two weeks in the hope that she will become fit for work again; if not, she will be selected for the gas chamber. Her fate is uncertain at best. Even if the *durchfall* resolves, the killing factories might be short of their daily quota and she will be selected anyway.

Rosa does not want to die, but she no longer fears it. She has seen too much death in the camp to be afraid any longer. Her overwhelming feeling is not of fear, but of weariness. When she first arrived she was employed in the *Krankenbau*, but after a few months somebody decided there were too many nurses and not enough munitions workers, so now she is assigned to a *Kommando* that is taken every day to a poorly ventilated factory where she and perhaps a thousand other women make shells for the artillery. It is summer and the heat inside is stifling. The air is dry and thick with dust from the gun-cotton, which gives all the women hacking coughs. Rosa is better off than many. Handling gun-cotton is not her job. She inserts fuzes into the ends of the shells. At first, whenever she twisted a fuze into its mounting she would say a prayer that it would fail to go off. It was as far as she was able to take any attempts at sabotage. Now she is indifferent: her actions are purely mechanical; she saves her prayers for herself.

In the K-B Rosa knows she has a much better chance of recovering if she is able to wash her hands after she uses the slop bucket, but although the doctors and nurses have asked repeatedly for a supply of water, there is none for washing. If she wants that, she must struggle all the way to the latrine. Even then it is not certain there will be any water. It is easier for the camp authorities to assign new arrivals to work than it is to connect a supply of clean water.

There is a commotion at the entrance to the K-B. An SS officer has arrived and is demanding a roll call. Everybody – doctors, nurses and patients – must show their tattoo with their camp registration number. It takes time to check off every prisoner.

When Rosa holds out her arm to reveal her number, the SS man smiles triumphantly.

'You,' he says, 'will come with me.'

32.

THE PHILIDOR POSITION

1962

Kerk de Krijtberg, Amsterdam

During the night Meissner's condition deteriorated. He endured a fever without complaining, but as soon as Mrs Brinckvoort saw him the next morning she summoned the doctor.

'How is he?' Willi asked the doctor when he came downstairs.

'Not good. It's like I said – he will have good days and bad days, but gradually he will have more bad days than good days until all he has left to him are bad days. All I can do is to make him as comfortable as possible. His main problem at the moment is pain in his bones and also in his abdomen, where his spleen has swollen. You will need to change his sheets – they are wet with perspiration. I will leave something for the pain, but it is only a matter of time before we have to take him into hospital.'

'Can we see him?' Emil asked.

'You can go up, but only for a few minutes. He's very tired.' He looked at the housekeeper. 'Mrs Brinckvoort, I expect you to make sure that the bishop follows instructions this time. If he insists on going out in his condition, I cannot answer for the consequences.'

They went up, but Meissner was sleeping. Back in the kitchen Emil pulled on his coat, for the walk to the Krasnapolsky.

'I'll come with you,' Willi said.

'No. It's all right. I'm not intending to play. I'm going to ask for a post-ponement.'

'What if they won't agree to it?'

'I don't know. I haven't decided.'

Willi reached into the closet for his own coat. 'Then I'm definitely coming with you.'

By the afternoon, Meissner was sitting up in bed drinking sweet milky tea and gently scolding Mrs Brinckvoort for fussing over him. It was well into the evening before Emil and Willi returned.

Standing beside the bed Emil seemed subdued, but Willi was jubilant.

'I take it,' Meissner said between coughs, 'that you beat the Englishman?'

'Beat him?' Willi smiled broadly. 'Paul, you should have seen it. The Englishman is good – very good, as you saw for yourself, but Emil? Pah. Let me tell you, I have never seen such nuanced play. The way he forced the Englishman to concede was magnificent. This is Emil's tournament, and, if he wants it, the world championship is his for the taking.'

Meissner turned to Emil. 'A man who has done so well should look more pleased with himself, no?'

'I am pleased, of course I am. But somehow it seems less important to me now.'

Mrs Brinckvoort put her head around the door. 'There's a fish pie and potatoes in the oven, if you haven't eaten,' she said.

'Thank you,' Willi replied. 'We haven't. We came straight here.'

'I'll come down,' Meissner said, hopefully.

One look from Mrs Brinckvoort was enough to tell them she would not permit it.

'The doctor said you must rest,' Emil said.

'The doctor is a lunatic. He knows I don't have much time left but instead of letting me make the most of it, he wants me to sleep or dribble the rest of my days away. Well, I won't have it.'

'I can bring food up on a tray,' the housekeeper offered.

'Good. And please, stop acting as if you have to protect me from knowing the worst. I know it already. I've known it for months. The only question is when. I've received absolution, and I'm ready to meet my maker so let's stop pretending, and talk about what's important.'

'Which is?' Emil asked.

Meissner looked him straight in the eye. 'Your wife.'

August 1944
Konzentrationslager Auschwitz-I

Rosa Clément is in a solitary confinement cell in the prison block. She has been there for days with no idea of why she was taken there. Ordered to follow the SS man from the K-B, she was made to climb onto the back of an open-topped lorry and driven away from the stark chimneys and the death stench of Birkenau to another camp, where the blocks are tall and made of brick and the prisoners do not have quite the same look of starved hopelessness.

Nobody speaks to her. Three times a day her cell door opens and the normal rations given to the *Häftlinge* are pushed in: for breakfast, the bitter liquid that passes for coffee, coarse black bread and a smear of margarine; and noon and evening, a bowl of soup made from cabbage and potato peelings. In the morning she carries her slop bucket to a latrine and pours its contents in. At least she is not made to work. After a few days the *durchfall* stops, but she is no closer to knowing why she is there.

'She's disappeared,' Eidenmüller said, mystified. 'According to my pal,

Connie Lammers, she was taken from the K-B in the women's camp by an unknown SS officer. It has to be Hustek. But where she is now, he has no idea.'

'She's in the prison block in the *Stammlager*,' Meissner said, 'She has to be.'

'You can't just take someone and put them in there, sir,' Eidenmüller objected. 'There are procedures that have to be followed – grounds for detention, records that have to be completed. Even Hustek couldn't get away without sticking to at least some of the rules.'

'You want to bet? The Watchmaker is a Jew. That means his wife is, too. They have no rights. So what if Hustek has broken the rules? Who's going to discipline him over it? Bär? I think not. But that gives us an advantage. Hustek thinks he's safe. He has no idea that we know what he's done, and in war, as he's about to find out, intelligence is the key to victory. We'll have her out of there in no time.'

'We?'

Meissner was smiling. The adrenaline of battle was already coursing through his veins. 'Yes, Ernst, *we*.' Eidenmüller looked at him askance; the Hauptsturmführer had never called him by his first name before. 'Look,' Meissner continued, 'we have to face facts. The war is lost. Anyone with half a brain knows it. And what do you think the Allies will do when they discover what we've done at Auschwitz? Pin a medal on us? We all of us need to think about what's going to happen to us after the war. We are going to need friends. Friends who will be prepared to testify that we weren't the ones herding helpless Jews into the gas chambers. Friends who will testify that, on the contrary, we tried to help them. If we rescue his wife from Hustek's clutches, don't you think the Watchmaker might be grateful?'

Eidenmüller shook his head. 'But Hustek? He's Gestapo. It doesn't do to cross those bastards. What if we get caught?'

'I'll take full responsibility. You were only following orders. But it won't come to that. Brossman despises Hustek too, and he's promised to help. Between us we can do it. Trust me.'

Night watch in the prison block is easy duty. A Scharführer is in overall command, plus two troopers on each floor, making a total of seven. Nothing ever happens at night. Apart from whimpers and occasional howls, there is not a sound to disturb the balmy August air. The SS men take it in turns to sleep – strictly against standing orders – but this is Auschwitz, and all its enemies are contained within its electrified fences. There is simply nothing to fear.

Hauptsturmführer Brossman's night inspection is a complete surprise. He arrives with a squad of ten troopers and angrily demands an explanation for why the Scharführer is asleep on duty, along with three of his men. Brushing aside the Scharführer's protestations, he insists on conducting an impromptu inspection.

The Scharführer protests. 'I'll have to get permission first.'

Brossman feigns outrage. 'Permission? From whom?'

The officer nominally in charge of the prison block is a Gestapo Obersturmführer, but everybody knows it is Oberscharführer Hustek who calls the shots.

'Oberscharführer Hustek, sir.'

'If I have anything to do with it,' Brossman growls, 'you've just signed your request for a transfer to the Eastern front.'

Despite the subdued light, the Scharführer pales visibly. To hell with Hustek. 'At y-your service, H-Herr Hauptsturmführer,' he stammers.

'What can I do to assist you?'

Brossman actually smiles. 'That's better. Now, it has come to my attention that a prisoner is missing from the women's camp. The Rapportführer concerned has been somewhat dilatory in bringing it to my notice and has been disciplined. According to him, the prisoner was brought here, but I cannot ignore the possibility that she has escaped. As I'm sure you're aware, the Kommandant takes a very dim view of escapes, and it's my responsibility to prevent them. So I want to see the paperwork for every prisoner detained here, while my men inspect the cells.'

'I assure you, sir,' the Scharführer says solemnly, 'at this moment, there are no women in the cells.'

'I hope you're right, Scharführer, for your sake.'

It takes only minutes to go through the detention records. The Scharführer has spoken the truth. There is no record of any female prisoner.

'Thank you, Scharführer,' Brossman says. 'It looks like we've been sent on a fool's errand.' Then a shout comes up from the lower level.

'There's a door down here, sir, but nobody seems to have the key.'

'A door with no key?' Brossman looks at the Scharführer, who shrugs. 'That doesn't seem right. Let's take a look, shall we?'

The door is solid wood and is set flush into a metal frame. There is a peephole near the top, and hinges and a lock made of what looks like cast iron.

'Who's in there?' Brossman asks.

'According to the records, nobody, sir.'

'Then why is it locked? Unlock it at once.'

'I don't have the key, sir.'

'Who does?'

'Oberscharführer Hustek.'

Brossman nods, as if the answer to an elusive mystery has been revealed.

At the end of the lane that leads to the prison block, Meissner and Eiden-müller are waiting in an SS staff car. Eidenmüller is on edge, but Meissner is feeling better than he has for months.

'If we get caught, sir, we'll both be for the high jump, I know it,' Eiden-müller says, through clenched teeth.

'Relax. What's the worst that can happen?'

'We could be sent to the Eastern front.'

'Don't worry about it. I've been there. It's better than here, I promise you. Someone with your talents would be a godsend. You would be in your element.'

Eidenmüller cannot believe what he is hearing. 'In my element? Getting shot to fuck by the fucking Bolshies? Not on your life – sir.'

'Get down,' Meissner hisses. The two men sink low in the car as one of Brossman's troopers jogs by.

'Where's he going?' Eidenmüller whispers.

Meissner does not answer. Moments later, the trooper runs back carrying a sledgehammer.

Inside her cell, Rosa Clément is listening to the commotion in the corridor with mounting apprehension. Suddenly somebody hammers on her cell door. 'Who's in there?' a voice yells. 'Answer me.'

Rosa does not know how to reply. She is not sure who she is any more. The light goes on. She blinks, trying to adjust to the brightness. Then she sees an eye at the peephole.

'Take a look for yourself,' Brossman says to the Scharführer, who is beginning to realize how much trouble Hustek has landed him in.

'According to your records, there is nobody in the cell, but quite clearly there's a woman in there. Even the Gestapo cannot imprison people without due process. I can only conclude that Oberscharführer Hustek has abused his authority with regard to this prisoner for his own personal reasons.'

'There'll be hell to pay over this.'

'How right you are,' Brossman agrees. He turns his attention to the door again. 'You, in there – what is your name?'

They can barely hear the reply. 'Rosa Clément.'

'How long have you been in there?'

'I'm not sure. A week, perhaps longer.'

It takes the trooper only a few minutes to return with a sledgehammer. The lock is smashed off and the door opened. The woman seems confused that her rescuers are SS men. 'Be silent,' Brossman orders. 'Follow me.'

He leads her to the waiting car. 'You took your time,' Meissner says.

'A slight problem with the door.'

'How long will it take to get to Mauthausen?'

'Ten or eleven hours, I would guess. But take your time.' Brossman looks back towards the prison block. 'I'll keep these beauties out of harm's way until you return.'

They headed south and east, towards Austria. In the back of the car, Rosa struggled to understand what was happening. Everything seemed unreal, as if she were in a dream. Her senses were heightened: voices too loud, lights bright, colours vivid. The glass of the window against which she rested her face seemed strangely cool and yielding. She tried to focus on the blur of shadows that streamed past but everything was moving too quickly. Until a week ago, her life in the camp had been brutal but mostly predictable; then the SS had put her in a cell and now other SS men had taken her out. It made no sense. Questions raced through her mind: was she to be freed? Or, more likely, was she simply a puppet in some game the Germans were playing? She wondered where she would be by morning, whether she would still be alive.

It was some time before she asked, 'Where are you taking me?'

The SS man in the passenger seat did not turn around when he answered: 'We are going to the K-Z at Mauthausen, in Austria. It's a work camp. You will be safer there.'

'Safer? How?'

'There are no gas chambers in Mauthausen.'

'Why are you doing this?'

'I can't tell you. It is better that you do not know.'

The answer made Rosa feel a little calmer. Wherever she was going, it could not conceivably be worse than the horror that was Birkenau.

The SS man offered her coffee from a thermos and a hunk of bread. This small act astonished her; tears rose to her eyes. Saying nothing, she blinked them back and reached hungrily for the bread.

It was the second miracle of the night, as unexpected as the first: real bread, soft and white, aromatic; not the hard, sawdust-filled pig-food that she had become used to. She held it, hardly daring to believe what she possessed. It was like treasure – if only there were somewhere safe she could hide it... but she was too hungry for that. Still she hesitated. It was such a simple, everyday thing, yet so utterly out of reach; if she put it in her mouth it would be gone... Then she was chewing ravenously, her heart beating quickly and her breathing heavy, as if she were with a lover. The bread was soft, moist and delicious; she wanted it to stay in her mouth for ever. As long as she had bread in her mouth she would never be hungry again. And the taste…she had never tasted anything so good. It tasted of breakfast in her favourite café on the corner of the Rue de Maine, of a rich dark sauce mopped up from a plate, of the sharpness of mustard spread thick on roast beef; it tasted of before the war, of summer evenings when she would promenade with friends along the Tuileries, of the heady scents from the perfumerie on the corner of the Rue Danton, of coffee in Montmartre, of champagne in Le Chat Noir.

It tasted of freedom.

'More bread?' Meissner asked.

She stared suspiciously as he passed the loaf, stiffening herself like a cat ready to pounce in case he was playing with her, teasing only to snatch it back.

Now it tasted of the south, of a bright spring day strolling along a river path with Emil and Louis and Marcel, the boys yelling with delight as they threw bits of stale bread to the ducks.

The spell was broken. The bread congealed in her mouth to a claggy dough, which she had no saliva to soften. A wave of nausea threatened to overwhelm her, and she had to spit the bread out into her hands, coughing and spluttering. She had come back to the real world, to this car with its booming engine and two SS men headed for God alone knew where.

Dawn found them on the outskirts of Brno. 'We take the road south,' Meissner said, consulting a map on his knee.

Eidenmüller, at the wheel, disagreed. 'Don't you think we'd be better sticking to the main roads, sir? Less likely to be stopped.'

'You think so?' Meissner examined the map again. 'Possibly, but it would take us too far out of our way.'

'If we get caught with her, we've had it.'

'What are you saying? That we should ditch her and run?'

'No, sir. That's not what I'm saying. What I'm saying is...'

Rosa lifted her head. 'I need to pee,' she said.

They pulled off the road into a copse of trees.

Rosa got out of the car, making for the trees. Meissner followed. 'I'm sorry,' he said, 'but I must insist on going with you. I cannot take the risk that you might run away. Please do not try. It would give me no pleasure to shoot you.'

Rosa squatted behind a bush. To pass water is such a basic human act, but this was the first time since her arrest that she had been able to do it in a place that was not surrounded by barbed wire. It gave her a strange feeling of liberty, as if she could simply get up and walk away from this place and never stop until she reached the ends of the earth.

It was almost exhilarating, but it was short-lived.

'What's she doing in there?' she heard Eidenmüller muttering.

The men relieved themselves, then Meissner took over at the wheel, determined that they would follow the southern route.

From the back seat Rosa looked out on the countryside, mesmerized. The road was lined with trees in full leaf, swaying gently in the morning light; hedgerows brimmed with flowers; and fields were heavy with produce, nearly ready for harvest. She tried to think back to the last time she had been able to look upon such a landscape – was it really only a year ago?

She dozed on the back seat and woke only when they stopped to fill the petrol tank from the jerry cans strapped to the side of the car. 'Where are we now?' she asked.

They had been passing through hamlets with German place-names for some time. 'In Austria, heading for Linz.' Eidenmüller took the wheel again. Towns passed by: Hagenberg, Pregarten, Altenhaus.

Meissner was staring out over the countryside, trying to keep his eyes open, when Eidenmüller gave an almost inaudible groan: 'Oh, shit.'

Ahead was a patrol of soldiers, one of them waving a hand for them to stop.

'Get down, right down into the foot well,' Meissner ordered Rosa. Hurriedly, he pulled a blanket over her.

As they drew closer they could see it was a squad of four Feldgend-armerie, led by an Obergefreiter. 'Relax,' Meissner told Eidenmüller, 'even you outrank him. Besides, we're SS. He has no jurisdiction over us.'

'Thank Christ for small miracles,' Eidenmüller muttered, pulling the car to a halt.

Meissner rolled the window down. 'Yes?' he snapped.

The Obergefreiter jerked to attention and saluted. He was barely out of his teens.

Meissner raised his right hand, palm outwards. '*Heil Hitler*. Now what is it? I haven't got all day.'

'Beg pardon, Herr Hauptsturmführer, we are looking for some desert-ers. Somebody reported seeing them in this area.'

'Army deserters?'

'Yes, Herr Hauptsturmführer.'

'Then you're wasting your time with us, aren't you?'

The Feldgendarmerie NCO swallowed. 'Beg pardon, Herr Hauptsturm-führer, but I must ask to see your papers.'

The NCO was rewarded with a look of disdain. 'Eidenmüller, show him your papers.' Meissner made no attempt to retrieve his own. Instead, he reached for a cigarette and popped it between his lips. He gave the

NCO the full force of a glare from his ice-blue eyes. 'Well? What are you waiting for? Don't you have any matches?'

'Of course, Herr Hauptsturmführer. At once.' A match flared. Meissner reached out to steady the NCO's hand as he puffed to light the cigarette.

Eidenmüller passed his identity card over. The NCO perused it nervously. For long moments it seemed they were cocooned in a bubble of silence, but the slow ticking of the car's engine penetrated, louder and louder until, to Eidenmüller, it seemed as deafening as a steam-hammer. From the hedges along the road, the cheerful chirping of sparrows seemed unreal and out of place.

Meissner recognized the electricity that fills the air before battle, yet he drew steadily on his cigarette, with an air of irritation at the unnecessary and intolerable delay.

'Auschwitz?' the NCO eventually said. 'You're a long way from home. What are you doing here?'

Meissner reacted angrily. 'That is none of your business and I have had enough of this nonsense.' He flicked the cigarette at the NCO's feet and turned to Eidenmüller. 'Take this man's name and unit number.'

Eidenmüller was sweating. His head was pounding. He fumbled in his tunic pocket, but the Feldgendarmerie NCO knew when he was beaten. 'No need for that, Herr Hauptsturmführer.' He handed back Eidenmüller's papers. 'You're clear to proceed. I'm sorry we detained you.'

Meissner did not even glance at the NCO as he pointed a finger at the road ahead. Eidenmüller put the car into gear, gunning the engine to put as much distance between them as he could.

Meissner placed a hand on his orderly's forearm. 'Not too fast, Ernst,' he said, 'or they'll suspect they've been had.'

'Beggin' your pardon, sir, but you're mad.'

'Why do you say that?'

'All you had to do was show them your papers.'

'No. That was too great a risk. Nobody must know we were here.'

'But it was OK for them to see *my* papers?'

'In an hour they'll have forgotten your name, but an SS-Hauptsturm-führer? That's something they would remember and would be bound to report.'

'And they won't report what happened anyway?'

A gleeful smile appeared on Meissner's face. 'Not likely. They would have to report that they let me go without seeing my papers. They'd probably end up on the Eastern front.'

They had been told to look for a hamlet called Grünau. There, they would be met by an SS officer, a friend of Brossman's from his days in Lublin. They concealed the car in a small wood and waited.

At the appointed hour, they saw a *Kübelwagen* slowly making its way towards them. Meissner stepped out from behind the trees and waved it down. When the car stopped he called out, 'Otto Brossman sends regards from Lublin.'

The voice that came back was high-pitched and anxious. 'Brossman? I think I may know him. Where did he do his training?'

'Bad Tölz.'

'When was he there?'

'1940.'

A harsh grinding sound came from the *Kübelwagen* as the driver botched putting it into gear again, then the car crept forward until it was almost touching theirs.

The driver got out: an SS-Obersturmführer wearing thick-lensed glasses, which he took off and started to polish nervously. 'Quickly,' he hissed. 'There's not much time.' He used the glasses to point at what looked like a heap of ragged clothing lying on the back seat. 'I have to get back before this one is missed.'

Eidenmüller bent to pull out the rags and grunted. They were heavier than he expected. His hands met resistance, cold and clammy. 'Shit.' He let go instantly and stood upright. 'What is this?'

'A body of course – one in, one out. That's the only way it can work.'

Eidenmüller looked aghast at the corpse. 'Is it a woman?'

'Of course it's a fucking woman. What did you expect, a monkey?'

'What happened to her?'

'Died of a fever.'

'Christ. Was it anything contagious?'

Meissner brought Rosa Clément over. 'How will you get her in?'

'Easy. She'll be passed off as this one.' He jerked his head at the body that Eidenmüller was pulling out of the *Kübelwagen*. 'Nobody knows she's dead yet. I'll have the new one allocated to a work *Kommando* in a different part of the camp. The prisoner count will tally and nobody will be any the wiser.' The Obersturmführer peered short-sightedly at Rosa. 'She's about the same size. We'll need to get their clothes switched.'

With a rapid gesture Meissner indicated to Eidenmüller that he should remove the clothes from the cadaver. With obvious distaste he set to his task, rolling it onto its back to unfasten the jacket buttons. The corpse's eyes were open and they stared at him accusingly. 'Holy Mother of God…' He jumped back, almost toppling over in his desire to get away from the body. Instinctively, he crossed himself. 'Sorry, sir, I can't do this. I really…'

Rosa was there, a hand on his arm. She crouched down beside the woman's body. Its limbs were stiff and the skin had a waxy quality, making

300

it difficult to get the clothes off. Finally it was naked; she looked vulnerable and pitiable, like a lost child. A tear slid from Rosa's eye and fell on the woman's face, a connection between their two existences that crossed the barrier that death had put between them. Under her breath, Rosa said a quick prayer, the first in months: 'Eternal rest give unto her, O Lord, and let perpetual light shine upon her...'

'Well?' the Obersturmführer demanded, looking at his watch.

It was Rosa's turn. In her months at Auschwitz she had suffered the humiliation of being forced to undress many times, not least during the frequent *Selektionen*. She had been stripped of her dignity along with her clothes to the unpleasant remarks of leering SS guards who openly ogled the women lined up for their inspection like vegetables on a market stall: 'Nice tits for a Jew...too hairy...too bony...' She had learned to make her mind go elsewhere so that she was not the one they were staring at, slavering over. But now, being told to undress by these men, this was different. These were her rescuers – had they restored her dignity, or was it only a loan that they could call in whenever they wanted?

'Come on, you stupid Jewish bitch.' The Obersturmführer was polishing his glasses again. The anger in his voice was palpable – or was it anxiety? 'Get your fucking clothes off and get hers on so I can be on my way.'

Rosa's hand moved to the top button of her jacket. 'Turn around,' she said, not knowing where the courage to say these two small words came from.

When Rosa was hidden in the foot well of the *Kübelwagen*, Meissner held out a hand to the other officer. 'Thank you. I know you're taking quite a risk over this.'

'I only hope it's worth it.'

'It will be. After the war you can say you were one of the few SS who saved the life of a Jew.'

'What now?' Eidenmüller said, once the *Kübelwagen* had departed.

'Back to Auschwitz, where our friend Brossman will have filed a report that, after freeing the unknown prisoner in the prison block, she was tragically shot trying to escape. And, lucky for us, we'll have a body and the paperwork to prove it. Unfortunately, an administrative error will send the body to the crematorium before Hustek has the chance to see it. Shame, eh?'

'What'll happen to her?'

'The Watchmaker's wife? She'll have to make do as best she can, same as all the other prisoners. But at least we've given her a fighting chance.'

1962
Kerk de Krijtberg, Amsterdam

It had taken Meissner some time to get his story told, between frequent bouts of coughing.

Emil sat transfixed, his supper untouched. 'So that's how she got to Mauthausen,' he said finally.

'You didn't know?' Willi asked.

'I never told him,' Meissner said. 'If Hustek had found out, it would have been the end of her and everyone involved.'

'I assumed that she had left Auschwitz with everyone else in January '45. Quite a few prisoners ended up in Mauthausen,' Emil said. 'When I found her in the autumn, she was ill and confused. When she told me that an SS officer had broken into the prison at Auschwitz in the middle of the night and taken her away, I thought she was delirious.'

'I have always wondered,' Meissner said, 'whether she survived. I'm glad she did, God be praised.'

Emil could not hold back the wave of bitterness that broke over him. 'Why would you praise your god for such a thing?' he spat. 'I cursed his name for what he did to her.'

'But I thought you and she were—?'

Emil stood, shaking his head, not bothering to wipe away the tears that had started down his cheeks. 'Oh, yes, we were reunited. For six days. Then she was taken from me a second time.'

Willi reached out to grasp Emil's wrist but Emil pulled his hand away.

'I'm so sorry,' Willi said. 'Truly. How—?'

Emil slumped back into his chair, the anger leaving him as quickly as it had come. 'Scarlet fever. She was too weak, you see, and by then she had lost the will to go on.'

'Dear God, dear God,' Meissner whispered, beating his chest. '*Mea culpa, mea culpa, mea maxima culpa.*'

33.

KING'S INDIAN ATTACK

The next morning Emil woke early. He wasn't sure what time it was but daylight was filtering around the edges of the curtains. He had not slept well. His night had been spent wrestling with memories. He had wanted to recall the good times he'd had with Rosa, but his mind had refused to cooperate. Instead, it had taken him to the miraculous day he had found her name on a Red Cross list, then to all the bureaucrats in their petty fiefdoms whom he had had to fight in order to get to her; then how he had found her, in bed number 117 in the makeshift hospital in Sankt Georgen an der Gusen: such a pretty name to disguise the enormity of what had happened there.* He remembered holding her hand, white and bloodless, so frail, like an old woman's. At first she hadn't recognized him; later, she could not trust herself to believe that he had also found a way to survive and that now he had found her. He had told her that he would never leave her side again. A smile had flickered across her face only to be replaced by pain. 'Forgive me,' she had said.

He remembered his last words to her. 'Louis and Marcel,' she had asked, her eyes wide but not seeing, her fingers suddenly locking his

* Sankt Georgen an der Gusen was very close to the Mauthusen concentration camp.

304

hand in hers. 'How are they?' He hadn't been able to bear telling her the truth. 'They're fine,' he had whispered. 'You'll see them soon, very soon.'

Another lie that had emanated from the kingdom of lies. Its intentions were good, but it was still a lie. He had vowed then that there would be no more lies in his life.

Emil got up. Quietly he looked into Paul's room, but he was in a deep sleep. He decided to go down to the kitchen, put on some coffee and have the first cigarette of the day on the bench overlooking the canal.

Willi was already at the kitchen table, smoking and staring vacantly ahead, a half-empty cup in front of him. He looked as if he hadn't slept, either.

'Is everything all right, Willi?'

'No. In fact, nothing is right at the moment.' He spoke in a dull monotone.

'What are you talking about?'

'It finally hit me last night.' Willi raised his head to look directly at Emil. 'What you and Paul have been talking about. It's all real, isn't it? It's not a story. It's not ancient history. It happened, and you and Paul were in the thick of it. And now I find myself caught in it too, and I realize how horrific it was, how cold and calculating and evil it was, and that it was done by Germans and that the victims were innocent women and children, and I don't know what to think about it and I don't know if I can deal with it.'

Emil sighed. 'What you are feeling is the legacy of Auschwitz. It is a burden that Paul and I must carry for the rest of our lives, and now I think that it has fallen upon your shoulders too. There is nothing you can do but bear it as best you can.'

Willi did not seem convinced. He ground out the stub of his cigarette in an ashtray and immediately took another from the packet. His hands shook as he lit it. 'The thing is,' he said, 'when you were playing chess against the SS it was not like other games, with only an intellectual duel at stake – they were the most real and vital games that have ever been played. Only a few years ago there was a game so extraordinary it was dubbed the game of the century. You must know it – the American master, Byrne, against the young prodigy, Fischer. It was a masterpiece of sacrificial play. Breathtaking. But it is insignificant beside your games in Auschwitz, and yet the world will never know of them.' He turned to look squarely at Emil. 'And if Paul had not almost knocked down my hotel room door, I would not have learned of them either, nor would I have come to know you, and so I would have continued to convince myself that what you had to say about Auschwitz was the product of the embittered imaginings of a man who feels guilty because he survived.'

Emil pulled out a chair and lit a cigarette for himself. 'Surely enough evidence about the death camps has emerged since the war to convince you they were more than imaginings, Willi?'

Willi stared at his hands, avoiding Emil's gaze. 'During the war I worked in the propaganda ministry. One heard things. We all knew that something was happening. We knew that the Jews of Germany had been sent east – but then they disappeared. Where could they have gone? Tens of thousands of people don't just disappear into thin air. We were told they were sent to work camps. Then stories about the camps began to circulate. They were not told openly, you understand – that was not possible, the Gestapo had ears everywhere. But behind closed doors, between people who trusted one other, things were said.' He drew deeply on his cigarette and let the butt fall from his fingers into the dregs of his coffee. 'It's not possible to keep such a secret. Men come home on leave and tell their

families, and word gets out. I knew what was happening; everybody did.'
Absently, he reached for the cigarette pack again only to find it empty. He
crushed it in his hand and dropped it onto the table top. 'I told myself it
could not be true,' he continued, 'it was too wicked, too incredible. Conditions in the work camps were harsh, but that was to be expected – we
were at war with the Bolsheviks, a war to the death. Casualties could not
be avoided. War is cruel... but death camps? It was not only unbelievable,
it did not make sense – so much better to put the Jews to work than to
kill them. Why kill them? There was no profit in it for the Reich. So I told
myself the stories were not true. Could not be true.'

'And now?'

Willi bowed his head. Silent tears streamed down his face. When he
spoke, his voice was tremulous. 'Now I am ashamed. Ashamed of myself,
ashamed of my country. For the rest of my life, I must live with the knowledge that we are a nation of murderers.'

Willi's hands were still shaking. Emil felt a swell of pity for him. 'You're
right, Willi. And it's painful to realize and difficult to bear.'

'You said that no German who lived through the war could claim to
be innocent of the death camps... that there were no good Germans.'

Slowly, Emil shook his head. 'Yes, I did say that, didn't I?' He stood
and picked up the kettle, walking to the sink to fill it. 'You're not the only
one who is learning how wrong he can be.'

September 1944
Political Section, Konzentrationslager Auschwitz-I
The Buna *Werke* has been bombed. The bombers came in daylight, but
instead of running for shelter as fast as their legs would take them, many
of the prisoners waved their caps and cheered. The effect on prisoner

morale is extraordinary: now they talk endlessly about how the Allies will bomb the gas chambers and crematoria in Birkenau.

The Gestapo is convinced that the factory has become a target because Polish partisans have managed to get information to the Allies. Oberscharführer Hustek has been ordered to find the prisoners who are communicating with the partisans, and it has presented him with an opportunity. In the technical workshop where the Watchmaker works, he has daily contact with Polish workers; that makes him a suspect.

Two of Hustek's men have been sent to bring him for questioning.

Hauptsturmführer Meissner is in the Kommandant's office. For twenty minutes he has been on the receiving end of a barrage of questions about the midnight 'inspection' of the prison block. Sturmbannführer Bär is not convinced by Meissner's insistence that he had nothing to do with it.

'Sir. I wasn't there. I wasn't even in the camp at the time.'

'Where the hell were you then?'

'I told you, sir. I had a couple of days' leave. You authorized it. I went to Kraków.'

'Then why can't you say where you went in Kraków, or who you saw? In fact, anything at all about your leave in Kraków?'

'Because, sir, as I've already explained, I took a wrong turning and then my car broke down. I spent the night in the forest. The next day it took me hours to walk to where I could find a telephone and call for help.'

'Hours? You could have walked to Kraków in a day if you had to.'

Meissner holds up his walking stick.

'Don't get clever with me, Meissner.' His superior's voice is sharp. 'How did you manage to find out the woman was in the prison block?'

Meissner shakes his head wearily. 'I knew nothing about it until after I got back. From what I have been told, Hauptsturmführer Brossman

308

decided to check the block on the off-chance she might be there. That he found her was pure luck.'

The Kommandant scowled. 'Brossman, yes. I don't know how you managed to involve him in your scheme, but I'll find out.'

'Sir, I'm sure you'll find Hauptsturmführer Brossman's motives were entirely genuine. The woman had gone missing. Brossman was duty-bound to search for her, and Hustek was holding her without authorization and for no legitimate reason. She wasn't even entered into the log as being there. Holding a prisoner for personal reasons flies in the face of all sorts of regulations, and it's against the law.'

'Don't be so ridiculous,' Bär snaps. 'Hustek's Gestapo. He's above the law.'

Meissner can feel his anger rising. 'But with the woman as his prisoner, he would have had a hold over the Watchmaker. Surely you can see that?'

'Does it matter, as long as he wins?'

'It matters to me, sir,' Meissner retorts. 'Hustek is a disgrace to the SS. He's not fit to wear the uniform.'

'That's not for you to say, Meissner. I'm satisfied that Oberscharführer Hustek's work makes a significant contribution to the war effort.'

Before Meissner can stop them, the words are out: 'If you think kidnapping a helpless woman makes a significant contribution to the war effort, then you're as bad as he is. Don't you understand? The war is over. Germany has lost. It is only a matter of time before the Russians are in Berlin. I've fought them, I know. There's no holding them back. Not any more.'

Bär's face pales with anger. 'You forget who you are talking to, Meissner. I *won't* have defeatist talk here. You are an officer in the SS. You should be ashamed of yourself.'

Bär's words break the thread that has been holding Meissner's temper in check. Before he knows it, he is shouting: 'I won't take that from you, sir, or from anyone else who's spent *their* war lording it over women and children, herding them from cattle trucks into gas chambers at the point of a rifle. Only someone who's seen the enemy close enough to smell them knows the truth of this war. The Waffen-SS know the truth of it, and we'll carry on fighting until our last breath; but, by God, we know the truth of it.'

When Meissner stops, he realizes the Kommandant is staring coldly at him. 'Finished? Good. Do you still want that transfer? If you can find a unit desperate enough to take you, then you can have it. Now get out.'

Meissner was shaking as he walked down the administrative building steps. Walking stick or not, going back to Monowitz on foot would help him to calm down.

He had not gone as far as the main gate when he found Eidenmüller waiting for him.

'What are you doing here?' Meissner asked, sharply.

'Sorry, sir, but you need to get back quickly.'

'Why?'

'Hustek's after the Watchmaker, sir. His men are in the camp now.'

Hustek had sent two agents to the Buna factory. Neither of them had been there before. It was vast: pipes ran everywhere in a seemingly inextricable tangle; some were suspended from overhead gantries, others ran at ground level. In the distance, the agents could see a large, square building with a row of tall, black chimneys pushing into the sky.

The bomb damage was extensive. At various points they could see men in civilian clothes carrying clip-boards, assessing the destruction; around them gangs of men in striped uniforms were clearing away rubble or removing damaged piping or machinery. Others scurried backwards and forwards, some heavily laden, still more pushing trucks along narrow-gauge rails or pulling hand-carts; others were digging. Everywhere, the furious activity was being driven by the clubs or thick, knotted ropes wielded by the *Kapos*.

'This is hopeless,' one said. 'We'll never find him here. It's chaos.'

'We should ask someone,' replied the other. 'The Rapportführer might know where he is.'

'Forget it. I know the Rapportführer here. Gessner. No point asking him. Him and Hustek don't get on.'

'Does anyone get on with Hustek?'

The first one rolled his eyes. 'Let's go to the camp. Bound to have better luck there.'

In the records office they found Unterscharführer Hoven.

'We're looking for the prisoner called the Watchmaker.'

Hoven looked up from the file on his desk that he was studying. 'Really? And who exactly is "we"?'

'Gestapo.'

The word alone was sufficient to generate a spasm of anxiety in Hoven's bowels.

'What exactly is it you want?'

The two men exchanged a knowing glance. They had the measure of Hoven. 'Just tell us where to find him.'

Hoven turned back to his file. 'Block 27,' he said, without looking up.

As soon as they were gone Hoven closed the file and left his office. Eidenmüller was in the next building along. He would want to know that the Gestapo was after the Watchmaker.

*

The two Gestapo men threw open the door to Block 27 and, unannounced, entered the day room. Two men were sprawled on wooden benches along the wall, asleep. Both had green triangles on their jackets. Without ceremony, the first Gestapo man pulled their legs up, tipping them onto the floor. With a rush of expletives the prisoners picked themselves up, rubbing gingerly at flesh that would soon bear bruises.

'Who the fucking hell are you?' one of them demanded angrily.

'Gestapo.'

Sullenly, the prisoners glared at their tormentors.

'We're looking for the Watchmaker. We were told he is in this block. Where is he?'

Neither prisoner spoke.

The Gestapo man pulled a cosh from his pocket and slammed it onto a table. 'We don't want to make life difficult for you. Just tell us where he is.'

The prisoners maintained their silence.

This time the cosh was waved beneath the chin of one of them. 'Only we haven't got too much time, see?'

'He's in the Buna *Werke*,' one of the prisoners said. 'They're all in the Buna *Werke*. They'll be back tonight.'

There were chairs around the table. The Gestapo men settled themselves down to wait. 'What have you got to eat?' one asked.

The prisoners shook their heads. 'Nothing. We had the soup ration at noon. There's nothing now until after roll call.'

'Shit,' the Gestapo man said. 'I'm fucking starving.'

Eidenmüller took the road from the *Stammlager* towards Oświęcim. Meissner was deep in thought. At length he said, 'This friend of yours, Hoven – do you trust him?'

'I don't really know him that well, sir. He doesn't like Hustek, I know that much. He's frightened of him.' Meissner went back to his thoughts. 'What are we going to do, sir? If Hustek gets hold of the Watchmaker, we'll never see him again.'

'Yes, I know that,' Meissner said irritably, 'but I don't know what we're going to do. I'm trying to think of something.'

By the time they got to Monowitz, a plan was starting to form. The problem was one of organization. There was no way a prisoner could be hidden for more than a few hours: the twice-daily roll call would imme-diately reveal he was missing. No, if Hustek wanted the Watchmaker he would find a way to get him.

Hustek had to be distracted by something bigger.

When they arrived they went straight to Hoven's office. 'Shut the door,' Meissner ordered. The Unterscharführer looked alarmed.

'What can I do for you, sir?'

'Where do you stand regarding the Watchmaker?' Meissner asked.

'The Watchmaker? I don't know what you mean, sir.'

'Hustek's men have come for him. You know what that means.'

'Yes, sir.'

'Do you want to let Hustek get him? Or do you want to stop him?'

'Yes, sir. I mean, no, I don't want that bastard to get his hands on him. But what can I do?'

'It's very simple. Forget you ever saw Hustek's men. They were never here. Understood?'

Understanding registered on the Unterscharführer's face.

'But—'

'No buts, Unterscharführer. Just stick to your story. You never saw them. If you keep to that you'll be safe. If you waver, you're a dead man.'

The opportunity to get back at Hustek beckoned. It was now or never. 'Yes, sir. I never saw anyone, sir.'

'What next, sir?' Eidenmüller asked, when they were outside again.

'Into the camp. We need to find Brack.'

Brack was near the kitchens, watching a couple of prisoners tending the vegetable plot. The harvest looked bountiful: beans, tomatoes and cucumbers – luxuries the prisoners could only dream of.

Brack pulled himself to attention when he saw Meissner.

'Don't bother,' Meissner said, 'this isn't a formal visit, and you haven't seen us. Is there anywhere we can talk privately?'

Brack smiled and pointed to a nearby block. 'In there. I'll see you in five minutes.'

Brack had sent them to the camp brothel. It was empty. Meissner explained the situation, adding, 'For all we know, Hustek's men are in your block right now.'

Brack's dream of a fortune amassed in a Swiss bank started to dissolve. His face creased into an angry frown. 'Hustek is a pig. He won't get away with this. Not if I can help it.'

'I didn't know you knew Hustek,' Eidenmüller said.

'Oh, yeah, I know him all right. I've got a score or two to settle with Hustek.'

Block 27 was on the northern perimeter of the camp, next to the wire.* It took little time for Brack to gather a few cronies, though Widmann was

---

* The Monowitz camp was divided into two sections, north and south. Between them, a service road ran east to west, bordered by a double fence of barbed wire, with the inner fence electrified for good measure, and a gate at each end. The service road did not extend all the way to the eastern perimeter, so at this point it was possible to walk between the sections.

nowhere to be found. In ones and twos they met behind the block, hidden from the guard towers.

'Right,' Brack said. 'Everybody ready?' He waited for everyone to show a weapon. 'No knives, remember. And no messing about. Straight in. Right,' he said again. He was feeling nervous. This was new territory. 'Let's get in there and do this.'

The Gestapo men were surprised when four men in prisoner garb came from the dormitory into the day room and took up positions barring the main door. More men followed. They were all carrying heavy wooden clubs.

A glance was all it took for the Gestapo men to work out what was going to happen to them. One of them, his face a mask of shocked disbelief, tried to bluster: 'If you know what's good for you, you'll leave now,' he said loudly.

'Well, that's the problem, isn't it?' Brack said menacingly, as he pushed the door closed. 'I've never known what's good for me.'

The other Gestapo man pulled out a pistol. With an angry yell Brack brought his club down on the Gestapo man's wrist. There was a momentary howl of pain before a blow to the head silenced him.

The first Gestapo man held his hands up in a gesture of supplication. 'No!' he begged. 'No, please—'

It was over quickly.

'Jesus,' one of Brack's men said, licking lips that had suddenly become parched. 'You realize what we've done, don't you?'

'Stop whining,' Brack said. 'There's no going back now. I know Hustek. He's an evil bastard. If he gets wind of this he'll have us thrown into the ovens while we're still alive.' He pointed at the bodies with his bloody club. 'These two were never here. None of us knows anything about them.' He glared at the two who had been caught in the block by the Gestapo men. 'That includes you. Unless you want to join them—?'

For an hour they worked harder than they had worked in all their time at Auschwitz. The room was scrubbed and the corpses were stripped and swung into a handcart outside.

One of Brack's men looked longingly at the pile of discarded clothing. 'Pity,' he said. 'Specially the boots – almost new.'

'Into the stove with them,' Brack ordered. 'I want no traces left.' The pistol could not be disposed of so easily. He would have to think about what to do with that.

'What about the bodies?'

'Don't worry, it's taken care of.'

Every day prisoners died in the Buna factory. They were hauled back by their fellow inmates to be counted in the roll call. Afterwards, their remains were thrown onto a lorry and taken to Birkenau for cremation. They were not counted again. Today would be no different, except that there would be two more. If anyone had bothered to look, they might have noticed two freshly cropped heads and physiques that were not skeletal. That might have aroused suspicions, and a closer examination would have revealed hands that were not calloused from hard labour, and feet that had not been rubbed raw by the wooden clogs that the inmates wore. But who would look? Two more among thousands were neither here nor there. Besides, the only people who would handle them were the Birkenau *Sonderkommando*, prisoners whose job it was to empty the gas chambers and put the carcasses into the crematoria.

They would have rejoiced to know they were putting the bodies of Gestapo men into the furnace.

*

Two days later, Meissner had a visitor.

He was announced by Eidenmüller. 'Oberscharführer Hustek to see you, sir.'

Meissner looked up from the papers that were spread across his desk. 'Take a seat, Oberscharführer,' he said. 'What can I do for you?'

'Two of my men have gone missing,' Hustek said, as he sat down. 'I was wondering whether you might know where they are.'

'Me? Why would I know where they are?'

'They were here, in Monowitz. They were here on my instructions. They were here to pick up the Watchmaker.'

Meissner leaned back and steepled his fingers. 'I still don't understand why you might think I would know where they are. I'm not in charge here: Obersturmführer Schottl is the Lagerführer. You should speak to him.'

'I already have. Nobody saw either of my men. Nobody. Don't you think that's strange? You would have thought *somebody* would have seen them.'

'I don't know.' Meissner concentrated hard on keeping his expression deadpan. 'There are always people coming and going, in and out of the camp. Someone might have seen them, but taken no notice of them. That wouldn't be so strange, would it?'

'Look, Herr Hauptsturmführer.' The Gestapo man tried giving a friendly smile, as if he were taking Meissner into his confidence. 'I know we got off on the wrong foot, and I know you see yourself as the Watchmaker's protector, but I do have a genuine reason for wanting to question him.'

'Really? What about?'

'About the bombing raids on the Buna *Werke*.'

Meissner laughed. 'You think the Watchmaker is working for the Americans? Oh, that's priceless.'

Hustek compressed his lips into a sneer. 'It's only recently that Buna has become a target. We're convinced the Polish underground have passed information about it to the Allies. But they must have had someone on the inside to tell them about the factory in the first place. The Watchmaker works in one of the instrument shops. He speaks to Polish workers every day. He's an obvious suspect.'

'For God's sake, man! Buna is full of Polish workers. Thousands of them pass through the factory gates every day. They don't need the Watchmaker to tell them what's going on inside. Besides, if you knew him as I do, you'd know it couldn't be him.'

'Why's that?'

'Because the only thing that interests him is chess. Nothing else matters to him any more.'

'But I still have two men missing.'

'They're bound to turn up eventually. Men go absent without leave all the time, even in the SS.'

'Not in the Gestapo.'

'I take it you've checked with their families?'

Hustek responded with a disdainful look.

'I'm afraid I really can't help you.'

'Can't or won't?'

Meissner ignored the question. 'If there's nothing more, I have work to do.'

Hustek stood and strode to the door. Putting his hand on the handle, he turned back. 'Do I have to play against the Kike?'

'If you don't, you lose by default.'

Hustek nodded, with a look that said he had known that this was how it would be. 'Well,' he said, 'far be it from me to be the one who saves a Yid from the gas chamber.' A sinister smile formed on his face. 'You know, Herr Hauptsturmführer, you should pay a visit to Birkenau yourself sometime, see what it's like. It's quite something to see the gassing – hundreds of people so alive one minute and so still, like a tableau in a waxworks, the next. And the screams, you should hear the screams. Gives you a real sense of a job well done.'

The mask of impassivity that Meissner had been wearing fell away. 'I wouldn't know,' he replied, his voice tight with suppressed rage. 'The only death I've ever seen is the kind where men get blown to pieces or roast to death in a burning tank. And the more I think of it, the more I realize what a fitting end that would be for you.'

Hustek was determined to have the last word: 'A word to the wise, Herr Hauptsturmführer. That journal of yours... I would keep it in a safe place if I were you. You wouldn't want the wrong people to know what was written in it.'

'How do you—?'

But Hustek had gone, leaving Meissner with the answer to a question that had been eating at him for months.

1962
Kerk de Krijtberg, Amsterdam

'I realized then,' Meissner said, 'that I could not put off applying for my transfer any longer. I immediately wrote to my comrade, Peter Sommer, in my old regiment. By then they were back on the Eastern front, so it took nearly a month before I got his reply.'

'What did he say?' Willi wanted to know.

'That the fighting was as brutal as ever, that he had been promoted again, and that yes, if I wanted it, there was a place for me as an adjutant in the staff HQ.'

'When would that have been?' Emil asked.

'Early October, perhaps a week before your game with Hustek. I had thought he would have been back for you, but he never came near. And then there was the uprising in Birkenau.'

'An uprising? By the prisoners?'

'Yes. The *Sonderkommando* at one of the crematoria rebelled. There was a small battle. They killed several guards and NCOs, and blew up the crematorium. Then they broke through the wire and ran off.'

'What happened to them?'

'I don't think many of them escaped. Those who were caught were brought back and executed. But the question on everyone's lips was how could Jewish prisoners in Auschwitz have managed to get hold of weapons and explosives? It was inconceivable. Bär was apoplectic with rage, and Hustek bore the brunt of it. He'd been so distracted by his determination to neutralize Emil that he'd completely missed what had been going on under his very nose. He was told in no uncertain terms to get to the bottom of it. I think he even forgot about his missing men.'

'So everything went quiet in the run-up to the game?'

'Not quite. Oberscharführer Hustek still had one roll of the dice left.'

34.

The Grünfeld Defence

October 1944

Konzentrationslager Auschwitz-III, Monowitz

The camp is subdued. At daybreak the sun in the east is red, a sure sign that bad weather is on its way. The camp has been trying to ignore the creeping approach of winter, for it knows the majority of the inmates will not live to see the spring and that, for all of them, each day will be purchased in suffering, and measured in icy clouds of breath, the stamping of feet on the ground, and the hunching of shoulders against the chill wind.

Among the inmates there is a growing unease – it is like a caged tiger, pacing restlessly from side to side, snarling. By now everyone knows of the uprising by the *Sonderkommando* in Birkenau and of how it was suppressed with a savagery that was notable even by the savage standards of Auschwitz. Now the inmates watch the SS in their towers around the camp and their patrols along the wire, wondering whether this same savagery will be turned upon them as well.

But that is not the main source of the unease. In the summer, to boost construction in the Buna factory, 2,000 extra prisoners were brought into the Monowitz camp. They were housed in tents near the parade ground. Now that winter is near, these men have been moved into the blocks, making the already overcrowded quarters even more squalid.

During the summer, *Selektionen* among the prisoners had come to a standstill while the gas chambers and crematoria of Birkenau had worked overtime on the slaughter of the Hungarian Jews. Now that the Hungarian *Aktion* is over, the old hands among the prisoners predict that the *Selektionen* will begin again: although it is of their own making, the SS will not tolerate such overcrowding for long.

Each inmate assures his neighbour that they will not be among the ones selected: only the old and the weak and the sickly will go. It does not matter if the neighbour is old or weak or sickly, they are told they are not old enough or weak enough or sickly enough. Everybody knows that these are empty words. The Germans are very thorough.

The *Selektion* comes without warning on a Sunday afternoon. The inmates are lining up for the soup ration. The bell sounds. All must return to their blocks.

Brack knows it is coming – he has gone through the procedure many times. Only Jews are selected, and he has their *Häftling-Karten* ready with their number, name, nationality and age and whether they are a specialist worker.

Brack wants everything to go quietly. He tells everyone to undress, and get into their bunks. He strolls to bunk number three, where the Watchmaker has a new companion to share his sleeping space.

'You know what's coming, eh?' Brack says.

Emil nods. 'Of course.'

'Don't worry, you're safe. Even if your card wasn't marked "protected", you are a specialist, and in good health.'

It is perhaps two hours later when an SS doctor and guards arrive at the block and the *Selektion* begins.

Starting at the furthest end of the dormitory, Brack and his minions move along the rows of bunks, striking them with wooden clubs, driving the fearful prisoners into the day room. Soon more than 200 naked men, each holding a card tightly in his hand, are herded into a space that is too small for them.

Now, the door to the outside is opened. Waiting there is an SS doctor. Brack stands to his right, and on his left the *Blockschreiber*, Widmann. Along the alley between the blocks, the outside door to the dormitory is opened. One by one, each prisoner must exit the day room, give his card to the *Blockschreiber* and then, naked, run along the alley and back into the dormitory. During these few seconds, the doctor decides whether each man will live or die.

After it is finished, Brack looks with disbelief at one of the cards. He takes it back to the SS doctor.

'Herr Obersturmführer,' he says, 'I think there has been a mistake.'

The doctor looks coldly at the prisoner with his green triangle and his all-too-clean uniform. 'Mistake? How so?'

'*Häftling* 163291. He is a specialist and in good health. Also, he has *Schutzhäftling* status. He is not for *Selektion*.'

The doctor hesitates for a moment, then says: 'Show me.'

Brack passes him the Watchmaker's card. The doctor looks closely at it.

'Where does it specify that this prisoner is a specialist or that he is in protective custody? He is for *Selektion*. Now get on with it.'

Brack stares at the card. It is not the one he prepared earlier. He goes back into the block to find the original. There is no trace of it. With an oath he goes in search of the *Blockschreiber* but he is nowhere to be found.

He finds one of his cronies. 'Where is Widmann?' he asks.

'I don't know. I haven't seen him since the *Selektion*. Maybe he's gone to the latrine.'

'I bet he's gone a lot further than that. Get the word out. I want him, and I want him *now*.'

But Widmann is not to be found. He is on his way to the *Stammlager* and freedom. In return for doctoring the Watchmaker's record card, Hustek has promised Widmann his liberty. Tomorrow, when the selected prisoners are sent to Birkenau, Widmann will be on a train to Stuttgart, and from there, with luck, to Switzerland.

But there is nothing Brack can do about Widmann now: he has a far more pressing problem. At dawn the next day, trucks will come to take the selected prisoners to the gas chambers. Before that happens, Hauptsturmführer Meissner must be told what has happened. But it is Sunday. He will not be in his office and there is no way to contact him. There is only one thing to be done.

The Watchmaker must be hidden.

It will not be easy. In the morning, after the work *Kommandos* have departed for the day, there will be a second roll call for the selected inmates. It will take time to conduct two roll calls, giving Brack a little breathing space to find Meissner. But when the roll call count does not tally, the SS guards will search the camp. It will not take long: the dogs will soon sniff out the hidden prisoner.

Two hiding places come to Brack's mind: the camp brothel and the forge. The brothel because it is the last place the Germans will look, and the forge because the smell of the place may put the dogs off.

If the Watchmaker is found before Brack can get to Meissner, it is likely he will be shot on the spot.

But the Watchmaker is reluctant to cooperate.

'It is Hustek's doing,' he says. 'Why fight it? He will get me in the end, anyhow. I have nothing left. My family is gone; the only friend I had is gone. At least this way I won't have to go through another winter watching the people around me dropping like flies.'

Brack is appalled. For years he has lived in a world where moral values have been extinguished; but in the Watchmaker he has seen something rare. It is more than his incomprehensible devotion to chess: it lies in his dogged determination not to succumb to the dead weight of indifference that Auschwitz hangs around every inmate's neck, and in his rejection of the idea that he might profit from the lives he has saved. Above all, it is evident in the way that the Watchmaker has refused to surrender his dignity. None of these things is clear in Brack's mind, nor does he conceive of any of them as 'good', for in Auschwitz there is no good; but, as he struggles to understand, he sees it as something that is *right*, how the world ought to be if it were not for the barbed wire within which they are all confined. A quiet voice within tells him that this is something he must fight for.

Brack cannot articulate any of this. His response is to slap the Watchmaker and bellow: 'Do you want to die?'

'Of course not,' Emil replies, rubbing his cheek.

'Then do as I say.'

'No.'

Exasperated, Brack raises a hand to strike Emil again, but he knows that Emil will not respond to violence so he lets it fall.

Abruptly, Brack leaves the block and steps into the cold evening air. He does not go far – just past the punishment block to Block 30. He is looking for somebody.

A short time later he is back. 'There is someone I want you to meet,' he says. He pushes a prisoner towards the Watchmaker.

'Who is this?'

'This is the life you will save when you win against Hustek. Talk to him. I want you to understand that if you throw away your own life, you will almost certainly be taking this one with you.'

The Watchmaker refuses to look at the prisoner; he fixes his gaze on Brack. 'No. You cannot put this responsibility on me. This scheme was not of my devising.'

'It doesn't matter. All that matters is that it is within your power to save this man's life. I want you to look him in the eye and tell him why you won't do it.'

Emil reluctantly contemplates the man. He is short, his head is shaven, and his face is riddled with sores, perhaps the result of vitamin deficiency. Like everybody, his uniform is patched and filthy, but he does not have the defeated look that many of the prisoners have. His eyes are alert and searching.

'What is your name?' Emil asks.

'Daniel. Daniel Farhi.'

'You are French?'

The man shrugs. 'Not exactly. My wife is French and my father is French-Egyptian. I'm from Cairo. In 1940 we were visiting my wife's family in Paris when we got caught by the German advance. It's a long story, m'sieur, but here I am.'

'What did you do in Cairo?'

'I was a dealer in gold.'

Emil nods. That explains Brack's interest in this man. 'What about your family?'

'My wife escaped to Spain. My children are in Egypt. As far as I know, they are well.'

'Do you understand the risk you are running? The man I'm up against in this game has no scruples. None. If I lose, he won't be satisfied with waiting until you are taken by a *Selektion* – he's the kind to take you to the gas chamber himself and laugh all the way home afterwards.'

Farhi smiles. 'But you will not lose. You are the Watchmaker.'

Emil sighs. He turns to Brack. 'And how much have you extorted from this one?'

Farhi interrupts. 'If it is a question of money, m'sieur...'

'Monsieur Farhi, it is not a question of money. But don't let yourself be fooled into thinking that our esteemed *Blockältester* is doing this because he cares for your welfare. He cares about himself.'

Emil bows his head, defeated by the inescapable logic of Auschwitz. 'All right then, tell me what I must do.'

The brothel is constructed of wood, the same as every other building in the camp. In one of the rooms on the upper level there is a hollow space beneath the floorboards. It is a hiding place for various items of contraband that are smuggled in and out of the camp. Using it to conceal the Watchmaker is likely to mean the end of its usefulness, but that cannot be helped.

It is a tight fit, but Emil manages to squeeze in.

'No matter what,' Brack says, 'make no sound.'

At 6:50 a.m. the sun rises. Brack immediately sends one of his trusted lieutenants to find a friendly SS guard. He must get a message to Eiden-müller. The prisoners are not allowed to march to Buna in the dark so they do not set off until 7:15. Ten minutes later, the prisoners picked out in the *Selektion* start to assemble on the *Appelplatz*. They are slow to form ranks – understandably so. They can see the trucks waiting for them on the service road, between the gates that are locked at both ends.

Despite the cold wind the SS guards are in no hurry, and it is nearly eight o'clock before the Rapportführer is told they are one short. He orders a recount. This time the count is done briskly, and the guards pay closer attention. The result is the same. The prisoners are left shivering in the cold while a search of the camp is mounted.

Meanwhile, Eidenmüller is waiting anxiously outside Meissner's office. On Mondays Meissner is in the habit of coming in early. But not today. The night before, Meissner was in Solahütte talking to Brossman about his plans to rejoin his unit, and urging his fellow officer to go with him. He sees no reason to pursue his duties with the same diligence as before. He does not arrive until shortly after eight.

'It's the Watchmaker,' Eidenmüller tells him breathlessly. 'There was a *Selektion* yesterday. I don't know how, but he was included. Brack's hidden him, but it won't be long before he's found.'

Lips tight with anger, Meissner storms outside, Eidenmüller following in his wake. At the gate they are let through under the watchful eye of the Lagerführer, Obersturmführer Schottl. He goes into the guard room and picks up the telephone.

Meissner and Eidenmüller hurry past the parked trucks and through the second gate. Brack is leaning against the wall of the sick bay, watching for them.

'What the hell happened?' Meissner asks.

Brack explains as they walk to the brothel. Through the wire they can see two teams of guards with dogs searching the clothing store on the north side of the camp.

'This way,' says Brack.

Inside, he pushes aside a bed and pulls up a floorboard to reveal the Watchmaker.

Meissner nods. 'Follow me,' he says.

Together, they take the path past the kitchens to the *Appelplatz* where Meissner presents the prisoner to the Rapportführer. 'I believe this is the one you are looking for.'

The Rapportführer is under the command of Obersturmführer Schottl. He is about to order the Watchmaker to join the ranks of other prisoners when the Lagerführer arrives.

'Thank you, Herr Hauptsturmführer,' Schottl says to Meissner, 'for finding our escaped prisoner. I don't know how we would have managed without you. Now we can get on with sending these scum where they belong.'

'Not this one,' Meissner says. 'This prisoner is in protective custody and is not for *Selektion*.'

'Of course,' Schottl says silkily. 'He can go back to his block as soon as you show me his *Häftling-Karte*. Until then…' He gives a pointed look at the Rapportführer.

Meissner looks at Brack. 'Do you have his card?'

Brack shakes his head. 'It's been switched. Otherwise I would have got this sorted last night.'

Meissner turns to Eidenmüller. 'On my order. Take the prisoner to my office. Now.'

'Yes, sir.'

Schottl is no longer smiling. 'I can't permit that, sir. This prisoner has been selected for liquidation.' He gives an order to the Rapportführer. 'Get that stinking Yid onto the transports – now.'

*

329

1962

Kerk de Krijtberg, Amsterdam

'Dear God,' Willi said. 'Then what?'

Emil glanced at Paul. 'What happened next took everyone by surprise, especially me. It was unbelievable.'

'What?'

Meissner grinned. 'I pulled my gun on him.'

Willi was stunned. 'You pulled your gun on a fellow SS officer?'

'Yes. You should have seen the look on his face.' Paul started to laugh.

'How did you think you would get away with that?'

Paul's laughter turned into a coughing fit. It took a while to subside. 'I had no idea,' he said, between coughs, 'but it was the only thing I could think of. It would've taken hours to do what Schottl was telling us to do, and by then it would have been too late.'

'What did he do?'

'What could he do? He looked at me in total and utter amazement. "Put the gun away," he said. "You're not going to use it."'

'What did you say?'

'I think I said, "Are you sure you want to take the risk?"'

'And he let you take Emil away, just like that?'

'No,' Emil said. 'That's not how it ended. While you and the other SS officer were having your stand-off, somebody else came over.'

Paul remembered. 'My God, you're right. Hustek.'

'What did he do?' Willi asked.

'Nothing,' Paul answered. 'It was very strange. Afterwards, I realized he must have been behind it all along. At first he did not appear angry or even disappointed that his scheme had failed; on the contrary, he seemed to have expected it. Then he saw Brack. In an instant his manner changed.

He looked thunderous. "Brack," he said, "I wondered where you had got to. I never thought you of all people would become a Jew-lover." Then without another word he turned and walked away. Schottl shouted after him, "What should I do with the Jew?" Without looking back Hustek called over his shoulder, "Let him go with his new friends."'

'So,' Willi said, 'out of all those men who were selected, you were the only one to survive.'

The three suddenly became very solemn. 'Yes,' Emil said. 'Out of them all, I was the only one.'

35.

THE CARO-KANN COUNTERBLOW

1962

Kerk de Krijtberg, Amsterdam

The next morning, Meissner was ailing badly. He had to be supported by pillows to sit upright, and his breathing was raspy and laboured; when he tried to shift his weight, his face contorted with pain. The doctor was called and a nurse was arranged to come and administer morphine, but after only one injection the patient refused to cooperate: the morphine clouded his thinking. The doctor tried to insist, but he reckoned without Meissner's tenacity. In the end he had no choice but to relent: if Mrs Brinckvoort would leave a measuring phial and the bottle of laudanum next to the bed, the bishop could help himself whenever the pain became too much.

Emil was restless. He played with his lunch, prodding the food on his plate aimlessly until, with a clatter, he let his fork drop.

'What's the matter?' Willi asked.

Emil didn't answer. He pushed his chair back and walked to the door. 'I'll see you later,' he said.

Willi sat at Paul's bedside for most of the afternoon, chatting or reading to him. When Emil returned, Willi was in the kitchen.

'How's Paul?' Emil asked.

'He's asleep. But he was awake on and off most of the time you were out.'

'That's good. He should rest while he can.'

'He's been asking for you. He wanted to know where you were. I told him I didn't know.'

'I've withdrawn from the competition.'

There was a short silence. 'I had a hunch that's what you were going to do,' Willi said. He stood up and laid a hand on Emil's shoulder. 'It's a big decision. You could have won. I think you would have. You would have had your shot at the World Championship.'

'Perhaps. But my heart's no longer in it.' Emil moved towards the door. 'I'll look in on Paul,' he said. 'There are more important things than chess.'

When Meissner awoke, the two men took their places at his bedside. Emil told him of his decision.

'It was the right thing to do,' Meissner said, his voice weak and thready.

'You think so? I thought you would have been disappointed.'

Meissner shook his head. 'No. You've already played the most important game of your life.'

'You mean the one against Hustek?'

'What else? How could anything ever come close to that?' Wincing with pain, Meissner pushed himself up on his pillows. He looked ashen. The laudanum was untouched. 'I'm so tired,' he whispered. 'You'll have to tell Willi about it. But don't leave anything out – I'll be listening.'

'The first thing to tell,' Emil said, 'is about the place where the game was played. It was the SS country club and, after nearly a year in the camp, it seemed I had been transported to paradise.

'I was taken there by Eidenmüller. He had been promoted to Scharführer.

His attitude towards me had changed quite a lot and he treated me quite decently. Whether this was due to Paul's influence, or for some other reason, I really don't know. Before we left he had me showered and given fresh clothes, and brought me some food – white bread and a little cheese and sausage. For a short while I felt better than I could ever remember. Then he drove me into the forest and up to the SS summer retreat.

'It was built on the side of a hill above a river and looked out across a valley. You came upon it quite suddenly – one second you were in thick woodland, and the next there was this marvellous view. Eidenmüller escorted me inside and told me not to respond to anything that was said to me unless it was a direct and sensible question.'

The bed creaked; Paul had moved to shift his weight, his face creasing with pain. Emil looked pointedly from Willi to the bottle of laudanum, but Paul motioned with a finger for him to carry on.

'You should understand,' Emil continued, 'that after three games in which I had beaten their SS comrades, emotions were running high. I was not permitted to wait in the room where the game would be played. Instead, I was taken to a balcony and left there alone until it was time to start. The weather was glorious, not a cloud in the sky, but bitterly cold. As I stood there, it struck me as a cruel irony that there could be such an idyll so close to so much suffering and death.

'After a while Eidenmüller came out. "It's time," he said. He seemed subdued, or perhaps he was angry. Inside, there was an air of almost desperate defiance, as if everyone knew the end was not far off but were determined to go out with a bang. After the previous games I thought I knew what to expect. I had steeled myself against the hostility, the jostling and the jeering, but nothing could have prepared me for the sight that confronted me.'

Friday, 13 October 1944
Solahütte, SS country club, German-occupied Silesia

The country club lounge was packed. Standing room only, the air thick with cigarette smoke. Waiters in white jackets made their way to and fro carrying trays laden with drinks. The only space was at the centre, where a table and two chairs had been set up. On the table was a simple wooden chess set; only the players were missing.

When the Watchmaker appeared in the doorway, a hush fell on the room. Emil hadn't expected that – he had expected to be assailed with shouts of *Kike, StinkJude, Jewish scum*. The silence was worse. He followed Eidenmüller across the room, his head bowed and his eyes fixed on the floor. Still, the oppressive silence; the whole room waiting, holding its breath.

He stopped at the table. Still no shouts, no threats, no sounds. Then, a snigger. Slowly, the Watchmaker raised his head. The SS men were struggling to hold back laughter. Emil followed their gaze; what he saw made his stomach churn.

It was another prisoner. He was in heavy manacles and around his neck somebody had strung a cardboard placard that read: *Don't speak to me. I am already dead.*

With a start, Emil realized who the prisoner was: it was Daniel Farhi. He looked terrified.

The room exploded in hoots of laughter and applause, and glasses were banged on tables in appreciation of the joke.

Unseen by the Watchmaker, Hustek was on the margin of the crowd, watching his reaction, a scornful smirk on his face.

Meissner was on the porch outside to greet the Kommandant. On his arrival, Meissner asked him to take a prominent place among the crowd, but Bär refused. He would observe proceedings, he said, from a distance.

When Meissner entered the lounge he saw the Watchmaker standing next to the chess table. Hustek was speaking to him, but he couldn't hear what was being said. Determined to prevent the Gestapo man from intimidating the Watchmaker any further, Meissner put all his weight into pushing through the crowd.

'Take a good look, you piece of Kike shit,' Hustek was saying, jerking his head towards Farhi. 'You know who he is, don't you? Aren't you wondering how I know about the little scheme you and Brack have got going together? How you're going to get rich after the war is over...? Listen carefully – I'm going to beat you, and when I do, I'm going to take that one over there and put him into the gas chamber myself. Then I'm coming for you.' He paused to let his words take effect. 'You're not so cocky now, are you?'

'What's going on?' Meissner demanded.

'I was merely spelling out a few home truths for your Jew friend, Herr Hauptsturmführer,' Hustek replied.

'Ignore him,' Meissner said to the Watchmaker. 'Your protected status has been confirmed by the Kommandant. There's nothing he can do about it.'

Hustek grinned, a self-assured leer. 'As you say, Herr Hauptsturmführer, but there's more than one way to skin a cat, if you know what I mean.' He took his seat.

Meissner indicated the Watchmaker should do the same, and waited for the noise in the room to subside.

As in the previous game, the Kommandant had insisted that Hustek be given choice of colour. He chose white and moved his king's pawn forward two spaces. Immediately he lit a cigarette, inhaled deeply and blew smoke into the Watchmaker's face. 'Oh, pardon me,' he said, before doing it again.

The Watchmaker showed no reaction and calmly moved his queenside bishop's pawn forward one square. The pulse pounding in his ears was deafening.

Hustek advanced his queen's pawn to stand next to its brother. The black queen's pawn moved forward two spaces to meet it. Ignoring the gambit, Hustek advanced his king's pawn one space. Emil brought out his queen's bishop to the middle of the board. The white king's bishop advanced to the third row. The black bishop swooped to take it.

'Thought that was clever, didn't you?' Hustek said, and moved his queen forward to capture the black bishop.

Emil said nothing. He moved his king's pawn forward one square.

Hustek responded by staring at Emil. He knew few people could bear the pressure of that gaze. But Emil looked back without flinching. At the front of his mind burned the Hebrew letter Zayin, representing the order of angels called Principalities and whose essence is in conquering. This was his shield against Hustek's viciousness.

The Gestapo man turned away, flicking ash from his cigarette onto the floor before advancing his kingside bishop's pawn two squares. Emil brought forward his bishop's pawn one more space. Again, Hustek ignored the sacrifice. Instead, he moved his queenside bishop's pawn one space. Emil's fingers hovered over his queenside knight.

'I know about your wife,' Hustek said, almost amiably, as if this were the most ordinary conversation imaginable. Emil looked at him sharply, but remained silent, advancing the knight so that with the next move he would threaten the white queen.

Hustek responded by bringing out his kingside knight. 'Did Meissner tell you – she was shot trying to escape.' He sniggered. 'At least that's what the report said.'

Emil closed his eyes, forcing Zayin back to the centre of his consciousness. Seemingly of its own volition, the black queen moved diagonally three spaces.

Hustek castled, pushing his king into a corner and releasing his kingside rook. 'I did what I could to help her. I had her in protective custody, but your chum, Meissner, got wind of it and decided she needed to be rescued. Bungled it, of course.'

Emil brought out the second black knight.

Hustek seemed to have been leading up to a concerted attack, but now all he did was to advance his queenside knight's pawn one space. Black bishop's pawn took white queen's pawn, stopping ahead of the white queen. With a contemptuous shake of his head, Hustek took the black bishop's pawn.

'She'd still be alive now if he hadn't interfered.'

Emil brought his kingside knight forward.

Hustek moved his queenside bishop one square on the left diagonal. His attack was taking shape, with a phalanx of pawns dominating the centre of the board and a formidable triplet of queen, knight and bishop behind. Black's position seemed disorganized and purposeless in comparison. Emil moved his queenside rook sideways two spaces.

Hustek advanced his own queenside rook's pawn one space. 'Has he told you he's applied for a transfer away from Auschwitz?' Emil tried to keep his features impassive, but Hustek saw immediately that his words had struck home. 'Oh, I see he hasn't. No, it seems he craves a return to active service. Life in our little camp is not exciting enough for the good Hauptsturmführer. But if you ask my opinion, I'd say he was running away from something.' He ground out his cigarette and lit another. Again he blew smoke into Emil's face.

Emil brought up his queenside knight to take the pawn standing before the white queen. The board now seemed set for a quick-fire exchange of pieces.

Hustek lifted his kingside knight. 'I wonder why he didn't tell you. Do you think it's because he knows he won't be able to protect you when he's gone?' With a disdainful flick of his fingers he took the black knight.

Emil brought up his kingside bishop to threaten the white knight. Hustek could not move it: it would put his king in check. For a moment his confidence slipped, then he smiled. 'A little obvious, don't you think?'

He moved his kingside rook sideways until it stood behind his queen. Emil took the knight that was protecting the king. Hustek scowled. Without pausing to think, he advanced his remaining bishop to take the knight. Despite the loss of the knight he was still in a strong position, with his queen behind his bishop, and a rook in a direct line behind to support it.

Black bishop immediately took the white bishop.

'Check.'

Angrily, Hustek took the bishop with his queen. Only then did he see the danger.

The Watchmaker's strategy had been masterful. He had made his moves look disjointed, disorganized, as if there was no real thought behind them, as if all along all he had been able to do was react to Hustek's superior strategy. But now, out of nothing, he had conjured a winning move.

The black rook moved the length of the board to the back row on the white side.

Frantically, Hustek looked for a way to counter this move, but there was nothing. He did not understand. Only moments ago his had been the stronger position. How had the Watchmaker managed to reverse their positions without him seeing it?

Meissner, seated to the side, sensed something momentous had happened.

The Watchmaker spoke. 'It's your move, Herr Oberscharführer.'

36.

THE GREEK GIFT

1962

Kerk de Krijtberg, Amsterdam

'Extraordinary,' Willi breathed. 'I was with you every move. So you beat the champion of the SS, and you won another life. But you must have known that Hustek would not honour the bargain that Paul had made with you. Was it true that Paul had requested a transfer?'

Meissner raised a hand from the bed. 'I'm afraid it's true,' he said, his voice frayed from coughing. 'And I knew it was selfish of me: I was running away, but I did not expect to survive the war. Casualty rates in the Waffen-SS were horrific, much higher than in the Wehrmacht, and I thought that in death my honour would be restored.' He was taken by another spasm of coughing. Willi helped him to sit up and Emil passed him a glass of water. After a few sips the spasm eased, but Meissner's face was grey with pain.

'Do you want some laudanum?' Willi asked. 'The doctor said it would help the coughing as well as the pain.'

Meissner shook his head. 'It was the Kommandant who, quite unwittingly, gave Emil the protection he needed after I had gone. And it was through him that the final character entered the Watchmaker's story.'

'Another character, so late in the game? Who?'

Meissner took another sip of water before replying. 'It was you, Willi. You also had a part to play, and you were probably instrumental in saving Emil's life.'

'Me?' spluttered Willi. 'It would be nice to think so, but I don't see how. I never went near Auschwitz.'

'Precisely.'

Friday, 13 October 1944
Solahütte, SS country club, German-occupied Silesia

With a furious shout, Hustek up-ended the board. Chess pieces flew into the air and scattered across the floor. In the stunned silence that followed they could be heard rolling to a halt. Hustek was standing, with his arm extended and his pistol pointing at the Watchmaker's head but, suddenly, the Gestapo man forced a smile and lowered the gun. 'No,' he said, his voice quietly menacing. 'Shooting is too good for you, Watchmaker.'

Without another word he forced his way through the packed ranks of spectators, not caring whom he pushed out of his path.

Then there was uproar.

Harsh words were shouted, and angry looks directed at the Watchmaker. One man spat at him; a woman threw her drink over him. Some stood, looking as if they intended to give him a beating, or worse.

Emil tried not to look at them. He was scanning the room for Daniel Farhi, who seemed to have disappeared. Then he saw him – crouched down in a corner, his hands clasped over the top of a head, trying to hide. It was the best thing he could have done: the crowd continued to direct its fury at Emil until Meissner placed himself in front of him.

Meissner stared down the crowd, daring them to include him in their invective.

Across the room, Eidenmüller steered Farhi along the front of the bar towards the exit.

'Let's go,' Meissner said softly, to Emil. Holding his walking stick before him, as if threatening to use it if necessary, Meissner edged his way through the crowd, the Watchmaker on his coattails.

The doorway was blocked by the Kommandant, his face red with anger. 'Well?'

'Sir,' Meissner replied, 'I think this is not the time. We should wait until tempers have calmed.' He glanced behind. The noise had not abated. Somebody yelled, 'Jew-lover!'

'I don't think we have the luxury of *that* much time, Meissner. I will see you in my office first thing on Monday.'

'Yes, sir. *Heil Hitler.*'

Monday, 16 October 1944
Kommandantur building, Konzentrationslager Auschwitz-I
Sturmbannführer Richard Bär read and reread the file on the desk before him. He was searching for anything that would provide a clue to Meissner's disloyalty. Before July there was no doubt that the Hauptsturmführer had been one of his best officers: conscientious, and capable; but he had changed. Where, Bär wondered, had Meissner's defeatist attitude come from? More importantly, what had happened to transform him into a Jew-lover?

Absentmindedly, he scratched a pimple that had erupted on the end of his nose and winced as he took the top off. A drop of blood fell onto the open page. He pulled out a handkerchief and dabbed at it, but all he managed to do was smear blood across the neat, type-written words. It was Meissner's request for a transfer: Bär took his pen and signed it.

There was a knock at the door.

'Hauptsturmführer Meissner, sir,' his orderly said.

Bär was much calmer than he had been on Friday night: he thought he had found a solution to the problem of the unbeatable Jew. It would be Meissner's last duty before he left.

'Send him in.'

Meissner entered and brought his heels together, raising his arm in salute. '*Heil Hitler*.'

The Kommandant ignored the salute, and did not invite Meissner to sit down. Instead, he leaned back and observed his troublesome officer closely, as if by doing so he could discover the cause of his disaffection. 'That was quite a stunt you pulled on Friday night,' he said eventually.

'You'll pardon me for pointing it out, Herr Sturmbannführer, but it was not my idea for the game to be played at Solahütte, nor was I the one who arranged for a prisoner to be manacled in the corner. If anyone is to be accused of pulling a stunt, surely it is Oberscharführer Hustek.'

'The funny thing is, Meissner, now that I've had time to think about it, I find I'm much less concerned with the uproar you caused than I am with your disloyalty.'

Meissner was indignant. 'Disloyalty? How have I been disloyal?'

'You have been disloyal to your fellow SS officers, to the SS, and to the Führer; and above all, disloyal to the blood of the German *Volk*.'

'Why? Because I arranged a few chess games against a Jew?'

Bär pursed his lips and shook his head. 'Of course not. You are disloyal because you have taken the Jew's side.'

Meissner's eyes narrowed in anger, then he did a double take – was that blood on the Kommandant's nose? 'Sir, no. I will not take that,' he replied. 'I have never taken the Jew's side.'

A drop of blood fell onto the Kommandant's tunic. He seemed not to notice. 'No? Then prove it to me: have him liquidated. I don't care if you do it yourself, or have him sent to the gas chamber.'

Meissner's reply was immediate. 'No, sir. I can't do that.'

Another drop. 'That's what I thought.'

'Sir. All I have ever sought was to maintain my honour in my dealings with him. I gave him guarantees if he won his games. Surely you would not have me break my word?'

Only now did the Kommandant seem to notice the blood. Irritated, he held the handkerchief to his nose. 'I don't expect you to break your word, Meissner, but you helped him to win, didn't you? That's what is so unforgivable.'

Meissner watched, fascinated, as the rich, dark blood of the German *Volk* seeped through the Kommandant's handkerchief. He made himself look away, to the photograph of Himmler on the wall, so fond of invoking the *Volksblut* himself. 'How?' he replied, evenly, trying not to rise to the Kommandant's provocation. 'How did I help him win?'

Bär removed the handkerchief from his nose to examine it. Meissner caught himself staring again. *Yes*, he thought, *take a good look – it's blood; and it's about as close as you will ever come to being wounded in action.*

The Kommandant's words cut across his musings. 'You can't deny that it was your actions, Meissner, that prevented Oberscharführer Hustek from beating the Jew.'

'With respect, sir, I did nothing to prevent Hustek from winning. All I did was to stop him cheating. Look what he managed to do with me trying to stop him – what would he have done if he'd had a free hand?'

The Kommandant dabbed at his nose again. The bleeding seemed to have stopped. He turned his attention back to Meissner. 'I've seen this

345

happen before, Meissner, where an unscrupulous Jew corrupts an otherwise blameless German. What you need to do is recognize what he's done to you and get yourself out from under his influence.'

Meissner had to work hard not to show his exasperation. 'Sir, I protest. I am under no Jewish influence. If anything, my fault was having too much faith in the supremacy of the SS.'

Bär regarded his subordinate coolly. 'This is getting us nowhere.' He picked up a sheet of paper from the desk and passed it across. 'I've made my decision – two, actually. Here is your transfer request. I've authorized it. As soon as you've been assigned to a new unit you can leave. However, before you go, we must have a solution to our little local Jewish question.'

There was a book on the desk. The Kommandant pushed it over to Meissner. 'Do you know what this is?' Meissner shook his head. 'It's a copy of the register of the Grossdeutscher Schachbund – the German Chess Federation. It contains the names and addresses of all its members. What I've decided is this – we will invite the chess champion of Germany to Auschwitz. He will play our unbeatable Jew and put an end to his pretensions once and for all.'

Meissner was appalled. 'That's hardly fair, sir. The Watchmaker has never played chess at that level.'

Bär slammed his fist down on the desk. 'Fair?' he roared. 'I don't care whether it's fucking *fair*, Meissner! This thing has gone too far, so now I must put an end to it.' He paused for breath before continuing more calmly: 'Don't you understand? Here in Auschwitz we are the front line fighting international Jewry. We cannot afford to lose a single battle, or we will be devoured. In war, everything is fair.'

Meissner knew he had to choose his words carefully. 'Don't you think you're taking this a bit too seriously, sir? Don't forget, Obersturmbann-führer Höss himself supported the idea. He said it was good for the SS to be challenged, that it would keep us from becoming complacent.'

'I'm not interested in what Höss or anyone else has to say,' the Kommandant said angrily. 'I'm the one who will be held to account if anything goes wrong. I'm concerned only with the good order of this camp, which your ridiculous ideas and your notions of fair play have disrupted. We've already had to put down one rebellion this year – this Watchmaker has given the prisoners hope. They've seen him beat the previously unbeatable SS. Well, I have to take that hope away and remove their illusions. So you will find this chess champion and bring him here. That is an order.'

October 1944
Ministry of Public Enlightenment and Propaganda, Berlin
Willi was late back from lunch. He was late for everything these days. With the relentless Allied bombing and all the shortages, even the Ministry of Propaganda could not guarantee food in the canteen. Besides, nobody cared any more, least of all him. The war was as good as lost, though nobody dared to say so.

His colleague, Georg, was gone: an English bomb had taken out his apartment block one moonless night about two months ago. At first, Willi had missed the older man's harping about his being late and how important it was to look busy, but that had passed. Now there was merely a pretence of work in the department, and the only men left were the cripples: Willi and others like him who weren't capable of holding a rifle. He hadn't had a woman in months. Women looked askance at men his age wearing civilian clothes. They would taunt him: 'Why aren't *you* at the front?' He had been tempted, once or twice, to pull off the glove that covered his artificial hand and wave it at them, but in the end he couldn't be bothered. What was the point? The war was getting to everyone. All he wanted now was for it to be over.

There was a scrap of paper on his desk – a note from his boss, Falthauser. As Willi scanned the note, he mused sourly, *Why hasn't an Allied bomb taken* him *out, instead of Georg? There's no justice.*

It made no sense. Apparently an SS officer had been looking for him. What could the SS possibly want with him? Pocketing the note, he set off to find his supervisor.

The increased intensity of the bombing had not improved Falthauser's temper. 'I have no idea what they want with you,' he told Willi, 'but you are ordered to report to the SS economic-administrative sub-office on Prinz Albrecht Strasse, immediately.'

Willi did not delay his visit. It wasn't as if he had any work that couldn't wait.

The SS headquarters had been hit by the bombing, but people were still working inside. He was directed to a young Untersturmführer, whose office consisted of a desk in a passageway.

'Are you Wilhelm Schweninger?' the officer intoned.

'Yes, that's me.'

'Wilhelm Schweninger the Reich chess champion?'

Willi rolled his eyes. Like many in the Propaganda Ministry, he did not like the SS – perhaps a reflection of the prejudices of his master, Goebbels. 'Yes,' he replied. 'I am Wilhelm Schweninger, the Reich chess champion.'

The SS officer peered at him as if he found it hard to believe that such a poor specimen could be champion of anything. 'We have received a rather unusual request,' he said, 'from the Kommandant of K-Z Auschwitz. I have instructions to induct you as an honorary member of the SS, and arrange transportation to the camp.'

'Auschwitz? What possible reason could there be for me to go to Auschwitz?'

'Apparently your presence is required for a game of chess.'

1962
Kerk de Krijtberg, Amsterdam

'I couldn't believe my luck.' Willi chuckled. 'At last I had a uniform. True, it was an SS uniform, and people in my building would look down their noses at it, but outside the ministry it would stop all those sneers and muttered comments. I might even get a woman or two again, especially seeing as I was given the honorary rank of Sturmbannführer.'

'When did this happen?' Emil asked.

'The end of October, beginning of November.'

'But you never got to Auschwitz, did you?' Emil asked. Willi shook his head. 'Why not? Were you reluctant to come?'

'Not at all – I would have done almost anything to get away from the bombing, even if it was only for a short time. No, every couple of days I would go back to the SS building – in my new uniform, of course – only to be told there was no transport.'

Meissner lifted a hand from the counterpane, waving it feebly. 'And it was because you were not able to come that Emil survived, of that I am sure,' he said, his voice barely audible.

'But why?'

Meissner's breathing was laboured and he struggled to reply. 'My transfer was overdue. My old comrade, Peter Sommer, was now the Division commander's chief of staff. I had been ordered to go west and take up duties as his adjutant in Koblenz in preparation for the *Ardennenoffensive* in December, but like you, Willi, I too was delayed by a lack of transport.'

Emil didn't understand the point Paul was making. 'Why would Willi's failure to reach Auschwitz have had any bearing on what happened to me?'

Meissner tried to push himself up on the bed and groaned with pain.

'Here,' Willi said, reaching for the bottle. 'For God's sake, man, have some laudanum.'

'Later. I'll have some when it's time for me to sleep.' Meissner waved the bottle away. 'Don't you see, my friend?' he continued. 'Once I had left the camp, I could no longer protect you. But you were not harmed because Bär was waiting for Willi to arrive and teach you a lesson: the only way to destroy the legend of the unbeatable Watchmaker was for you to be defeated by one of the SS.'

'When did you finally leave to rejoin your old unit?' Willi asked.

'Not until the tenth of November. It was a time of great confusion. Bär even asked me to reconsider my transfer request. The Russians had reached the suburbs of Budapest, which was only about four hundred kilometres away. I think by then even he could see what was coming. But I couldn't stay. I knew Hitler would never give in, and I wanted to face the end with my old comrades, not a shameful surrender in a camp surrounded by thousands of starving prisoners.' He took a ragged breath. 'But there was one last thing I was able to do to protect Emil.'

'What was that?'

'Something I gave to Eidenmüller.'

'What did you give him?'

But all Meissner could do was to shake his head. He was exhausted and, with a muted gasp, fell back into the pillows.

Emil and Willi exchanged a worried glance.

'I wish he would take the bloody laudanum,' Willi whispered.

Emil nodded, but said, 'I can understand why he won't.'

Meissner did not open his eyes but croaked hoarsely, 'I can still hear you, you know.'

Willi grinned. 'Don't worry, old man, we're not going to force it on you. But you need to rest. We'll come back later.'

'Give me some now, before you go,' Meissner whispered. 'But promise me you'll be back. I want to know how it ends.'

Emil helped Paul to sit up while Willi measured a dose of the narcotic. Meissner choked on the bitter liquid, and a little dribbled down his chin. Emil took a handkerchief to wipe it off. Meissner reached up a hand to grasp Emil's arm. The strength of his grip took Emil by surprise.

'Promise me,' Meissner hissed.

'Don't worry, Paul. I promise.'

A minute later, Willi reached across to touch Paul's arm.

'I think he's asleep,' he whispered. He stood and crept towards the door. Emil followed.

But Paul is not asleep. He is striding through the Buna *Werke* frantically searching for somebody, though he doesn't know who. Then it comes to him: the Watchmaker. He must speak to him urgently. He calls to everyone he sees: 'Where is the Watchmaker?' Nobody has seen him. He should be in the instrument workshop, but he is not there. Paul turns into a blind alley. Facing him is one of the wooden watchtowers that are usually spaced at intervals along the camp perimeter. There is a man standing on the platform at its top; a man in a long black leather coat and wearing a SS cap. Paul shouts to him: 'Where is the Watchmaker?' The man turns to face him. It takes a moment for Paul to recognize him. It is Hustek, but not Hustek. His face has turned into a death's head, its lidless eyes staring, and the teeth and jaws locked in a hideous grin. 'The Watchmaker?' it says. Hustek's voice echoes along the alley, filling the air, as if coming from a loudspeaker. 'He is not here; he has gone up the chimney. Where he belongs.'

37.

ENDGAME: FOUR KNIGHTS

1962

Kerk de Krijtberg, Amsterdam

Though his bedroom is warm, Meissner cannot stop shivering. He is not sure where he is. He raises his head expecting to see the familiar items that define his life: the prie-dieu, the crucifix, his breviary at the side of the bed, but there are none of these things. He is in a large room where the walls are covered in maps, with arcane symbols drawn across their surface. Light comes from antique crystal chandeliers suspended from the ceiling and through large mullioned windows, where each small pane of glass is taped to prevent it from splintering in the event of an explosion. He can hear the shrill sound of telephones ringing and all around there are men in military uniform. Now he knows where he is. All night he has been trying to get through to the logistics command in Dietrich's VI Panzer Army HQ. The Second SS Panzer Division has performed miracles: they have broken through the Allied lines and are advancing fast, but now, less than forty kilometres from Namur, they are running out of fuel. The field telephone is down. No matter what he does Meissner cannot get through, yet he must get fuel for the Panzers.

There is only one thing for it: he will have to go in person. He looks for Sturmscharführer Schratt, who'd saved his life at Voronezh. Like him, Schratt is a survivor, wounded and then assigned to administrative duties.

Schratt hates it; he tells everyone it is like serving a prison sentence.

'Schratt!' Meissner yells. The NCO appears out of nowhere. 'Find us some transport. We're going to Dietrich's HQ.'

The only available vehicle is a motorcycle and sidecar. Schratt drives it through the freezing mud like a man possessed. Meissner crouches low in the sidecar, a machine pistol cradled across his knee in case they meet the enemy. But the enemy they encounter is not one that can be fought off so easily: an American Mustang fighter zooms in low over the trees and strafes them with a long machine-gun burst. Schratt veers from side to side and Meissner empties the magazine of his weapon ineffectually. The aeroplane turns for a second pass. This time Schratt cannot avoid the hail of bullets. His body is cut almost in two and the bike somersaults into a ditch. Meissner is thrown clear and comes to hours later in a field hospital.

Miraculously, Meissner's injuries are superficial. The doctor says he can go. But there is no transport. Meissner is furious. The outcome of the offensive depends on getting fuel for the Panzers. Eventually he manages to reach his division on a field telephone.

'I was trying to get through to the logistics group at Dietrich's HQ,' he says, 'but I didn't get there. We were strafed by an American plane.' Then he remembers. 'Schratt is dead.' Old Schratt – old, indestructible Schratt. No time now to mourn. 'Somebody must get through to them. Without fuel, the attack will grind to a halt.'

'Calm yourself, Paul.' It is Peter Sommer. 'I'm sorry Schratt is dead. We'll have to manage without the fuel. There's none to be had.'

'Manage without ... but how?'

'Just get yourself back here, Paul. You're needed.'

*

Emil jerked awake to find himself still in the chair beside Paul's bed.

Father Scholten was at its foot, quietly telling his beads. 'He's delirious,' Scholten said.

Paul was shivering with fever, muttering and mumbling. He cried out: 'Schratt!'

'What time is it?' Emil asked, blinking away sleep.

'Late.'

'It's all right, Father,' Emil said. 'I'll look after him. Just give me a minute to wake Willi. I'm sure he would want to be here too.' He went to Willi's room and knocked. 'Willi? Paul's not too good. I think you'd better come.' He went back into Meissner's room.

Willi arrived, pulling a robe around his rotund stomach.

'Dead . . .' Meissner muttered. '. . . manage . . . needed here . . .'

'What's he talking about?' Willi asked.

'I have no idea.'

'He's raving. How much laudanum did he have?'

The next morning Meissner was pale, and his skin had taken on a waxy hue. His breathing was laboured and he could speak only with great effort. Mrs Brinckvoort insisted he take more laudanum. He was too weak to argue, but would not take all that she measured out.

'Emil,' he murmured, 'my part in your tale is done. But I want to know what happened in the last days of the camp, and on the death march.'

'Death march?' Willi asked.

'The SS did not want the prisoners to fall into the hands of the Russians,' Emil explained. 'As far as they were concerned, we were still capable of work. So, days before the Russians arrived, the prisoners were marched out of the camp.'

'In the middle of winter? How did they manage to survive?'

'Thousands didn't. They either fell by the wayside and froze to death or were shot if they couldn't keep up.' Emil stopped. The air in the room suddenly seemed stale. He crossed to the window to raise the sash a little. 'Nobody knows how anyone managed to survive,' he said, resuming his seat. 'Least of all the survivors.'

'And you were on this death march?'

Meissner reached out a hand to tug feebly at Willi's sleeve. 'Why don't you let him tell his story?'

16 January 1945
Konzentrationslager Auschwitz-III, Monowitz

It is cold. In the three years he has spent at Auschwitz, Eidenmüller cannot remember it being so cold. A thick blanket of white hoar frost covers the trees, and icicles hang from eaves and window ledges. It snowed a couple of days ago and the roads and paths are covered in dirty slush. They are short of everything: food, fuel, even coal, and Eidenmüller is getting sick of tinned beef or pork. In the distance he can hear the booming of guns. He is not sure how close they are, but he is getting nervous; he does not want to hang around to meet the Russians. Meissner has told him that when they encounter the SS they do not take prisoners.

A new officer, Untersturmführer Walter, has taken over Meissner's duties, but he is fresh from the Hitler Jügende* and has no idea of anything apart from shouting and throwing his weight around. Fortunately, it is not difficult for Eidenmüller to keep out of his way.

Even the prisoners know the end is near. The gas chambers have been

* Hitler Youth.

shut down and explosive charges have been placed ready to demolish them.

The Buna factory is a deserted wasteland. It was bombed repeatedly in the autumn and, with the Russians so near, there is no point attempting repairs. Until a week ago, work *Kommandos* were sent every day to salvage what could easily be dismantled and shipped out, but no longer. Even if it were possible to remove more material, there is no transport. The prisoners are shut up in their blocks in enforced idleness, an intolerable situation for the camp authorities but one they are powerless to remedy. The SS have their belongings packed, awaiting only the command to abandon the camp. But though they have been expecting the order for days, it has not come.

The SS barracks have become like the front line: most of the NCOs are drinking heavily, and arguments are frequent occurrences. Eidenmüller seeks refuge in the empty Monowitz administration offices. The files have all been burned and most of the equipment removed. All that remains is the furniture – desks and chairs – which he has been breaking up and putting into the stove for fuel. He wonders how Hauptsturmführer Meissner is getting on. He has heard about the offensive in the Ardennes that will throw the Allies back to the coast, and he knows that the Hauptsturmführer's division is in the thick of it. He hopes Meissner does not get killed. He is the best officer Eidenmüller has ever had.

He hears footsteps on the stairs. Quickly he folds a cloth over the pistol he has been cleaning and puts it into a drawer. It was a parting gift from the Hauptsturmführer – a Russian Tokarev T-33 semi-automatic, a souvenir from the Eastern Front. It is a simpler design than the Luger, the standard handgun of the SS. It has a solid feel, and its weight in his hand is reassuring, as if to tell him he can trust it never to misfire. When Eidenmüller had asked why the Hauptsturmführer was giving him such a thing, he had replied only that he had a feeling it might come in useful one day.

The steps are coming closer. A board creaks outside the door and Untersturmführer Walter walks in.

'Eidenmüller,' he says. 'What are you doing here?'

'Not much, sir. I was making sure that we hadn't missed any of the files that were supposed to have been destroyed.'

'Very commendable,' says the Untersturmführer. 'Now come with me.'

'Yes, sir. I just need the latrine. I'll meet you downstairs.'

The Untersturmführer retraces his steps. Not knowing when he'll be able to return, Eidenmüller retrieves the pistol and puts it in his pocket.

Outside, the officer tells Eidenmüller of the plans to evacuate the camp: the prisoners will be distributed among other concentration camps in Germany and Austria; the sick will be left behind to fend for themselves. Eidenmüller asks how transport will be provided for so many prisoners. 'They will have to march,' the officer says.

The plan is foolishness. The recent snowfall was heavy and it seems likely more will come soon. How will prisoners in their ill-fitting wooden clogs and threadbare uniforms be able to march in such conditions? But that is not the Untersturmführer's problem. His only concern is to ensure his men are ready for the journey. When? The day after tomorrow.

Walter does not stay long: he is anxious to be seen to be performing his duties diligently, and the best place to do that is in the vicinity of a superior officer.

When he is sure Walter is gone, Eidenmüller enters the camp and walks to the Watchmaker's block. In the day room, Brack and his cronies are gathered around the stove. Most of the inmates are in their bunks trying to keep warm.

'Anywhere we can talk?' Eidenmüller asks Brack.

Brack follows him outside and they walk briskly along the slush-covered paths, great clouds of vapour billowing from their mouths.

'We've got our marching orders.'

Brack raises an eyebrow. 'Yeah?' he says. 'When?'

'Not just us. Everybody. Day after tomorrow.'

Brack stops. 'Everybody? No. It's not possible. These men won't make it far in this weather – it'll kill them. It's bad enough walking to the Buna factory and back.'

Eidenmüller agrees. 'Look,' he says, 'there's a chance for some of them to survive. I know about the deals you've done with a few of the Yids – but if they die, I'm guessing all bets are off.'

'What do you suggest?'

'Get them into the *Krankenbau*. You, the Watchmaker, and a few others. The sick are going to be left behind. The officers think the cold will finish most of them off, but once we're gone, you can start breaking the barracks apart for fuel. What do you say?'

'It sounds like a good plan, but what's in it for you?'

'I've been thinking. After the war, people like me, you know – ex-SS – are going to find it hard. I'll get you into the sick bay too and keep any nosy parkers out of your hair when our men come to empty the camp. After the war's over, I'll find you and we can come to an arrangement.'

Brack smiled. 'Funny, I never took you for the trusting type.'

'I'm not. If you don't play fair with me, you won't like the consequences, I promise.' Eidenmüller spat on his palm and held out his hand. 'Deal?'

Brack did the same. 'Deal.'

*

359

1962

Kerk de Krijtberg, Amsterdam

'Of course I didn't know any of this at first,' Emil said. 'Brack told me, later, when we were in the infirmary.'

'Brack,' Meissner wheezed. 'He was a complicated character. Out for number one. But there was more to him than that, I think.' His eyes closed.

'Next morning we went to the *Krankenbau*. Obviously we were not ill, but Eidenmüller had concocted a story about an SS doctor who suspected us of having typhus. The Jewish doctor was unconvinced until a packet of cigarettes appeared and with that, his concerns seemed to vanish.'

'So you and Brack and these others went into the sick bay and waited for the Russians to arrive?'

'If only it had been that simple, Willi.' Emil turned to Meissner. 'Are you still listening, Paul?' A squeeze of a hand showed that he was.

'That night we had a visitor.'

'Who?'

'Hustek.' Emil felt Meissner stiffen at the mention of this name. 'He was looking for me. Brack tried to stall him by telling him I had typhus. "Bring him out here then," Hustek said. "If he's got typhus, he's as good as dead anyway; better to let the cold finish him off, it'll be kinder in the end." But Brack shook his head. "Nothing doing," he said. But his words were empty and he knew it.

'When I came out, Hustek was there holding a pistol. I almost expected him to shoot me there and then, but he waved the gun and said, "This way." I had hardly moved when he had second thoughts and pointed the gun at Brack. "You as well," he said.

'He walked us at gunpoint through the camp, up the service road, through the gates and into the SS administrative building. It was empty, and he marched us up the stairs into Paul's old office.'

Hustek made Brack and the Watchmaker stand in the two corners furthest from the door. There was a paraffin lamp on the desk. He lit it, then settled himself astride a chair with his back to the door, and took out a pack of cigarettes.

'Smoke, Brack?' he said. When he got no reply he shrugged and put the cigarettes back in his pocket.

'Why have you brought us here?' Brack demanded.

'I would have thought that was obvious.' Hustek used his unlit cigarette to point at the Watchmaker. 'Killing your Jew friend here – that wouldn't cause me any problems at all. But killing you, Brack? Questions might be asked. I could hardly say you were shot trying to escape, could I? No, I needed somewhere where you wouldn't be found until it was too late to matter.' He smirked, struck a match and inhaled deeply, blowing the smoke at the ceiling. 'I suppose,' he continued, 'I should ask if you have any last requests.' He seemed to find that very funny, and laughed so hard he started to cough. When he had recovered, he said, 'By the way, Brack, I thought you would want to know that Widmann told me all about the deal the two of you cooked up. Your idea, of course – Widmann wasn't clever enough for that, but he was clever enough to realize he needed a new partner. Me.'

Brack glowered at Hustek, but said nothing. His brain was working feverishly: there was a slim chance he might survive, providing Hustek fired at the Jew first. Then, in the corridor outside, a floorboard creaked.

*

Eidenmüller hadn't wanted to spend the night in the SS barracks – it had been bad enough the night before, with most of his fellow NCOs drunk and whining repeatedly about having to escort prisoners in this weather; so he had brought a cot up to his old office.

He had been awoken by the sound of someone laughing. There was a light on in the Hauptsturmführer's office. Quietly, he had eased himself up and crept to the door.

In the flickering light, Eidenmüller could see the Watchmaker in the far corner. Holding the Soviet handgun tightly, he took a step forward.

Hustek spun round, peering into the darkness.

'Put the gun down, Hustek,' Eidenmüller said.

Hustek recovered quickly. He swung his gun to point it at the Watchmaker. 'You won't shoot me,' he said. 'Not for the sake of a stinking Yid.'

'I wouldn't be so sure.' Eidenmüller's face glistened in the lamplight. 'I've sort of taken to him. He's not a bad sort – for a Jew. On the other hand, nobody likes you Gestapo scum – not even your own mothers.'

Hustek did not waver. He kept the pistol aimed at the Watchmaker. 'Don't be so fucking stupid. You might win – for now. But in the morning, I'll be back with a squad of my men and I'll have him, whether you like it or not. It'll be a lot easier for you if you walk away now. I'll forget you were even here.'

Eidenmüller shook his head. 'You are a cocky bastard, aren't you? I knew that's what you would say, and I knew what I would have to do as soon as I saw it was you.'

Hustek's mind was raging. Why hadn't he checked the other rooms? The chances were the SS arse-wipe couldn't hit the side of a barn from five metres, but it was a sure thing that Brack and the Yid would be on him before he could say *Heil* fucking *Hitler*.

'You can shoot me,' he said, trying to keep his voice even. 'But as soon as I sense your finger squeezing that trigger I'll kill your precious Yid. No matter what you do, he'll be dead, so let's be sensible, eh?'

Hustek sensed a flicker of movement. With a snarl of rage, he pulled the trigger.

Within a fraction of a second, three shots were fired and two men fell to the floor. One was Hustek: Eidenmüller's bullet had taken him cleanly in the head. The other was Brack.

Brack had had a pistol of his own, nestled in the waistband of his trousers: it was the Luger he had taken from the Gestapo man that he and his cronies had murdered. He had known that Hustek intended to kill him, but he was no Jew to go to his death meekly.

Watching the exchange between Hustek and Eidenmüller, he detected a momentary hesitation as the Gestapo man's gaze wavered and pulled out his pistol. Seeing the danger, Hustek switched his aim. They fired at each other almost simultaneously. Brack missed his shot, but took a bullet in the stomach.

Emil felt a sudden pressure on his hand. 'Eidenmüller,' Paul murmured, struggling to rouse himself. 'What happened to Eidenmüller?'

'As far as I know, Eidenmüller is alive and living somewhere under the name of Leon Nadelmann.' He caught Willi's dubious glance, but continued. 'Brack wasn't dead, but he was in pain and bleeding heavily. We stripped off Hustek's shirt and used it to try and staunch the flow of blood. Then, between us, we carried him back to the infirmary.

'He died about an hour later. There was nobody to mourn him and, as was usual, his body was dumped outside to be sent for cremation. By morning it would have been frozen solid. Eidenmüller saw his chance – "One out, one in," he said. Several prisoners died that night. He assumed the identity of one of them.

'The next day the camp was evacuated. The prisoners were lined up in the snow and marched off. I never saw any of them again. A week or so later, the Russians arrived.'

The Watchmaker's story had reached its end. A ragged breath passed Meissner's lips. 'Thank you,' he whispered, so quietly Emil could barely hear him. 'The last time we parted I neglected to say goodbye. Not this time. Go with God, Watchmaker.'

The artillery battery – three self-propelled Wespe light howitzers commanded by a young SS-Obersturmführer – had taken position behind the Russian village to shell Soviet positions about three kilometres distant. The officer had sited the guns behind a low ridge, which was why nobody saw the approach of a squadron of Russian T-34 tanks as they advanced through the village. If not for a gust of wind that had carried the sound of their engines, the surprise would have been complete.

In an instant, the officer's remarkably blue eyes took in everything. Calmly he ordered a retreat and mounted the rear-most vehicle. 'Call HQ,' he shouted to the radio operator. 'Tell them we need a Stuka strike or we're done for.'

The first tank came over the ridge. With a loud *crump*, its gun fired. A mound of earth flew into the air beside the first Wespe. The Russian's tactics were sound: if the first Wespe was disabled, the others would have to slow down to get around it. A second tank appeared and fired at the retreating Wespes. Another miss. But the Obersturmführer knew their luck could not hold for long, the tanks were faster than they were. Then a third and a fourth tank appeared. They did not continue the chase but halted.

'Fuck,' the Scharführer commanding the Wespe said. 'They don't need to chase us. They'll pick us off before we reach the next ridge.'

Two shots were fired almost in unison. One kicked up a shower of earth in front of the first Wespe; the other hit the second. The howitzers were only lightly armoured and the shell from the T-34 gouged a hole in its side and tore away the track below. Amid shrieks of pain from the crew, the Wespe ground to a halt.

'Schratt,' the Obersturmführer yelled to his second in command, 'get to gun number two! Help them get out. I'll take over here.' The officer squeezed into his place. 'Driver,' he shouted, 'turn this thing around. Aim us at the first tank.' He turned to the gunners. 'Get the gun loaded and depress the barrel fully. As soon as you're done, we'll shoot over open sights.'

The driver locked the left track and turned the Wespe. The manoeuvre took the Russians by surprise. The Wespe fired at point blank range and blew the turret off the first Russian tank, detonating the ammunition within, creating a maelstrom of fire and smoke.

'Next one,' the officer ordered. The driver peered through the smoke, trying to line up his vehicle with the next T-34.

'Fire.' Another hit: not a killing hit, but the tank was immobilized.

Then – an explosion beside the T-34s that had halted. The first Wespe had followed their example and had also turned upon their attackers.

The officer whooped, the joy of battle upon him.

And then his world was torn apart. There was a thunderclap so loud it made his ears ring and the Wespe was tossed up from the ground as if by a giant's hand. He was thrown clear – when he looked up, he saw the Wespe was on its side and burning. *Christ*, he thought. He had better move before the flames reached the ammunition.

He tried to stand but where his left foot should have been, all that remained was a bloody stump; oddly, he felt no pain. Around him the battle raged: two Tigers had crested the hill and had started firing on the T-34s. He was in the centre of a whirlwind of white-hot metal, but seemed immune. Everything appeared to be moving in slow motion.

Then he saw Schratt walking towards him. The Scharführer was waving. When he got close he was smiling, his hand extended to help him up. Meissner took it; Schratt's grip was firm and cool. He pulled Meissner to his feet.

To Meissner's amazement, his foot was no longer injured.

'Obersturmführer Meissner,' Schratt said, 'I've been sent to get you.'

'Get me?' Meissner said. 'How is this happening? I thought you were dead.'

Schratt shook his head. 'Old soldiers never die,' he said.

Meissner did not seem able to grasp the idea. 'Never?'

'No, sir. Never.'

37.

The Immortal Game*

Konzentrationslager Auschwitz-II, Birkenau

It is early. Beyond a long line of concrete fence posts, rows of barrack blocks rise like dark, primeval creatures out of the morning mist. Crumbling chimney stacks stand stark against a pale sky, like the masts of stranded ships.

Emil rubs condensation off the car window to peer out. They are on a narrow road that runs beside the remains of a long fence. Every so often he can see the stumps of a watchtower sticking up out of the ground like broken teeth, black and rotten.

This is not the Auschwitz he remembers. He had thought the Monowitz camp was big, but this is *vast*.

The driver brings the car to a halt beside a red-brick tower that stands above an arch, through which a railway spur runs. He points to the building beside it. A man is waiting there, stamping his feet in the cold.

'*Dzień dobry*,' Emil says, trying to remember the little Polish he picked up in the camp. '*Nazywam się Emil Clément.*'

---

* 'The Immortal Game' was played by Adolf Anderssen and Lionel Kieseritzky in London in 1851. In a series of seemingly rash moves, Anderssen sacrificed most of his major pieces – queen, both rooks and a bishop – but then achieved checkmate with his remaining bishop and knights. It is considered to be a chess game without peer.

'Good morning,' the man replies. 'Fortunately, I speak German.'

The man is a professor from the University of Kraków, the supervisor of the preservation work that is being carried out. Birkenau is to become a museum. Monowitz is all but gone. The Buna factory is being run by the Polish government.

The professor is not at all happy that Emil and his companions have arrived to disturb his work. 'Could we hurry, please?' he says. 'All this is most irregular.'

Everything since Paul's death has been irregular. According to the Catholic authorities in the Netherlands, it was irregular for a German priest to be sent 'home' to die in Amsterdam. Then there was the question of the will. Paul had had few possessions, apart from his beloved coffee set – which he left to Mrs Brinckvoort – and his journals, which he bequeathed to Emil.

His desire to be cremated caused consternation.

'The Catholic Church does not hold with cremation,' Father Scholten explained, stiffly.

'But it is what Paul wanted,' Emil insisted.

'But he was a priest,' Scholten objected, in turn.

Willi intervened. 'Exactly,' he said. 'He understood what he was asking for. Surely the Church would not deny his dying wish?'

In the end, it was Paul's final request that caused the greatest problems.

Emil and Willi made enquiries through the Polish Consulate in Amsterdam. It was out of the question, they were told. As for visas, obtaining them was rarely straightforward, even less so with what they had in mind.

For several days Emil and Willi racked their brains for a solution. 'What we need is a fixer,' Willi said, after a few drinks.

Emil slapped his hand to his forehead. 'That's it, Willi! You've got it. And who did Paul say was the best fixer he ever knew?'

'Eidenmüller.'

They found him in a bar in the small Dutch town of Simpelveld, only two kilometres from the German border, near Aachen.

The barman looked up from polishing a glass as two men walked in. 'Good afternoon,' he said. 'What can I get you gentlemen?'

Emil recognized him at once. He extended a hand. 'Eidenmüller,' he said, quietly, in German. 'It's been a long time.'

A shadow crossed the barman's face. 'I think you must be mistaken,' he said quickly. 'My name is Nadelmann. I've never heard of this ... what was his name?'

'Eidenmüller,' Willi said, then, more loudly: 'We're friends of Haupt-sturmführer Paul Meissner.'

A look of alarm crossed the barman's face. 'Keep your voice down,' he hissed. 'Who are you?'

'Do you really not recognize me?' Emil asked.

The barman shook his head. 'Should I?'

'Yes. I'm the Watchmaker.'

The barman stopped his polishing. 'My God,' he said. 'Why have you come?'

'We're trying to carry out the dying wish of an old friend, and we're hoping you will be able to help us.'

Eidenmüller seemed confused. 'Old friend? Who?'

'Paul Meissner. He died a few weeks ago.'

The news took Eidenmüller by surprise. 'Really? Paul Meissner? He was in the Das Reich Division, you know. Hard bastards they were – not many of them left after the Russians finished with them. But my old Hauptsturmführer made it. Well, I'll be…' He nodded to himself. 'Still, I'm sorry to hear he's dead. He was a good sort – for an officer.' He looked up. 'But hang on. You said he was an old friend. I wouldn't have thought…'

'Nor me,' Emil said. 'But he helped me find something precious that I thought was lost for ever.'

'Oh? What was that, then?'

'Myself.'

Fortunately the bar was empty. Eidenmüller flipped the sign on the door to *Closed*. 'What exactly is it you think I can do?' he asked.

'We're not exactly sure,' Willi replied. 'But Paul said you were the best fixer in the SS.'

Eidenmüller smiled self-consciously. 'Please don't let anyone hear you saying that,' he said. 'I've tried to put those days behind me.'

The solution to their problem, Eidenmüller decided, was twofold: first, they needed a story that was plausible and would stand up to cursory scrutiny; second, they needed money.

'Money? Why do we need money?'

'Communism,' Eidenmüller replied. 'It seems wrong, I know, but what Communists want more than anything is money. I bet there aren't many real Communists in Poland, but you can be damned sure there's an awful lot of poor people. We used to say a Pole is always good for a bribe. I bet that hasn't changed since the war – worse, if anything, I would have thought. But we might need to bribe a lot of people, so we'll probably need a lot of money.'

'We're finished then,' Willi said. 'I wouldn't say I was badly off, but I don't have much to spare.'

'That makes two of us,' Emil said.

'Three,' Eidenmüller added. 'All I've got is this place. And there's not only me to think of.'

'You're married?' Emil asked. Eidenmüller nodded. 'Does she know, about, you know…?'

'Yes. I told her everything.'

'Children?'

'Yes. Two boys.'

'What did you call them?'

'Paul… and Freddy. That was the Hauptsturmführer's second name.'

'I didn't know.'

'I once had a peek at his service record. He was a brave man.'

'Yes, he was,' Willi said. 'Right to the end. So,' he continued, 'we need money, but we don't have any. Short of robbing a bank, where are we going to get it?'

'I think I might know where,' Emil said.

The house seemed out of place. The street – Oudedijk – was pleasant enough, with trees along its length and broad pavements, but in the midst of ranks of modern apartment blocks, the large, detached, nineteenth-century villa seemed to have been planted on an anarchic whim. However, the name on the brass plate below the bell was the one that Emil remembered: *Kastein*.

'May I speak to Mijnheer Kastein?' he asked, when a maid in an old-fashioned black uniform with white collar and cuffs answered the door.

'Who shall I say is calling?'

'Tell him… Tell him it's the Watchmaker.'

Kastein was as good as his word of nearly twenty years ago: he almost hurtled through the door to drag Emil inside, shaking his hand and refusing to let go.

Coffee was served in a sumptuous lounge. 'I'm sorry I lost contact with you, Watchmaker,' he said. 'But now that you're here, we must make sure not to let it happen again.'

'If you had followed the world of chess you would have found me easily enough.'

'I never knew there was a world of chess to follow. All I knew was our little chess club in Auschwitz. You, me, Brack, and that SS officer and his flunky.'

'It may seem a little strange, but that's why I'm here.'

Kastein was a godsend. Not only did his money smooth their path, he had contacts. Within days, four visas had been arranged.

'Four?' said Emil, surprised.

'I'm going with you.'

Kastein offered to charter a private plane for them, but on this point Emil was adamant. A plane was not right, he said. This was not merely a journey; it was a pilgrimage. They would go by train.

And now they are standing at the gates of Birkenau.

'Which of you has the money?' the professor asks. This is why they have come so early – so there are no witnesses. Kastein is to make a substantial donation to fund the restoration work: US$10,000. If it goes through official channels it will disappear; corruption is as endemic among the Communists as typhus was in the camp. The professor promises it will be spent wisely.

Now he leads them along the side of the railway track to the ruins of the crematoria. Ground mist swirls like phantoms around their feet as they walk.

They enter a grove of birch trees. It is very quiet, almost silent; even the singing of birds is absent.

To their right is a jumble of shattered concrete and bricks – a building that has been demolished and abandoned.

'It was blown up by the Germans. You see it exactly as they left it,' the professor explains. 'There are some who say it should be restored so that people can see what went on inside. There are others, including me, who think it should be left as it is as a monument to those who died.'

For Emil, the answer is obvious. 'It should be left as it is. Everyone knows what went on inside.'

'I'll leave you to do what you came for,' the professor says. 'I'll see you back at the gate. But don't take too long.'

Don't take too long . . . The professor's words seem misplaced. He doesn't understand that time has no meaning for the inmates of Auschwitz, living or dead.

Emil walks apart from the others, to the edge of the trees, wondering at the unearthly quiet. The silence is oppressive, not peaceful. If he listens very hard, will he be able to hear the screams of the ghosts who inhabit this place? Will he hear the last utterances of his mother and his children? He tries to listen to the voices that mill about him in the silence. But they are all talking at once, and he cannot hear what any of them is saying.

And, now he is here, a new uncertainty pushes itself forward – an unwelcome addition to the many he has nurtured since leaving Auschwitz. This grotto is a sacred place. It is home to the thousands who perished here. What right does he have to add to their numbers one who was among their oppressors?

He had wondered what it would be like to return, but now he is here, he is not sure what he feels. He is back, but he is not back. Nothing about this place is familiar.

This is a different Auschwitz, and the memories that permeate this place are not his.

All that is left is his conviction that he must honour Meissner's last request. From his rucksack he takes a metal canister. Hands trembling, he pulls at the lid and some fine, light-coloured powder spills onto the ground.

For long moments, Emil holds the canister as if not knowing what he should do with it. Then he walks into the birch grove, scattering the ashes as he goes. He does it hurriedly, far more quickly than he had intended, as if fearing he might change his mind before he has finished. When the canister is empty he stands there, following with his eyes the patterns the ashes have made upon the ground. They will not be there for long: a strong breeze or a shower of rain and they will be gone.

There will be no memorial stone for Paul Meissner. The only trace that his ashes have been laid here will be in the memories of four men. Emil feels a pang of guilt: he should have scattered the ashes slowly; it would have been more respectful, but it is too late now. The others – Willi, Eidenmüller and Kastein – are silent witnesses. Nothing is said until Emil rejoins them.

'I suppose one of us should say something,' Willi suggests.

Eidenmüller cannot. Tears are streaming from his eyes.

'We should say Kaddish,' Emil says.

But this is too much for Kastein. 'I made a promise to you, Watchmaker, and I have kept my word, but this—' He walks apart to stand next to the ruins of the crematorium. When he speaks again his voice seems to shout into the silence. 'Not for him. I cannot say Kaddish for *him*.'

'Not only for him,' Emil says, mildly. 'For all of them.'

It is a great deal to ask. Kastein's memories are not Emil's memories. He has no knowledge of the journey Meissner has made. He has only his own recollections – of death, of loss, of privation and suffering, injustice and hatred, and, for him, it is among these that the memory of Meissner belongs.

Reluctantly, he turns away from the ruins, and rejoins the others.

'Thank you,' Emil murmurs. From his bag he takes a book. Reading from it, in a sonorous voice he starts to chant in Hebrew. The others bow their heads. It does not take long.

'What does it mean?' Eidenmüller asks, when it is over.

'It is the prayer for the dead. It's not easy to translate exactly, but it's something like: "*May the name of God be lifted up and praised by all creation according to His will. May His reign be established and may His saving grace be made manifest and His anointed one be found among you during the days of your life and during the days of the house of Israel, quickly and without delay. Amen and Amen.*"'

'What I don't understand,' Kastein says, struggling to keep his voice even, 'is why an SS officer would want to have his ashes scattered here. I would have thought it would be the last thing he'd want.'

'Meissner was a changed man,' Emil says. 'He said that he could think of no more fitting place on earth. He said he would spend eternity asking for forgiveness.'

Kastein raises his eyes to look wonderingly at the iron-grey clouds overhead. Eternity is beyond his ability to imagine.

Eidenmüller pulls back his sleeve to glance at his watch. 'We should go before the professor comes looking for us.'

'There's one more thing we have to do,' Emil says. He reaches into his bag, pulls out a small box, and passes it to Willi.

'What is it?' Kastein asks.

'It's pocket chess,' Willi says, starting to smile. 'Are we going to play here?'

'We are. The game we should have played all those years ago. Can you think of a better way to honour him?'

'No. We had better make sure it is a good one.'

Willi picked white. He moved his king's pawn forward two spaces. Emil did the same. A faint breeze stirred the trees. Willi glanced over his shoulder to where Emil had scattered Meissner's ashes. 'Do you think he's here now, watching us?'

Emil smiled. 'I'm sure of it.'

SS RANKS USED IN
The Death's Head Chess Club

SS Rank	British Army Equivalent
Reichsführer-SS	None. Throughout the war, this position was held by Heinrich Himmler
SS-Gruppenführer	Lieutenant General
SS-Standartenführer	Colonel
SS-Obersturmbannführer	Lieutenant Colonel
SS-Sturmbannführer	Major
SS-Hauptsturmführer	Captain
SS-Obersturmführer	1st Lieutenant
SS-Untersturmführer	2nd Lieutenant
SS-Sturmscharführer	Regimental Sergeant Major
SS-Hauptscharführer	Battalion Sergeant Major
SS-Oberscharführer	Company Sergeant Major
SS-Scharführer	Sergeant
SS-Unterscharführer	Corporal
SS-Rottenführer	Lance-Corporal

Historical Note

Introduction

The Death's Head Chess Club is a work of fiction, but its setting is the worst crime against humanity in recorded history. Hans Frank, the governor-general of Nazi-occupied Poland during the Second World War, said, 'Jews are a race that must be completely exterminated.'

Of all the death camps, Auschwitz had the biggest role to play in this genocide. An estimated 1.1 million people died in Auschwitz during its four and a half years as a concentration and death camp, the vast majority of them Jews from across Europe.

Auschwitz – the camp

Auschwitz was originally conceived of as a concentration camp, a place where the enemies of the Nazi state could be incarcerated away from public view. These included political enemies (mainly Communists), homosexuals, gypsies, Jehovah's Witnesses and Jews.

Concentration camps in Germany (such as Dachau and Sachsen-hausen) and the principles on which they were run were long established. Prisoners were subject to brutal, sometimes capricious discipline, housed in primitive conditions with inadequate nutrition, and hard labour was imposed mercilessly. This was what was expected when SS-Hauptsturm-führer Rudolf Höss was appointed as the first Kommandant of Auschwitz to establish one of the first concentration camps in the newly conquered territories (Silesia), arriving on 30 April 1940.

Auschwitz was established as a penal work camp on the site of a former Polish army barracks. Its beginnings were inauspicious: the barracks were extremely dilapidated and infested with vermin, and the resources available to Höss were meagre, but his appointment as Kommandant was well judged: he was resourceful, hard working and completely dedicated to his task.

As the number of camps included in the Auschwitz umbrella expanded, this first camp would be designated Auschwitz I, the *Stammlager*. Eventually, there would be three main camps: Auschwitz-I, Auschwitz-II Birkenau and Auschwitz-III Monowitz.

It was with the expansion into Birkenau that the role of Auschwitz evolved to become a combined work camp and death camp (unlike other sites in Poland, such as Chełmno, Sobibór and Treblinka, which were solely extermination camps). In the late summer of 1941, while Höss was away from the camp, his deputy, Fritzsch, conducted an experiment, killing Russian prisoners of war using the pesticide *Zyklon Blausäure* (Cyclone cyanide) which until then had been used to kill infestations of insects. When Höss returned, Fritzsch demonstrated the new method of killing, of which Höss approved whole-heartedly, writing later that he was relieved that this method had been found as it would spare him a 'bloodbath'. Between then and the summer of 1942, Höss supervised the construction of the first purpose-built gas chambers in Birkenau for mass murder using Zyklon-B.

During this time, the German industrial giant IG Farben put forward a proposal to build a factory in Silesia to manufacture synthetic rubber and oil from the poor-grade coal that was abundant in the area. The factory would be part of the Auschwitz complex and would be built using slave labour from the camp. This was designated Auschwitz-III Monowitz.

It is here that the Watchmaker's story unfolds.

The life of Auschwitz as a concentration camp came to an end in January 1945. On 18 January, with Red Army units within a few miles, the SS force-marched around 60,000 prisoners who were considered fit enough out of the camp, westwards, on foot, in appalling weather conditions. This was the infamous death march. Already debilitated by starvation rations and wearing only their ragged camp clothing and camp-issue clogs, thousands died: some collapsed and froze to death, others were shot if they lagged behind. When Russian soldiers arrived at the camp on 27 January they found nearly 8,000 prisoners who had been left behind: close to 6,000 in Birkenau, a little more than 1,000 in the *Stammlager* and about 600 in Monowitz. Among the Monowitz survivors was Primo Levi. Orders had, in fact, been given by the SS area commander, Obergruppenführer Schmauser, that prisoners considered too weak to be included in the mass exodus should be shot, but the rapid advance of the Russians had made the camp SS nervous and, in the end, they had been more concerned with saving their own skins than with the fate of a few prisoners who they thought were likely to die of disease or starvation anyway.

Historical characters in The Death's Head Chess Club
The main characters – Emil, Paul, Willi, Bodo Brack – are fictitious. Some of the supporting characters are historical figures. These are:

- Rudolf Höss – first Kommandant of Auschwitz
- Arthur Liebehenschel – his successor
- Richard Bär – the third (and last) Auschwitz Kommandant
- Otto Brossman – guard commander

- Eduard Wirths – chief garrison physician at Auschwitz
- Vinzenz Schottl – Lagerführer of the Monowitz camp
- Richard Glücks – head of the Concentration Camps Inspectorate

Klaus Hustek's character is based on SS (Gestapo) Oberscharführer Josef Erber.

After the war, a series of war crimes trials took place. Between 1946 and 1948 about 1,000 former members of the Auschwitz SS were extradited to Poland where a number of special courts were set up, including the Supreme National Tribunal which tried the most important criminals. In March 1947, the first Auschwitz Kommandant, Rudolf Höss, was tried in Warsaw and sentenced to death. In November and December of the same year, in Kraków, forty former members of the Auschwitz SS were tried. Of these, twenty-three were sentenced to death, including the second Auschwitz Kommandant, Arthur Liebehenschel. Others received sentences ranging from three years to life imprisonment. In 1950, following numerous appeals, the former SS Hauptsturmführer Otto Brossman was acquitted of war crimes by the Kraków court.

Some former SS personnel from Auschwitz were tried and convicted for crimes other than those that were committed at Auschwitz, including Vinzenz Schottl who, as early as 1945, was convicted by a US war crimes tribunal and sentenced to death.

Eduard Wirths and Richard Glücks committed suicide.

Between 1949 and 1980 other former SS personnel were tried in the Federal Republic of Germany. The last Auschwitz Kommandant, Richard Bär, was arrested in 1960 and died in detention awaiting trial. Former SS Oberscharführer Josef Erber (who had changed his name from Houstek) was arrested in 1962 and brought to trial in Frankfurt in December 1965. He was sentenced to life imprisonment and released in 1986. He died one year later.

Chess

Most of the chapter headings relate to chess moves. The moves were chosen to reflect some aspect of the chapter content. I do not know whether or not there was a chess club for the SS in Auschwitz, and in my research I have found no evidence to confirm it either way. The unofficial Chess Olympiad did take place in Munich in 1936, in circumstances as described in Chapter 21, though, of course, Wilhelm Schweninger's involvement is fictitious. The teams from Poland and Hungary were made up of Jews, and they both beat the German team. Hungary won the tournament with ease with twenty wins in a row, something that wasn't repeated until 1960. Poland finished second, with Najdorf winning an individual gold medal.

Acknowledgements

I am indebted to many who have inspired or helped me on this journey. I found great inspiration in the harrowing and courageous personal accounts of those who survived Auschwitz, particularly Primo Levi, Filip Müller and Elie Wiesel, and also of those who did not survive and whose names are all but forgotten today: Zalman Gradowski, Dayan Langfus and Zalman Leventhal were among the numbers of the Sonderkommando; their diaries were unearthed after the war. In addition, I could never have written this book without the meticulous scholarship of numerous historians who have documented various aspects of the Nazi state, the SS, the Holocaust and Auschwitz.

I would like to express my thanks to the people who helped to make this book a reality: my agent, Carolyn Whitaker, for having faith, Ravi Mirchandani, for giving me a hearing and James Roxburgh, Belinda Jones and Ileene Smith for their endless patience and constructive editing suggestions.

And to my family – Barbara, Hannah, Laura, Andrew and Jack – thank you always for your constant love and understanding.

To all those who suffered or died as a result of the Holocaust, this book is respectfully dedicated.

Note on the Author

John Donoghue has worked in mental health for over twenty years and written numerous articles about the treatment of mental illness in a variety of medical journals. He is married and lives in Liverpool